MY OWN WORST ENEMY

by

James Anthony Goble

© James A. Goble. All rights reserved.

No part of this book may be reproduced, stored in a retrieval system, or transmitted by any means without the written permission of the author.

First published by Authorhouse   09/23/2011

ISBN: 978-1-4567-1072-9 (sc)
ISBN: 978-1-4670-3311-4 (hc)
ISBN: 978-1-4670-3312-1 (ebk)

ISBN-13: 978-1481987301

Library of Congress Control Number: 2011907130

Printed in the United States of America

Any people depicted in stock imagery provided by Thinkstock are models, and such images are being used for illustrative purposes only. Certain stock imagery © Thinkstock.

Because of the dynamic nature of the internet, any web addresses or links contained in this book may have changed since publication and may no longer be valid. The views expressed in this work are solely those of the author and do not necessarily reflect the views of the publisher, and the publisher hereby disclaims any responsibility for them.

This is a work of Fiction. The characters and events portrayed within this book are either products of the author's imagination or used fictitiously. Any similarity to persons living or dead is strictly coincidental.

To my loving mother without whose
love and support I would never
have survived this wretched
ordeal. And to my family
for always being there
when I needed them.

Contents

CHAPTER 1   Armed Robbery and First-Degree Murder 1
CHAPTER 2   Brookens' Treachery 33
CHAPTER 3   Lapeer County Jail and my Trial 51
CHAPTER 4   Jackson Prison 67
CHAPTER 5   Preston's Trail and his Final Betrayal 83
CHAPTER 6   Escapes from Jackson Prison...................................99
CHAPTER 7   My Escape from Hospital 107
CHAPTER 8   California..135
CHAPTER 9   Back to Jackson Prison..159
CHAPTER 10 Michigan Intensive Programming Center 173
CHAPTER 11 Marquette Branch Prison 179
CHAPTER 12 Huron Valley Men's Prison...................................213
CHAPTER 13 Thumb Correctional Facility 247
CHAPTER 14 Hiawatha and Kinross Temporary Facilities 267
CHAPTER 15 Back to Thumb Correctional Facility 279
CHAPTER 16 Saginaw Correctional Facility 309
CHAPTER 17 Riverside Correctional Facility..............................317
CHAPTER 18 Carson City Correctional Facility..........................327
CHAPTER 19 E.C. Brooks Correctional Facility 337
CHAPTER 20 Macomb Correctional Facility...............................355
ACKNOWLEDGMENTS 365
ABOUT THE AUTHOR 367

ABOUT THE BOOK

The author has written this book as a caveat to all those who are naive and hardheaded, as he once was: sometimes unwittingly making choices without ever considering the possible adverse consequences and repercussions of those choices. This is his story of thirty-eight years behind bars, replete with detailed accounts of prison escapes, inmate violence, unethical prison guards, inadequate prison health care, and a brief commentary on the old felony murder law as it existed prior to 1980. The book also contains events and significant emotional experiences of the author's childhood and family members.

This is the story of a young man in his early twenties who chose the wrong friends, started using drugs and subsequently, made several tragic errors in judgment that literally cost another young man his life. The first chapter is a thorough narrative of his crime, which began as a drug deal, evolved into a rip off and resulted in armed robbery and first-degree murder. Although three individuals committed this crime, only the author was convicted and sent to prison for life. His two accomplices used and betrayed him. One testified against him and walked away with virtual immunity, while the other was acquitted of all charges.

The author gives an account of many interesting survival experiences, including his own escape and cross country trek to California, where he was arrested by the FBI after four months of freedom. While being transported back to Michigan, he once again attempts escape by breaking his handcuffs and jumping out of a vehicle traveling at seventy miles per hour. Once back inside prison walls, he spends the next eighteen months in the hole, where he finally realizes that he has always been his own worst enemy and begins making a conscience effort to become his own best friend.

CHAPTER 1

ARMED ROBBERY AND FIRST-DEGREE MURDER

It was September 20, 1972, when I was arrested. The charges still reverberate in my head today.

Count I: Feloniously, deliberately, willfully with malice aforethought, while in the perpetration or attempted perpetration of a robbery, did kill and murder one Alexander Blake.

Count II: Did assault Alexander Blake, Terry Brookens and William Sutton while armed with a dangerous weapon, a shotgun, and did then and there feloniously rob, steal and take from Alexander Blake, Terry Brookens and William Sutton, while in their presence, their respective wallets and contents therein.

I was tried by a jury in Lapeer County Circuit Court and on January 17, 1973, I was found guilty as charged.

On February 13, 1973, I was sentenced to life in prison for first-degree murder and to a term of twenty to thirty years for armed robbery.

----- SEPTEMBER 18, 1972 -----

For the past two months, Ron Preston, Terry Brookens and I had been sharing an apartment in Pontiac, Michigan. Pontiac was a city whose streets once gleamed with towering oak trees in the front yards of neat brick colonials. Shiny cars were parked in the driveways and children played on the sidewalks.

But that was about twenty years earlier. The city owed its then success mostly to the booming automobile industry, which had expanded north from Detroit to conveniently set up manufacturing plants in which good paying jobs abounded. Middle class families from all over the state descended upon the city and filled its streets with life.

Things weren't as shiny and successful as they once were for the city, which now had its fair share of slums — abandoned homes, seedy businesses and a plethora of darkened alleys. It also had an overabundance of apartment buildings. With the supply greatly outweighing the demand, rent was much cheaper than in the outlying suburbs. It was one of the reasons that Preston, Brookens and I had decided to move there. Plus, it was only about 20 minutes south of our hometowns and had more to offer in terms of nightlife.

I was the youngest of the three of us at twenty-two years old. Bell-bottoms were all the rage then and we wore them in all the colors of the rainbow — red and blue, green and yellow, even purple and pumpkin orange. I'd grown to my full height, about five-foot-nine, a little on the skinny side and wore my wavy hair shoulder-length, as did most young guys.

Both the other guys were twenty-four and I'd met them first in my hometown of Lake Orion, but I'd known Brookens a lot longer than Preston. My first encounter with Brookens was seven years earlier, when I was just fifteen, at a pool hall in downtown Lake Orion, which was the main hangout for all the young kids like ourselves.

Oddly enough, I met Preston at the same place, only years later. It was Brookens who'd introduced him to me. Preston was an unmistakable sight — a taller guy, maybe six-foot or six-foot-one, and probably about two hundred and thirty pounds. Making him stand out even more was the shoulder length, blaring red hair he had with a long, wavy and wild red beard to top off the look.

Brookens, on the other hand, was clean-shaven with straight, brown shoulder-length hair and tried to keep a very suave look about him. He was probably about my height and build, perhaps a bit stockier, and had a tendency to walk around with a sense of arrogance in his posture.

Preston worked on the line at one of the automobile manufacturing plants in Pontiac, a common job for young guys like us. Brookens on the other hand, worked at a fiberglass boat manufacturing plant just north of our hometown. Meanwhile I worked at a small automobile parts manufacturing plant in Pontiac, where I spent most of my time as a hi-low driver.

I mostly worked a regular nine-to-five shift at my job. I remember it was a mild day, the leaves on the trees still mostly green, when I left work that Monday. I made a quick stop by a fast food joint on my way back to the apartment. It was just before six o'clock when I walked in the door.

Preston was sitting on the sofa watching television and when I asked him where Brookens was, he replied that he was in the bathroom taking a shower.

After we talked for a couple of minutes, Preston began telling me about a drug deal that Brookens was making with one of his coworkers who lived in Lapeer County, a mostly rural county about twenty-five miles north of Pontiac.

"I guess the guy's name is Alex Blake," he continued. "He called Brookens earlier wanting to buy some weed."

Brookens had told Blake that he and his roommates didn't have anything, but that he could probably find what Blake wanted if he made a few telephone calls. Brookens then instructed the guy to call him back in an hour — an hour in which Preston and Brookens had discussed ripping off Blake for his money rather than actually selling him any drugs.

They thought it would be easy money.

"It's not like he can go to the cops and complain about getting ripped off while trying to buy illegal drugs," they reasoned.

When Brookens came out of the bathroom, they continued to discuss what their plan would be. And for this, there wasn't much planning anyhow — it wasn't like they were going to rob a bank.

Preston suggested to Brookens that when Blake calls back, he should set up a meeting with him at the bar on M-24 in Metamora, a little town just over the county line into Lapeer. Up there was nothing like being in Pontiac; farm fields, dirt roads and dingy diners dotted M-24, which was the main thoroughfare running north and south in the county.

Preston walked over to the kitchen cabinet, opened the drawer and pulled out a small brown paper lunch bag. He grabbed two sticks of butter out of the refrigerator, put them in the bag and handed it to Brookens.

"What the hell do we need butter for?" Brookens asked, holding the bag.

"It's a dummy, to fool them," Preston said. "Just put it in the trunk of your car."

"What if they want to look at it before the deal goes down?" Brookens inquired.

"Just tell 'em it's hidden in the trunk," Preston said nonchalantly. "Blake is only going to see the bag; he won't even get the chance to see what's inside it before I pull up."

Preston did have his concerns about the plan to meet in the parking lot of a bar that's alongside the busiest road in the county.

"Can't you convince him to meet you somewhere else?" Preston asked. "I mean, the parking lot's got lights and people coming and going."

Preston paused for a moment, thinking.

"Hey man, you know where Kyle Road is?" Preston asked Brookens, but Brookens was already shaking his head no.

"It's right before the bar, you can't miss it," Preston said. "It goes to the left of M-24 and its perfect, fuckin' perfect — there's no lights, no houses by the road. Nobody'll see what's going on."

Preston continued with the instructions.

"Drive down the road a bit and then stop, say 'Here's good, doesn't look like anyone's around. I'll grab the bag from the trunk,'" Preston devised. "And right then, I'll pull up behind you guys all fast and slam on the brakes, get out of the car and start screaming at you guys to give me your money."

The idea, then, was for Brookens to meet up with Blake at the bar, invite him into Brookens' car and drive down the road. Blake had never seen or heard of Preston before, so he'd have no clue that Preston wasn't actually a seasoned robber. Preston would act like he was robbing Brookens too, and Brookens would play along and give up his wallet so Blake wouldn't suspect it was a set up.

When Blake called back, I overheard Brookens telling him that he'd found the two ounces of marijuana. He asked Blake to meet him at the bar in Metamora at eight o'clock that evening.

Then Blake said something that made Brookens look momentarily uncomfortable.

"Yeah, I guess that's OK — I know that guy," Brookens said into the phone and then added, "Yeah, he's cool. That's fine."

Evidently, Blake didn't feel like coming alone. He'd asked Brookens if it was okay to bring along his friend, William Sutton. Brookens was definitely surprised — it was not, after all, a part of their *plan* — but apparently, he knew the guy and decided it wouldn't screw things up.

After Brookens hung up the telephone, Preston asked us if we wanted to get high. He wasn't talking about pot.

For the past couple of months, the three of us had been shooting heroin on a regular basis and we were beginning to spend more money on dope than what we were earning from our weekly paychecks. In fact, this was the reason Preston and Brookens were planning the rip off — they wanted the money to buy more drugs.

"Funny thing is, I did have two ounces of weed earlier today," Preston said, laughing. "I just took it to the dealer today and swapped for something better."

He tossed two dime bags of heroin on the kitchen table.

"Go ahead and enjoy yourselves," he said.

After we shot the heroin, Brookens and Preston continued to talk about the rip off, discussing the details of their plan. Practically in mid-sentence, Preston stopped talking and looked directly at me.

"Hey man, do you want to come along for the ride?" he asked me.

I was high and didn't really think about it, let alone digest the seriousness of the crime that would be taking place. Naïvely, I agreed to go along.

As we were getting ready to leave the apartment, Preston went to the closet in the living room and got out his old army fatigue jacket. Then he reached back into the closet, this time grabbing a black trench coat from another hanger and holding it out to me.

"Wear this, it'll be like a disguise," he said. I nodded and reached out my hand to take the coat.

We were ready to go. Brookens had already left the apartment and Preston and I were on our way out the door.

"Wait," Preston said, turning around just as he reached the door. "I have an idea — go grab the 20-gauge shotgun."

I stood there a moment, a little surprised. While I had known about the shotgun, it hadn't crossed my mind since we first moved into the apartment. I'd asked him about it back then. He'd told me it was his father's gun, which he'd borrowed a couple months earlier to go pheasant hunting with and that he just hadn't gotten around to returning it to him. I knew Preston did occasionally go hunting so I never gave it another thought.

"If these guys see that we have a gun, they'll be intimidated for sure," Preston mused. "Just think of it as insurance that nothing will go wrong. They'll be so scared, there's no way they'd try to be tough and start some shit."

The shotgun, then, was meant only to frighten these guys.

I went to the dining room where the shotgun was kept out of sight in an antique cabinet that I'd brought with me when I moved in. I carefully removed the shotgun from the cabinet and placed it underneath the trench coat where it couldn't be seen. The coat was big on me anyhow, its length passing beyond my knees and completely concealing the shotgun.

As we were walking to our cars, Preston reached into his coat pocket, pulled out a shotgun shell and handed it to me.

"When we drive up behind Brookens and stop, all you have to do is step out of the car and fire the shotgun into the air," Preston told me.

I must've looked stunned and he immediately told me not to worry.

"Insurance, man. It's just insurance. They're going to shit their pants," he said reassuringly. "Just stay back behind the car door. We can't have them getting a good look at the shotgun or else they'll notice it's only a single shot."

I laughed. "Okay man, whatever you say," I said.

Brookens drove past us as we were getting into our cars and he motioned with his hand for us to follow him. We were going to meet in Lake Orion, our hometown, where I'd park my car and ride with Preston.

The drive to Lake Orion was uneventful, except for the fact that I couldn't stop thinking about exactly what role I was about to play in this harebrained scheme.

This whole stupid mess started out with me going along for the ride, but I'd somehow let Preston talk me into doing something that I'd never have considered doing on my own.

I'd committed a few misdemeanor crimes when I was a juvenile, but this was sheer stupidity on my part. I was about to actively participate in an armed robbery, which I knew was a very serious crime that could possibly send me to prison for a long time. I wanted to tell Preston that I was having second thoughts, but I couldn't.

I was very insecure, worried of how my friends perceived me. I was afraid if I told Preston that I was having second thoughts, it'd either be the end to my current social circle or the beginning of years of taunting, or both. None of which appealed to me.

So, I kept my mouth shut. I didn't want to deal with another insecurity.

When we got to Lake Orion, Brookens was parked at the Clark gas station buying gas and when Preston pulled in, I drove in right behind him. I heard Preston tell Brookens to proceed up M-24 and that we would follow him to the bar in Metamora, but I told Preston that I needed to make a quick stop at my mother's house to pick up something.

"I'll meet you there instead," I said, and he nodded.

My mother lived in a big gray house on the corner of M-24 and Flint Street, which was right next to Lake Orion's quaint and historic downtown area. It only took me a couple of minutes to get there from the gas station.

I walked in the house and saw my mother sitting at the dining room table, meticulously applying her makeup just as she always did before she went anywhere. She worked the afternoon shift at a small factory in a growing community about 15 minutes southeast of Lake Orion. She was preparing to leave for work when I arrived.

I said hello, gave her a quick kiss on the cheek and asked her if my younger sister was home or if she was still at work.

"Oh, no, she's not home," my mother replied. "She's still at work."

"Okay, well I just needed to grab something from my old bedroom," I told her. "I'll be back tomorrow to see you."

I went up the stairs to where the bedrooms were located, but instead of going to my bedroom, I went into my sister's room. I went to her bureau, pulled out the drawers and started digging through her belongings. Nylon stockings were what I was looking for — they'd work better than the coats alone. Preston and I could pull them over our heads to make our faces unidentifiable.

I didn't want to take any chance that these guys might be able to identify us at some point in the future.

I found the stockings and went back down the stairs.

"Jim, I need to get some gas in the car," my mother said. "Would you mind taking it to the station next door?"

I wanted to tell her that I didn't have time, but before I could get a word out of my mouth she was holding out her car keys and a five dollar bill. At that point, I couldn't say no.

Just as I walked out the front door, Preston was pulling up and I told him that I needed to get some gas in my mother's car.

"It'll only take a minute," I told him.

I'd expected him to say we didn't have time, but he surprised me.

"Hey, put it on my credit card and we can use the cash for something else," he offered.

It didn't matter to me one way or the other, so I told him to go ahead and I gave him the car keys and the money. When Preston returned with my mother's car, he suggested we use it for the drive to Metamora.

"If someone does see us, it'll be harder to trace her car back to us," he told me.

At the time, it made sense to me. Plus, I was still high on drugs.

Nevertheless, I gave my mother some story about using her car and she bought it.

"Just have it back by the time I need to leave for work," she said.

Leaving my mother's house, I was in my own car and Preston was driving my mother's vehicle.

"I'll drive until we get to Oxford and you follow me," I told him as we were leaving.

Oxford was Lake Orion's neighbor to the north. In a matter of minutes, we had passed through Oxford's downtown strip lined with historic, brick buildings. I turned off on to a side street just north of the downtown and parked my car, then joined Preston in my mother's car.

In about 15 minutes, we'd be at our destination in Metamora. I spent the time asking Preston as many what-if questions as I possibly could.

Nothing stumped him, though. Preston had the ability to put people at ease; he could talk a person into making compromises they wouldn't otherwise consider. He would've made an excellent salesman with all his charisma, and a rich one too, I'm sure.

"I don't think anything can possibly go wrong," he reassured me. "Just think about it, what are these guys going to do?"

He made a face and started mocking our soon-to-be victims.

"Uh, officer, we were just trying to buy some drugs when these guys pulled up and robbed us," he mocked. "They'd be in handcuffs too — the officers would be laughing at them, probably tellin' 'em they got what they deserved."

He was probably right about that, but as we would soon find out, that was only one of about a hundred things that could go wrong.

We pulled into the bar's parking lot. It was a classic "watering hole" looking place, a rustic log cabin façade with very few windows. There weren't many vehicles in the parking lot, seeing as how it was a Monday night, and we noticed right away that Brookens' car was nowhere to be seen.

"We're running a few minutes late," Preston said. "Brookens is probably already en route to Kyle Road with our guys."

We turned around in the parking lot, got back on M-24 and headed south to Kyle Road. Once we got on Kyle Road, it was only a short distance before we spotted Brookens' car. I pulled out the nylon stockings I'd grabbed from my sister's dresser and tossed a pair to Preston. As I pulled the nylons over my face, I remember hearing my heart thumping wildly with nerves.

We saw Brookens standing at his trunk with Sutton and Blake, the trunk open and its light shining dimly on the men. Preston sped up, turned on his brights and then slammed on the brakes. The car came to a skidding stop on the loose gravel, its back end kicking out as we slid to a stop about twelve feet from Brookens' trunk.

Preston jammed the gearshift in park, threw open the car door with a menace and leapt out as if the car were about to burst into flames.

"Don't fuckin' move or I'll blow your fuckin' guts out!" Preston screamed at them.

I was a bit shocked by Preston's energy and dire threats — it seemed a little extreme and over the top for our plan.

I'd gotten out of the car too and was standing behind the front passenger side door. I knew this was when I was supposed to fire the shotgun in the air, but looking into the faces of Blake and Sutton made me realize it wasn't necessary.

It wasn't just a look of shock or surprise I saw — not like a deer caught in headlights. No, if these guys were deer, then the look in their eyes said they were staring down the barrel of a hunter's rifle. In their eyes, I saw terror.

There was no need to fire the shotgun and for the first time that day, I was making my own decision about my role in this scheme. I didn't shoot.

Preston didn't skip a beat; didn't even turn around to shoot me a look about my decision. Instead, he proceeded in his role as the menacing robber.

"Turn around and put your hands up!" he yelled at them. "Turn around — I said turn the fuck around! Face the goddamn car!"

The three men complied mostly in silence. Only Brookens, playing along, had the guts to make a sound.

"Whatever you want, man. Whatever it is, you can have it," I remember hearing him say.

Preston wasted no time approaching them, shoving them into the car and digging his hands into their pockets to take everything they had.

He grabbed wallets from Blake and Sutton and made sure to get Brookens' wallet too. He gave Brookens an extra shove into the car — assuring that the other two guys saw Brookens as a victim as well.

"Where are the fuckin' drugs at, huh? Huh?" he interrogated the men. "Get over here; get the fuck over here by the trunk. Where are the fuckin' drugs?"

"We don't have any drugs, man," Sutton said, probably wanting the whole ordeal to just be over with.

"You think I'm a fuckin' idiot? Give me the goddamn drugs," Preston barked.

Brookens obligingly spoke up, quietly telling Preston the drugs were in the trunk behind the spare tire while he kept his head down, his eyes focused on the gravel under his feet. Brookens played a good victim.

Preston pushed Sutton aside. "No drugs, huh?" he sneered, and pushed Blake away too. Then he leaned into the trunk and grabbed the brown paper bag with the two sticks of butter in it.

If my heart wasn't pounding so hard from nerves, I might've had to laugh at the entire ordeal. All this pushing, shoving and barking orders, and for what? Two sticks of butter.

But the rip off was complete now. We could go, and I was antsy to get back in the car and head home.

"Just go, get the fuck out of here," Preston yelled at the men. "Make yourselves disappear — go!"

He motioned for the men to take off into the woods across from the roadside while yelling at them. Brookens and Sutton didn't waste any time, running into the dark woods and disappearing in a flash.

Blake, though, just stood there. It was like he was frozen.

"Get the fuck out of here man!" Preston yelled at him. "Did you hear me, motherfucker? I said go!"

But Blake didn't move. He was still standing there, just a few feet in front of the vehicle.

I tightened my grip on the gun and thought that maybe if I prodded him with the end of the barrel, it might just jolt him out of his shock and get him to take off running.

I was still standing behind the car door, so I stepped around it and walked over to the front fender. It all happened so fast — not even a second, I'm sure — but to this day, it plays back so slowly in my mind.

I was going to reach the gun out and jab him with its end, not getting myself close enough to make physical contact with him.

As I stepped forward, perhaps a bit clumsily, that's when it happened — I just remember seeing a flash of fire shoot out from the muzzle. I had inadvertently squeezed the trigger when I pushed Blake with the gun's barrel and as I realized what happened, a rush of shock and horror washed through my body.

Like in slow motion, my eyes watched the wadding from the shotgun shell as it exploded from the barrel and then instantly disappeared when it hit Blake.

Every time I close my eyes, I can see that split-second moment replay in my head — the wadding disappearing and Blake's back arching forward with the impact of the shot, his legs taking a couple stumbling steps forward in the gravel before he dropped to his knees and slowly fell face down in the dusty dirt road.

I could see a hole in the back of his flannel shirt where the pellets and wadding had struck him. The pellets hit Blake in the small of his back on the left side, about waist-high, and as would later be verified in court, the pellets entered his body at a thirty-degree angle.

In the midst of what felt like great chaos, I too had fallen to my knees, but I quickly clamored to my feet and stumbled over to Blake, trying to get a feel for how bad he was hurt.

"Oh God, let him be okay, let him be okay," I prayed under my breath.

But what I saw didn't indicate that would be the case. Blood was pumping out of the hole in his back, darkening and drenching his flannel shirt. I could see blood dripping out of his mouth too, falling in big, red drops and coloring the gravel as they hit.

I can close my eyes and still hear his shallow, labored breathing. With each breath, there was a wheezing, almost whistling noise. I wanted to roll him over, to see his face — some innate desire telling me that if I could just look at him, maybe he'd be okay. Maybe he'd say something.

But common sense told me better, that moving him could actually do him more harm than good. I'd already done enough harm.

One look at Blake lying there and I think anyone could've known that this was a serious, life-threatening wound. But Preston was already shouting in the background.

"Get in the car, man," he yelled nervously. "We gotta get out of here, now! Right fuckin' now!"

Now full of terror myself, I ran back in the car and jumped in the passenger seat. I didn't even get the door closed before Preston floored the gas pedal in reverse. We zipped backwards down the road, Preston's head cranked around so he could see out the rear window.

When we could no longer see Brookens' car in the headlights, Preston jammed on the breaks, spun the steering wheel around and we made a sliding u-turn in the middle of the road. With the car now facing forward, Preston stomped the gas pedal and we jolted forward, racing at a breakneck speed back toward M-24.

We went back the same way we came, heading south toward Oxford as fast as we possibly could. I knew there was a small party store on our side of the road and as we got close, I urged Preston to stop.

"Come on, man, we gotta stop," I pleaded with him. "I didn't want to kill nobody; we gotta call an ambulance for that guy."

"No way, man," he said. "Someone'll see you make the call and the cops'll come down here and be all over the place — they'd be on top of us in no time."

He continued, "We can't fuckin' get caught man. This is serious shit."

"That's what I'm saying dude — if Blake doesn't get help and dies, then I'm in for fuckin' murder!" I said, flipping out.

"Even if he doesn't die, you're in deep fuckin' shit if we get caught so you'd best be worried about yourself," Preston told me. "Besides, Blake will be fine. The pellets didn't hit 'em anywhere serious."

"I don't know, man, it looked pretty fuckin' serious to me," I spoke, my voice still shrill with fear. "I saw the hole in his back, man, and there was blood coming out of his mouth — his mouth! That's bad, you know that's bad."

"It doesn't fucking matter," he yelled at me. "It doesn't matter. Either way, we're both fucked if we don't get the hell out of dodge and pretend this never happened."

Maybe if Preston had seen the hole in Blake, the blood running out of his mouth and splattering on the gravel, maybe then he'd have felt different. Maybe if he'd been the one holding the shotgun, or if he'd just stood there for a second rather than immediately running back to the car, maybe he would've stopped. Maybe.

Preston was, however, always looking out for himself first. It probably wouldn't have made a difference. It doesn't stop all the what-ifs and maybes from running through my head though, even nearly 40 years later.

Preston was driving like a madman, keeping the gas pedal pressed to the floor as he sped down M-24 and then turned off onto Oakwood Road — a winding and paved but less traveled road — just before we got into Oxford.

He kept to the back roads all the way into Lake Orion, where we had to drop my mom's car off to her.

When we got back to her house, Preston gathered up the coats, nylon stockings, the shotgun and the wallets he took from Blake and Sutton and put them in his car.

"I'm going to make sure that none of this shit is ever seen again!" he said. "I'll be back."

As strange as it may seem, I never asked Preston and he never told me how much money he took from Blake and Sutton.

After Preston left, I went inside my mother's house to wait until he got back. I held out the car keys to my mother and sat down on the living room couch, staring blankly at the television set. I couldn't move, but my mind was racing with a million thoughts. Fear and guilt consumed me and a disquieting knot of anxiety was growing in the pit of my stomach.

It was only about a half hour until Preston returned, though it felt a world longer. I joined him in the car and sat down silently. He kept the engine running, but never pulled the car out of park.

"It's taken care of," he told me. "No one will ever find that stuff."

I didn't bother to ask him what he did with it; just nodded my head and continued to stare forward blankly. I didn't really want to know where it was.

He was right, though. Whatever he did with those things remains a mystery. No one ever found them.

We sat in silence for a while. Consumed by the knot of anxiety and guilt weighing my stomach down like a rock, I couldn't think of a thing to say.

"I'm not going back to the apartment tonight," he said. "I'm going to stay away for a while, but if you need me, I'll be at my wife's apartment."

He and his wife were newly separated. In fact, it was one of the reasons the three of us decided to move in together. They maintained a somewhat cordial relationship, though. Since the separation, she had moved into a relatively new apartment complex on Walton Road, which was the very northern border to the city of Pontiac.

"It's probably best that we aren't seen together for the next few days, though, so you probably shouldn't come by," he told me. "And you should probably stay away from the apartment too, at least until we know what Brookens told the police."

My car was still parked in Oxford and I asked him if he'd drive me up there to pick it up.

"I don't think that's a good idea; we should probably stay away from M-24," he said. "The police are probably on the lookout for two men, especially two guys driving down M-24."

I nodded my head again and reached for the door handle to open the car door. He told me to be careful as I stepped out of the car. I still didn't have any words.

I watched him pull out of the driveway and then walked to the gas station next door. I knew they ran a towing service out of the station and figured I could get them to give me a lift to my car.

I felt lost without my car. Of any time to be stuck somewhere, to have no way to escape quickly, now was not the time.

Walking under the lights over to the gas pumps, I tried to square my shoulders and told myself to look normal and act normal. I wondered if I somehow looked different, if shooting a man could perhaps change a person and make him look automatically suspicious.

Be normal, I told myself. *Just be normal.*

I approached the counter and attempted to smile and kind of grimace at the same time.

My Own Worst Enemy

"Hey there," I said. "My car stalled out on me earlier today, just on the other side of downtown Oxford. Just couldn't get the darn thing to start again."

"Any chance you'd mind driving me up there and taking a look at it for me?" I asked, and added, "It probably ain't nothing big, she's a pretty solid car."

"I'm closin' up here at ten o'clock," he said to me. "If you don't mind waiting until then, I can drive up there and give 'er a look."

"Yeah, that'd be fine," I agreed. "Thanks a lot, man."

"No problem," he said, and I walked away from the counter.

I hung around the station until the attendant closed up and was ready to go. It only took us about ten minutes to drive the short distance to Oxford and when we got to my car the attendant told me to first try to start the engine like normal.

"Maybe the carburetor just flooded with too much gas," he suggested. "After they sit for a while, sometimes, they'll just start right back up."

I got in my car and when I turned the key, the engine started just as I knew it would.

"You must've been right about that carburetor," I said to him. "It was probably just flooded with too much gas."

He charged me five dollars for the service call.

"You get any more problems with that car, just bring it in and I can check her out for ya," he offered and returned to his car.

I didn't know exactly where to go or what to do. I wanted to listen to the news — a person getting shot, especially in a normally quiet farm town, would make big headlines on the local stations. As I approached my mother's house, I decided I'd stop back in. My mother had already left for work and my sister was nowhere to be found either.

I turned the radio on to one of the local stations that gave news headline updates every fifteen minutes. Commercials played for a minute or so and then the newscaster's voice came over the airwaves.

Immediately, I heard what I didn't want to hear.

"We have breaking news. It is being reported that one person has been shot and fatally wounded in Lapeer County," the newscaster said. "There is very little information available at this time but police do suspect the victim was shot during a robbery."

My ears were pounding with the pulse of my blood rushing quickly through them. My stomach sank as if I was riding a rollercoaster and suddenly, I felt I was going to be sick.

What do I do, I asked myself silently, *what the hell do I do?*

The gravity of the situation crashed down around me like a ton of bricks. The room went away, its furniture and walls and windows, the radio and coffee table — it all disappeared as my head spun and my stomach turned.

I killed a man. I am responsible for the death of another human being, I thought.

This was without a doubt the biggest mistake of my life. I should've jumped out of the car at that party store and called the paramedics. Better yet, I shouldn't have gone along with them in the first place, or at least disagreed with taking the gun along. I could've thrown the shotgun shell out the window during the drive up. I could've stayed behind the door and let Preston deal with making Blake run. I could have, and I should have, done so many things differently.

It was an accident, I told myself. *Just turn yourself in. Tell the police everything. They'll believe you. It was just an accident.*

But I didn't believe that. We were robbing these people; worse yet, we were drug addicts robbing these people. Telling them that we hadn't planned nor remotely even thought of hurting anyone wouldn't matter, because we did hurt someone. Or more to the point, I did. I killed a man.

I was acutely aware of the fact that I'd made a tragic error in judgment that was undoubtedly going to adversely affect the lives of many people for an indefinite number of years to come.

I wanted to say that I was sorry, to undo what we'd done, but it was too late.

I decided I needed to talk to Preston again. I had to know exactly what he was thinking. Perhaps he'd also listened to the news and heard that Blake died. If he didn't, I needed to tell him. Maybe he was having second thoughts. Maybe the seriousness of the situation was settling in for him like it was for me.

From my point of view, we didn't have many viable options. Sooner or later, we would have to face the consequences of what we had done.

I left my mother's house and began heading back to Pontiac. I made a right onto Walton Road and turned into the newly built apartment complexes on the corner, where Preston's wife lived. Pulling into the parking lot, I spotted Preston's car and felt relieved knowing he was there. I'd never been to her apartment before and wasn't sure which one was hers, but it was a simple matter of checking the mailboxes in the foyer of the apartment building until I found her name and apartment number. She was on the first floor.

I rang the doorbell and Preston's wife opened the door. Before I could ask her if Preston was there, she said he was.

"He's sitting in the living room watching the football game," she said. "You want to come in?"

"Yes, please," I said and stepped through the doorway.

Preston was sitting on the sofa in the living room watching television. When he looked up and saw it was me, he invited me in.

"Come on and sit down," he said.

I sat in a chair next to the sofa and tried to act as if everything was normal. I was sure Preston didn't tell his wife about what happened and I didn't want her to notice that anything was wrong.

We made small talk about the football game for several minutes and then Preston asked his wife if she wouldn't mind getting him something out of the kitchen.

As soon as she left the room, I scooted forward in the chair, leaned closer toward Preston and in a low voice, I whispered, "Blake is dead."

"Are you sure?" he asked.

"Yes I'm sure," I said. "I heard it on the radio before I left my mother's house."

I was expecting some sort of reaction from Preston — shock, fear, guilt, just something. But the look on his face didn't change. He didn't seem the least bit concerned or worried about what I'd just told him.

"Calm down, man. Just take it easy," he said quietly. "We need to wait until we hear from Brookens and find out what he told the cops."

"I don't know, Preston," I agonized. "This is serious shit, and if we don't come clean and just let them know the whole thing was an accident, it'll be even more serious."

"We just gotta tell them everything, man. Everything," I added.

Preston didn't want to hear that.

"It doesn't matter if it was an accident or not," he retorted. "It happened during a robbery, that makes it first-degree felony murder, you jackass."

He wasn't going to budge and so, still uncertain about what to do, I drove back to my mother's house. I spent the night there, but that's not to say I got any sleep.

The robbery, the shooting, all the events of the day kept replaying in my head. The guilt was overwhelming. The knot in my stomach never eased and questions of what to do kept me awake most of the night.

By the time the sun rose the next morning, I felt and looked like crap. Even so, I got dressed and made my way downstairs.

My mother was standing in the kitchen, drinking a cup of coffee.

"Do you want a bite to eat, Jim?" she asked me.

"No thank you," I said politely. "I'm not hungry, and I really need to get going."

"Is everything okay?" she inquired.

"Yeah, everything's fine," I tried to say nonchalantly. "I'm just supposed to be in Pontiac in like 20 minutes."

"Okay," she said. "And you're all right?"

"I'm fine," I told her.

I'm sure she sensed that something was wrong. I desperately wanted to tell her everything, but I couldn't. She'd seen me in all sorts of trouble, but not like this. Nothing like this. There are just some things a son can't say to his mother, things that are too heartbreaking. Shooting and killing a man is one of them.

I needed to find out if Brookens had returned to the apartment. I had to know exactly what he told the police. I got in my car and headed back to Pontiac.

Still not wanting to show myself around the apartment, I decided to park my car several blocks away. I walked to a gas station that was just down the road from the apartment and decided I would call instead to see if Brookens was there. The phone rang and then picked up, but it wasn't Brookens on the other end — it was Preston.

"Hey man, it's ..." I started to say my name, but Preston cut me off.

"He's here now, but he's with a couple guys from Lake Orion," Preston told me. "So we can't talk now."

"Do you know anything about what Brookens told the cops? Are we suspects?" I asked.

"Dude, I told you. I can't talk about that right now," he hissed. "There's people here."

"Okay, just tell Brookens to meet me on the bridge down the street in twenty minutes," I said and hung up the phone.

I walked down to the bridge and paced back and forth a couple times. Turning around, I spotted Brookens heading toward me and he was smiling. Smiling. I couldn't believe it.

How in the hell can he be smiling? Does he realize what fucking happened last night?

I should've known right then that something wasn't right, but my mind was preoccupied. Maybe he has good news. It didn't matter. I just wanted to hear what he told the cops.

With the smile fading from his face as he got closer, he said, "What the hell happened? How the fuck did you shoot Blake?"

"He was just standing there," I told him. "He wouldn't run off like you guys did; Preston even yelled at him twice and he was just fucking standing there, in the middle of the goddamn road."

It felt slightly relieving to finally be speaking the details of what happened last night out loud. Every little action had been running through my head for hours, but I hadn't said a single thing aloud. But as the words came out of my mouth, the shock set back in after hearing my voice and my words verbalize all those actions.

"I thought if I just nudged him with the gun it'd grab his attention, scare him away," I told Brookens. "But when I went to push him, I must've accidentally squeezed the trigger."

I took a breath and continued: "I didn't mean for it to happen. I didn't want to hurt anyone, man — you know that."

Brookens sighed. "That's fucked up man. Just fucked up," he said.

He said that he and Sutton had been questioned by police for most of the night and that they'd been released only a couple of hours ago.

"They told me to go home and get some sleep, but I've got to go back in later today for more questions," he told me. "They impounded my car for evidence and said the state police crime lab is already dusting it for fingerprints. I'm hopin' they're done with it by the time they finish questioning me tonight."

Brookens said that he and Sutton told nearly the exact same story when first questioned by the police. They both said that they couldn't identify either of the two people that had robbed them and shot Blake, but instead gave police a general description — height, weight, clothing, the nylon masks. Nothing that would pinpoint us.

Sutton was asked first about the vehicle and described it as a white 1972 Plymouth with a black top. Sutton told Brookens how he had described the car, so Brookens repeated the same description, knowing it wasn't entirely accurate.

My mother's car wasn't white, but actually a dark brown color with a black vinyl top.

"Do the police know that the three of us live together?" I asked Brookens.

"I told them about Preston, because his name's on the lease," Brookens said. "But they don't know anything about you. I didn't mention your name; they don't know you live with us."

He could tell I was on edge.

"Everything will be okay," he said. "The police don't know or even have any reason to think we might be involved. As far as I know, we aren't suspects at all."

He paused for a moment and looked down at the ground.

"You probably should stay away from the apartment, though, just in case the police are watching it to see who's coming and going," he added.

I felt a little jolted by him saying that, knowing that he and Preston would be there like normal but I had to stay away. It almost seemed like they were blaming me when it was their stupid idea from the start. I didn't say anything though and reassured myself that we were all in this together.

"If you need to get in touch with me, then, I guess I'll be at my mom's house," I told him.

Brookens and I parted ways but instead of heading back to my mom's house, I went straight to the dope house and bought a couple packs of heroin. I thought, and hoped, the heroin would help me get through the day. I wanted it to numb me, and to numb my guilty conscience. I was only fooling myself, though. Deep down, I knew that the drugs wouldn't make my problems go away.

In fact, the drugs had only served to make every aspect of my life a living hell and it'd only taken a few months to do so.

Growing up in Lake Orion, kids pretty much separated into one of three crowds once they hit their teenage years — hippies, frats or squares. The hippies, of course, weren't exactly all deadheads who tripped out all day and never took a shower. Mostly, it was just the kids who rebelled more than the rest, wearing their hair long and their bellbottoms big and trying out whatever drugs might be floating around in the local community.

It was an easy crowd to fall in with and so, I did. I tried smoking weed as a teenager and drinking beer like the rest of them, but I never cared much for it. For the most part, I stayed away from the drugs and alcohol and just enjoyed the easygoing company of the crowd I hung around with.

When I turned twenty, I tried out some prescription drugs: mostly painkillers like Demerol and such. I liked it much better than I did the marijuana and alcohol.

By that time, Brookens had introduced me to Preston and the three of us hung around a lot. One day, Preston and I were cruising around when he said he had to drop off an ounce of marijuana at a friend's house. He asked me to come inside with him and as I had no reason not to oblige, I followed him in.

A handful of people were sitting around on the sofas in the living room. Preston introduced me and we sat down too. They all started talking about heroin and apparently, there was some in the house. Before I knew it, Preston and his smooth talking ways — selling the drug to me like a salesman selling a car — persuaded me to give it a shot.

One time can't hurt, I told myself. *You can't get addicted from one try.*

I remember Preston inserting the needle in my arm for the first time. As soon as the drugs hit my vein, the high was instantaneous

— it felt like a slice of heaven was coursing through my veins with every beat of my heart. It was incredible.

I began using on the weekends with Preston and Brookens. It was purely recreational, I told myself. Pretty soon, though, we were shooting up in the evenings after work. I quickly gave up seeking any sort of regulation of my newfound drug habit, though in my own brain, I didn't see that I was addicted.

We had lived in the apartment for about two months at the time of the botched robbery. All three of us were shooting up on a daily basis when we moved in together and our new living situation was only encouraging and enabling the growing drug habit that the three of us shared.

Now, as I sought out another high, I reflected on all that had transpired.

During the past two months, I'd managed to destroy any chance for a decent life that I might have had. The stupid and harmful things I'd done to myself — I had truly become my own worst enemy. I'd have never allowed anyone to do the things to me that I did to myself. I knew that I had a problem, but it seemed like I was powerless to do anything about it. And now, I'd killed a man. But even that wasn't enough; I just couldn't give up the dope.

I got in and out of the dope house as fast as I could and pulled into the first gas station I came to. I had to get my fix. I needed it. So I walked quickly inside and into their bathroom, shutting the door behind me and making sure it was locked.

I backed myself up in the corner, my back leaning against the crumbling, cold and dirty tiles that lined the walls and floor. As I focused on preparing the heroin and getting my arm ready to shoot up, I'm sure I didn't even notice what a despicable place I was in — a rusty sink and toilet partially full with the feces and toilet paper of people who apparently couldn't hold it until they found a more sanitary place. None of it mattered as I pushed the heroin into my arm and let myself slump down in the corner, not caring about the dirty floor I sat on or the filthy cold tiles I leaned my head against.

I didn't have any place to go. I really didn't want to see my mother. She knew something was wrong. I couldn't have her prying it out of me, no matter how much I wanted to tell her everything.

I drove around aimlessly for a few hours after that. My high was unable to mask my worries as I passed one street after another and the consequences of what I'd done really began to sink in. I wanted so badly to just stop and call the police, but I couldn't bring myself to do it.

Eventually, I decided to stop at the Firebird Lounge in Pontiac and have a drink. Although I never really cared for the taste of alcohol, my high was wearing off and I hoped that a couple of drinks might help to ease my troubled mind.

The bar was practically empty; there weren't more than a dozen people in the whole place. I reminded myself that it was a Tuesday night — not exactly the hottest bar night in town.

The lounge was a happening place on the weekends, drawing the best in local bands to perform on their stage. The booths and barstools were a bright red fake leather material set against black walls and black tables with a polished wood bar that ran the length of one whole wall. Smoke swirled throughout the joint, though it was much less smoky on that night than during the weekends.

I sat down at the bar, ordering a shot of Tequila.

"With a Budweiser to chase," I added.

When I really wanted to get drunk, this was my drink to do it — liquor and beer.

I looked around the room, perhaps a bit nervously but trying to act normal. I noticed a girl I knew from high school sitting at the other end of the bar and thought about buying her a drink.

My insecurities made me question if she'd even recognize or remember me.

I was feeling miserable, though. I needed someone to talk to; something to keep my mind off the events of last night. I picked up my drinks and walked down the length of the bar, settling on a stool next to her.

In fact, she did remember me and we sat together, talking and drinking for quite some time. I was beginning to feel the intoxicating effects of the alcohol, but even after all the alcohol and heroin, I still couldn't suppress the overwhelming sense of guilt that remained pitted in my stomach.

With my tongue loosened by the drinks and my mind incapable of thinking of anything other than the events of the night before, I slipped up.

"I'm thinking about leaving the state," I said grimly. "I might have gotten myself into a lot of trouble. I'm seriously thinking about leaving."

She gave me a look of inquisitive indulgence.

"I'm curious, Jim, what kind of trouble could possibly be so serious that you would consider leaving behind your family, your friends, your everything?" she asked.

I looked up and into her eyes, but then turned and shook my head.

"Does it have something to do with a woman?" she asked.

"No," I said, still looking away. "It's a lot more complicated than that."

I had an overwhelming urge to tell somebody what was really on my mind, detail by detail. It was becoming harder and harder to keep the words from coming out of my mouth.

"Don't say anything, but I was at the scene of a robbery and shooting in Lapeer County," I said, and she looked at me dumbfounded. "Now, I didn't rob or shoot anybody, but I was there."

And then I added, with a grimace, "In fact, cops might be looking for me right now."

She kept asking me more questions, and more questions, until they were all blurring together. I sat there silently, coming to the realization that I had said too much. Way too much.

"I have to go to the bathroom," I told her, getting up. "I'll be right back."

It was an easy way out. I walked unsteadily past the bathroom and out the front door of the bar, and then found my way to my car. I was going home, to my mother's, to get some sleep.

I actually did sleep — I'd apparently consumed enough booze to allow my weary body to finally rest. When I woke the next morning, all my troubles came rushing back and I called Preston right away. I had to know the latest.

"I haven't heard from him, man," he told me very matter-of-factly. "I drove him back to the Lapeer County Sheriff's yesterday, and I haven't heard from him since."

He continued on, telling me that Brookens never returned to the apartment last night.

"I'm starting to wonder what the hell is going on," he said.

"Do you think the police arrested him?" I asked Preston. "And what about, I mean, have you considered that Brookens might've told them everything? What if he cracked?"

Preston was quick to defend Brookens.

"He wouldn't give us up," he told me. "Brookens is not that kind of guy."

I made no comment on what I thought Brookens might do and instead told Preston to call me as soon as he heard anything, and then hung up the phone.

I'd never told Preston about my past experiences with Brookens and I'm quite sure Brookens never told Preston what type of guy he really was — a liar, a snitch and a rapist. Preston really had no clue of what Brookens was actually capable of. I'd never told Preston that Brookens was a piece of shit. I was always afraid that if I said anything bad about Brookens, everyone would just turn on me and defend him, leaving me with no friends.

In my mind, though, there wasn't the smallest snippet of doubt that Brookens would indeed give us up to save his own skin.

I hung around my mother's house, hoping to hear something from Preston or Brookens. Around noon, the phone finally rang. It was Preston.

"Brookens called, he said he's still at the sheriff's and wanted to know if I'd come pick him up," Preston told me. "I guess the crime lab is still going over his car so he needs a ride back to the apartment, so I'm taking off right now to go get him. I'll call you back as soon as we get home."

Four hours passed, and by the time four o'clock arrived, I was getting restless. I hadn't heard from either of them. I needed something to do, but I didn't want to get too far away from the phone just in case Preston called back.

I decided to drive down to the self-service quarter car wash that was right down the street and blow the dust off my car. When I got there, I gave the car a quick wash and I decided to wipe it off when I got back to my mother's house.

I headed back, but as soon as I turned on to my mother's street I noticed an unmarked sheriff's car in front of my neighbor's house. It was an Oakland County Sheriff's car, since that was the county where we lived, but nonetheless, it was a cop. And I knew instantly that they were there for me.

The thought crossed my mind that I should keep going, but I knew it would only delay the inevitable. But I couldn't stop just then. I drove past the house, turned around at the next street and then drove back and parked across the street. I didn't see any police when I first drove up, but I knew they were there. They were somewhere close by.

They're probably waiting for me inside my mother's house, I thought.

I got out of my car, but instead of going inside I began wiping the droplets of water off the car windows as if nothing were wrong; as if I had no idea as to what was going on.

Out of the corner of my eye, I saw two men dressed in suits and another in a sheriff's deputy uniform walking out of my mother's front door. They walked directly over to me. I ignored them as best I could, continuing to wipe my car dry until they were a matter of feet from me and I could ignore them no longer.

The two men in suits identified themselves as detectives with the Lapeer County Sheriff's Office. I could see deputies dressed in the Oakland County uniforms standing by their vehicle now, watching as their counterparts from the county to the north approached me.

"Is your name James Anthony Goble?" one of them asked me.

I nodded my head and replied, "Yes."

"Sir, I have a warrant for your arrest on the charges of armed robbery and first-degree murder," he said, and before I knew it, I was being placed in handcuffs.

While one detective tightened the handcuffs, the other pulled a small card out of his pocket and began reading me the Miranda rights.

When he finished, he asked me if I understood my rights.

"Yes," I said solemnly.

"Do you wish to make a statement?" he asked me.

"No," I replied, and just like that, they grasped me by my upper arm and walked me across the street to the cop car, placing me in the back seat.

Before they closed the door, one of the detectives asked me if I'd give them permission to search my vehicle. Obligingly, I told them to go ahead. There was nothing in my car that could be used against me.

My Own Worst Enemy

A lot of things raced through my mind on the drive to the Lapeer County Jail. We went back up M-24, the same path we'd taken on the fateful trip to Metamora two days ago.

When we arrived at the county jail, a gray and dreary looking square building, the sheriff's deputies didn't waste any time booking me on charges of first-degree murder and armed robbery. Immediately, I was whisked into a small room where a deputy grabbed my hands and took my fingerprints, then lined me up against a wall and took several mug shots.

When that was done, he handed me a pair of white coveralls and a pair of white rubber shower shoes.

"Put these on," he said, then he handed me a large brown paper bag. "And put all your civilian clothes and shoes in the bag."

Now dressed in my jailhouse apparel, I was taken inside the main cellblock and placed in a four-man cell all by myself. The jail itself was a pretty small place, much smaller than its outward appearance made it look. The cells were also small. Two bunks holding cot-sized mattresses were bolted to one wall. A toilet, steel sink, and showerhead were mounted to the opposite wall. And unlike the rear of the cell that was enclosed with steel bars, the front of the cell was totally enclosed with the only point of entry being a solid steel door.

After the deputy left I stood there, looking around, until I heard the inmate in the adjoining cell calling out to me from the crack underneath his cell door. "Whatchya in here for?" he asked me.

I got down on the floor next to the door, "Armed robbery and first-degree murder," I said, the words sounding surreal coming out of my own mouth.

"That's strange — guy across the hall got brought in for the same thing," he said, and immediately I assumed it was either Preston or Brookens.

I called out Preston's name, to which he answered right away.

"Where's Brookens?" I called out to him.

"I have no idea," Preston said.

We began asking all the inmates around us and none of them had heard the name. We even asked some of the jail staff members too, but he was nowhere to be found.

"So, what happened? I thought you were coming to pick him up?" I asked Preston.

"I was on my way here and a bunch of police cars came up on me, surrounded me and forced me off the road," Preston said. "They ordered me out of the car with their guns pointed directly at me."

Preston too was arrested for armed robbery and first-degree murder.

It was difficult for Preston and I to communicate through the solid steel doors of our cells. We had to lay face down on the cold concrete floor and talk through the small crack at the bottom of the doors, and we had to be careful of what we said. In a jail, someone is always listening.

We began passing notes back and forth if we needed to communicate anything important; anything we had to keep private.

Preston suggested that we not talk to the police, if they tried to question us, until we had attorneys present.

"I already called my wife, she's going to have an attorney at the courthouse tomorrow morning for our arraignment," Preston said.

All inmates are allowed one phone call, and I hadn't yet made mine. When the deputy walked by, I got his attention and asked if I could make my one call.

"I'll need to check with the sergeant," he said and walked away.

In a matter of minutes, he returned and told me I could make one, five-minute phone call.

The only person I knew to call was my mother and I was sure, after the police were at her house looking for me, that she'd be worried about what had happened to me.

The phone rang and she picked up right away.

"What in the world is going on?" she asked, sounding exasperated. Her voice trembled as she began asking me question after question and it was clear how worried she was.

"I only have five minutes to talk," I told her. "I just wanted to let you know that I'm okay. I'm being arraigned early tomorrow morning in Lapeer County District Court, can you make it there?"

She told me she could, and then I told her what I'd been arrested for. She gasped hearing the charges, and I quickly added: "I'll explain everything when we have more time to talk, but don't worry about me. I'm okay, really."

"I love you very much, Mom," I said and hung up the phone.

When I got back to my cell, I laid down on the floor and scooted close to the gap under the door.

"I just called my mother," I told Preston and I heard footsteps approaching. It was the deputies, and before I could say anything else, they took Preston out of his cell and escorted him down the hallway to a small room at the end.

A few minutes later, he was back — the deputies leading him down the hall and putting him back in his cell. He waited until the deputies left and then filled me in on what happened.

"There were two detectives in there," he said. "They were asking all kinds of questions about the robbery and shooting, but I wouldn't answer a single one."

He added: "I just told them I wouldn't say a word without an attorney present, just like we talked about."

The detectives kept prying and added that they knew Preston was involved because Brookens had already confessed.

"They said, 'We just want to hear your version of what happened,'" Preston said to me.

I wanted to hear what else they told him, exactly what Brookens had confessed to and what else they knew. But before Preston could finish talking, the deputy came back — this time for me. He unlocked my cell door, opened it and escorted me down the hall to the same room Preston had just been in.

The two detectives, the same ones who had arrested me, were in the room. Both were wearing dark suits and while one sat behind a desk, the other was sitting on top of it with his legs crossed. They both stared sternly at me as I walked in.

"Take a seat," said the detective sitting at the desk, motioning toward the lone chair across from him. I sat down apprehensively.

"Things'll go a lot easier for you if you cooperate and answer some questions for us," the detective continued saying.

The other detective piped in, "We know you're the one who shot Alex Blake."

The detective behind the desk quickly added, "But we just want to hear your side of the story. Are you willing to make a statement?"

I looked down at the desk and thought about it for a moment. I considered just coming clean now, letting all the little details pour out. But then I thought of Preston — he hadn't said a word. I reminded myself that anything I said could be used against me.

"No," I said. "No, I want to speak with an attorney first."

I was returned to my cell, where I called out to Preston as soon as I could and told him exactly what the detectives said to me, and that I didn't answer any questions.

We soon found out that Brookens had helped the police to set up Preston. Brookens had apparently spilled his guts to the cops, confessing to everything. The cops then asked him to call Preston and ask if he'd pick him up from the jail and give him a ride back to the apartment. The cops needed to get Preston into their jurisdiction in Lapeer County in order to arrest him without another agency's help, so they waited for Preston's car to pass the county line and then surrounded him with police cars to make the arrest.

Supposedly, Brookens had made the same phone call to my mother's house, but I wasn't there to answer it.

CHAPTER 2

Brookens' Treachery

Brookens was a real piece of work; the epitome of a dope fiend. He was the type of addict that would betray his own mother for a syringe of heroin. Brookens had, after all, set up his own friend and coworker to be robbed — which resulted in a death, and then, two days later, he betrayed both Preston and I on top of it all.

Brookens' treachery and duplicity was nothing new to me. Seven years earlier, I'd gotten a good taste of what type of person Brookens truly was. Looking back now, I see I should have cut my ties with him then. I just never had the guts, always afraid of how our circle of friends would react if I called out Brookens on who he really was.

In 1965, the popular hangout and meeting place for local teenage guys was a pool hall in downtown Lake Orion. There wasn't much else to do in the small town of Lake Orion, so all the teens would descend on the pool hall on Friday and Saturday nights.

The pool hall was located in the heart of downtown Lake Orion. Like Oxford, the town to the north, Lake Orion's downtown was centered around a four-corner strip with historic two and three story brick buildings. All the buildings had been built in the early 1900s and boasted all the charm and detail that buildings from that era were known for. It was within walking distance of my mother's house and I almost never missed a weekend night at the pool hall. Six pool tables were the focal point of the place and tall chairs lined the wall in front of them. The opposite wall was lined with racks of cue sticks. And the interior was dimly lit — like a bar — where the only light came from fixtures that hung about four feet above each table.

On a Friday or Saturday night, there weren't enough tables and chairs for half the people who packed into that place. Just about everyone smoked back then and by the end of the night, it looked like a dense fog had moved into the pool hall.

That's where I first met Brookens. He was seventeen at the time, a high school student. I was only fifteen and still attending junior high.

From the very first moment I met him, something about Brookens rubbed me the wrong way. He was always putting on a show, trying too hard to impress everyone and be the center of attention. He tried to portray himself as the ultimate cool guy. I always saw through the act. From my point of view, Brookens was just trying to hide who he really was — a kid full of insecurities and operating with a deviant nature.

All the kids in the small, suburban community complained of boredom. There wasn't anything — aside from the pool hall — for teens to do. And so, that led most teens to seek out trouble in one way or another.

On Friday nights, the local General Motors car dealership would close up for the entire weekend. Not a single employee would be left on the lot. Back then, General Motors' keys were largely interchangeable and I'd collected quite an array of them, probably about two dozen total.

Myself and a bunch of my teenage friends would sneak on to the lot, jiggling each key in a car door until we found one that worked on a car we wanted to drive. If the key opened the door, it usually worked for starting the engine too.

One of us would take the license plate from the front of another car and put it on the back of the car we wanted to drive, and then we were good to go. In our minds, it wasn't a serious crime — we were only borrowing the vehicles, simply appropriating them for a night of teenage fun cruising around in a car.

We were meticulous about bringing the vehicles back, making sure we parked it exactly the same way in exactly the same spot. We'd put the license plates back the way they were before and had our routine down pat — no one ever suspected the cars were taken..

We usually took a car just for a night of cruising, but sometimes, if it was a car we really liked, we'd keep it for the entire weekend and return it late Sunday night before the dealership reopened on Monday.

One Friday evening, Brookens and I appropriated a 1964 Pontiac Catalina 2+2. It had a 421 cubic inch engine with tri-power and a four-speed transmission. We picked up a bunch of friends and headed down to Woodward Avenue in Bloomfield Hills, the cruising mecca for all people in metro Detroit.

Brookens, being older than the rest of us, was driving. He was the only one who had a valid driver's license at the time.

Like the idiot he truly was, Brookens valued showboating in front of his friends over using common sense. He started talking about drag racing and got all the guys in the car riled up.

It was a busy Friday night on the most happening strip in Michigan and we were driving a stolen car. And despite it all, drag racing seemed like a good idea to him.

Not long after Brookens began driving like a mad man, the police sirens went on behind us and we were busted. The Bloomfield Hills officer walked up to us and summarily asked Brookens for his driver's license and vehicle registration.

Brookens, of course, didn't have the registration.

"Sit tight, I'll be back," the officer said, and then returned to his police cruiser to run a check on the license plate registration. We knew that we were busted, but we didn't say anything to each other about what we were going to tell the police. The other guys in the car had no idea it was stolen. Brookens had told them earlier it was my parents' car.

The officer returned to the car with a stern look on his face.

"This license plate here is registered to a different make and model," he told Brookens. "Why is that?"

I was sitting in the back seat at the time and watched in horror as Brookens turned around and pointed his finger directly at me.

"He did it!" Brookens said vehemently. "He stole the car from a dealership in Lake Orion and picked me up. I had nothing to do with it, officer."

What the hell was I supposed to say to that? I couldn't believe my ears. I just sat there, stunned. Brookens was just as guilty as I was — all I'd done was given him the keys and switched the license plates. It was Brookens who drove off the lot in the damn car.

The officer asked me to step out of the vehicle and I obliged. I was fifteen and terrified.

"How old are you, son?" the officer asked me, his eyes running up and down my lithe body as if he were sizing me up.

"Only fifteen, sir," I replied quietly.

"You sure are lucky you're a minor — otherwise, I'd be cuffing you and taking you to jail for automobile theft," he told me.

Of course, that didn't mean I got off scott-free. The officer still handcuffed me and placed me under arrest. It's just that rather than being taken to jail, I was taken to a juvenile hall and spent a weekend there. Juvenile hall wasn't all that starkly different from a jail.

For two days, I sat in a cell with nothing but a steel bunk bed. The mattresses were only handed out at night and taken away first thing in the morning. I had to beg to use the bathroom, pounding on my cell door to try and grab someone's attention. Those two days seemed like the longest days of my life, but then Monday came. A hearing was held and at that time, I was released into my parents' custody.

Naturally, my parents were furious. They gave me a verbal tongue lashing that seemed to go on forever — my father scolding me and telling me I was raised better, I was raised to know right from wrong, and my mother getting teary-eyed and fretting that I was growing up too fast. I told them that we never intended to steal the cars or do anything bad with them.

"It was just supposed to be for fun," I told them. "We were just taking the car for a joy ride."

They both made me promise to never do it again, and never to be involved in any other joy riding incidents whether it was the prettiest girl in town or my best friend who took the car.

I kept the promise, but it had less to do with their tongue-lashing and more to do with the fact that after the car dealership found out what was going on, they hired a night watchman to guard their lot.

After my parents had calmed down, I asked if I could go see my girlfriend Cathy. She lived on the other side of town and it took me about forty minutes to walk there, but I really cared about Cathy. I knew she'd be wondering why I didn't call or stop by to see her all weekend and I wanted to explain to her in person.

When I finally got there, Cathy had no sooner opened the door than tears began falling from her eyes. At first, I assumed she was crying tears of joy because she was so happy to see me and then, it crossed my mind that perhaps she'd found out I'd gotten in trouble and was upset with me.

As it turned out, though, I was wrong on both counts.

Through her tears, she told me that Brookens had come to her house on Saturday night and told her I'd been arrested for stealing a car.

"He said he had no idea the car was stolen and that you tricked him into driving it," she cried. "He said that you got him in trouble, that he was almost arrested and taken to jail himself."

Cathy's fine, ivory skin was reddened over the cheeks from tears streaming down her face, making her sharp blue eyes stand out even more. She was a beautiful girl with light blond hair, which now hung straight and was pushed back behind her ears. She had great dimples when she smiled, but Cathy was far from smiling as she continued telling me what happened.

Her parents weren't home at the time, but Cathy said she was instantly worried about what had happened to me and invited Brookens in to hear the rest of the story. She had no reason to even think that Brookens would harm her or her five-year-old little sister, who was sleeping in the bedroom.

Brookens' anger at me continued once he was inside her house. She said he ranted and raved, his voice getting louder and face redder with every sentence.

"He kept saying, 'Your boyfriend owes me a favor, and I'm about to collect it from you,'" she told me. "I was getting scared; I didn't know what the hell he meant."

She continued, barely taking a breath, "So I told him my parents would be home any minute and he had to leave or we'd both be in big trouble. Then he grabbed my wrist and twisted my arm behind my back —

Cathy's body started heaving with sobs as she recounted the story.

"— and he, he grabbed my throat, threw me on the floor and," she gulped. "He raped me."

"He what? He fuckin' did what?" I yelled; I was the angry one now, I was the one red in the face and ready to pulverize Brookens, the despicable piece of shit.

I was ready to go right then. There'd be no waiting. I'd hunt down Brookens until I found him and I'd beat him until he needed a trip to the hospital.

As my plans to pulverize him began pouring out of my mouth, Cathy collapsed to her knees and clutched my hands, still crying.

"No, Jim, please," she cried. "You have to promise me not to do anything to him. Please — you can't say anything at all, nothing. Promise me Jim, please!"

It was the 1960s, when being a rape victim was far different than it is today. The stigma was terrible; girls were often accused of "asking for it" or blamed for acting slutty. Girls had no good reason to come forward — they'd be ridiculed, their friends would turn against them, fellow students would ostracize them and make their life miserable. As Cathy pleaded with me, I tried to look at things from her perspective. I wanted to be a good boyfriend; I wanted to do what would make her happy.

And so, I never told a soul of her ordeal. Not even a word to Brookens.

It was difficult at first. I tried to keep my distance from him, but I didn't want to act weird to the point that he suspected Cathy had told me. God only knows what he'd have done to her if he'd suspected that. Every time I was around him, I had to remind myself to stay calm and just let it go. Act normal, for Cathy's sake.

About two months later, Cathy had another big surprise to share with me. She was pregnant — and distraught. Being an unwed teen mother created as much of a stigma as being a rape victim.

I immediately had my doubts about being the father. During the past year, we'd indulged in unprotected sex many times, but nothing like this happened. I thought about the timing of everything — Brookens raping her, and now this.

I wouldn't have dared suggest to her that I wasn't the father, though. That was the last thing she needed to hear. My doubts, my uncertainty, it could all be totally unfounded, I told myself. The timing of the rape could be nothing more than a mere coincidence, so I kept my mouth shut and fully accepted that I was about to be a father.

About a week later, I went over to Cathy's house and she had a look of optimism on her face.

"I know how we can solve our little problem," she whispered to me. "But before I tell you, you have got to promise that you won't tell anyone — and I mean, no one — about what I'm going to say."

I promised her once, which didn't satisfy her.

"I swear, Cathy, I won't tell a soul," I reassured her. "Not a single soul."

"Okay, well, you know Susie, right?" she asked me.

I nodded. Of course I knew Susie; Susie was her best friend and lived just a few doors down from her.

"Susie was pregnant too; in fact, she was pregnant up until just a couple months ago," Cathy said.

"What?" I said in disbelief. Susie had never once looked like she was pregnant.

Cathy told me that Susie had accidentally gotten pregnant by her boyfriend last year, but was able to hide her pregnancy for several months. Like Cathy and I, she was only fifteen — too young to get married, too immature to handle the responsibility of a baby and too fearful of the stigma she'd have to endure.

"Well, Susie's boyfriend came up with this plan to cause her to have a miscarriage," Cathy said. "He brought over a bunch of beer to get her drunk — so she wouldn't feel any pain, you know — and then punched her in the stomach a bunch of times."

Cathy smiled at me after saying it. Looking back now, I realize how morbid it all sounds. Back then, though, when we were fifteen and faced with such a huge problem, it seemed like the perfect solution. Our immature, teenage selves didn't see it as a life, but rather as a problem. A big problem.

"And that actually worked?" I asked her, feeling a bit grossed out.

"Yeah, it did," Cathy said. "Susie told me she miscarried and afterwards, wrapped the fetus up in newspaper, put it in a brown paper bag and stuffed it into a garbage can — she wasn't even sick or nothing afterward. Just went on with her life like normal."

"So this is what you want to do?" I asked her. She nodded her head.

I didn't like the idea. It sounded too risky, like too many things could go wrong. What if I really hurt Cathy, or if she died from the miscarriage? And how can anyone just 'go on with life like normal' after something like that? Wouldn't the image of that baby, that premature, wrinkled little body being wrapped up in newspaper stick in our heads forever?

"What if something goes wrong, Cathy?" I asked her softly. "What if you get seriously hurt?"

"So what? Pick up a phone, call the police and tell them you think I'm having a miscarriage," she said nonchalantly.

I sighed. I wasn't in favor of the plan, but I tried to empathize with her. I needed to be sensitive to her needs; this was a much more desperate situation for her than for me. Reluctantly, I agreed to give the plan a try. She leapt up and hugged me, holding me tight.

"Thank you, Jim," she whispered into my ear.

A couple of weeks later, Cathy called me at home to tell me her parents were going away for the weekend.

"We should do it then," she said. "It'll be perfect; we'll have all weekend to take care of it."

The days leading up to Saturday were nerve-racking. I tried to push my anxiety aside, telling myself I had to do this for Cathy and that after Saturday, this entire ordeal would be done and over with. Things would be back to normal.

I'd arranged for one of my older friends to pick up a six-pack of beer for me on Saturday afternoon. Armed with the six-pack, I made my way over to Cathy's house.

I had no reason to think she'd change her mind, but I nonetheless hoped that was the case.

"Are you sure you want to do this?" I asked her after walking in the door.

Without hesitating, she exclaimed, "Yes! I'm sure."

We went into the living room and sat down on the sofa. Cathy turned on the record player and we listened to music while she began downing the beers.

By the time she'd polished off her fifth beer, her eyes had the unmistakable drunk look to them and every word that came out of

My Own Worst Enemy

her mouth was terribly slurred. Her mood had gotten more excitable and melodramatic.

"Come on Ja-Ja-Jim," she stuttered. "La-lets ah-do this nowww — I think I'm a dru-drunk enough, don't you?"

I helped her off the sofa and we sat on the floor, both of our backs against the sofa.

"Tell me when you're ready, Cathy," I said softly to her.

"Ga-go ahead," she slurred. "Jes hit me in the stomach."

I drew in a deep breath, hesitating for a moment before clinching my fist. I pulled my arm back and starting to push it forward, but I couldn't do it. Just before I made contact with her stomach, I pulled my arm back. I just couldn't bring myself to hit her. I even tried again, but again, I just couldn't make contact.

Cathy started crying, drunkenly sobbing.

"Pah-pleeaase, Jim," she pleaded. "Please hit me, harder. Please Jim; pah-leeze just hit me."

Her face turned red with her tears, her sniveling nose dripping snot onto her lips.

"Please, Jim, please," she cried, grabbing my arm. "We gotta do this. Got to do this."

Her pleas didn't matter anymore. I just couldn't do it.

"This isn't going to work, Cathy," I consoled her. "There has got to be another way."

I didn't honestly have the slightest clue what other way there was. I didn't know what we should do. We were fifteen. Our options were severely limited — I didn't have a driver's license and no means of supporting myself, nonetheless a family. It didn't matter though. I thought about it and thought about it. There was only one thing I could do, the only right thing to do, and that was to marry her.

"We can get married, Cathy," I offered to her. She looked at me with big eyes.

"I don't know what we'll do, but we'll figure it out," I added. "This isn't right; it's just not the right thing to do."

She didn't say anything.

"Well, just think about it," I said and kissed her on the forehead. "It's up to you."

I felt better knowing the miscarriage attempt was over and not to be repeated. I knew the next thing I had to do now was tell my parents I got my girlfriend pregnant.

They were distraught at the news, to say the least. My mother kept herself calm and collected and dealt with things rationally. But my father got really upset, and began yelling at me.

"I offered to marry her," I told them, thinking they'd be proud of me for stepping up and being a man about things. I was wrong.

"Are you crazy?" my father yelled. "Marriage is out of the question — no way. You are not marrying that girl. I will not let that happen; I am not going to just stand here and watch you ruin your entire life."

The situation was becoming dire. It was clear that my parents weren't going to change their minds and now, I had to come up with something dramatic, something that would force them to reconsider.

My mother was standing in the kitchen, leaning against the sink. My gaze fell upon the cabinet drawer next to her. It was where we kept all the different household painkillers and medications.

I walked over to the drawer and took out a full bottle of Aspirin as if all the drama had given me a headache. But when I popped the top off, I held the bottle's mouth to my lips and sucked down nearly the entire bottle before my mother snatched it out of my hands.

My theatrics got me nothing except a ride to the hospital and a wretched stomach pump.

Cathy, on the other hand, didn't tell her parents about the pregnancy until nearly a month later. She was beginning to show and there was no more hiding it from the world. The father, she told them, was me, and naturally, they were outraged. From their point of view, I'd taken advantage of their little girl.

Her father was extremely disappointed with me, and rightfully so. He never told me to my face that I was no longer welcome at his house — perhaps he was afraid of what he might do to me if he had to see me in person. So, I got the news from Cathy when I called her a few days later.

"He's forbidding me from seeing you," she said. "I'm not supposed to have any contact with you at all, not even on the phone like this. I've got to go, Jim."

It wasn't long before practically everyone in school assumed that I was responsible for getting Cathy pregnant. It was, after all, the most natural assumption seeing as how everyone knew that we'd been going steady for about a year.

Seemingly overnight, I became a pariah. Everyone at school shunned me. I could hear them whispering as I walked by and talking behind my back. I just kept walking. What was the point in defending myself against the scathing and malicious rumors — it wouldn't have changed any of their minds about me. I did my best to ignore and endure all the gossip and innuendo.

For the next five months, I didn't see or hear a thing from Cathy. Her parents had taken her out of school right away and kept her at home, hiding her from the public.

I resisted the urge to call or try to see her, but I couldn't resist forever. I kept thinking about her, wondering what was happening to her and what she was going through. Finally, one day, my curiosity got the best of me and I decided to skip out of school early and go over to her house so I could see for myself how she was doing.

The usual forty minutes it took me to walk from my house to Cathy's was extended to nearly an hour as I zigzagged up and down side streets that I thought Cathy's parents were less likely to travel. I didn't want either of them to spot me. My route allowed me to keep an eye on both lanes of traffic and gave me plenty of places to hide in case I did catch sight of one of their cars.

When Cathy's house finally came into view, I didn't see either of her parents' cars in the driveway, a generally surefire indication that they weren't home. I thought about going to the front door, but I didn't want to take a chance.

Who knows if they've asked a neighbor to keep an eye on the house and make sure no fifteen-year-old boys were sneaking around while they're away, I thought. The last thing Cathy needed was for me to get her in even more trouble.

I instead went around to the back door by the kitchen and knocked, knocked, and knocked again. No one came. But as I stood there knocking, I became more and more certain Cathy was home. I could hear a vacuum cleaner running inside the house — obviously why she couldn't hear me knocking. I turned the doorknob, expecting it to be locked, but it wasn't. Cautiously, I cracked the door open just enough to stick my head inside and crane my neck around, looking to see if anyone was in sight. The kitchen was empty.

Going inside uninvited was a scary thought. *What if, by some chance, her dad was sitting around the corner on the sofa?* I was apprehensive, but I needed to see Cathy. After a year of being together, I knew the family's schedule pretty well and could be damn near sure that her parents would both still be at work and her little sister still at school.

Nevertheless, my heart pounded nervously as I stepped inside the kitchen and cautiously tiptoed across the floor and to the side of the living room doorway. I peeked around the corner and again saw an empty room. The sound of the vacuum cleaner was louder now, clearly coming from down the hallway near the bathroom and bedrooms.

I crept closer to the hallway and peeked my head around the corner. I could see the vacuum cleaner sitting in front of the bathroom and then I caught a glimpse of Cathy, just inside the bathroom vacuuming its floor. She was oblivious to the fact that I was in the house, the vacuum's loud whine drowning out all other sounds. I walked slowly to the vacuum, just a few feet from her, and pushed its off switch. There was a sudden and somewhat deafening silence that permeated throughout the house.

She turned around with a puzzled look on her face, probably wondering if something on the vacuum had broken. When her eyes settled upon me though, the puzzled look changed to one of shock and surprise.

"What are you doing here?" she scolded me.

"I just wanted to see for myself that you're okay," I told her.

Just then, a car pulled into the driveway and she immediately began to panic. Running toward the window, she saw it was the worst person to possibly be arriving home while I was in her house — her father.

She turned around and shot me a panic-stricken look.

"You've got to get out of here, *now!*" she said. "If my father finds you here, Jim, there's no telling what he might do."

She didn't have to tell me twice — I was in a dead run to her back door, out in the yard and several blocks down the street before I even allowed myself to slow down. Eventually, I paused, hunching my back over and putting my hands on my thighs to hold myself up while I caught my breath. I checked behind me, making sure dear ol' dad wasn't chasing me down with his twelve gauge Browning automatic shotgun that he kept hanging on his bedroom wall.

After that near disaster, I never tried to see Cathy again. Luckily, my mother discovered she worked with a lady who lived directly across the street from Cathy. Her name was Janice and she knew about my relationship with Cathy and the situation we'd gotten ourselves into. She always caught my mother up on anything she heard about Cathy.

When Cathy had her baby, our baby, she told my mother about it. We felt good knowing that Cathy gave birth to a healthy baby girl with no complications.

My Mother told me the baby was immediately given to Cathy's aunt and uncle. They didn't have any children of their own and had been trying to adopt for several years.

A little while later, Janice would tell my mom, who then told me, that the baby was named Christy. That was the last little bit of information Janice would pass on to us.

It'd be four years before I saw Cathy again. We were walking the opposite ways on the same narrow sidewalk in downtown Lake Orion when our paths finally crossed.

We both smiled warmly at each other and exchanged cordial hellos, but both of us had, by then, put our past together well behind us. I'd heard that Cathy, now nineteen, had already married. I wanted to ask about Christy. I wanted to know how my daughter was, but I didn't want to bring up those painful memories. So, we parted ways amicably without saying a word about our past.

I'd later find out that Christy grew to be a young adult before learning she was adopted. For years after that, Christy would know she was adopted, but not know that her mother was actually her aunt. It was on Christy's twenty-first birthday that she would find out who her biological parents were.

Christy contacted Cathy and they developed an amicable relationship. Cathy had been married for almost twenty years by that time and had three other children. Cathy's husband knew about Christy before they got married, but they hadn't told their children.

Christy started asking questions about me and was told that I was serving a life sentence in prison for murder. She didn't try to contact me at first, but a few years later her adoptive father passed away and she felt it was time to meet me.

It was 1994 and I was incarcerated at the Thumb Correctional Facility in Lapeer County when a letter showed up for me from an unfamiliar address. It was Christy. She wrote to tell me that she was my biological daughter. She wrote that she'd like to arrange a visit to meet me in person, if I didn't mind.

"I understand if you do not want to meet me, however, I am hopeful that you do. There are so many questions I'd like to ask you, even to find out family medical history. I am very much looking forward to finally meeting you," she wrote.

For the past twenty-nine years, I'd held on to the belief that Christy was my daughter. Sitting in prison for so long, I spent countless hours thinking about her; wondering what type of person she was, if she had any of my features or characteristics. I wondered what life was like for her growing up and what she had chosen to do with her life. I wondered if she had married, if I could possibly even have grandchildren by now.

I'd always hoped that one day she would contact me. I'd stew upon what I would say to her and wonder if she'd accept me.

Opening that letter from her was one of the best things that had ever happened to me, I thought.

I wasted no time writing a letter back to her. I tried my best to relay just how happy I was to hear from her, writing that I'd been waiting a lifetime for this very moment and it was difficult to express, on pen and paper, just how elated I was. I told her that I would love to meet her whenever it was convenient for her.

I had never seen Christy, not even a picture of her. The days leading up to her visit were some of the most exciting, albeit anxiety-filled days of my life in prison. I wondered and wondered what color her hair was, what her voice sounded like and more.

My Own Worst Enemy

The day finally came and when I walked into the visiting room, there was no mistaking who Christy was. She was the spitting image of her mother and looked exactly as Cathy had twenty-nine years earlier. They looked so much alike — same blonde hair, blue eyes and dimples in their cheeks — that they could've passed for identical twins.

From the moment we first met and looked into each other's eyes, we felt comfortable with one another. She was warm and talkative; it was as if we'd known each other all our lives. Our visit lasted four hours and we talked nonstop through every minute of it.

In great detail, Christy explained the many obstacles she'd had to overcome in her search for her biological parents. She told me that she'd been desperate to meet me, and yet she'd been somewhat apprehensive that I might not be interested in meeting her. She also said she had great respect for her adoptive father, which made me feel good that she'd been raised by a man worthy of her respect. She added that it was out of her respect for him that she'd waited so long to contact me. He'd passed away recently and I expressed my condolences to her.

"I'm very happy, and relieved, to have finally met you," she told me.

When the visit was over and we said our good-byes, I could barely contain the overwhelming sense of pride I had for her. She was beautiful, kind and thoughtful. For the first time in my life, I felt I had really contributed something not just great, but something downright wonderful, to this world.

During the next month, Christy came to visit me every Sunday afternoon. It was one of the best months of my life.

I enjoyed getting to know my daughter, and it became quite apparent that truthfulness and honesty was of the greatest importance to Christy. It was understandable why. For most of her life, people had been hiding the truth from her.

Not to say that anyone had ill intentions to do so. Christy's adoptive parents hid the truth from her thinking that they were doing what was best for Christy. Inadvertently, though, it had caused a great deal of confusion and anxiety in Christy's life.

As we talked about truth and honesty, I thought perhaps a paternity test would put any doubts that I was her biological father behind us. I didn't want any what-ifs to hinder our relationship. I asked her if she'd like to have a paternity test done to confirm that I was indeed her father.

"No!" she exclaimed. "I have no reason to doubt what I've been told."

I nodded my head during a brief silence, and then she asked the question that I was not prepared to hear.

"Do you have any doubts about being my father?" she asked me with a look of concern.

I sat there for a moment, thinking back twenty-nine years to all that had transpired and the seed of doubt that had immediately cropped up when Cathy told me she was pregnant. At this point in my life, the last thing I wanted was to find out Christy was not actually my daughter. She'd brought so much joy into my life. She meant so much to me. She'd made me happy and proud. Thinking about losing her was gut wrenching.

I reminded myself, though, that I owed it to her — my daughter or not — to be completely honest with her. Nothing was more important to her than honesty and in the back of my mind, there was that nagging sense of uncertainty that I had invariably tried to ignore for almost thirty years now. At the very least, I owed Christy an explanation as to my reason for that doubt.

And so, I decided to reveal to her the secret of her mother's rape, which I'd been keeping locked up inside myself for twenty-nine years. It was a long time to keep a secret, but I don't know if that made it any easier to tell her about it.

As I told Christy the complete story, from beginning to end, I held nothing back. I told her about how much I had cared for Cathy, dating her for a year, and of our intimate relationship. I told her about stealing the car with Brookens and getting in trouble. I told her what Cathy told me of Brookens coming to her parent's house and raping her. I told her everything that had happened before and after Cathy discovered she was pregnant. When I finally finished, Christy looked somewhat stunned.

"I understand why you don't feel you can be one hundred percent certain that you're my father," she said quietly.

It was a sad visit.

Christy later contacted Cathy and told her what I said. She wanted Cathy to confirm or deny the story and Cathy reluctantly admitted that I was telling the truth, that she had been raped by

Brookens. Cathy conceded that she couldn't totally rule out the possibility that Brookens might be her biological father, but she continued to insist that I was Christy's father. I'm sure she wanted to believe it as much as I did.

Days passed, and then weeks, without a word from Christy. She stopped coming to visit me and wouldn't accept my phone calls. A few weeks later, I tried to call her again and Christy's adoptive mother answered the phone.

"Christy is very upset and confused right now," she told me. "Cathy never told her about the rape. I'm sure you can understand. She just needs some time to sort everything out and then she'll contact you."

Christy began searching for Brookens and finally, she found him living in another state. When she contacted him by phone, she wasn't greeted warmly. Brookens wasn't receptive to the possibility that he might be her biological father; he had no desire to meet her in person or even establish any type of relationship with her. He did, however, agree to have a paternity test done.

Two months later, I received a short letter from Christy. She wrote that she had received the results of the paternity test and it came back ninety-nine percent positive that Brookens was her biological father.

My heart sank as I read that.

She apologized for any inconvenience or hardship that she may have caused in my life and she wished me well and that was that — I never heard from her again.

I thought about the irony of the whole situation. Me, a supposed scum of the earth, piece-of-shit convict, was the only person willing to reveal the truth to this young lady. I remembered the saying, "We learn from our mistakes and we grow from our misfortunes."

Even though I was profoundly hurt inside, I tried not to give it any energy. I kept telling myself that you can't miss what you never had. Despite it all, I still miss having a daughter —
especially one as sweet and beautiful as Christy.

CHAPTER 3

Lapeer County Jail and my Trial

I wish I had been smarter about dealing with Cathy's rape. I still tell myself I did the right thing in respecting Cathy's wishes and keeping everything a secret, but I wish I had at least permanently ended my friendship with Brookens.

As fate would have it though, Brookens would continue to be a thorn in my side. From my point of view, Brookens was just as guilty as Preston and I were, but he would never spend one day in jail. By agreeing to testify against Preston and I, he was freed of serving any time.

Preston and I were arraigned in district court on the morning that followed our arrest. His wife had retained a notable criminal attorney who specialized in murder cases and he was at the arraignment to represent Preston.

My mother had also retained an attorney to represent me, however, he wasn't known for winning criminal cases. The attorney was a nephew of my stepfather and he worked primarily as a corporate attorney for a publishing company in Detroit. He was licensed to practice criminal law, but prior to representing me, he'd only had one other criminal case. And unfortunately, his client was found guilty.

The arraignment was held to determine if there was sufficient evidence to bind Preston and myself over to the circuit court for trial. In order to establish that, it had to be determined that a crime had actually been committed and several police officers who were at the scene of the crime were called to testify.

The most incriminating evidence though, came from Brookens. He testified that the three of us had planned and committed the crime and by the time he was finished running his mouth, there was no doubt that we were going to trial. The judge ruled accordingly; that there was indeed sufficient and probable cause to suggest that we'd committed the crime and therefore, we were bound over to circuit court and would stand trial on charges of first-degree murder and armed robbery.

Preston and I were returned to our cells in the Lapeer County Jail and it didn't take long for me to realize that jail was one hell of an inconvenience, to say the least.

My first week in jail was extremely difficult. I found myself suddenly thrust into a totally controlled environment and deprived of everything familiar to me. Adjusting to that wasn't my only problem though — I had a heroin addiction to deal with as well.

Jail forced me to deal with the reality that I'd become severely addicted to heroin during the past few months. Without the daily injections of heroin that I'd become dependent on, I began experiencing withdrawals. This is when I began to fully understand what a truly wretched drug heroin is.

The symptoms were similar to those of a severe cold or flu — nausea, lethargy, fatigue, and a runny nose — but were tenfold greater. The intensity of the symptoms was greater than I'd ever experienced with a cold or flu and seemed to take over my entire being. For three days, I was sicker than a junkyard dog. During the worst of it, I laid there wondering if I'd live or die.

My sinuses were constantly running and every inch of my body ached — even my hair hurt. How lethargic I felt was unbelievable, as if I had no strength or energy whatsoever. I was constantly nauseated and vomiting, but that wasn't the worst of it. After I had thrown up too many times to keep track of and there wasn't a single morsel of even my own snot left in my stomach, I began dry heaving. I couldn't stop my weakened body and its tortured stomach muscles from continuing to heave and heave. The pain was so intense that I was sure my stomach lining and even my stomach itself were being heaved up.

I felt as if I'd been run over by a fully loaded semi truck towing two trailers and I wanted nothing more than to lie down and sleep for the next week. But sleep was no escape either. During the rare moments I could shut my eyes and drift away, I inevitably drifted into the most vivid and terrible nightmares I'd ever had. I'd wake up in a cold sweat, shivering, and with every piece of clothing and my blanket drenched in my own sweat. I'd never felt so tormented and frightened in my entire life.

On the third day, the terrifying symptoms of withdrawal began to slowly subside. With each passing day, I began feeling more and more like a normal person. Oddly enough, I remember thinking that despite the fact I was sitting in jail, I felt good. For the first time in three months, I was drug free. I felt normal and clear-headed and that, by itself, was enough to make me feel good.

That first time Preston persuaded me to try heroin is still a vivid memory for me. I remember the other people in the room smiling and laughing, practically cheering me on as Preston lowered the needle to the skin on my forearm. I can see the needle's point breaking through my skin and then, that feeling of incredible warmth entering my body and washing over me.

When I first began using heroin, I'd inject myself with two penny-caps of it. It cost two dollars and was enough to get me and keep me high for the entire day. That, of course, didn't last long.

At the time of my arrest, I'd been shooting two ten dollar packs of heroin every day, and that was just enough to make me feel normal. If I wanted to actually get high, I'd have to shoot an additional ten dollar pack or more.

I'd heard the stories about how easy it was to become addicted to heroin, but I was one of those hardheaded individuals who wouldn't listen to anyone. I had to learn things the hard way. I thought I knew it all, even though in retrospect, I was nothing more than an ignorant, arrogant and naïve young fool. I thought I could regulate my drug usage, which was a joke. I was just fooling myself.

The drugs took total control of my life and consumed my very being. I lost all self-control and self-respect. I'd gotten to the point where I'd consider doing almost anything to get more heroin. It was the first thing I thought about every morning and the last thing I thought about at night — my whole world revolved around getting my next fix.

Ironically, what was so obvious to others who knew me wasn't so readily apparent to me. In fact, there was one guy who had been a neighbor of mine growing up who'd tried his own intervention on me. We'd long since parted ways, realizing we belonged with different crowds when we were both young teenagers. But we'd grown up together and had, for many years, been the closest of pals.

One day, not long after my heroin problem became a daily habit, he approached me and asked if the two of us could go out together one night.

"For old time's sake," he told me. "We can catch up on things."

I had no reason to say no and so, I didn't. At the bar later that night, he told me he was worried about me; that he knew I was running with a bad crowd and that, even from a distance, he could see a huge change in me.

Unfortunately, I pretty much wrote him off. I see now he was probably the only true friend I'd ever had.

My family members told me I'd become quite the Dr. Jekyll and Mr. Hyde, which usually just made me angry — especially when I was feeling the need to shoot up.

People told me I'd become a totally different person, but I didn't believe it. I couldn't see through the false sense of well being that the heroin provided, nor did I see that I was losing my soul. I had, in effect, become my own worst enemy.

It didn't take years in prison for me to realize that using heroin was the biggest mistake I'd ever made. As soon as I became clear headed again, I could see the chain of events. If I had never allowed Preston to talk me into trying the drug, so many things would've never happened. As a direct result of that mistake, I made a tragic error in judgment that literally cost another human being his life.

I've asked myself countless times, *what was I thinking?*

I often wonder what in the world ever possessed me to think that I needed to alter my state of consciousness. Undoubtedly, a large part of my problem was the way I perceived drugs, thinking that they were cool and getting high was fun.

I had my share of everyday problems, just like everyone else. I was acutely aware of my faults and insecurities and I kept them hidden from everyone, but for the most part, I had a good life. There was no justifiable reason for my drug abuse. My behavior was totally irrational and irresponsible and I had no one else to blame but myself for the mistakes that I'd made.

Someone once said that each choice we make is the death of all other possibilities. I often think that the day I chose to put that syringe of heroin in my arm was the day I lost my life. I might as well have put a loaded gun to my head and pulled the trigger, for the end result would've caused a lot less pain and suffering for many people, including myself.

Knowing what I know now, even if given the opportunity, I'd never use drugs ever again. I'd rather commit suicide first and save myself and everyone else from the unremitting heartache, grief and stupidity I'd create by using drugs.

I believe that one of the key elements to having a good life is to live in a way that will leave you with as few regrets as possible. Personally, I have many regrets and the type of life that goes along with it. Every day of my vile existence, I think of all the things I regret having done or not done.

The most profound regret, obviously, is being responsible for the death of Alex Blake. There are no words to adequately express the remorse I feel. I suppose the only way to understand how I feel is to know what it is like to cause the death of another human being. To this day, I still find it entirely sickening.

I can offer the most sincere, heartfelt apology to the family of Alex Blake for all the pain and suffering I caused them, but it doesn't change what happened. It doesn't bring him back; it doesn't mean I can move on. There is no moving on for me; what I did is done and I will live with it forever, enduring the guilt and shame of being responsible for the death of another human being whether I am rotting in jail or sitting on a nice sofa in the free world.

The only consolation I have is knowing that I did not kill him intentionally. In my heart, I remind myself that I am still a good person. I've never had murderous intent, never wanted or planned or meant to kill another human being. It's a small consolation, though, because no matter what, this tragedy remains indelibly etched in my mind and it will be there for as long as I live.

After the miserable symptoms of withdrawal subsided and I could again do something other than lay down or vomit, Preston and I began working on a secure way to communicate privately. We tore strips of cloth off our sheets and tied them together to make a long string. At one end, we'd tie our hand written notes and then would slide the string under the cell doors, carefully tossing it until it was within reach of the other's cell door. Then we'd simply pull the notes across the hallway.

We were making an attempt to get our stories straight and come up with an alibi. I figured it was our only hope. I filled him in on how I'd ask my mother to testify about when she saw us and how long we were gone, perhaps even the attendant at the gas station. I hoped it was enough of an alibi to persuade a jury.

Whenever Preston sent a note to me, I'd always make sure that his notes didn't fall into the wrong hands. I meticulously tore the notes into tiny pieces, flushed them down the toilet and would continue flushing and standing there until I was certain that not even a fleck of one of the shredded pieces came back up.

Preston was supposed to be taking the same precautions with the notes that I wrote to him, but something went wrong. Preston had gotten a bit careless, he wasn't tearing the notes into pieces nor did he bother flushing them down the toilet. I soon found out from my attorney that one of the other inmates in Preston's cell had actually reached his hand into the toilet and snatched out one of my notes, handing it over to the police.

The inmate thought this was his opportunity to make a deal with the prosecuting attorney; he'd hand over the note in exchange for an early release from jail. He told one of the sheriff's deputies that he was in possession of incriminating evidence against Preston and I.

The note wasn't exactly a smoking gun, but I'd written certain phrases in reference to our alibis about where we were on the night of the crime. It was definitely subject to interpretation, but the prosecutor saw it as another piece of circumstantial evidence to use against us. He'd bring in an expert handwriting analyzer to prove that I had indeed written it. In the end, the prosecutor did make a deal with the inmate.

I confronted Preston about his lax attitude creating even more trouble for us and he offered me an apology.

"I'll be more careful next time," he promised me.

"It's a little too late for that now," I said. "The damage is already done."

I asked him how he could've been so careless.

My Own Worst Enemy

"I'm sure I flushed it down the toilet, Jim," he told me. "I guess it must've come back up, but I never would've thought one of the other guys would do something like that."

At our next court appearance, Preston's attorney submitted a motion requesting that Preston receive a separate trial. He argued to the court that some of the evidence obtained by the prosecutor couldn't be used against his client, referring to a female witness who would give testimony in regard to a conversation that she had with me at a bar in Pontiac the night after the crime occurred.

"Any conversation that took place between this female witness and the codefendant must be considered hearsay in regard to my client," I remember him saying. "Therefore, any testimony that she may give cannot be used as evidence against my client."

This wasn't the end of his argument.

"Additionally, the note that was allegedly written by the codefendant during his stay at the Lapeer County Jail cannot be considered evidence against my client," he continued. "This note cannot be definitively linked to my client and therefore, it cannot be used as evidence against my client."

The prosecuting attorney argued that it could, even citing case law that the note was admissible as evidence against Preston. Nonetheless, after due consideration, the judge ruled in favor of Preston's attorney and granted his motion for separate trials.

At that point, the judge asked the prosecuting attorney which one of the defendants — Preston or myself — he wanted to proceed to trial with first. The prosecutor answered by saying that he believed he had a stronger case against me and therefore, wanted to proceed with my trial first.

My attorney made no objection to this and the judge then scheduled a court date for the jury selection process to begin. After summarily denying our motion to allow for bail, we were taken back to the county jail.

Sitting in jail for the next week, I tried just about everything imaginable to occupy my mind. I spent hours doing sit-ups and push-ups, anything that would pass the time and help relieve the ever-present boredom. Finally, I was placed in another cell with two other prisoners. The three of us spent most of our time playing cards and the occasional chess game. We also had a few jigsaw puzzles that we laid out and assembled on the cell floor.

Those who have never been in jail cannot begin to truly comprehend what it actually feels like to be deprived of their freedom. Words alone cannot convey the true depth of despair and hopelessness that one must endure. The psychological experience of being locked in a cage twenty-four hours a day, seven days a week, defies any attempt to accurately describe what it's really like. Only those individuals who have actually served time in jail have acquired this insight. Its true nature cannot be imagined.

Weeks later, the process of selecting a jury for my trial finally began. For this, I was taken back to the courthouse and was allowed to wear my street clothes again. After being clad in nothing more than a pair of white county jail coveralls for the past few months, it felt great to be in my own clothes again — I actually felt like a different person.

I also found the short ride to the courthouse to be strangely pleasant. I hadn't seen the outside world for the past couple of months and looking out the windows of the police cruiser, it was somewhat comforting to see the free world and know it was still there as I'd left it.

It took only a few days to complete the jury selection process. My attorney asked each potential juror if they'd read about the case in the newspapers; attempting to make sure they hadn't already formed an opinion as to my guilt. The prosecuting attorney, on the other hand, asked each potential juror if they'd have a problem finding me guilty, knowing that a guilty verdict would automatically result in a mandatory life sentence in prison.

Each attorney was allowed a set number of preemptory challenges that could be used to dismiss unwanted potential jurors without having to show cause as to why that person was being dismissed. I was a little surprised when my attorney didn't use all his preemptory challenges to dismiss several jurors that I would have classified as "unwanted." Instead, he settled for what he believed was about as fair and impartial jury as we were going to find in Lapeer County. With the prosecuting attorney and my attorney agreeing upon the selection of the twelve jurors and their two alternates, my trial was scheduled to begin the following week.

The day before my trial began, Preston sent a note to me expressing his concern that I might make a deal with the prosecuting attorney and turn state's evidence against him. He asked me not to make any plea bargain that would require me to testify against him and he attempted to justify his request by telling me that he didn't think that I'd be convicted.

"If, by some chance, the jury does find you guilty, that doesn't necessarily mean the jury at my trial will automatically find me guilty as well," he wrote. "And if you're found guilty, but I'm acquitted, I promise I'll do whatever it takes to get you out."

He had a plan that he thought would work if he were acquitted, writing me in a note to say that law prevents anyone from being tried twice for the same crime.

"So if I'm acquitted and you're not, then I can admit to the crime and I'll tell them that you had nothing to do with it," he wrote me, and then promised, "You have my word. I'll do whatever it takes to get you out."

I believed Preston. Call it naïvety or perhaps ignorance, but once again, I let Preston talk me into going along with another of his egotistical and stupid ideas. To this very day, I still don't completely understand how or why I let Preston talk me into sacrificing myself.

Perhaps it was my misguided sense of loyalty, or maybe the fact that even in the midst of the most serious thing that'd ever happened in my life, I was still worried of what my so-called friends would think of me. I could hear everyone calling me a snitch, saying I'd sacrificed Preston to save myself. If I had used my head and really analyzed the situation, maybe I'd have seen that Preston was planning to do essentially the same thing to me.

Nevertheless, I gave Preston my word that I wouldn't testify against him — a mistake that I'd regret for the rest of my life. In the years to come, I'd find myself wondering what the hell was I thinking and dwelling on how I'd become a victim of my own bad judgment. The saying, "Fool me once, shame on you; fool me twice, shame on me," would come to make all too much sense to me.

On the first day of my trial, I entered a plea of not guilty on both counts of armed robbery and first-degree murder. Once the judge accepted my plea, he told the prosecuting attorney that he could proceed with his opening statement to the jury.

"I will present to all of you an unbroken chain of circumstantial evidence that will prove beyond a reasonable doubt that this man,

James Anthony Goble, is indeed guilty of armed robbery and first-degree murder," he told the jury, his voice rising and falling dramatically.

"I know circumstantial evidence is often not enough, but it's appropriate in this case because there are no eyewitnesses in the actual, and fatal, shooting of Alex Blake," he continued. "However, there is a co-conspirator to this crime, Terry Brookens, who will take the stand."

He paused for a moment, taking in the jurors' reactions.

"Terry Brookens has admitted to being one of the individuals who planned and perpetrated this senseless crime along with the defendant, Mr. Goble," the attorney said. "And, in addition to Mr. Brookens, I will also present a female witness who met Mr. Goble at a bar in Pontiac the night after the crime was committed."

He then told the jury that Preston's fingerprints were found in the trunk of Brookens' vehicle, and that those fingerprints would be introduced as evidence during the course of the trial.

"These fingerprints are significant because Mr. Brookens, as you will hear throughout the course of this trial, will testify that he placed a brown paper bag in the trunk of his vehicle to fool the victims into thinking that it contained marijuana," he told the jurors. "And therefore, the only other persons whose fingerprints that could have possibly been found in the trunk of Mr. Brookens' vehicle was the person who removed this paper bag during the robbery."

When the prosecutor finished laying out his case to the jury, my attorney was given the opportunity to present his opening statement.

"My client, James Anthony Goble, is innocent of the crimes he has been charged with," my attorney told the jury. "There is no possibility that he could've been at the scene of the crime during the time it was alleged to have taken place, and I will present an alibi to show that Mr. Goble was indeed somewhere else at the time the crime occurred."

He continued, adding: "I will present several witnesses who will testify as to Mr. Goble's whereabouts at approximately the same time the crime was supposedly taking place."

After my attorney concluded his opening statement, the judge allowed the prosecutor to begin presenting his case.

During the first two days of my trial, most of the testimony was given by police officers who were the first responders to arrive at the crime scene. Their testimony was harmless enough, as it was used basically to establish that a crime had indeed been committed.

The next witness to testify was the doctor who performed the autopsy at the hospital. He testified that the victim had died as a result of a gunshot wound to the lower left-hand side of his back and concluded that Blake had been shot at close range, as can be determined by the powder burns on the victim's clothing and skin.

"In my opinion, the gun was fired from no more than a distance of six feet away," he said.

The doctor also testified that twenty double-aught pellets from the shotgun blast had entered the victim's body at an upward angle of thirty degrees. Two of the pellets struck the lower ribs and ricocheted upward into the chest cavity. One pellet had exited through the chest while the other pellet had pierced the heart, fatally wounding the victim.

The next person called by the prosecution to testify was an expert witness in analyzing tire tracks. The witness testified to the similarity of the tire tracks found at the crime scene to the tires on my mother's vehicle. He said that the tire tread patterns were of a similar design, but that was about all he could say with any degree of certainty.

When cross-examined by my attorney, he was asked to be more specific as to the extent of similarity and said that the tread patterns were of a standard design used on most makes and models of cars.

"There are probably over a million tires with that same particular tread pattern currently being used on many other vehicles," he admitted on the stand.

Upon further questioning, he also admitted that when he did a comparison of the tire tracks taken from the crime scene and those on my mother's vehicle, he was unable to find any distinctive characteristics that could positively identify the tires on my mother's vehicle as being the vehicle at the scene of the crime.

After that, a state police crime lab technician was called to the stand to give testimony in regard to fingerprints. He said that the only fingerprints found at the scene, other than those belonging to the victims, belonged to Preston.

Preston's fingerprints had been found inside the trunk of Brookens' vehicle and the technician testified that they couldn't have been there for more than a few days.

The Lapeer County Sheriff's deputy who had executed a search warrant of our apartment in Pontiac also testified that during the search, he had discovered an empty box of shotgun shells in one of the bedrooms.

The prosecutor purposely never asked the deputy what gauge shells the empty box previously contained, because written on the box was the type of gauge and it was not the same gauge as used by the murder weapon.

I'm sure the prosecutor was hopeful that the jurors weren't familiar with shotguns, but my attorney made sure to inform them of what they needed to know during his cross-examination of the deputy.

"Do you know what gauge of shotgun shells the empty box had previously contained?" my attorney asked the deputy.

I already knew the answer but was relieved to hear the deputy say it.

"Yes, the box was marked for containing twelve-gauge shells," the deputy said.

"Now tell me, sir, as a deputy, you're quite familiar with guns, right?" my attorney asked.

"Yes, sir, I am," the deputy answered.

"Then, can you tell me if it would be possible to use a twelve-gauge shell in a twenty-gauge shotgun, such as the one used to shoot Alex Blake?" my attorney asked.

The deputy's answer was an emphatic no.

When Brookens took the stand, his testimony covered everything he actually did know about the robbery, which was damning. In keeping with the type of person he was, though, he also made up answers to questions that he knew nothing about.

This helped my attorney during his cross-examination of Brookens, as he was able to catch Brookens in numerous lies. My attorney was able to effectively characterize Brookens as being a duplicitous, backstabbing dope fiend.

My attorney also asked Brookens if the prosecution had granted him immunity for his testimony.

"No sir," Brookens said, once again lying.

My Own Worst Enemy

He was never prosecuted; never spent one day in jail.

While I was worried about the testimony of the girl I'd spoke to at the bar in Pontiac, it wasn't as bad as I had thought.

She did testify that I told her I was at the scene of a crime where a robbery and shooting had taken place.

"But he said that he didn't rob or shoot anyone," she added.

My attorney asked her what her motive was for coming forward to testify.

"I wanted to try and help Jim," she said.

When the prosecution finally rested its case, my attorney then presented his argument in my defense. He called a number of witnesses — my mother, sister, even the guy from the gas station — who testified as to my whereabouts around the same time as the crime was supposed to have taken place.

However, the prosecution would point out that there was a small gap of time — about thirty minutes — that couldn't be accounted for by the witnesses.

I'd never told my attorney the whole truth about my involvement in the crime. I believe that he did the best he could with the information he had to make my defense.

On the sixth day of my trial, both attorneys were given the opportunity to make their closing statements to the jurors — their last opportunity to convince the jurors of either my guilt or my innocence.

"I ask all of you to carefully scrutinize the credibility of each witness, to weigh all the testimony and evidence as carefully as you can before arriving at a verdict," my attorney asked of them.

After both attorneys were done speaking, the judge instructed the jurors as to the law in regard to armed robbery and first-degree murder.

Part of what he said, as I remember it, was:

> There is no evidence here of premeditation to kill anyone, therefore, for the purpose of this trial and to enable you to better understand the issue, the statute as it applies to this case may be paraphrased as follows: All murder which shall be committed in the perpetration of any robbery shall be murder in the first-degree. If you, the jury, are convinced beyond a reasonable doubt that Alexander Blake

was being robbed and that one of the robbers shot him, that he died as a direct result of the gunshot and that the defendant was a participant at the scene, then it is your duty to return a verdict of guilty of murder in the first-degree.

It matters not whether anyone actually intended to shoot and kill another and it matters not who held the gun that caused the death. He paused a moment before concluding, then said: "The conflict and variations in the circumstances of the affair are legitimate factors for consideration in determining the defendant's guilt or innocence."

I was nervous and anxious to have the jury begin deliberating, but by the time the judge finished reading the jury's instructions, it was getting late in the afternoon and he decided to dismiss the jurors for the evening.

"By law, you are bound not to discuss this case with anyone," the judge told the jurors. "You are to report back to the courthouse at eight o'clock a.m. tomorrow morning to begin your deliberations."

Early the next morning, I was taken back to the courthouse to await the jurors' verdict while they deliberated.

I didn't have to wait long.

The jury had only been deliberating for about three hours when they informed the bailiff that they'd reached a unanimous verdict. The court was called back into session and I was led into the courtroom and seated at the defense table.

I watched as the jurors filed into the courtroom and were seated.

"Has the jury reached a unanimous verdict?" the judge asked the foreman of the jury.

The foreman stood up from his seat and said, "Yes, your Honor, we have."

The verdict was passed to the bailiff, who then handed it to the judge. After he read the verdict silently, he asked the foreman of the jury to read their verdict out loud to the courtroom.

The courtroom was eerily quiet as the jury foreman began reading the verdict.

"On count one of the indictment armed robbery, we the jury find the defendant guilty as charged. On count two first-degree murder, we the jury find the defendant guilty as charged," he said.

My mind immediately went blank. I vaguely remember hearing the judge's voice as he spoke to the courtroom, but my mind didn't comprehend a word of what he was saying. I was in a state of shock.

The next thing I remember was walking down a flight of stairs with two sheriff's deputies escorting me across the street to a police car, where they placed me in the back seat.

When I arrived back at the county jail, I was placed in a cell by myself. Preston was nearby and as soon as the deputy left, he hollered at me from across the hallway.

"Jim, what happened?" he asked. "Did the jury reach a verdict?"

I didn't feel much like talking, nor did I think I could muster a loud enough voice to reach him. I felt defeated and alone.

Still, I managed to holler back, albeit weakly, that I'd been found guilty.

He said something else, but the words were mush in my ears.

"I don't want to be bothered right now," I said.

It had been one of the worst days of my life — a day that would remain indelibly etched in my mind forever. I remember feeling as though I were totally alone in the world, complete and utter loneliness. There was an inextricable emptiness inside me that I'd never before imagined and I knew there wasn't a single soul in the world that could help me now; the realization that all my rescues were gone sank in.

I didn't sleep much at all that night. I was overwhelmed with fear and anxiety. There were a million thoughts and questions of uncertainty running randomly and uncontrollably through my confused and troubled mind.

As reality sank in, an unsettling knot grew in the pit of my stomach, one that was similar to having butterflies — fearful anticipation, to say the least. It was a disquieting feeling that I'd occasionally experienced when I was anxious, scared, or apprehensive about some uncertain turn of events; however, this visceral feeling was more intense. It was as if the muscles in my stomach were being squeezed ever so tightly. As my state of anxiety and uncertainty heightened, the knot seemed to grow, twist and turn. Little did I know then, that disquieting knot in the pit of my stomach would become my only constant and inseparable companion for the rest of my life.

CHAPTER 4

JACKSON PRISON

After having been found guilty, my last court appearance for sentencing was scheduled for January 17, 1973.

I already knew what the sentence would be. In fact, everyone knew that I was going to receive a mandatory life sentence for the first-degree murder conviction. Whatever I received for the armed robbery was irrelevant.

On the day of my sentencing, I was taken to the courthouse under tight security and escorted into the courtroom by several sheriffs' deputies. They seated me in the defendant's chair and removed my handcuffs. Then I waited, the seconds ticking by slowly until the bailiff appeared.

"Court is now in session, all rise for Honorable Judge James P. Churchill," the bailiff announced as the judge entered the courtroom.

The judge customarily asked everyone to be seated and waited for silence to open the proceedings.

"Are you both ready to proceed?" the judge asked the attorneys.

They both nodded and the judge made his obligatory comments about the court having no discretion in sentencing so far as the first-degree murder was concerned.

"In regard to the sentencing for the armed robbery charge, however, this court does have an area of discretion," he added.

Judge Churchill continued, stating:

> With respect to the murder charge, it's the law that all murder committed in the perpetration of a robbery shall be murder in the first-degree and should be punished by solitary confinement at hard labor in the state prison for life. In any event, the court, therefore, sentences Mr.

Goble to prison for life on the mandatory first-degree murder conviction.

I don't know what effect it will have in the years to come. The situation with respect to subsequent dispositions, subsequent action by appropriate boards and the governors and so forth is not directly within the control of the court. I'll say this, while there was evidence of a very serious intentional crime, there was really no evidence of intent to kill. There was premeditation with respect to the robbery, but we have no evidence whatsoever as to why a trigger was pulled. It could have been intentional; it could have been accidental. Nobody, based on the record that's before the court, and so I put that in the record for whatever future benefit it might have, that I recall can't say anybody could have determined that there was an intention to kill. And that might make a difference, in a long time, perhaps.

With respect to the robbery conviction, and when I say that, that's not in any way being critical of the jury verdict because the jury has no choice. If they determine that there was a robbery being committed and someone was shot, one of the victims was shot, that's murder in the first-degree, but premeditation is not an element, and it wasn't alleged, and it wasn't proven, and it wasn't necessary for it to be proven. With respect to the robbery charge, the circumstances are different. The sentence can be life or for any term of years. I really don't know what extent the court's sentence will affect the defendant's future in this respect. I have given a great deal of careful thought to what the sentence is, and should be, and I have tried to make a determination, almost independent of the fact that someone was killed and that there was a murder.

While there was no premeditation on the record with respect to the killing, and I think one can pretty much construe there was no premeditation with respect to the killing, there's no reason why one man would be killed and the other living under these circumstances. There had to be some kind of a fortuitous circumstance that resulted in the trigger being pulled.

However, with respect to the robbery, this was a planned robbery. The jury obviously believed that it was a planned robbery, that it occurred and the planning began clear down in an apartment someplace in Oakland County. It was carried out over a period of an hour or two. A shotgun was used. The gun was obviously loaded; it was a deadly weapon. The entire robbery was perpetrated under such circumstances that the people who perpetrated the robbery showed an utter disregard of the risks to the lives of those involved.

For that reason, I believe that quite apart from the murder conviction, the circumstances of the robbery require a very substantial sentence.

It's the judgment of this court that the maximum sentence which is determined by the court be thirty-years, the minimum sentence twenty-years.

I don't think any of us know how horrible it must be to be a defendant, to be his wife and family, to be going to prison for an extremely long period of time during a young man's youth. I don't know what the future holds. However, society has pretty much disregarded and left to others, society has washed its hands almost of what happens in the post-conviction process. Such humanity as occurs in the correction process once somebody is sent to prison is because of a few, relatively few, very dedicated people in the corrections system and in the parole system.

In the case of people serving life sentences there has to be a public hearing before there can be a parole. In the case of people who are serving a mandatory life sentence under the present law, the parole board doesn't have the authority to parole — all they have the authority to do is make a recommendation of the commutation to the governor. However, I hold that out because while it's not the kind of a future that any of us relish ... there are possibilities of future parole. There are possibilities of improvement in the prison system in some ways which are foreign to what we have thought of in the past.

The judge also said that, in the years to come, he thought we would be likely to see a great deal more humanity towards prisoners. There was no nice way to be confined, but he hoped that there would be a great deal of improvement in the manner in which society deals with people convicted of serious crimes. Then he thanked the attorneys for their diligence and professionalism in representing their clients throughout the course of the trial and adjourned the court.

I was taken back to the county jail, where I would await transfer to the state prison in Jackson, Michigan.

I knew all along that I would receive a mandatory life sentence since the court had no discretion in the sentencing of first-degree murder cases. I thought I had mentally prepared myself to hear the words, "life in prison," but I had not. After hearing them, though, I began to realize that the life I once knew was over. The days ahead would bring many drastic and dramatic changes to my life; changes I did not expect to be pleasant.

"Jim!" I heard Preston call out from across the hallway, but I wasn't in the mood to talk to him. I had a lot to think about, and only one thing left to look forward to — a visit from my family the following day.

In the whirlwind of thoughts running through my mind that night, I'd break from my worries and anxieties to think of seeing my family. I told myself to hold their hands and feel the touch of another human being who loved me for the last time. I thought of what I would say to them and wondered if I might cry.

I finally drifted off to a restless sleep, but was awakened early by the sound of one of the deputies pounding on my cell door and calling out my name.

"Get up and get dressed!" he barked. "You're being transferred to the state prison within the hour."

Suddenly, I was overwhelmed with a sense of uncertainty and foreboding, but there was nothing that I could say or do. I wanted to ask about my scheduled visit with my family, but I knew the deputies would do nothing but laugh. I was now a permanent ward of the state and they could do just about whatever they wanted with me.

They quickly cuffed my hands and placed me into leg shackles, wasting no time hustling me out of the jail and into a waiting police cruiser. As they put me in the back seat, I thought of how disappointed my family would be when they arrived at the jail only to discover I was already miles away, en route to the Jackson State Prison.

I knew it would be a long and depressing ride there, as the prison was several hours away, but I told myself to take a long look around at the world outside the windows.

It'll be years, and maybe never, that you'll see the outside world again, I told myself.

My heart was racing and I could feel a surge of adrenaline pumping through the veins in my head. I was apprehensive as to what might await me in prison and really had no idea what to expect. My head was spinning, thoughts running so uncontrollably through my mind that I was unable to concentrate on any one thing. Never before had I felt so alone and so scared.

Hours later, I got my first look at my new and foreboding home. I'd come to learn the place's nickname was Jacktown, the world's largest walled prison. The sheer size of the place struck me with awe — it was impressively massive and sprawling with an unmistakable, sinister look to it. With its towering walls and numerous gun towers, the sight of the prison was both intimidating and ominous.

This was the big house at the end of the road, the last stop for some and the beginning of the end for others, and yet society refers to it as a place for the rehabilitation of criminals.

After the police cruiser was parked, I was led into what's called "the bubble" — a nickname for the prison's reception center building. In the bubble, I was placed in a large holding cell with several other prisoners. One at a time, our names were called and we were directed to go through a gate into an adjoining room where all incoming prisoners were processed.

When it was my turn, I stepped through the gate and was met by a prison guard wearing a forest green suit coat with a white shirt, black tie and black trousers — an outfit I found a bit surprising. I was expecting the stereotypical, drab uniforms I'd so often seen in the movies and his uniform reminded me that this was no movie; it was my life now.

"Strip down, get in the shower," he said coldly.

The so-called shower was nothing more than four shower heads mounted on the wall. I did as I was instructed and when I was finished, a trustee handed me a towel to dry off. Then I was left to stand there, buck-naked, for several minutes until another trustee walked toward me with a handheld pump sprayer. He sprayed me down with a delousing powder and then handed me a set of state prison blues — my new clothes.

"Get dressed and go stand behind the yellow line across the room," a guard directed me.

From there, I was directed to a desk in the corner of the room where another guard took my fingerprints and mug shot. Finally, I was issued a six-digit prison number and told by one of the trustees that the reception process was complete.

I'm officially a convict now, I thought.

One of the other trustees made the offhand comment that I wouldn't have to worry about doing time on the installment plan — a reference to guys who were always in and out of prison — since I'd managed to get a life sentence the first time around.

Several other prisoners and myself were led through a door and escorted down a long corridor that sloped downward until we came to a solid steel door with a very small window.

Mounted on the wall next to the door was a button and a sign that read, "Ring bell for guard!"

The guard leading us pushed the button, activating a loud, ringing bell that sounded like a fire alarm. Almost immediately, the guard on the other side unlocked the door and we continued our journey inside the prison walls to seven block, one of two cellblocks used as a quarantine area.

We entered the cellblock through the kitchen area, where all the meals were served to the quarantine inmates of seven and eight block. From there, we walked up a flight of stairs to the first gallery bulkhead where the guard's station was located. There were two desks; one with a guard sitting behind it and facing the interior of the block and the other desk was off to the side, where the inmate block clerk was sitting. It was the clerk who assigned each of us to a cell and gave us a copy of the rules. We were issued a bedroll along with a few toiletries and then escorted to our assigned cells.

I was amazed at the enormous size of the cellblock — it was huge. Beside the base area, there were four additional tiers of cells that they called galleries. Each gallery contained about one hundred cells. When I stood on base and looked toward the end of the cellblock, it looked like a massive cargo ship with one big difference — the cargo hold in this ship was filled to capacity with steel and concrete cages to house human beings. The sight was downright eerie.

The cells themselves were furnished sparingly. Each had a small sink about the size of a dinner plate and above the sink was an eight-by-twelve-inch mirror. There were no faucets, just a hot and cold button like on a drinking fountain. A push of the buttons made the water trickle out and as soon as the pressure was released, the water stopped.

The toilet was situated right beside the sink and at first, it didn't look any different from any other toilet. I soon realized, though, one big difference — there was no lid and not even a toilet seat. In this prison, toilet seats are a luxury item afforded only to the guards' restrooms.

The bed was exactly like an old army-type bunk, complete with squeaky springs, and the mattress was literally in piss poor condition. Unsightly stains covered the mattress on both sides, no doubt a gift from the several tenants who'd used it before me.

A single, 100-watt incandescent light bulb was the only lighting for the cell. There was no switch to turn the light on or off. If you wanted the lights off, you unscrewed the bulb with your hand.

My new accommodations would definitely take some getting use to. And as if all this wasn't enough to deal with, directly in front of my cell was the dining area where the inmates sat and ate their meals. Three times a day, a steady stream of about 900 inmates from seven and eight block filed past the front of my cell. There was absolutely no privacy whatsoever. It was noisy, dirty, and it smelled terrible.

This prison wasn't at all like something out of the movies — it was more like something straight out of a nightmare.

I soon learned that all incoming prisoners were placed in quarantine for a period of thirty days, during which time each prisoner was medically screened for any health related issues including any possible communicable diseases. In addition, prisoners were required to undergo psychological testing and evaluations to determine if they needed counseling or treatment. Academic, vocational and IQ tests were also given to ascertain whether an inmate needed school placement or a work assignment. When all the testing and evaluations were completed, every inmate was given a security classification screening to determine his appropriate security level placement.

My first week in quarantine seemed to go by ever so slowly. It was difficult trying to adjust to the strict regimented order of prison life. Unlike the county jail, we were allowed some movement outside of our cells but everything was supervised and tightly controlled.

To occupy my mind and alleviate some of the ever-present boredom, I tried to sleep in whenever possible, but it was almost always impossible because each new day brought back the same loud level of noise.

In the afternoons, I was given one hour to spend in the yard, which turned out to be the highlight of my day. The yard was quite small, only about the size of a basketball court. At that particular point in time, though, size was of no consequence to me — I was just glad to get out of that cell and be able to walk around.

For the past five months, I really hadn't been outside except for the short trips from the county jail to the courthouse. It was especially nice to see the sky again, breathe the fresh air and feel the warmth of the sun on my face.

Prisoners weren't allowed to make telephone calls from quarantine, which meant that my only means of communicating with my family and the outside world was by mail. I'd never written many letters before, not even in the county jail, but I began writing every day with the hope that someone would write back to me. I desperately needed a few reassuring words; something familiar to hold on to. I had many uncertainties as to what the days ahead would bring, but I knew that whatever challenges lay ahead, I'd have to deal with them entirely on my own. There was no one around that I could count on or trust if I needed help.

Quarantine was rarely ever quiet. During the day there was a constant, cacophonous din from hundreds of voices talking at the

My Own Worst Enemy

same time. The noise level would taper off in the evenings to a low murmur, but even in the middle of the night there were strange sounds that echoed through the cellblock.

Talking wasn't allowed after ten o'clock at night, which was lights out time. From what I had observed, though, it was a rule that the guards seldom enforced — or at least that's what I thought until I was caught talking to my neighbor after lights out.

On that particular night, the cellblock was more noisy than usual. Some of the guys were showcasing their amateur talents with animal vocalizations ranging from howling wolves to cows, pigs, and all kinds of bird sounds. The guards weren't impressed and decided to end the talent show before things got totally out of control.

I was lying in my bunk when one of the guards told me to get out of bed and get dressed.

"You're getting a major misconduct ticket for these animal noises — it's a disturbance of the block," he said sternly. "I'll be back for you."

Instead of getting dressed, though, I rolled over and pulled the blanket over my head, laying there quietly and hoping that he would forget about me. But that wasn't the way things worked in prison.

About fifteen minutes later, he came back with another guard.

"Get dressed, you're going to the hole," he barked, unlocking the door to my cell and stepping inside. "Turn around and put your hands behind your back."

The other guard placed me in handcuffs and they walked me over to five block — the segregation area. They gave me two days in the hole, which actually wasn't as bad as I'd expected. It was kind of like being back in the county jail and it was exceptionally quiet. The only time I even saw another person was when my meals were delivered.

Nevertheless, I learned a valuable lesson — keep my mouth shut.

Initially, I tried to avoid any interaction with the other inmates. I didn't know what to expect; I didn't know the first thing about life in prison. I'd decided before I even got there that it'd be in my best interest to stay away from the other inmates until I learned more about prison etiquette. As the weeks went by, though, I found myself slowly beginning to adjust to my surroundings and the daily routine of prison life. I began accepting the fact that I had no other choice, literally, than to live with my current situation. I could only hope for the best and try to be prepared for the worst.

After returning from the yard one afternoon, I discovered that my cell had been ripped off. I didn't have much, but someone had managed to enter my cell and take what precious little I did have. The cell door had been locked, but the locking mechanisms were old and didn't function properly. Clearly, some of the inmates knew all too well about the locks and took full advantage of the situation — popping the doors open by grabbing the bars at the top and giving a quick, hard pull.

There was absolutely nothing I could do about the items that were taken from me. I had no idea who was responsible and complaining to the guards wasn't an option. I knew enough about prison etiquette to know that was snitching, and I knew too that snitching in prison could very well get you killed. If you wanted to survive in this environment, you kept your mouth shut.

Before prison, I hadn't given much thought to understanding the old saying, "There is no honor among thieves." In the past few months, though, I not only understood it, but was convinced that it was indeed an accurate saying.

I was already aware of the intimidation and manipulative tactics that some inmates tried to use on other inmates to get whatever they wanted. It was usually the inmates who were new to the system that were often singled out as targets because they were naïve and generally perceived as being weak.

A few of these individuals were constantly harassed and tested for signs of weakness. One of the con games was to try and verbally intimidate an inmate until he gave up whatever he had that might be worth something, be it a wrist watch, wedding ring or his street shoes. Most of the time, if the newbie inmate stuck to his guns and made it appear that the items would have to be taken by force, the harasser would give up, considering it not worth their trouble. I'd somehow managed to avoid most of the idiots, their con games and all the other bullshit that went on in quarantine. I'd even learned a few valuable lessons along the way and I was just glad that the madness of quarantine was almost behind me.

Within a matter of days, I was expecting to be sent inside the walls and from what I'd been told, it was supposed to be a lot better than quarantine.

My mother and younger sister Emily were allowed to see me once the thirty days in quarantine was over, and they came the first day it was allowed.

When I walked into the visiting room, we greeted each other with hugs and kisses — I was ecstatic to see their familiar smiling faces. It seemed like it had been years since I'd last seen them. We talked about everything that had taken place since I left the county jail and my mother told me that she'd hired an appellant attorney to appeal my case.

"I just don't know what else to do, Jim," she said.

It wasn't long before our conversation got around to the crime.

"Tell me the truth about what really happened that night," she said softly.

I'd always been able to tell my mother anything without fear of punishment or condemnation. She was the most patient and understanding person I'd ever known, but even so, this was going to be a difficult story for me to tell and probably even more difficult for my mother to hear. I felt profoundly ashamed of myself — ashamed not only of the crime and all the ways I'd been so stupid, but ashamed of knowing that telling her the truth would break her heart.

Nevertheless, I took a deep breath, let out a long sigh and began telling her about my drug use.

I told her everything that happened, leaving out only the most minor of details, and I tried to answer all of her questions directly and honestly. Eventually, I got to the details about the shooting — deciding I wasn't going to shoot the gun as planned into the air and then how Alex Blake just stood there like he was paralyzed, so I thought I'd give him a little scare by showing him the gun. And then, how I watched in horror as the gun accidentally discharged.

I looked up and saw my mother's eyes watering with tears, as though her heart had just broken inside of her. It made me feel sick to cause her so much pain.

"I'm so sorry Mom," I said at the sight of her tears. I knew she was devastated by what I'd just told her. "I really am; I am profoundly sorry about every last bit of this."

Not surprisingly, though, she looked directly into my eyes and said, "Nothing will ever change the fact that you're my son. And no matter what happens, I'll never give up on you because I love you unconditionally."

It was at that very moment when it dawned on me that even though I was in prison, I still had many things to be thankful for. And I knew that there were some things in life that not even prison could ever take from me.

A sudden wave of anxiety surged through my entire body when our visiting time was over and my mother and sister had to leave. I had the overwhelming feeling of being completely alone once again, despite the fact that my mother and sister hadn't even left the visiting room. More than anything I wanted to go home with them and it hurt inside knowing that I couldn't. As we said our goodbyes, my mother reassured me that she'd do everything humanly possible to obtain my release from prison.

"I am going to come and visit you at least once a month, dear," she told me, and that made me feel somewhat better about my situation.

The following day, I was classified to general population and that afternoon, I was sent inside the walls. Getting out of quarantine was a huge relief — it was one of those experiences that you hope you'll never have to go through again and one you can never forget. Thankfully, that was behind me now. When the guard came to my cell and told me that it was time to go, I was ready and didn't waste any time. I grabbed my bedroll along with the few personal belongings I had and I was out of there.

Four block was located on the other side of the compound and in order to get there I first had to go through six block, which was where they housed all the inmates on protective custody status, the mentally ill and the sissies. Once through there, I had to go through the control center and down the sub-hall corridor that led to the main yard.

When I first stepped out of the sub-hall, the size of the yard caught me by surprise. It was big.

Besides the gymnasium, there was an outside weight lifting pit, four handball courts, two tennis courts, two horseshoe pits, a softball diamond and a hardball diamond where they played varsity league hardball with teams from the outside. There was also a small area enclosed by a chain-link fence where the inmates were allowed to jog. Most surprising of all was the in-ground, Olympic-sized swimming pool. I totally was not expecting that.

The yard was usually open to inmates every day, seven days a week after breakfast, lunch and supper. The only exception was foggy days, and that's because the fog reduced visibility from the gun towers.

Whenever the yard was open, all of the special activities were usually open as well — the auditorium, barbershop, library, hobby-craft and the inmate store. We were only required to be in our cells for the four mandatory counts and at night, unless you had a third shift job assignment.

The first thing I noticed about four block was that the design of the cellblocks was completely different from those in quarantine. For starters, they were back-to-back rather than facing each other, which not only provided some semblance of privacy but also noticeably reduced the noise level. My cell was on the first gallery along the backside of the block.

From my cell, I was able to see the employee parking lot through one of the broken eight- by ten-inch panes of glass that made up several large windows, which extended the length of the entire block. It was nice to see the cars — they were something familiar, a part of the free world that I'd left behind but not forgotten. As the months passed, I often found myself standing at the front of my cell, staring out the window. I'd occasionally get so lost in my thoughts that I'd suddenly find myself engulfed in pensive reflection of days gone by and daydreaming of what might have been.

When I was in the county jail, my mother would leave toiletries for me every Wednesday, which was visiting day. I sincerely appreciated these items, but the paper bag that the toiletries came in meant much more to me. The bag itself always emitted the pleasant scent of my mother's perfume, which was something familiar and reminded me of home. Every day I'd hold that bag to my face and breathe in the familiar scent of home. But the familiar scents, sounds and objects from my life in the free world were becoming more elusive with each passing day.

One of my neighbors in four block was an Italian guy who was a couple of years older than me. His name was Peretti, but everyone called him by his nickname, Batman. I always wondered how he got that nickname but I never got around to asking him. During the next two years, Batman and I would become good friends.

He'd already served six years on a breaking and entering charge but still had another two years to serve. When I first told him that I had a life sentence for first-degree murder as well as twenty to thirty years for armed robbery, he raised his eyebrows, shook his head at me and slowly said, "Damn ...."

During my first few weeks in four block, Batman filled me in on all the important things I needed to know about living in prison. He explained how they ran the block activity schedule for laundry, showers and movement. He also schooled me on the pitfalls of prison life, offering advice on how to avoid getting caught up in the bullshit prison scams. His philosophy was rather simple.

"Stay away from the drugs, gambling, spud juice and the homosexuals," he told me. "If you can stay away from all that shit, your time here will be a lot easier and you'll probably live longer."

Being in four block and having the chance to purchase things from the inmate store was a lot better than quarantine. The store was open five days a week with the exception of holidays. We were allowed to purchase toiletries, tobacco, writing supplies and a limited selection of food items. The store also stocked a few items of personal clothing and casual shoes, but they were available only by submitting a purchase order form to the business office. We could also submit a purchase order form for a seven- or twelve-inch black and white television set, a small portable AM/FM radio and a small cassette player. One of my first priorities was to order all three of these appliances. They were essential in providing entertainment and keeping abreast with current events in the free world. They would also provide me with a temporary escape from the ubiquitous, daily boredom of prison life.

The currency we used at the inmate store was called script. Every two weeks we were allowed to order a maximum of seventy-five dollars. Script was nothing more than printed pieces of colored paper, kind of resembling movie tickets, with the denomination printed on each ticket. The tickets were stapled together inside a printed cover that denoted the amount enclosed, called a script book. To receive script, an inmate had to sign and submit a disbursement to the business office denoting the amount of money he wanted deducted from his personal account. The following week, script books would be delivered directly to each inmate's cell by the third shift guards.

Nothing is free in prison, though. The way inmates earned script was through work assignments. As the days passed by, I decided I needed to find myself an assignment — both to occupy my time and financially support myself. I couldn't even brush my teeth or wash my butt without a source of income. Just like everyone else, I had to purchase my own toothpaste and soap from the inmate store.

I'd been told that there were lots of job assignments available to choose from. The license plate factory paid the highest wages, but I really wasn't interested in being stuck inside all day long at a tedious and repetitious job. There was also the print shop that printed all the institutional forms and many of the official state forms as well, but that was pretty much the same as the license plate factory. A kitchen assignment was the last thing I was interested in, since I'd done more than my share of time in the kitchen while I was in the army.

Batman was assigned to the butcher shop, but I wasn't interested in that either. I was thinking about requesting an institutional maintenance job. I'd noticed that the inmate maintenance workers were allowed to go almost anywhere inside the compound, they even had access to areas that were off-limits to most other inmates. With my past experience in small engine repair and auto mechanics, I really didn't think that I'd have a problem getting a maintenance job as a mechanic.

Before receiving an assignment, the inmate requesting one is interviewed by the classification committee. At my interview, the first thing they asked me was if I wanted to work in the license plate factory.

"Most lifers want the factory jobs," one of the men said to me. "They pay the highest wages and help establish a daily routine."

I had no desire to pursue a career in the fine art of making license plates and the wages wouldn't change a thing for me.

"I'm not really interested in that," I told the committee. "I've got a lot of experience working as a mechanic; If possible I'd like to get an assignment doing that type of work."

About a week later, I received a work detail for institutional maintenance.

The maintenance department was located in the basement beneath the kitchen and gymnasium. I was assigned to the machine shop along with two other inmates who already worked there. One of the inmates was the kitchen mechanic, who repaired all the kitchen equipment and was on call twenty-four hours a day. The other inmate was the machinist, who operated all the different machinery. It was his job to make whatever replacement parts were needed to repair the kitchen and laundry equipment.

The machine shop was fully equipped with lathes, mills and other machines that could make practically any replacement part that was needed in the prison. Our supervisor was an amiable and laid-back kind of guy. He'd worked at the prison for more than twenty years and started out as a guard. Throughout the years, he'd pretty much seen it all and didn't get excited about too many things. His philosophy, he said, was, "Eight and the gate."

"I put in my eight hours and then I walk out that front gate," he said to me.

He also told me that so long as I didn't start any shit, there wouldn't be any shit — not in the machine shop.

I was assigned to be the laundry mechanic and it turned out to be a fairly decent assignment. All I needed was a work order and I was allowed to go virtually anywhere I wanted within the prison complex.

"If you run into any problems you can't handle, just let me know," my boss said.

CHAPTER 5

Preston's Trial and his Final Betrayal

Preston's trial started in April of 1973 and my mother kept me informed of how his trial progressed. His lawyer had petitioned for a change of venue, saying that it would be impossible to find an impartial jury in Lapeer County because of all the pretrial publicity, and also that my guilty conviction could have a prejudicial affect on potential jurors in the county. The court granted Preston a change of venue and so, his trial was taking place in Tuscola County, the adjoining county to the north.

I'd written to Preston several times since I left the county jail, but my letters were cordial and nothing more. I mostly wrote about what it was like in prison and avoided mentioning anything about my trial or his trial that might be misconstrued. I asked him to keep me posted on what was happening with his trial and to let me know the outcome. But the entire time he was in the county jail, he wrote only one short letter to me.

I was able to make weekly telephone calls to my mother and during one of them, she told me that Preston's trial had resulted in a hung jury.

"Apparently, the jury wasn't able to reach a unanimous verdict," she told me. "But Preston isn't being released; the prosecutor still believes he can get a conviction so he has to stay in jail and stand trial again."

The prosecutor was certain that Preston was guilty and he wasn't about to let him just walk away a free man.

The whole process would start all over again for Preston's second trial. Another jury would have to be selected and that was scheduled to begin in two weeks. In the interim, Preston's attorney had filed a motion asking the court to release him on bond until his next court appearance, but the judge denied the motion at the request of the prosecutor.

"Inmate Goble," yelled a guard approaching my cell. "Your attorney called here requesting that you be allowed to call him at his law office in Detroit, as soon as possible."

I'd only spoken once with this new attorney hired by my mother to appeal my case, and based on that conversation, I wasn't the least bit impressed.

My mother and I talked about it and she said that when she first retained this attorney, she'd spoken with the senior attorney at the law firm and was given the impression that he'd be personally handling my appeal. But he wasn't. Instead, his son was handling my case and he had practically no experience.

"I did have mixed feelings about this law firm," she told me. "It was like a sales pitch when I went in there, it made me feel uneasy."

She said the man boastingly showed her a file cabinet, claiming that it contained numerous examples of murder cases that he'd successfully won on appeal. He never actually pulled those files out and showed her the appeals, though.

"I wasn't convinced this was the right firm, but Jim, I just had no other clear options," she told me.

Out of sheer desperation, she hired the attorney.

In my opinion, the guy was too young and inexperienced to be litigating an appeal in a murder case. Worse, though, was that something about his demeanor made me feel very uncomfortable.

He kept bothering my mother about getting his fee and called her frequently, asking that she pay him cash for Xerox copies, postage and filing fees. He was more worried about getting paid than getting me out of prison and I simply didn't trust the guy.

Nevertheless, he was about the only hope I had, so I called his office collect from one of the telephones in the block that were designated for inmates' use.

The phone rang a couple times and then the attorney's secretary picked it up and asked me to hold for a moment. When my attorney finally took the call, he told me that he'd been working on my appeal when he unexpectedly got a telephone call from Lapeer County's prosecuting attorney.

"He wants to make a deal with you, Jim," my attorney said. "Since the jury couldn't reach a unanimous verdict in Preston's first trial, the prosecutor is worried and he thinks your testimony will help."

He continued: "If you'll admit complicity in the crime and agree to testify against Preston, they'll set aside your first-degree murder conviction and let you plead to second-degree murder, which is a lesser crime with a sentence of no more than ten years in prison."

I personally thought that this was a reasonable offer.

"What is your professional opinion?" I asked my attorney.

"Don't do it," he said, much to my surprise. I thought he'd be glad to have this settled. "I'll have you out of there in less time than what the prosecutor is offering."

My gut feeling was to take the prosecutor's offer, but my attorney was essentially giving me a guarantee that he could get me out of prison even sooner and that sounded even more appealing to me.

But the prosecutor's offer is a sure thing, I thought to myself. Ten years was nothing compared to the life sentence without parole that I was already serving. I had nothing to lose and everything to gain.

I also thought about the promise that I'd made to Preston and I couldn't help but wonder if he'd keep his promise to me. I remembered how Preston had shown how irresponsible he can be, letting my handwritten notes fall into the hands of the prosecutor.

There were a number of other questionable issues that made me uncertain.

"Are you absolutely sure you can have me out of here in less than ten years?" I asked him.

"Yes, I'm sure!" he said. "Without a doubt, Jim."

"Well then, I'm not interested in making any deal that requires me to testify against Preston," I told him, and we both said our goodbyes and hung up.

Once again, my propensity for making the wrong decisions prevailed over my God — given common sense. Not helping my situation was this young attorney who had just given me the worst possible advice.

Years later, I learned that attorneys are not legally permitted to instruct their clients to accept or deny any plea bargains. Attorneys must inform their client of any plea bargain offered by the prosecution, but they specifically weren't allowed to advise clients the way my attorney advised me. Doing so is completely unethical. The decision to accept or deny a plea bargain is supposed to be made independently by the defendant.

In retrospect, I can see how naïve I was. Hindsight is twenty-twenty, after all, and nowadays, I can see that my attorney wasn't the least bit concerned with representing my best interests. His only interest, in fact, was to line his pockets with every hard-earned penny of my mother's money that he could get his greedy little hands on. It was so obvious; I have a hard time understanding why I didn't see that then.

Several years later, I filed a delayed motion for appeal and was sent written documentation from the prosecuting attorney and the trial judge stating that a plea bargain had indeed been offered to my appellant attorney. Nevertheless, my greedy attorney denied that the prosecutor had ever offered any such deal or plea bargain: lying to cover his own ass, of course.

Had I known then what I know now, I would have filed a complaint with the Attorney Grievance Commission in regard to his unethical conduct.

It wasn't long after I turned down the prosecutor's offer that I heard Preston had been acquitted of the armed robbery and the first-degree murder charges. The jury had deliberated for less than an hour before returning a verdict of not guilty. To say I was surprised is an understatement.

Practically the same evidence was used at both our trials — Preston's fingerprints were even used as evidence against me at my trial — and yet a different jury found him not guilty. Without a doubt, Preston's attorney played a huge role in his acquittal.

His family had retained the attorney for a price of fifty thousand dollars. There was no way my family, at that time, could've afforded such a price, but the difference between our two attorneys was unmistakable. Preston's attorney had a great deal more trial experience in defending murder cases. I've heard it said that this country has the best judicial system that money can buy and there is most definitely a great deal of truth to the statement.

In all the years that I've been locked up, not once have I ever met a wealthy or rich person in prison. They say that justice is blind, as depicted by the blindfold on Lady Justice. But more often than not, the amount of justice you receive depends on who you are, who you know, and how much money you have.

I was feeling somewhat ambivalent about Preston's acquittal. I found myself wondering if he'd keep his promise to do whatever it took to get me out of prison now that he was a free man. After all, I'd kept my promise to him by turning down the prosecutor's deal and refusing to testify against him. If it wasn't for me, he would have been sitting right next to me in a prison cell. If I'd testified against him, it wouldn't have mattered if he had the best attorney in the country — my testimony would have put him behind bars for life.

A couple of weeks later, my mother called to tell me that she'd heard Preston was staying with his wife at their apartment in Pontiac. She'd somehow managed to get the phone number there and passed it along to me. I called him as soon I could.

Preston's wife answered the telephone.

"Hello," I said to her. "May I please speak to Preston?"

"Sure," she said. "Hang on a sec and I'll grab him for you."

A moment later Preston's voice came over the line.

"Hey man, how ya doing?" he asked me.

"I'm okay, how are you?" I replied.

"I feel great — God it feels good to be a free man again after being locked up for the past seven months," he said.

My stomach sank a bit; I wanted so badly to have that feeling. Even so, I wanted to be cheerful for him.

"I'll bet it does!" I said back to him. "You know, after your first trial, the prosecutor offered me a deal of just ten years if I'd testify against you."

"Wow, I didn't know," Preston said. "Well, thanks, man. I'm really glad you didn't take the deal."

"So, you know how you said that you'd get me out of this place if you were acquitted?" I asked him. "When do you think you'll be able to do that?"

He hesitated for a moment, drawing his breath in deeply.

"I don't think I can do what we originally talked about, Jim," he told me. "I'm really sorry, but it's just that my family went through so much to support me through all of this. They even mortgaged their house to pay for my attorney because they believed I was innocent."

Preston added: "I just don't think I can tell them now that I am guilty."

"So, just what do you plan on doing to get me out of here?" I asked him.

"Don't worry!" he told me. "I'll do everything I can. I'll come up with something!"

When I hung up the phone, the old saying, "Fool me once, shame on you. Fool me twice, shame on me," popped into my head. While it stung that Preston had betrayed me, it came as no great surprise. I let myself be manipulated because I thought that Preston was my friend. Evidently, we had a different understanding of exactly what a friend was.

I should have known better; it seemed like every so-called friend I'd ever had in my life betrayed me sooner or later.

Either way, I couldn't lay all the blame on Preston. No one had held a gun to my head and forced me to make the choices I made. I knew what I should have done from the very beginning. I should have listened to that little inner voice, my conscience, which was screaming at me, demanding that I take responsibility for my actions and what I'd done. I'd been a fool.

On that day, I made a promise to myself to never again let myself be used by another person.

I tried to call Preston several times after our initial conversation, but I could never reach him. His wife would always tell me that he was working or give me some other excuse to cover for him. After a while, I finally just gave up and I didn't bother trying to call him anymore.

Every now and then my family would tell me that they'd seen Preston or Brookens somewhere, but that was all the knowledge I had of them. My sister told me that just after Preston was acquitted, he and Brookens held a celebration at one of the bars in Lake Orion.

"Oh Jim, it was awful," she told me. "They were telling everyone their own version, the wrong version, of things — saying that you'd tricked them into going along with you on a drug deal and that everything was supposedly your idea and your fault."

I tried to hold in my anger. It wouldn't have been right to get upset with my sister on the phone. It'd only make her more upset about the whole deal.

"Just forget about them," I said to her.

It's been said that what comes around goes around — karma, I believe it's called.

Both Brookens and Preston had a lot of bad karma to carry around, and evidently, Preston didn't learn a thing from the whole terrible ordeal.

Maybe he was on a suicide mission from the beginning, because as soon as he became a free man again, he went right back to using heroin. I couldn't believe it when I heard about it.

How could you be so stupid to not realize you'd been given a second lease on life? I'd feel so lucky if I were him; I'd treasure every day, I thought.

His luck was about to run out, though, and this time, he wouldn't walk away unscathed.

A couple years later, I was told that Preston developed some sort of stomach ailment that required professional medical treatment. Whatever the problem was, it was serious enough that his doctor recommended he undergo a routine surgical procedure necessary to correct it.

Preston set up the surgery, but made a fatal mistake when he neglected to inform the doctor that he was a heroin addict. In fact, on the day of his scheduled surgery he checked into the hospital while high on heroin. Consequently, when they took Preston into the operating room and the anesthesiologist administered the anesthetic, Preston experienced an acute adverse reaction and went into cardiac arrest. The attending physician attempted several different resuscitation procedures, but he was unsuccessful and Preston died right there on the operating table of a massive heart attack.

To be perfectly honest, I felt no remorse or grief whatsoever for Preston. I did feel sorry for his family. I knew something about the psychological hell and the huge financial burden Preston's family had been forced to endure — after all, I'd placed my family in the very same, precarious situation.

Preston had been given a second chance to do something with his life, but he foolishly chose to throw it away. He not only betrayed me, but he betrayed his own family as well.

In the end, I couldn't help but feel a sense of overwhelming futility and wretchedness. Preston's life and death, and all I'd been through, made me wonder if there was any real purpose to life or if life was nothing but a mere existence. I'd lost whatever blind faith I grew up with and I didn't know what to believe anymore. My parents had raised me to be religious, to believe in God and to trust that there was a divine purpose that created and guided humanity. I was taught to believe that every person was put on this earth for some special purpose in life.

But the more I thought about it, the more I found myself questioning this belief. I tried to apply my religious faith to the every day problems of my own life — the miserable existence I'd become forced to endure — and it never worked out. It didn't seem to make any sense to me. I felt empty and confused and I began to question whether God actually existed at all. I could never understand how God, supposedly being omnipotent and omniscient, could stand back and watch as his so-called children endure the insuperable adversities of every day life — hunger, sickness, disease, old age, war, man's inhumanity to man — without interceding on his children's' behalf as any loving parent would do.

I guess most people inherently have a need to believe in something greater than themselves. A belief, though, is not necessarily the truth.

For the first couple of years after Preston was acquitted, I admittedly held onto the slightest hope that he'd eventually make some kind of effort to help me get out of prison, but that hope turned out to be nothing more than wishful thinking. He never so much as took the time to write me a single letter.

Now, with Preston resting six feet under the ground, I knew beyond a shadow of a doubt that Preston couldn't keep his promise to me if he wanted to. I had no choice but to accept the fact that I was going to be in prison for at least the next few years of my life.

I still held out hope that my appeal would be successful, but I also had to be realistic about my current situation. The best thing to do was to keep my mind occupied as best I could and try not to give up. I continually reminded myself of the saying, "Being defeated is usually only a temporary condition. Giving up is what makes it permanent."

My work assignment started at seven o'clock every morning and count time followed four hours later at eleven o'clock. The inmates assigned to the maintenance department were allowed to remain on their assignments during count time instead of returning to their cellblocks.

When count cleared and every inmate was accounted for, usually around noon, they started running the chow lines.

Instead of going to chow, I'd meet Batman in the weight-pit. Batman was an old hand at weightlifting with years of experience behind him and it was obvious from his muscular build. For me, on the other hand, weightlifting was something altogether new. I was surprised to discover just how weak and out of shape I really was.

When I first started working out, I struggled with one hundred and thirty five pounds on the bench press. I'd look over at Batman benching three hundred and fifteen pounds and making it look easy. The first week was incredibly painful; my muscles were so sore that I could hardly move. But once the soreness was gone, my muscles quickly adapted and responded to the strenuous exercise. Within three months, I was able to bench press two hundred and twenty five pounds for eight repetitions. I even got to the point where I actually liked lifting weights and looked forward to the days I worked out. In fact, after I'd been at it for a while, I began feeling guilty whenever I missed a day.

To occupy my time in the evenings, I started taking music theory classes two days a week. I'd had an interest in learning how to play the drums as a teenager and at one time, even owned a complete drum set. I was never all that good, though. I could keep a steady beat and do a few drum rolls, but I played by ear and that severely limited my repertoire.

However, now that I had the opportunity and lots of extra time, I decided to learn how to read sheet music in hopes that it would help me to become more proficient at playing the drums. Music theory and beginner's band classes were held Monday through Friday in the basement of the auditorium. On the weekends, we were allowed to use the classrooms for informal group practice, which was actually a lot of fun. I always enjoyed participating in those impromptu group sessions — it was almost like not being in prison for a couple of hours.

Almost every day, there was some kind of drama taking place within the prison. One morning I was standing in the weight-pit waiting for Batman when I noticed an inmate and a guard coming down the walk from the license plate factory. The inmate was walking behind the guard and every few steps he'd take a swing at the guard with his clenched fist. The guard was doing all he could to stay ahead of the inmate, but every now and then the inmate would land a good punch and the guard would drop to one knee.

The weight-pit was located in the yard, right across from the kitchen loading dock where there were three gun towers positioned on top of the building. One on each corner and the other was directly above the kitchen back dock entrance.

When the inmate and the guard were almost in front of the weight-pit, the inmate came running into the weight-pit, picked up one of the ten pound weights and then went back after the guard again. The guard was now on the loading dock trying to get inside the kitchen, but in his rush to get away from the inmate, he fumbled with the keys and couldn't find the right one to unlock the door. He turned around at the last moment; I could see the terror in his eyes as he realized the inmate was almost on top of him. With no place left to go, the guard ran over to where they steam clean the kitchen equipment and he frantically began yelling and waving his arms at the guard in the gun tower, trying desperately to get his attention.

The guard in the gun tower finally heard the commotion below and saw that the inmate was about to attack the guard.

"Stop immediately or I'll shoot," he called out to the inmate over the speakerphone.

The guards in the gun towers were armed with high-powered 30-30 caliber rifles that could stop a man in his tracks and every inmate knew this. Despite the warning, the inmate continued to pursue the guard. Following procedure, the guard first fired a warning shot to signal his lethal intent. But again, the inmate chose to foolishly ignore the warning. The next shot was meant to take the inmate out, and it did. The bullet ripped through the inmate's right shoulder with such force that he did a somersault off the back dock and landed flat on his back.

He was lying there still, not moving a muscle, and I was sure he was dead. Surprisingly, though, after a couple minutes passed the inmate slowly got his feet underneath him, staggered to the loading dock and slumped against the wall until several more guards arrived. The guards laid him on the ground and one of them began applying pressure to the bullet wound to prevent excessive blood loss.

When the nurses arrived they placed him on a stretcher, and began administering first-aid. The guards carried him to the infirmary and that was the last time I ever saw that inmate. I assume that if he lived, he was probably sent to Marquette Branch Prison, which was the maximum-security prison in the Upper Peninsula.

There were many times when I witnessed the gun towers firing warning shots, but that was the only time I ever actually saw an inmate get shot inside the walls. Most of the violence was usually inmate on inmate, which was frequently out of sheer frustration or over something as trivial as perceived disrespect. Depending on your transgression, you were always in danger of getting stabbed. More often than not, though, confrontations were settled by other means.

Two years passed by slowly as I lived in four block. As the second year came to an end, I decided to apply for a move to one of the so-called honor blocks, where inmates are given extra privileges. Eleven and twelve blocks were the designated honor blocks and an inmate could request placement in one of these blocks only if he had received no disciplinary tickets within the past year.

The honor blocks afforded the inmates a few extra privileges that the other blocks didn't allow. They had out of cell movement from six o'clock in the morning until the ten o'clock count at night, and the inmates were allowed to move around freely within the cellblock. They were also given unlimited access to the telephones, showers and the color television that was located on the base area. Locking in one of the honor blocks was indeed somewhat better than the other blocks, but just because these blocks were designated as honor blocks didn't necessarily mean that every inmate was a model prisoner. In fact, there were probably more illegal activities taking place in the honor blocks than any of the other blocks.

I had no disciplinary tickets for more than a year, so my request to be housed in the honor block was granted. One of the first things I noticed upon getting there was that most of the older guys locked on the base floor. I never asked why; just assumed that they probably had medical problems and it was difficult for them to climb the stairs.

One of these individuals was an older gentleman by the name of Jones. He'd been locking on base at the far end of the block for years. Most of the other inmates knew Jones to be a friendly and mild-mannered individual who never bothered anyone. He minded his own business and stuck to himself. The only illegal activity he was involved in was running a block store, which means he sold store items to other inmates to supplement his income. Jones routinely purchased a variety of items from the inmate store and resold those items on credit or at a slightly higher cost to make a profit. Although running a block store was against the posted rules, it was usually overlooked as long as it didn't get out of hand or come to the attention of the administration.

Most guys who ran block stores expected to take a loss every now and again, and of course there was always the risk of doing business with an idiot or a psychopath who couldn't be reasoned with. Unfortunately for Jones, he discovered this fact a little too late when one of the guys who owed him a couple of dollars for items that were bought on credit refused to pay him. It would've been a small loss, but Jones was concerned that if he let it slide, the other inmates would perceive it as a sign of weakness and think that they could take whatever they wanted from him without fear of retaliation.

Jones had repeatedly tried to work out a compromise with this individual, but the guy just kept giving him the run-around. As a last resort, Jones tried to pressure and intimidate the inmate for payment, but the tactic backfired. The guy became so enraged that he stabbed Jones in the chest with an ice pick.

Jones didn't think the wound was serious because it was only a small hole and it wasn't bleeding very much, so he decided not to seek medical attention. About twenty minutes later, though, he started coughing up blood and realized that something definitely was wrong and he needed medical attention after all. Jones began walking the length of the block, which is about the length of a football field, to alert a guard. But just as he got to the front door, he fell over dead in his tracks.

Apparently, the ice pick had nicked Jones' aortal artery and caused internal bleeding. His chest cavity filled up with blood and as a result, Jones literally drowned in his own blood.

Whenever an inmate died inside the walls at Jackson, his body was taken to the infirmary and placed in the basement until an autopsy could be performed. One of the guys who worked in the infirmary was locking a few cells down from me. He'd previously mentioned that it was his responsibility to clean up after the autopsies had been completed. The day after Jones died, the inmate mentioned to me that he was there when the doctor was performing the autopsy on the old man.

"It was so gross, man," he told me. "They were removing the blood from Jones' body — they do that with these plastic tubes, you know — and the tubing came loose and sent blood squirting all over the room."

"It took me fuckin' forever to clean up the mess; the blood was sticking to everything and all gooey and shit," he added. "Two hours; two hours it took me to clean up after that old man."

"That sucks, man," I said back to him. "That's just gross."

"Yeah, and then, me and one of the other guys down there grabbed Jones' heart after the doctor left," he told me, laughing. "We used that fucker's heart to play a game of catch!"

I didn't laugh with him — that really disgusted me.

"How could you fuckin' do that?" I asked incredulously. "Don't you have any damn respect for the dead?"

My reaction just made the inmate laugh more.

"The guy was dead, Jim!" he said, smiling. "He didn't feel a goddamn thing!"

I was somewhat bewildered by his callous statement. I couldn't help but wonder if I too would become as hard-hearted and insensitive as some of the other inmates who had already spent a number of years in this wretched environment.

Prison was mostly filled with people you'd never seen or heard of before. But every once in a while you run into someone you did know on the outside. You just don't expect it to be your doctor or bank president.

A few years before I came to prison, my family doctor from Lake Orion was arrested and charged with second-degree murder. Apparently, the good doctor's wife had been having an affair with another man. When the doctor found out about his wife's infidelity, he was unable to deal with the matter in a calm and rational manner. I don't recall all the details, but supposedly, one evening the doctor waited for his wife's lover to exit a bar in downtown Lake Orion. As this man came out of the bar and was walking to his car, the doctor casually walked up to him and shot him in the chest with a 38-caliber handgun. I remember hearing that after the doctor shot this man, he sat down beside him and watched him die.

The doctor made a deal with the prosecuting attorney to plead guilty to the lesser charge of second-degree murder and in return he was sentenced to ten years in prison. Upon entering Jackson, I'd been pretty sure that the doctor was doing time somewhere inside its walls. Jackson was a huge prison, though, and if he locked in a cell in the infirmary or six-block, it was quite possible that we could be in the same prison together for years and never so much as catch sight of one another.

But when I requested a new pair of prescription eyeglasses and was sent to the infirmary for an eye examination, I was surprised to discover that the person performing the eye exams was none other than Doctor Mitchell, my old family physician.

I was even more surprised to see that the prison was still allowing him to practice medicine. Not to say he wasn't a good doctor, because he was, but he'd taken another human life and I knew that was a violation of the Hippocratic Oath he'd taken in order to practice medicine. All things considered, though, we were quite fortunate to have Doctor Mitchell working in the prison infirmary.

The doctor was in the middle of doing an eye examination when I walked in the clinic, but when he looked over at me, his face lit up with a big smile. He immediately stopped what he was doing and came over to shake my hand.

"I'm glad to see you, Jim," Doctor Mitchell said to me. "I wish it was under different circumstances, though, for both of us."

"I've been asking around about you forever," I told him. "I'd kinda figured that you were here somewhere, but no one seemed to know anything about you — I just assumed you were probably in trustee division."

He nodded his head at me and said he'd read about my trial in the newspaper.

"I was so sorry to read that you'd gotten a life sentence," he told me seriously.

We chatted for a few moments and I gave him the short version of what had happened that night and how my so-called friends had used and betrayed me. He got my eye exam underway and upon finishing up, I told him it'd been nice to see him.

"I hope I get to see you again sometime, Doc," I told him. "I'll tell my family you asked about them."

We wished each other the best of luck in getting out of prison and after that, I never saw the doctor again. About a year later, I heard that he was sent to the trustee division and then paroled a few months later. The only other thing I ever heard about the doctor was that he moved to California and was once again practicing medicine.

Not long after hearing of the doctor's move to the west coast, I made a little move of my own — to twelve block. One afternoon, the block was called to lunch and as we were filing out the doors, I noticed an inmate in line just ahead of me who looked vaguely familiar. At first I couldn't place his face, but then it clicked for me.

Community National Bank in Lake Orion, I thought. *That guy was the bank president!*

I'd done my banking there and was sure it was him. I caught up to him on the sidewalk a few moments later and tapped him on the shoulder. He turned around, but the blank look in his eyes made it clear he didn't recognize me.

"Did you used to be the bank president of Community National in Lake Orion?" I asked him.

"Used to be," he said nonchalantly and a bit coldly.

"I thought you looked familiar," I told him. "I used to do my banking there; I'm from Lake Orion too."

We talked briefly on the way to the chow hall, but after that, I didn't see him again. I assumed that he must have been paroled or sent to trustee division. I never did find out why he was in prison, but I've always been curious. You just don't see too many bank presidents in state prisons.

CHAPTER 6

Escapes from Jackson Prison

The possibility of escape is ever present on the minds of some inmates, but few have the balls, resolve, or the inclination to actually surmount their fears of failure and punishment to ever attempt such a feat. Most just lie down and passively accept their plight without even the slightest whimper of dissent or defiance.

During the five years that I spent behind the walls of Jackson, I witnessed several attempted escapes and several more that were successful. One that sticks out in my mind is when an inmate named Alan attempted to hide his six-foot, four-inch body in one of the fifty-five gallon drums of garbage that were sent out of the prison twice a week.

These barrels weren't filled with the common, everyday type garbage, but were instead full of the leftover food scraps from the kitchen. After the barrels sat around for a couple days at room temperature, the hodgepodge of garbage food items inside them quickly turned into a rancid, foul-smelling slop that was used to feed the hogs raised on the prison farm.

Alan spent several months planning his escape. He'd slightly modified one of the garbage barrels by using a lag-bolt to punch a small hole in one side of the barrel.
Through this hole, he planned to insert a piece of rubber hose that would allow him to breath for an extended period of time. He also planned to take an extra set of clothing in a sealed plastic bag, so if he were successful, he'd have some clean clothes to change into. Alan knew that his plan wasn't foolproof, but he figured that he just might get lucky. To him, it was worth taking the chance because he was serving a life sentence. At that point in time, the guy just didn't have anything to lose.

On the days when the garbage was being picked up, the sally port guard would always call the kitchen guard to notify him that the garbage truck was on its way in to make a pick-up. One afternoon when Alan heard that the truck was on its way in, he set about making his final preparation. Another inmate helped him climb inside the barrel, which was already half-full with the wretched food mixture. He placed the air hose securely in its hole, crouched down as far as he could and braced himself as the other inmate began filling the barrel with more of the foul-smelling slop until Alan was completely covered.

It took the back-dock crew about ten minutes to load all the barrels on the flatbed truck before it pulled away from the back dock and headed for the sally port. Once the truck was inside the sally port, the guards were always supposed to check the contents of each barrel going out. They accomplished this by using a steel rod to probe down inside each barrel; however, not all of the guards checked each barrel. Some of the guards would occasionally just do spot checks, which was fairly common knowledge to those inmates who had been around for a while.

Unfortunately, this wasn't to be Alan's lucky day. On the particular day he put his escape plan into action, the guard working the sally port happened to be one of those overzealous individuals who did his job strictly by the book. Rarely, if ever, did he let a single thing get through the sally port without a thorough search.

Once the truck was secured inside the sally port, the guard climbed up on the truck and he began probing each barrel, making sure that the steel rod went all the way to the bottom. When he plunged the steel rod into the barrel where Alan was hiding, the rod struck Alan directly in his testicles.

We were told that Alan came out of that barrel like he'd been shot out of a cannon — gasping for air, vomiting and holding his nuts with both hands. The guards in the sally port were somewhat surprised, but only slightly amused by Alan's antics. They couldn't believe that a guy as big as Alan would try to hide himself in a garbage barrel.

For his attempt at escaping, Alan was given six months in the hole and then transferred to Marquette Branch Prison, the maximum-security prison in the Upper Peninsula.

Even so, it didn't deter Alan from trying again to escape. I heard that a few years later, he was caught in another attempted escape from Marquette. This time, he and several other inmates got to work on digging a tunnel under one of the walls.

Supposedly, one of the guards just happened to stumble across the tunnel entrance, which was carefully concealed next to the trash incinerator. It was rumored that another inmate had snitched on the guys, and that's more than likely the real reason they got caught.

Rocky was another guy who tried escaping from Jackson. The guy was only five-feet, five-inches tall and weighed all of one hundred and twenty pounds. His brilliant idea was to disguise himself as a female nurse and simply walk out the prison's main gates. Believe it or not, he almost pulled it off. The one flaw in his plan was that he didn't have any identification to show the guard at the main gate.

Rocky told me that he'd never seriously thought about trying to escape until the idea mistakenly arrived in the mail one day. He'd placed a catalog order for several items of men's clothing, but when the shipment arrived a few weeks later, Rocky opened up the package to find the company had mistakenly sent him female clothing.

He thought about sending it back, he said, but then wondered if maybe it was a sign — fate's way of mailing him a ticket out of prison. It seemed simple enough and during the next couple of months, Rocky set about obtaining several more items of female clothing and accessories to fully, albeit superficially, transform his appearance and conceal his true identity. About the only thing Rocky didn't need was a wig, since he'd been wearing his hair down to his shoulders for the past several years.

To complete the look, he paid the inmate barber to trim and style his long, red hair into a more feminine fashion. He applied lipstick and eyeliner, which he'd bought off one of the gay inmates.

Rocky's work assignment in the auditorium was a perfect location for him to implement his plan. It provided him enough privacy to apply his makeup and get dressed without having to worry about someone discovering him before he was able to complete his transformation into a female. Then, once he was satisfied with his appearance, he left the auditorium and made his way to the sub-hall gate.

When he got to the sub hall, the guard took one look at Rocky and opened the gate without any hesitation, letting him pass through unchallenged. He proceeded down the hallway, walking confidently and with a female's swagger in his step right past the deputy warden's office, through the control center and up the flight of stairs to the main gate without anyone giving him a second glance.

As Rocky stepped up to the main gate, the guard in the control room between the two gates activated an electrical switch that opened the first gate, allowing Rocky and two other people to enter. Apparently, the guard who was working the main gates recognized the other two people as employees, so he didn't bother to ask them for their identification. He stopped Rocky, though.

"Sorry to be a bother ma'am, but I just don't recognize you," the guard told Rocky. "Can you show me your employee identification card?"

At that point, Rocky knew he was in trouble. About the only thing he could do was to try and talk his way out of this predicament.

"I must've left that out in the car," Rocky said in his best woman's voice. "I'm a bit new around here, haven't quite gotten used to things."

The guard wasn't about to buy that old excuse, though.

"Well, I'm sorry ma'am, but I can't let you exit the gate without showing proper identification," the guard said.

Rocky kept on talking and the guard kept on believing him, although he wasn't about to bend the rules.

"I guess you'll have to wait here a few minutes," the guard said. "I'm going to have to call the control center sergeant and get some instruction on how to handle this."

The guard got his instructions and returned to Rocky with a second guard, who escorted him back through the gate to the control center.

"We're just going to have to check with employee personnel to get you verified," Rocky was told.

Of course, whatever fake name Rocky had given the guards was not in the prison's system. Consequently, they confronted Rocky with this information and he was finally forced to reveal his true identity.

Like the others, Rocky did some time in the hole and was then transferred to Marquette for five years. I'd see him again a few years later when I was moved there too.

One of the most notorious and well-publicized escapes from Jackson Prison was made by an inmate named Remling, who escaped from inside the walls by means of a helicopter.

It was around noon on the day that Remling escaped. I was standing in the weight-pit, getting ready to start my workout when I first heard the distinct and unmistakable sound of a helicopter somewhere off in the distance. As I continued to listen, the sound of the rotor blades grew louder and louder, so I knew the helicopter was getting closer to the prison. My area of vision was limited by the towering prison walls, though, and prevented me from seeing exactly where the helicopter was.

The sound seemed to be coming from the direction of the back forty, which was over by the license plate factory, but when I looked in that direction, I still didn't see anything. Nevertheless, I could tell from the deep thumping sound of the rotor blades that the helicopter was very close. Suddenly, it came into view — flying very low just above the top of the back wall. No sooner had it cleared the wall than the pilot made a one hundred and eighty degree turn while descending, skillfully landing in the small yard next to the swimming pool.

I stood there in the weight-pit, mesmerized and confused by what was taking place. I didn't really know what to think, but I wasn't about to take my eyes off the helicopter.

When I saw someone running toward the helicopter, I knew something was going down. One of the people inside the helicopter swung the door open and held it there until the man running toward it had jumped in. While the door was being shut, the helicopter began taking off and flew quickly back over the prison walls in the same direction it had come from.

It all happened so fast that no one actually realized what was happening until it was over. The guards in the gun towers never even fired a shot.

When the helicopter first came over the wall, it was flying so low that I thought it was making an emergency landing. I assume the guards had thought the same. But when I saw that person run to the helicopter and climb inside, I was almost certain that I'd just witnessed an escape.

It was only a matter of minutes until the emergency count siren began signaling a lock down was in progress.

"All inmates are to report to their cellblocks immediately for an emergency count," a voice said over the PA system. "I repeat, all inmates are to report to their cellblocks immediately."

At that point, there was no doubt in my mind that someone had indeed pulled off a great escape with great success. I was expecting us to be on lockdown for the rest of the day, but surprisingly, we were only locked down for about two hours. Once the headcount had been completed and they found out exactly who was missing, they cleared the count and allowed the rest of us to resume our normal routine.

Remling had indeed pulled off a great escape, but his freedom was short-lived. By the end of that same day he was back behind the walls and locked securely in five-block segregation.

The details of Remling's escape were soon common knowledge throughout the prison. Remling had supposedly promised to pay an old acquaintance of his a sum of ten thousand dollars to help him escape. The accomplice had gone to an air charter service under the pretext of hiring an aircraft to take aerial photographs of property that he'd recently purchased. He arranged to charter the helicopter for a specific date and time, and Remling had given him instructions as to the exact location within the prison where he'd be waiting.

Remling had also given him specific instructions to approach the prison from the back wall, where most of the gun towers were unmanned during the day.

On the day of the escape, Remling's accomplice arrived at the air charter service apparently giving no indication of his true intent. But shortly after takeoff, he brandished a large hunting knife, threatened the pilot and hijacked the helicopter. He then ordered the pilot to fly the helicopter to Jackson State Prison.

"We'll be picking up a passenger there," Remling's accomplice said crudely.

Everything went exactly as they'd planned. Once Remling was inside the helicopter, they ordered the pilot to fly them to a location several miles from the prison where Remling's accomplice had parked a vehicle in a wooded area. As soon as they landed, Remling and his accomplice got out of the helicopter and went directly to their getaway vehicle. They didn't bother to restrain the pilot in any way, nor did they disable the helicopter or the pilot's radio. Instead, they simply got in their vehicle and drove away.

Hindsight is always twenty-twenty, they say, and I'm sure in retrospect Remling and his accomplice had wished they'd done something about the helicopter pilot and his radio. Once Remling and his accomplice were out of sight, the pilot took off and contacted the authorities by radio, telling the police that his aircraft had been hijacked and he was forced to participate in a prison escape.

The pilot was also able to give the police a description of Remling's vehicle and what direction he last saw them heading in. The authorities immediately set up roadblocks within a specified area and began actively searching for Remling and his accomplice.

They found him within an hour.

Remling was sitting in a bar, only ten miles down the road from the prison. He was immediately taken into custody and returned to the prison. As for Remling's accomplice, he was arrested and charged with air piracy. He ended up having to serve more time in prison than Remling.

Remling was taken to the county courthouse for arraignment on escape charges the following morning and the news media was having a field day. They were all over the place; all of them trying to snap a photo as he walked up the steps and holding out their microphones and tape recorders. He gave them a short statement.

"I just wanted to see if it could be done," he was quoted as saying.

At first, I thought this guy must have been relatively intelligent to have pulled off such a well-planned and daring escape. After his statement, though, I came to the conclusion that at some point in his misguided life he must have been a flower child because he turned into a blooming idiot.

CHAPTER 7

My Escape from Hospital

In June of 1977, a new facility was opened at the Jackson prison and they called it the North Side Complex. It was a level-two facility for inmates who had served more than five years and had good records. Instead of building new housing units, though, they decided to seal off one and two blocks from the inside population and use those to house the level two inmates.

Since I'd already served five years of my sentence, I was eligible to have my security level reduced to level two and therefore, I was allowed to remain in one block when the facility opened.

One of the new things about the North Side Complex was the yard. The new trend in prison construction, which was also less costly, was to enclose the entire complex with two chain-link fences, electronic sensors and multiple coils of razor wire that were strung along the top of each perimeter fence. In addition to the two gun towers that already existed above one and two block, they also installed another gun tower on the far side of the complex next to the administration building.

After being inside the towering walls for almost five years, it felt strange walking outside and not being surrounded by a forty-foot tall concrete wall. Regardless of all the new security measures, it was nice just to be able to look out across the yard and see the horizon far in the distance. Even being able to watch a common, everyday thing like cars traveling up and down the highway was a welcome and enjoyable sight. This new environment seemed to be less oppressive and somewhat less confining. Now that I could actually see a small part of the free world again, I felt a renewed sense of hope for the future. It was as if I'd taken a step closer to the free world.

It wasn't long after I lost my freedom that I first began to realize I had never taken the time to really appreciate all the little, common, everyday things in life. I had always taken most things for granted; I was too busy or preoccupied with other things, like drugs, that provided me with instant gratification.

But prison was drastically changing my perception regarding the way I once viewed everything in my world, from the big things to the smallest of things. I was finally beginning to appreciate the little things more than I ever thought possible.

The main yard, which was located behind the school building and the gymnasium, was a lot smaller than the yard inside the walls. On the upside, though, it was still big enough to accommodate a baseball diamond and a football field. There was also a smaller common yard in front of one and two block with a basketball court, but most of the yard in front of two block was off limits because they'd installed two large house trailers in that area. The trailers were being used to house the steady flow of incoming level two inmates.

The outside of the new food service building looked like a modern fast food restaurant. The facade of the building was covered with an ash colored brick, giving it an overall grayish-white look. The front and north sides of the building were covered with large panes of smoked glass. Everything inside the kitchen was brand spanking new, including the plastic serving trays, cups, bowls and plates, which were a big change from the stainless steel cups and serving trays that were used inside the walls.

Across the yard from the housing units was the newly built administration building that housed the warden's office, business office, records office and the mailroom. The rear portion of the building, which faced the inside of the compound, was occupied by the control center and the prisoner visiting room. The gymnasium and the school building were located in the middle of the compound, but due to a shortage of bed space, the school classrooms were also being used to house the overflow of inmates.

The North Side Complex was certainly a big improvement and a welcome change as compared to my previous accommodations behind the walls. But even so, it was still just another prison.

The new inmate visiting room was definitely an upgrade from inside the walls. It was furnished with padded chairs and a coffee table at each visiting station. At one end of the visiting room there were several large tinted glass windows that offered the visitors a view of the inside compound. Vending machines had been installed and each outside visitor was allowed to bring in ten dollars in change to purchase soft drinks, sandwiches and other snacks from the vending machines — another luxury that they didn't have behind the walls. The visiting schedule was seven days a week from eight-thirty in the morning until eight-thirty in the evening and we were allowed to receive an unlimited number of visits. Inmates could receive several different visits every day and up to six outside people could visit an inmate at one time.

Unfortunately, I only spent about two months at the North Side. I was playing softball one afternoon when I threw the ball and experienced a sharp pain in my chest. Little did I know then, I'd become terribly sick.

At first, I didn't think much of it. I thought that perhaps I'd torn a muscle or strained something. The pain continued to get worse and about a week later, I started coughing up blood. The persistent, nagging cough seemed to worsen whenever I laid down and was making it hard to sleep at night. When I finally did doze off, it'd only be for brief periods and I'd wake up several times during the night in a cold sweat, shivering and soaking wet. It got so bad that almost every night, I had to get out of bed, towel myself off and even change my sheets.

I went to the infirmary to complain about my symptoms and told the doctors of the severe pain in my chest. The doctor ordered a couple x-rays and upon looking at them, told me it was nothing serious.

"It's probably nothing more than a torn muscle in your chest," the doctor said. "It can be very painful and sometimes, these injuries can take months to heal."

The pain in my chest continued to worsen, as did my coughing. A few days later, the coughing became so bad, with bright red blood readily coming up, that the infirmary ordered I be taken to an outside hospital. That turned out to be a waste of time because the doctor at the hospital didn't do much for me either. He probably thought I was just another convict trying to get some attention so he gave me a quick examination, a shot for the pain and then sent me on my way back to the prison.

My condition got progressively worse with each passing day. I kept going back to the prison infirmary, trying to convince the medical staff that my problem was more serious than a torn muscle. Even though I was coughing up a lot of blood and getting weaker every day, the medical staff continued to display deliberate indifference to my complaints.

A couple days later, with my condition still worsening, I went back to the infirmary again for another doctor's appointment. I was told that the regular prison doctor was on vacation and that I'd be seeing a different doctor. I didn't have much faith in this doctor either, but after he listened to my heart and lungs, he told the nurse that he wanted to see my chest x-rays.

Apparently, he knew exactly what he was looking for because he took one look at my x-rays and he told the nurse that I needed immediate medical attention at an outside hospital.

Once the control center was notified that the doctor was sending me to an outside hospital in Jackson, it took about fifteen minutes for the ambulance to arrive. This time, when I got to the emergency room, the first thing they did was check my vital signs and draw blood samples. One of the nurses inserted an intravenous line in my arm while another nurse placed an oxygen mask on my face. After the preliminary examination, the doctor told the guards that he wanted to admit me to the hospital for a couple of days, or at least until they could determine exactly what was wrong with me.

I was wheeled out of the emergency room and taken upstairs to the third floor, where I was placed in a semi-private room that was unoccupied. The nurse gave me one of those hospital gowns that was open in back along with a pair of red socks and then asked me if I needed any help getting changed. I said no, and when I finished changing, one of the guards put all my clothes in a plastic bag. While one guard stayed to watch me, the other took my clothes and went back to the prison.

I'd just gotten into bed when another nurse came in pushing a cart with a large glass bottle sitting on top that looked strangely like an empty, five-gallon water cooler bottle. She told me she needed to insert a tube down my throat to remove the contents of my stomach, just in case I needed to have surgery. But before putting the tube down my throat, she gave me a shot to ease the pain in my chest.

Later that evening, when the nurse removed the tube from my stomach, she placed a small oxygen tube in my nose to help me breathe and adjusted the bed to elevate my chest.

"This should help alleviate some of your coughing," she said. "And you should be able to sleep better too."

At that point, I was so sick and in so much pain that I didn't think anything was going to help me. Despite what the prison doctor had been telling me, I knew all along that I was seriously ill. I really wasn't sure if I was going to live or die.

I made it through the night and the next morning, the doctor came to examine me again.

"We need to do some more blood tests and take a couple more x-rays too," he told me, adding that I'd be given some kind of scan too.

"Do you know what's wrong with me?" I asked him.

He didn't answer me directly and only said that he couldn't know for sure until the test results came back.

"They should be back by the end of the day," he assured me.

Not long after the doctor left, one of the nurses helped me into a wheelchair and I spent the next couple of hours undergoing all kinds of tests. I didn't mind them too much, except for the one where I had to drink some horrible tasting barium dye.

The doctor came back later that afternoon and had terrible news, telling me I was in critical condition and my prognosis wasn't good.

"First off, you have a Staph infection in your blood," he said, pausing a moment. "That alone could have killed you."

"You also have pneumonia and all the havoc going on in your lungs gave you pleurisy as well," he continued. "What that means is that all that coughing has caused the membrane that lines your chest cavity, surrounding the outside of your lungs, to get very inflamed. This is what has been causing you so much pain."

"In addition to all this, you've also got some extensive blood clotting in both your lungs. It only takes one small clot to break loose, get into your heart and kill you."

The doctor's prognosis was dire, but he offered a solution as well.

"There's a new, experimental drug that's been used to treat pneumonia patients and it's having very promising results so far," he told me. "However, it is experimental and there are no guarantees that it will work. Nevertheless, I think it's probably your best hope given the severity of your condition."

He also said he'd need my written consent before he could start the treatments, since the drug was still considered to be experimental.

There wasn't much to hesitate about. From what the doctor said, it didn't appear I had any other viable options. He didn't think conventional treatments could cure my illnesses in their advanced stage and it really left me with no other choice except to trust that he knew what he was doing. So, I signed the consent form giving him permission to administer the experimental drug.

"I'll get the treatments started right away," the doctor told me.

Within the hour a nurse came in carrying two bottles of clear liquid that she hung on the IV pole at the foot of my bed. She inserted catheters in both my arms, connected the IV lines and then carefully adjusted the flow of the medication on both bottles. I trusted that the nurse knew what she was doing, but I was curious as to why they were pumping two different bottles of medication into my body at the same time.

"What's in both those bottles?" I asked her.

"One of them is a blood thinner, which will stop your blood from creating more clots and will help to dissolve the clots you already have in your lungs," she explained. "The other bottle is the experimental drug to treat the pneumonia."

When my mother found out that I'd been admitted to the hospital in critical condition, she immediately tried to get permission from the prison administration to visit me at the hospital. The prison summarily denied her request for security reasons, but my mother wasn't such an easily deterred woman.

She then made a call to the governor's office and spoke with one of the governor's aides, who promised to look into the matter and return her call as soon as possible. She received that call back the next day, and it was good news. The governor's office informed her that her request had been granted and the prison was being notified that she had permission to visit me at the hospital.

Both my mother and sister came to see me right away, but when they arrived, I was in a semi-conscious state from the pain medication. I could hear their voices, but I only understood about half of what they were saying. I was aware that my mother was holding my hand and when she spoke, I could tell that she was on the verge of crying.

She didn't mention anything to me at the time, but apparently, someone had told her that I wasn't expected to recover due to the advanced state of my illness.

I tried to reassure her that I was going to be okay.

"There's no need to worry about me, Mom," I mumbled, my eyes fluttering while I tried to keep them open. "The nurses here are taking really good care of me — they're doing everything they can to make me comfortable."

My mother and sister stayed at my bedside for most of the afternoon until it started to get dark outside and they had to leave. When they kissed me goodbye I could tell from the tears in their eyes and the woeful look on their faces that they weren't so sure if they'd ever see me again.

I don't recall much about the first week I spent in the hospital. They gave me pain medication every four hours to alleviate the pain in my chest from the pleurisy and it kept me in a stupor. Without the pain medication, though, it was unbearable to even breathe. It felt like there was a knife in my chest and with every breath; the knife was being twisted and turned into my flesh.

Remarkably, after only a week on the medication, I was feeling much better. I even began to notice that the adjustable hospital bed was comfortable, and much more so than what I'd become accustomed to in prison. I discovered that what the nurse had first said about keeping the bed elevated was true. If I kept the bed adjusted to where just my upper body was elevated, the fluid stayed down in the lower part of my lungs. Not only did I cough less, I actually did sleep better at night.

The room was semiprivate but the other bed remained empty. It was actually kind of nice having the room all to myself. I found it to be rather quiet and relaxing. A prison guard was always posted in the room with me, twenty-four hours a day. I wasn't handcuffed or restrained in any way, but if I had to leave the room for any reason, the guard always went with me. The only time I was out of a guard's sight was when I was using the bathroom.

Most of the guards just sat in the chair and watched the television during their eight-hour shift. They rarely said anything to me unless I initiated the conversation.

Surprisingly, after talking to a couple of the guards over the course of several days, I discovered that they were decent and amiable people just trying to support their families. There was one guard by the name of Adam who always treated me like I was a real person, not like a pariah or a scum-of-the-earth, piece-of-crap convict, as some of the other guards had a tendency to do.

Adam would often bring me books, magazines, candy and other small things that meant a lot to me. I sincerely appreciated his thoughtfulness. Occasionally, he'd even bring me food items like shrimp and delicious desserts from home, saying his wife had prepared them just for me. Adam was the exception when it came to guards; he was more like a friend. Even so, I respected the fact that he was my guard and never crossed that fine line between us. I believe that if a person is a true friend, he would never jeopardize that friendship by placing the other person in a compromising position, not for any reason.

Whenever the guards had to use the bathroom, they had no choice but to leave me unguarded. I'd occasionally tease Adam, jokingly telling him that if he stayed in the bathroom for too long, I wouldn't be here when he came out. Instead of taking me seriously, he'd just laugh and say that he didn't care.

"If I lose a prisoner, it's only a three-day suspension anyhow," he told me once.

Not that the thought hadn't crossed my mind — it had. Adam was the only thing standing between me and my freedom, but I'd never put Adam in a situation like that. He treated me with kindness and respect, and to a certain extent, I think he must've trusted me. My conscience and my morals wouldn't have allowed me to betray or violate that trust.

When I'd told my mother that first week that the nurses were treating me good, I wasn't lying. In fact, they were great to me. The nurses treated me as if I was someone special, regularly stopping by my room just to talk or to make sure I had everything I needed. They went out of their way to take good care of me and nurse me back to health. Without their exceptional medical care, I might not have survived the whole ordeal. I sincerely and profoundly appreciated everything they did for me and I've never forgot their extraordinary kindness.

I know people complain that hospital food is terrible, but I didn't share the sentiment and I doubt other inmates would've either. The meals I received in the hospital were the best I'd tasted in a very long time. In fact, there were many times when I requested double portions and that actually seemed to really please the hospital staff.

I suppose it could be argued that after eating prison food for the past five years, it would only be natural for anything else to have tasted better.

I was also getting better with each passing day. I tried to stay out of bed and walk a little every day to regain my strength. Even the doctor was pleased with my progress. He said that if my condition continued to improve, he expected me to make a full recovery.

"But even if you do make a full recovery, Jim, the healing process is going to leave a lot of scar tissue on your lungs from the pneumonia," he warned. "You'd do yourself a great help to practice taking deep breaths several times every day — it'll expand the scar tissue a bit before it completely heals. If you don't, the scar tissue will contract and actually cause your lungs to shrink, meaning your lung capacity will be greatly diminished for the rest of your life."

It sounded like some good advice, so I took it. Several times a day, I'd practice breathing in as deeply as possible and holding my breath for as long as I could. I even snuck a few push-ups in when I was in the bathroom, where the guards couldn't see me. I didn't want to do push-ups around them, figuring that if the guards saw me exercising, they'd probably think I was well enough to go back to the prison — I truly wasn't looking forward to that day. My stay in the hospital had been like a vacation at a five-star hotel. I didn't want to leave.

After spending almost a month in the hospital, I was feeling like my old self again. I knew that any day now, I could be released from the doctor's care and returned to prison.

The possibility of escape was definitely on my mind. In fact, I was thinking that escaping would be relatively easy. All I had to do was wait for the right moment when the guard was using the bathroom and then I could simply walk down the hallway to the fire escape stairwell and out the door to the parking lot.

It sounded simple, but there were a couple of problems I needed to work out. I didn't have any street clothes or a pair of shoes. I'd probably look somewhat conspicuous walking down the street dressed in hospital pajamas.

But, rather fortuitously for me, the hospital had recently moved an older gentleman in to the other bed in the same room as me and my eyes had not missed the fact that his street clothes were hanging in the closet at the other end of the room. As a last resort, I could always take his clothes. I wouldn't feel the least bit guilty about it either — that old jerk had complained to the hospital administration that I was receiving too many visits from the female nurses.

A few days later, one of those infamous, asshole-type guards was assigned to watch me. Every time I went to the bathroom he went along too. When I walked up and down the hallway, he grasped me by my upper arm and not to assist me, but rather to physically restrain me. That miserable jerk walked me around like you would a dog on a short leash.

With his grip on my upper arm practically cutting off my circulation while I walked slowly to rebuild strength, I casually suggested to him that he ought to lighten-up a little.

"After all, man, it's not exactly like you're guarding John Dillinger here," I said.

"No prisoner has ever escaped from me in the past twenty-two years and it's not about to happen now!" he barked back at me, clearly not amused with my suggestion.

I knew these types of guards and I knew not to push it, so I squared my shoulders and looked forward, deciding not to say another word. In my mind, though, I couldn't stop thinking about this guard's shitty attitude. It reminded me of all the other guards like him that I'd be faced with every day upon my return to prison. The more I thought about it, the more I dreaded having to go back there. This, in turn, made me think about escaping.

The doctor came by later that afternoon for what I thought was going to be just another routine examination. He flipped through my chart, briefly checked me out and then looked me in the eyes and said, "Jim, it looks like you're cured! You seem back to normal now, very healthy."

He then turned his gaze to the guard.

"I'm releasing him from the hospital now," he said.

The guard didn't waste any time, immediately phoning the prison to tell them that the doctor had just released me.

"I need a vehicle to transport him back to prison," I heard the guard say.

When he hung up the telephone, he curtly told me that I had about fifteen minutes to get my things together before a transportation vehicle arrived. My heart immediately began racing as my thoughts rushed back to earlier in the day, the guard's grip digging into my upper arms and all the hatred and dread I had for the prison. I felt a surge of adrenaline pulsate through my veins. If I was going to escape, I knew I had to make my move right then and there. My time at this hotel had run out — it was now or never.

The guard turned back to the telephone and was making another call. For the moment, he wasn't paying any attention to me. I couldn't see the patient in the bed next to me because the curtain was pulled around him for privacy, but his snoring was a good indicator that he was fast asleep. I quietly walked over to his closet and opened the door gently and carefully so it didn't make a noise. After it was cracked just wide enough for me to reach my hand in, I grabbed the shoes off the bottom shelf and shoved them down the front of my pajamas.

I glanced back at the guard out of the corner of my eye and saw that he was still on the phone. But just as I reached back in for the old man's clothes, I heard the sound of the phone clicking back into the receiver. I looked back over and saw the guard was taking out his handcuffs and walking toward me, so I assumed that he'd seen what I was doing.

"I don't want any trouble, now, but I'm not going back to that hellhole," I told him sternly, staring him down.

He didn't say a thing but instead reached around to the pocket on the back of his pants and pulled out a blackjack, the only weapon guards were allowed to carry inside the hospital. I thought about trying to make a run for it, that perhaps I could dodge most of the blows and make my way past him. But then I saw my IV pole, within reach at the end of the bed, and I grabbed it, pointing it menacingly at the guard.

"Stay where you are," I told him.

The IV pole was a half-inch solid steel rod shaped like the numeral seven. I used the horizontal end to try and push the guard farther away from me — I didn't want to risk him getting close enough to take a swing with the blackjack.

He was able to grab hold of my rod with his left hand, though, and he pulled me toward him. This guard was a big guy, standing about six-feet-two and probably weighing in close to three hundred pounds.

As he drew me closer, I pressed the IV pole against his throat and was trying with all my strength to keep him off of me, but I wasn't having much success. He was within reach to strike and wasted no time doing so, steadily pounding on the side of my head with the blackjack and trying to beat me unconscious.

I kept trying to pull away from him, but he had a death grip on me. No matter what I did, he wouldn't let go. About the only leverage I had was to try to pull him in the direction that I wanted to go, which was out the door. I finally managed to drag him into the hallway and when the nurses saw that he was beating me senseless, they began screaming at him frantically to stop.

Apparently, the nurses screaming had some effect on the guard because he abruptly stopped hitting me and looked down the hallway toward the nurses' station. At that point, I was almost totally exhausted. With what little strength I had left, I shoved him as hard as I could, causing him to stumble backwards and forcing him to release his death grip on me.

I dropped the IV pole on the floor and took off running as fast as I could, past the nurses' station and through a set of doors marked Maternity Ward/Fire Exit. The fire escape stairwell was just on the other side of the door and when I reached it, I quickly looked over my shoulder to see if the guard was chasing me. He wasn't, though — I could see him still standing in the middle of the hallway where I'd left him. Perhaps he was stunned. I didn't really have time to think about it and didn't really care.

I ran down the three flights of stairs to the bottom of the stairwell, where there was a door marked fire exit. I was greatly relieved that when I pushed that door handle, the door swung open and cool, fresh air rushed inside the stairwell. My worst fear, at that moment, would have been to have found that door locked and myself trapped inside that stairwell, awaiting certain capture and years of punishment.

Before I went outside, I noticed I still had the shoes with me. After all the commotion, I was surprised they hadn't fallen out and were still tucked tightly into the waistband of my pajamas. I slid them on my feet, finding out they were a couple of sizes too big. Even so, they were better than nothing.

I pushed the door open and stepped outside, where large raindrops were falling from a cloudy, gray sky. I scanned the area to see who was around, but there was only one person standing on the sidewalk and I was quite sure that she didn't see me, as she was cowering under her umbrella and hiding from the cold rain.

My first thought was to try to steal a car from someone in the parking lot, but I decided that I'd probably be better off if I didn't get an innocent bystander involved. Instead, I walked around the corner of the building to the parking lot and began looking inside vehicles, hoping that someone might have left their keys in the ignition. As I was peering into rain-streaked car windows, the thought crossed my mind that I was conspicuously out in the open, dressed suspiciously in my hospital clothes and wasting valuable time. If I couldn't get out of the immediate area quickly, then it was probably best to find a good hiding spot. It was only a matter of time before the whole area would be swarming with police searching for me.

There was a row of houses along the backside of the hospital parking lot, so I decided to go in that direction. I thought there would be less traffic and that it would probably be easier for me to find a place to hide. I stayed off the streets and sidewalks to avoid anyone seeing me, instead walking through peoples' backyards until I spotted an open crawl space under someone's back porch and decided to hide there for awhile. Luckily, there were a lot of old newspapers and rags under the porch and I used those to cover myself and keep relatively warm. I dozed off a couple of times, but was awakened by the voices of the people who lived in the house. I could hear their muffled voices and the sound of their footsteps above me.

When I left the hospital, I was only wearing a pair of flimsy hospital pajamas and a thin cotton bathrobe. The bathrobe hung down past my knees and was adorned with the same thin blue and white pinstripes as the pajamas, reminding me of a railroad engineer's hat and coveralls. I was cold and wet, but for the moment, I was free and that was all that mattered.

The rain, despite sending a chill down my bones, was actually a lucky break for me. I knew that it would be difficult for tracking dogs to pick up my scent in the rain. In fact, I'd find out later that the police did use a tracking dog in their attempt to find me. However, my zigzagging route through the parking lot was covered up, my scent obliterated by the carbon monoxide fumes from the exhaust of all the vehicles.

It must have been somewhere around midnight when I finally decided that it was probably safe for me to move from my hiding place. I figured that by then, the police had probably given up their search of the immediate area, thinking that I was long gone.

I had no idea where I was or in what direction I was headed. I knew I had to keep a low profile and avoid contact with anyone. So, I quietly left the crawl space and walked for about an hour through residential neighborhoods, keeping mainly to the sidewalks and avoiding the streets as much as possible. I didn't want to get caught out in the open on the side of the road. If I stayed on sidewalks, I had a better chance of jumping into a bush if I suddenly needed a place to hide.

I was also trying to keep an eye on every car that drove by, staying in the shadows until I could be sure it wasn't a police car. I wanted to make sure that I could see the police before they had a chance to see me.

The night was pitch black and it had to have been well after midnight when I saw a car coming slowly down the street in my direction. I kept my eyes focused on it, but I couldn't tell if it was a police car. There were no streetlights and the vehicle was driving with its high beams on, making it more difficult for me to see the shape of the car behind the lights.

I was hoping that it would pull into one of the driveways, but it kept coming and was almost right on top of me before I finally realized that it was a city police car. I didn't panic — I knew if I ran, I'd only give myself away. Dressed in pajamas, the only thing I could do was act like I lived in the neighborhood and was out looking for my lost dog. I started whistling and calling out loudly for my fictitious dog.

"Here Duke, come on boy," I hollered. "Here Duke, come on! Let's go home buddy!"

My heart was racing, but surprisingly, it worked. The police officer only gave me a cursory passing glance as he drove past. Nevertheless, as soon as the police car was well out of my sight, I made a quick detour through several backyards and counted my blessings.

I kept walking for what seemed like hours before I heard the sound of a train whistle off in the distance. The thought suddenly occurred to me that if I could catch a ride on a freight train, I could be well out of the area before daybreak. So, I turned on my heels and decided to head in the direction of the train whistle. It took a while before I finally found the railroad tracks, stumbling upon them in the black of night.

I followed the tracks until I finally came to a freight yard. More than a hundred boxcars were parked in the yard and there were eight different sets of train tracks. Workers were busy moving the freight cars from one track to another, but none of the trains appeared to be leaving. I was too tired to continue walking and the blister that had formed on the heel of my left foot was throbbing in pain.

I decided to find an out-of-the-way spot where I could sit down and rest until one of the trains started moving. It didn't really matter to me what direction the train was headed; my only concern was getting out of the immediate area.

I must have waited for close to an hour before I heard one of the trains finally begin to slowly pull out of the yard. I couldn't actually see the train because it was several tracks over, but I could tell from the sound — a slow chugging — that it was definitely leaving. It took me several minutes to make my way across the freight yard — I had to crawl under trains to get there and wanted to be careful. Getting stuck under a moving train would've been certain death. Luckily, when I got there, the train was still moving at a relatively slow speed.

I began running alongside it and suddenly realized that jumping into a moving boxcar wasn't going to be so easy. For one thing, the floor of the boxcar was level with my chest, making it a difficult angle to jump inside, and dangerous too since the train was picking up speed. I ran as fast as I could and threw myself at the boxcar, managing to jump far enough into it where I could pull myself inside without getting seriously hurt. I sat down and gathered my bearings, once again counting my blessings, and breathed a sigh of relief.

The boxcar was empty except for a few pieces of clear plastic wrapping that had probably been used for shipping. There was a steady stream of cold air blowing inside the boxcar and I quickly found myself to be freezing cold, my thin pajamas and robe still wet from the rain. I tried several times to pull on the heavy steel door, trying to close it, but it wouldn't budge. Realizing I wasn't going to get the door closed, I instead moved to the front end of the boxcar where I was at least out of the direct wind.

I gathered up the plastic wrapping scattered on the floor and huddled into a corner, pulling the plastic around me to act as a blanket and block the cold wind. It wasn't going to be a comfortable ride, but it was a ride out of town nonetheless. Unfortunately, the ride didn't last very long.

My Own Worst Enemy

About an hour later, the train suddenly stopped and the railroad workers began uncoupling cars and moving them to a side track. To avoid being seen, I stayed huddled in the corner until everything was quiet. By the time I climbed out of the boxcar, though, the train was already gone and I was back to walking once again.

About a half hour into my walk, I spotted another freight train heading my way but it was moving way too fast for me to even think about trying to jump inside a boxcar. But, both ends of each boxcar had a handrail and footstep, which allowed access to the couplings that connected the cars as well as the roofs. I thought that perhaps I could grab on to a handrail and then pull myself over to where I could stand on the coupling. The train was traveling fast and it wasn't easy to run in the crushed limestone beside the tracks, but I somehow managed to grab hold of the handrail and jump on the bottom rung of the footstep.

I climbed further up the footsteps, getting to where I could reach the handrail mounted above the coupling. I had to stretch my arm out to reach it and then, once my grip was secure, pulled myself over to where I could stand on the boxcar coupling. The train continued to pick up more speed, though, and it began rocking and bouncing around so violently that I wasn't sure I'd be able to hold on. I found myself being tossed around like a leaf in the wind, my knuckles white as I gripped the handrail for dear life.

At one point, I was jolted and bounced right off the coupling, my feet and legs dangling desperately. The only thing that saved my life was my death grip on the handrail. In moments like those, I was terrified. I thought for sure that I was going to die.

My hands soon began aching from having to grasp the handrail so tightly, but I knew that if I'd let go I'd most likely be sucked underneath the train and my body would be left in pieces for either the authorities, or for scavenging coyotes and birds, to find. I was stuck. There was no letting go; jumping off was far too risky and I'd likely just end up under the train if I tried. I summoned all the willpower and strength I had and continued to squeeze my hands around the rail.

Fortunately, the train began slowing down and I was able to regain my footing on the coupling. I'd never felt so grateful to be alive as I did in that moment and thanked God again for blessing me. I'd survived one hell of a scary train ride and I'd remember it for the rest of my life.

My whole body was trembling from the ordeal as the train continued to slow down. When it finally came to a complete stop, I was able to regain my composure and climbed around to the inside of one of the open boxcars. I gratefully sat down and thought about all that had happened to me in the past few hours. It had been a long day and I was physically and mentally exhausted.

It was just beginning to get light outside when the train started to move again. I sat on the boxcar floor watching the scenery go by and it was much more pleasant than my first ride, where I hid from the dark and cold winds whipping by the outside of the boxcar. I hadn't had any sleep yet and I was beginning to get hungry, but most of all, I was thirsty. I told myself that when the train stopped again, I'd take some time to find water.

Later in the morning, the train arrived at another freight yard. I climbed wearily out of the boxcar and took the opportunity to search for water. I'd decided during my ride that the best place to check would be the caboose, logically figuring that there'd have to be some sort of water supply for the workers. The first caboose I checked didn't have anything, but in the second one, I found a five-gallon water bottle dispenser that was half full. The water was warm, but it didn't matter. I was so thirsty that I drank as much as I could, drinking until my stomach began to hurt. And when I couldn't drink any more, I used the water that was left to wash some of the dirt and grime off my hands and face.

When I finished with my birdbath, I headed for the back door and was stunned when the door suddenly opened and a guy, holding a broom and dustpan in his hands, was standing there. I assumed he worked for the railroad and he must've been just as surprised to see me as I was him, since he just stood there with a puzzled look on his face. No doubt, I was a strange sight to see dressed in my hospital pajamas and a bathrobe. The poor guy probably thought I was a homeless person or someone with a psychological problem. We stared at one another for a couple awkward seconds before he finally spoke.

"Who do you work for?" he asked.

"Anyone that'll take me," I said nonchalantly, and with those parting words I walked past him and out the door.

Worried that this guy might report me to his supervisor, I decided that it would be in my best interest if I didn't hang around the freight yard. I quickly dodged out of sight and began walking along the railroad tracks again to take me away from the yard.

A while later, I came to several houses. I was hungry and hoping to find a yard with an apple or pear tree; even a patch of berries would suffice. While I didn't come across any such things, I instead discovered a vegetable garden in one of the home's backyards and helped myself to what was available, filling my bathrobe pockets with tomatoes, bell peppers and cucumbers. As I was leaving, I grabbed a small watermelon for dessert.

By the time I got back to the freight yard it was almost dark. After my long walk, I badly wanted to find somewhere to sit down and rest until one of the trains started to move. Much to my surprise, I noticed that one of the trains was loaded with new, 1978-model Ford cars and trucks. I hadn't seen a new car in years and was curious to check out how much the body styles had changed, so out of curiosity, I climbed up on the train to get a closer look and poke around. Peeking into the vehicles, I noticed that shipping invoices were attached to the inside of each vehicle's rear window.

I read several of the invoices and one after another stated the cars' final destination to be California, which just happened to be the place I really wanted to get to — far, far away from Michigan. As I looked closer at the interior of the cars, I noticed all the vehicles had their keys right in the ignition. I pulled up on the door handle of the car I was looking at, but it was locked. I moved to another and did the same, over and over again, finding out that every single door on every single vehicle was locked.

I wanted inside one of the cars — looking at the comfortable seats was agonizing. If I could get inside one of them, my travel accommodations would be greatly improved. No more huddling in the corner of a cold boxcar; I could be relaxing in one of the cushy seats of a brand new Ford.

I decided to climb down from the train to see if I could find a rock or something else to break one of the car's windows. I quickly came upon a piece of old brake shoes from a train wheel. The heavy steel would easily do the job.

I got back on one of the railroad cars, where there were two tiers of vehicles. I climbed up to the second level and chose a Ford Granada that was parked in the middle of the railroad car. Using the brake shoe, I broke open the window for the back seat on the passenger side of the car.

I finagled my way from the back seat to the front, settling comfortably into the driver's seat and looked at the dashboard. I started the engine to get a reading on the gas gauge, which looked to be about half full.

I didn't want to draw attention to myself, though — I was worried that someone may pick up on the sound of a running vehicle coming from the train. So, I turned the ignition off and decided to lay low until the train started moving.

I flipped up the center console, which opened up a good amount of space in the front seats for me to curl up and lay down. I closed my eyes and tried to take a short nap while I waited for the train to start moving, but I just couldn't get warm enough. There was a lot of cold air blowing in through the broken window and it was just too cold to sleep.

I thought about using my bathrobe to cover up the broken window, but then realized the clear plastic covering that was laid over the front seat was a better option. I rigged it up the best I could and it reduced the draft quite a bit. I still couldn't fall asleep, though.

When the train finally began moving, I started the engine and turned on the heater to its highest setting. I hadn't been warm since I left the hospital and the warm air blowing out of the car's heater felt great.

The antenna for the radio was conveniently lying in the back seat. I grabbed it and got it plugged in and situated on the dashboard, finding a spot with good reception and flipped through the radio stations until I found some music. Warm and comfortable, I laid down again in the front seat and fell fast asleep.

When I awoke, the car was still running and the train was still moving. It felt as though I hadn't been asleep that long, but the sun told me otherwise. It was coming up across the horizon and looked as though it was going to be a nice day.

From the top of the train, I had an excellent view of the countryside. I hadn't seen anything of the free world in the past five years. Superficially, it appeared that nothing had really changed; the grass and trees and what else I could see of the world looked pretty much the same as when I had left it. Change is inevitable, though, and nothing would ever be the same for me again. The world had moved on and just like the train was passing quickly by the landscape, I felt that life had passed by me. I was acutely aware that I was on borrowed time and therefore, I was determined to make the most of whatever time I might have.

For the next two days, my train ride was relatively comfortable. Whenever the train would stop, which was at least once a day, I'd leave the train and forage for food and water. I was managing to survive mostly on fruits and vegetables from backyard gardens, but what I really needed was to find a change of clothing.

It was inevitable that, sooner or later, my comfortable train ride would come to an end. This I knew, and it was exactly what happened the following day when the train stopped at another freight yard. While I took the opportunity to go looking for food and a change of clothing, the train left before I got back. I had no choice but to continue my journey on foot and so, I set out walking alongside the railroad tracks.

Late in the afternoon, I spotted several old junk cars sitting out in an open field far off in the distance. I thought that I might be able to find some old clothes or maybe something else that I could use, so I decided to go over and take a look.

I rummaged through the rusty, broken-down cars, but I didn't find any clothing. I did, however, find a few coins underneath the seats that I could use to make a telephone call. Before I could go into town and find a payphone, though, I needed to find some clothing that was a bit more inconspicuous.

I dropped the coins into the pocket on my robe and headed back to the railroad tracks, walking until I came to a trestle that spanned a small creek. It was almost dark and my feet were killing me, throbbing in pain from walking on the stones that lined the railroad tracks. I decided to stop and rest for a while, hoping that a slow moving train would come by and I could catch a ride, even though it didn't look promising. All the trains that had passed by me were traveling at a high rate of speed, making it far too dangerous to attempt jumping on and I had no desire to lose a limb or even my life by trying.

Eventually, I got up and started walking again. I walked through the night and by the next morning, I could feel the nails in the heels of my shoes cutting into the soles of my feet. The constant walking in the crushed limestone rocks along the railroad tracks had almost completely worn the heels off my shoes; exposing the nails and driving them upwards through the insoles.

About the only thing I could do was find a rock that I used as a hammer to bend the nails over and pound them down until they were flat. I tore strips of cloth from my bathrobe and folded them into square pads, which I then placed in the bottom of my shoes to cushion my heels and stop the bleeding. Surprisingly, the pads were rather comfortable and they kept the nails from cutting into my feet.

Later that morning, I finally came upon a clothesline full of clothes, but there was just one small problem — it was all women's clothing. I was desperate, though, and willing to take whatever I could get.

I pulled down a multi-colored sweater and a pair of brown stretch pants. I could only hope that I wouldn't be mistaken for a drag queen.

The pants must have been at least a size forty-two, and I wore a size thirty-two. They hung loosely around me and without a hand holding them up, fell quickly to my feet. That was only a minor problem, though, and I easily came up with a solution by tearing a long strip of cloth off my bathrobe to use as a belt.

I knew I looked peculiar, but I could live with it until I found something more appropriate to wear. It was, at least, less suspicious than my hospital pajamas.

With my new clothes on, I decided it was safe enough to go into town and use my coins to make a telephone call. I wanted to call my mother, but I thought the police would probably have her telephone tapped in anticipation of me doing just that. The only other person who I knew I could trust was my sister, Jenna.

As I got closer and closer to civilization, I knew my surroundings didn't look familiar, but I wasn't expecting them to. When I finally reached a telephone, though, I was surprised to discover that I was just outside of Omaha, Nebraska. I hadn't thought I'd actually traveled that far and with my few coins, I didn't have enough to pay for the call to Michigan.

I knew my sister wouldn't mind accepting a collect call, though, especially considering the circumstances. I dialed her number and then listened as the phone began ringing on the other line.

"Are you okay?!" my sister exclaimed as soon she picked up the phone.

"Yes, I'm fine," I told her.

"I am so glad to hear from you, Jim, we've been worried sick about you," she said.

"I'm okay, Jenna, there's no need to worry. I'm far out of Michigan now," I said. "But I do need a favor; can you send some money to the Western Union office in Omaha, Nebraska?"

"Yeah, sure," she said.

"I don't have any ID with me, but you can give them my old military service number," I told her.

"Okay, what is it?" she asked, and I recited the number to her.

"Tell Mom I'm OK," I said, and thanked her for everything. "I'll call you again when I reach California."

After I hung up the telephone, I went to a nearby gas station and I asked for directions to Omaha.

"It's about thirty miles south of here," the attendant told me, and gave me some road names to follow.

It took me several hours of walking and hitchhiking before I finally reached downtown Omaha and located the Western Union Office. For some reason, I kept thinking that Western Union was going to give me a hard time about identification when I asked for my money, but that wasn't the case at all. I simply gave them the number and they gave me the money.

My first priority was to buy some new clothes and a pair of shoes, which I desperately needed. I stopped at the first clothing store I came to and I purchased everything from underwear to toiletries, including some black hair dye to change my appearance. I even bought a leather satchel to carry all my newly acquired belongings. Once I had everything I needed, I checked into a hotel and nearly felt giddy over the idea of taking a nice, long, hot shower and sleeping in a real bed for the first time in years.

When I awoke the next morning, I felt like a new person. I showered, shaved and dressed like a normal person and finally, I felt like a normal person too. I checked out of the hotel and I spent a good part of the day just walking around the city, taking in all the sights and sounds. It was fascinating to watch the masses of people crowded together on the busy sidewalks. Everyone seemed to be in such a big hurry to get somewhere.

The whole experience seemed almost surreal, and yet vaguely familiar at the same time. It was late afternoon when I came across a Greyhound Bus Station and I decided to purchase a one-way ticket to Denver, Colorado. I wanted to get as far away from Michigan as I possibly could. I remembered someone telling me once that if you're on the run, never run in a straight line and never stay in one place for too long.

It made sense and so, I decided to adopt the philosophy as my own. I'd eventually make my way to California, but in the process I'd take an indirect route and enjoy a little sightseeing along the way. As long as I kept moving, I knew it would be difficult for the authorities to locate me.

I'd been to California once before when I was a teenager, but I'd only stayed there for a couple of weeks with some friends who lived in Bell Gardens. The last time I was in California, I wanted to visit Disneyland and see the Pacific Ocean, but I never got the chance. As I sat, waiting to board the Greyhound bus, I daydreamed about my final destination and I vowed to myself that this time, I'd make both things happen — I'd spend some time at Disneyland and see the mighty Pacific, up close and personal.

When I boarded the bus, I was hoping to find two empty seats that would allow me to stretch out and relax, but most of the seats were already occupied. I had to settle for an aisle seat toward the back of the bus.

"This seat taken?" I politely asked the man who was sitting in the window seat.

He didn't say anything back, merely shook his head to signify that it wasn't, so I sat down and settled in for the long ride ahead. It wasn't long after we left the terminal that the guy dozed off, but I was far too excited to sleep.

Even though it was getting dark and I couldn't see the landscape, I was thrilled to look out the window and see all the night lights — it was a sight I hadn't seen in years.

After a couple hours of listening to the steady drone of the engine, the excitement began waning and I could feel the tiredness settling in. I must've dozed off because when I opened my eyes again, the sun was just beginning to peek above the horizon, casting a warm orange glow on the landscape and letting streaks of light wash through the bus. The driver announced he was making a twenty-minute rest stop for those who wanted to grab a bite to eat or stretch their legs.

After sitting in that cramped seat all night, the rest stop was a welcome break. I was glad for the opportunity to get off the bus and walk around. My whole body was aching, especially my butt.

When I got back on the bus, the guy in the seat next to me seemed to be in a friendlier mood. He introduced himself as Jake and began telling me all about himself. I learned that he was originally from Canada and was on his way to Colorado, where a job was waiting for him as a ski instructor at one of the resorts.

To deflect him from starting to ask me questions, I asked him a couple things about Canada and he really set off on a roll. He talked about Canada and skiing for almost an hour, boring me half-to-death. When he finally shut up and went back to sleep, I was grateful for the silence.

I wasn't used to sitting down for long periods of time, though, and I couldn't get comfortable. After sitting in that seat all night, the cheeks of my butt were painfully sore. The morning break helped, but it was just minutes into sitting down again that they started hurting. I shifted my weight around, trying different positions, but I couldn't get comfortable. I even thought, at one point, that there was no way I'd be able to stay on the bus all the way until Denver. Walking was beginning to look like an appealing choice again, now that it was my butt and not my feet that were hurting.

Lucky for my aching ass, it wasn't long before the bus stopped at an airport. I still had plenty of money and decided that it was time to do a little sightseeing from the air.

By the time I got off the bus, the driver had already unloaded several bags from the luggage compartment and was just about ready to close the door when I asked him for mine.

Fortunately, in those days, the airlines didn't require any identification to purchase a plane ticket. The only thing they asked me for was a name, and I gave them a fake one.

I purchased a one-way ticket to Phoenix, Arizona, but my flight wasn't scheduled to depart for two hours. To pass the time I found a seat in the terminal where I could watch the planes taking off and landing, though I mostly stood until my butt stopped aching. After a while, I got bored and decided to go to the passenger lounge for a drink. I didn't have identification so I wasn't sure if they'd serve me, but I figured it was worth a shot.

It was just after one o'clock in the afternoon and the lounge was practically empty, except for two people who were sitting at one of the tables. I sat down at the bar and ordered a beer, and surprisingly, I had no problem getting served. By the time I finished my third beer, I was beginning to feel a little lightheaded — probably due to the fact that I hadn't tasted any alcohol in the past five years. Since I had no desire to become inebriated, I paid my tab and left the lounge, heading back to the boarding terminal to wait for my flight.

By the time they finally started boarding the plane, my buzz from the beers was all but gone and that was fine by me. Considering the circumstances, I needed all my brain cells to be in good working order. I had no business altering the state of my consciousness in the first place.

The stewardess directed me to a window seat just behind the plane's right wing and next to the emergency exit, where I had a spectacular view of the terrain below. For the most part, the flight was uneventful with the exception of when the pilot started making his descent to land in Phoenix. The ride got a little bumpy as we got closer to the ground, where apparently, the plane had run into several pockets of clear air turbulence.

We were bounced around for several minutes, which was almost like being on a roller coaster ride. When I looked out the window, I could see the plane's wing flexing up and down, almost like a bird flapping its wings. I knew that airplanes were typically designed and built for the wings to be somewhat flexible, so I wasn't worried about it.

After landing, I went directly to the baggage claim area to pick up my bag and soon discovered that it wasn't with the rest of the baggage on my flight. I waited around for about twenty minutes, hoping that it would show up. Finally, I went to the airline ticket counter and told them my bag was missing.

"Okay, sir, we'll need you to fill out a lost baggage form," the attendant sweetly told me. "Your bag may be on the flight from Denver, which should get here in an hour."

I didn't have much in the bag, but it was all I had and I didn't want to spend what little money I had remaining to replace the items. I waited patiently in the terminal for more than an hour before I was finally called over to the ticket counter and handed my bag.

Stepping out of the terminal and into the world outside was a shock to my system, as I was greeted by a blast of stifling hot air. The sun was blazing hot and the temperature that day in Phoenix had climbed all the way to one hundred and ten degrees, something I was not accustomed to as a lifelong resident of Michigan. Even so, I had every intention of walking all the way to downtown Phoenix.

It was just a couple miles into my walk that I realized I needed to get out of the sun before I was burnt to a crisp. I decided to stop at the next motel I came to and spend the night there, but by the time I reached one, I was already sunburned. I checked into a room and immediately turned on the shower, keeping the water cold, to cool myself down. The cold water felt so soothing on my painfully red skin.

I went back outside afterward to have a look around, but I couldn't bear to be out in the extreme heat for long. Despite the sweltering temperatures, I stayed outside long enough to notice the large palm trees lining both sides of the street for as far as my eyes could see. I was amazed at how all these palm trees appeared to be the exact same height and had been planted at precisely the same distance apart from one another. It really looked kind of neat and was especially pleasing to the eye.

I checked out of the motel early the next morning, trying to get started for downtown Phoenix before the midday heat reached its peak. Seeing as how I didn't have a lot of money — certainly not enough to keep renting motel rooms every night — I decided it'd be in my best interest to purchase some hiking and camping equipment and try to sleep outside whenever the weather permitted.

I stopped at an army-navy surplus store and bought a sleeping bag, pup tent and a backpack large enough to hold all the things I'd need for several days of camping.

I began making plans to leave Phoenix, but before I went on my way, there was one other item on my agenda I wanted to do — see the famous Maricopa County Courthouse. Back in the mid-seventies, there was a television show called *Petrocelli* that was about a criminal attorney practicing law in Phoenix. The Maricopa courthouse was prominently featured in almost every episode. I thought that while I was in the neighborhood, I might as well stop by and see one of Phoenix's famous landmarks.

I had thought about stopping by the Grand Canyon when I left Phoenix, since I'd never been there before, but I heard on the radio that it was snowing in Flagstaff. For the time being, I decided to skip that landmark and instead bought a bus ticket to Anaheim, California, where Disneyland was located.

CHAPTER 8

California

When the bus pulled into the Anaheim depot, I was somewhat bewildered by the dilapidated appearance of the Greyhound Bus Depot. The building looked more like an old wooden shack than a bus terminal. With Disneyland being the most famous theme park in the world, I'd expected a large, modern terminal bustling with crowds of people.

Nevertheless, as soon as the bus driver unloaded the luggage, I grabbed my backpack and I headed for Disneyland. Off in the distance, I could see a portion of the Disney hotel and the elevated train that was used to shuttle hotel guests back and forth to the theme park. As I got closer and the parking lot came into view, I was amazed at the size of it — I'd never seen a parking lot of that magnitude before.

I walked down Harbor Boulevard until I came to an entrance for the parking lot, but then I still had to walk probably another quarter of a mile before I got to the main entrance of the park itself. I placed my backpack in one of the security lockers outside the front gate and purchased fifteen dollars in tickets for the rides and entertainment.

It was supposedly the parks off-season, but there were still a lot of people mulling around. I walked around for quite a while, taking in all the sights and sounds, before finally deciding to go on several of the rides, including Magic Mountain, Pirate's Cove and the Jungle Safari.

Everywhere I turned, there were several Disney cartoon characters like Mickey Mouse, Donald Duck, and Goofy, who were greeting the public and obligingly posing for pictures. In addition to the characters walking around, the park also showcased all its Disney cartoon characters in a parade that went through the streets of the park several times throughout the day.

Most fascinating to me was the robotics used to animate some of the characters. I was most impressed with the animated performance of the Abraham Lincoln character, which looked incredibly life-like. Lincoln was on one of the exhibits that had a rotating platform featuring several robotic characters performing three different theme shows.

When the stage rotated and the curtain was raised, Abraham Lincoln was sitting in a high-back chair turning his head from side to side as if he was assessing the audience. I was amazed when he stood up out of the chair and began giving one of his famous speeches; it was like watching a real, live person talk.

I spent two days at Disneyland, which wasn't nearly enough time to see or do everything they had to offer. I reminded myself that I was on borrowed time, though, and made up my mind to reach my second goal and see the Pacific Ocean. I boarded a transit bus, asking the driver for a transfer slip because there wasn't a bus that went directly to Huntington Beach. It was about a forty-minute ride before the bus turned onto the Pacific Coast Highway and I got my first glimpse of the Pacific Ocean. Looking out the bus window, I could see giant whitecap waves rolling in towards the shore. The waves were much larger than what I'd previously seen in Michigan's Great Lakes. Even from the window, it was an awesome sight.

Huntington Beach was a small and rather quaint little town. The residential area and business district were situated on the east side of the coastal highway. On the west side of the highway was Huntington Beach State Park, which was well known as being a popular surfing location. From what I could see, surfing was a big business in Huntington Beach. I personally didn't have any interest in the sport, but out of curiosity I browsed through a couple of the shops that sold surfing equipment and specialized in making custom surfboards.

The most prominent feature of Huntington Beach was the large pier that extended several hundred feet out into the ocean, standing about fifty feet above the surface of the ocean. All along the pier, people were fishing or watching the surfers ride the waves, and many others appeared to be just taking a casual stroll and enjoying the many sights and sounds of the ocean. The pier provided an excellent view of the surrounding area for miles up and down the coastline. For those people who wanted to get an even better view, telescopes that accepted coins were mounted along the railing on both sides of the pier.

When the temperatures cooled down a bit later that evening, I went for a walk along the beach. I thought about the fact that I might never see the mighty Pacific Ocean again, but at least now I could say that I'd actually seen it with my own two eyes.

As the sun began to slowly disappear below the horizon, I sat down on the beach listening to the sound of the waves breaking on the shore. I thought about a lot of things, but the one thought that was constantly on my mind was how much longer I'd be able to hold on to my freedom.

The next morning I went into town, walking into a video arcade and playing video games for the first time ever. The whole idea of arcades and video games was new to me, since neither they nor personal computers had been around when I went to jail in 1972. I was amused with the games and spent several hours there.

By the time I decided to leave, it was afternoon and I went back to the pier to watch the surfers and enjoy the spectacular view of the coastline. When I looked straight down into the ocean from the pier, I could see a number of long, slender fish swimming in toward the shore. They looked to be about three or four feet in length.

"Are those Barracudas?" I asked a gentleman standing nearby fishing.

"Yep, they sure are," he said. "You ever seen one before?"

"No," I said. "In fact, I'd never seen the Pacific before my trip here."

"Ah, well, enjoy it," he said. "It's a beautiful sight."

I nodded and looked down again, getting another good look at the fish.

"Do the Barracuda live in the shallow water?" I asked him.

"No, not really, but they like to swim in real close to the shoreline looking for something to eat," he told me. "The shallow water is pretty much their feeding ground."

"Hmm," I said, nodding my head. "Have a good day, now, and good luck fishing."

I strolled away, leaving Huntington Beach and boarding a bus to go south on the coastal highway to Newport Beach. Newport was somewhat larger than Huntington Beach and it had a lot more vehicle and pedestrian traffic. Unlike Huntington, though, it wasn't a surfing town — more like a boating and yachting town. It was peppered with loads of small businesses that sold and repaired boats. Since I had previous experience at building and repairing fiberglass boats, I thought that perhaps I could find a temporary job in Newport doing the same.

After all, the money I had wouldn't last forever and I didn't want to risk getting in trouble with the law by trying to rob or steal anything. I didn't need much. Enough money to be able to rent a room and buy some food was all it'd take to make me happy.

I applied for jobs at several of the boat repair shops around town but the prospects weren't good. No one seemed to be hiring and I decided not to stick around, so the next day I boarded a transit bus with the intention of returning to Anaheim. I changed my mind mid-trip, though, and got off the bus in Santa Ana instead.

There, I found an apartment complex on Harbor Boulevard that rented rooms and apartments on a weekly basis for about sixty-five dollars. I paid for a room and decided to stop moving around for at least a week while I contemplated how to make things work.

I knew that keeping my freedom meant I needed to have a revenue stream, and I knew that I needed a job to make that happen. But, if I was going to get a job, I'd have to acquire a social security card and some form of photo identification.

I was a bit hesitant to ask my sister for additional help, but I couldn't think of anyone else who might be able to help me obtain the documents I needed. Her ex-husband was only four years older than I was — close enough in age for his identity to work as mine. If I could somehow get an original copy of his birth certificate and social security card, I could then apply for a California driver's license in his name. I didn't have any ill intentions of misusing his identity; I just obviously couldn't use my own.

I called my sister and told her exactly what I needed.

"I'm really sorry to ask you for all this," I told her. "It's just, I want to make things work out here. I don't want to get in trouble and go back to prison — if I could just get some identification I'm sure I could get a job and then I'll be all right."

"I just don't know, Jim," she said. "I don't have his paperwork or anything."

"Do you think you could talk to him and just see if he might be okay with it?" I asked her.

"I don't know if he'll agree to something like that, but I'll ask," she said. "Give me a name and address I can send it to, just in case he does agree."

I gave her the information and thanked her again for all her help.

"Really, you have no idea how much this means to me," I told her. "You're really saving my life, sis."

And she was. Evidently, she was quite persuasive with her ex-husband because about a week later, I was pleasantly surprised to find a letter from her. Inside the envelope was a copy of my ex-brother-in-law's birth certificate and social security card.

With that in hand, I didn't have to look very hard to find a job. A business named Ken's Wheel House, about four blocks down from the apartment complex I was staying at, was hiring. It was a small family business that sold tires and custom wheels for cars and trucks. They accepted my paperwork and I told them that I'd recently moved from Michigan and hadn't gotten a California driver's license yet. My job there was pretty simple — I mounted, balanced and installed tires and wheels on the customer's vehicles.

The family who owned the business was exceptionally nice. Ken Williams, the patriarch, owned the business and spent most of his time supervising their small factory and warehouse, where they made most of their custom wheels. His wife, Lauren, had been managing the Wheel House for the past ten years and she knew practically everything there was to know about the business. Not only was I surprised at the extent of her knowledge about tires and wheels, but I was also impressed.

The Williams had three children who all worked part time at the store. Their eldest daughter, Katie, was twenty years old and attended college full time, but she too occasionally came into the store to work. Their youngest daughter, Valerie, was seventeen and worked several days a week after school, taking care of all the paperwork. Their son Shawn was eighteen and he also was still in school, but usually worked Thursdays and Fridays after school let out.

Weekdays were pretty slow at the business and I kept myself occupied by doing a lot of cleaning and restocking. On Fridays, though, when most people received their paychecks, there was usually more business than we could handle and it was hard to keep up. Customers would be lined up and down the block, waiting to have their wheels and tires mounted on their vehicles. It felt good to be working again in the free world, even when it was busy to the point of being hectic.

One evening after work, I was sitting in the apartment complex laundry room waiting for my clothes to dry when a young woman came in carrying a basket of laundry. When she finished putting her clothes in the washer, she came over and sat down directly across from me.

"Hello, my name's Doreen," she said cheerfully, extending her hand forward and introducing herself.

I shook her hand and replied, "Hello, nice to meet you."

"You too," she said. "My husband Bill and I have been renting an apartment here for a few months now. Have you been here long?"

"Just a couple weeks," I said.

"You're probably like us, then— don't know anybody 'round these parts," she said, her southwestern accent revealing itself. "We're from Texas. My husband, he's in the Marine Corps, stationed over at the El Toro Air Naval Station."

She continued: "We've lived in Texas all our life and haven't really met anyone or made friends 'round here, 'cept for a few guys Bill knows from the Marine Corps."

My Own Worst Enemy

"How long do you guys have to be out here?" I asked her.

"'Til Bill finishes up his tour of duty," Doreen said. "Then we're going to go back to Texas — Bill plans to get a job in the oil business."

We chatted for a bit longer while my clothes finished up in the dryer. Once I was done folding my laundry, I told Doreen that I'd enjoyed talking with her.

"It was nice to meet you," I said. "I look forward to meeting your husband if I see him around."

I began to walk toward the door and just then, it opened and Doreen's husband walked in. Her face lit up when she saw him.

"Well, speak of the devil! Here comes my husband," she said cheerfully, getting up to stand by him. "Bill, this is our new neighbor."

I set my laundry basket down to shake his hand and we made small talk for a while. During our conversation, Bill mentioned that they were going to a lounge in Anaheim called the Sunshine Meat and Liquor Company. He said it was a great place with good food and assured me that I was more than welcome to come along. I was a bit hesitant at first, but figured that both Bill and Doreen seemed like nice folks.

"Well, seeing as how I don't know anyone in California either, I think I'll take you up on that offer," I said. "Maybe all three of us can meet some people and make some friends."

"That'll be great," he said. "Just meet us in the common area in, say, how about an hour? That'll give us some time to finish up the laundry here and get all cleaned up."

"Sure thing, I'll see you in an hour," I said.

The lounge was located on Harbor Boulevard, just down the street from Disneyland, which made it a popular nightspot for the tourists visiting the park. The place was absolutely packed when we got there, so we had to wait in line for about twenty minutes before we could even get in the front door. Once we got inside, we managed to find an empty table and Bill ordered drinks for the three of us.

He and I had some common ground to talk about, seeing as how I'd served in the military for a while too. I told him about some of my experiences being in the army back in the late sixties, during the Vietnam War, and asked him what it was like being in the Marine Corps.

"It's not all that different from having a regular, civilian job," he said. "Monday through Friday, I have to be on base by five a.m. for roll call and I work until four o'clock in the afternoon, just like any other job."

"What do you do around there?" I asked.

"I'm the company clerk, which is actually one of the better assignments to have," Bill said. "Most of the time, I'm excused from having to participate in the daily physical training routine."

He paused for a moment, glancing over at Doreen.

"You know, the only reason I even enlisted is because my father had been a Marine and he really wanted me to follow in his footsteps," Bill told me. "Once I finish my tour of duty, Doreen and I are moving back to Texas 'cause I got a job lined up for me with one of the major oil companies."

"That's pretty lucky," I said. "How do you come by getting a job all lined up and waiting for you?"

"My father and grandfather have worked in the oil business all their lives," he said with that Texan drawl. "I got a lot of contacts in the business."

"I don't really have any big plans for a career," I told him. "I just knew I wanted to be in California, so I came out here and got the first job I could."

"You said you work down at that tire place, right?" Bill asked.

"Yep, it's really not a bad gig," I said. "Pays the bills, the hours aren't bad at all and the work itself is pretty simple."

He nodded, took a drink of his beer and signaled with his hand as though he had something to say.

"I gotta tell ya, though, man, the oil business is where it's at," he said. "There's a lot of money to be made in the oil business. You look like a man who could master an oil rig."

"I don't know a whole lot about it," I said. "There's not much of an oil business out East, where I'm from."

Our conversation went on for a while and as we talked, I got the picture that both he and Doreen couldn't get their minds off what the future held for them. For a moment, I wished I had their kind of freedom to dream of the future in such a way, but then I reminded myself to simply be grateful that I was out in the real world and not locked away behind bars.

Doreen was one of those individuals who could strike up a conversation with anyone, making friends practically instantly and effortlessly. She wasn't drop dead gorgeous, but what she lacked in looks she made up for with her amiable personality.

She stood about five-foot-eight and weighed maybe around a hundred and twenty pounds. Her eyes were hazel and she had long brown hair that hung down well past her shoulders. With her shapely, slim and trim body, she actually wasn't all that bad to look at.

After we had a few drinks, Doreen began trying to coax Bill out on to the dance floor. Bill continually resisted.

"I just want to sit here and relax with my drink," he told her. "I don't wanna do no dancin' tonight."

Doreen persisted though, refusing to give up until Bill finally suggested that she ask me to dance with her. At first, I sat there silent, unsure of what to do or say.

"Oh, I don't know about that," I finally said, hesitant about dancing with another man's wife — especially someone I'd just met.

"I don't mind, man," Bill said. "You'll be doin' me a favor, really — that woman won't give up 'til she gets her way and I'd rather it be you out on that dance floor than me. I ain't much for dancing."

"I'm not either, but I guess I owe you a favor for bringing me out here," I said.

Doreen jumped up excitedly, clearly happy that someone was going to dance with her. She grabbed my arm and led me to the dance floor, practically running there and tugging on my arm the whole way.

After the first dance, I was ready to sit down. It was awkward dancing with another man's wife, even with his blessing.

"Just one more dance," she'd beg after each song ended, and I'd inevitably oblige. I didn't want to hurt her feelings, so I tried to think of something to say.

"You know, I've actually got to go use the bathroom," I told her. "Maybe you oughta check on Bill while I'm gone."

When I got back to the table, I was happy to see Bill and Doreen talking and laughing. It appeared that Doreen had gotten the dancing out of her system and for that, I was grateful.

The three of us sat there for a while, drinking and talking and laughing.

"I think I'm drunk!" Doreen exclaimed at one point, her Texan drawl exacerbated by her slurred speech.

"You're not alone, sweetheart," Bill said, laughing and holding his glass forward to toast. Doreen and I put our glasses forward too and as we tapped them together, it was evident how drunk all three of us were — the glasses clanging together with too much force and the beer spilling over the top of them.

Not one of the three of us was in any sort of condition to drive, but we didn't broach the subject until we reached the parking lot and started heading for the car.

"I ain't drivin' tonight," Bill said, laughing. "All ya 'all got a lot less at stake than I do — I'll get kicked outta the Marine Corps if I get caught swervin' all 'round."

I thought to myself that no, he didn't have less at stake than me. He'd get kicked out of the Marine Corps and be on his way back to Texas, where he really wanted to be anyhow. I'd be back to rotting in prison.

I kept my mouth shut, though, and when we reached the car, Bill immediately fell into the back seat of their Volkswagen, passing out on impact. I looked at Doreen, who was stumbling back and forth while trying to make her way around the front of the car to the passenger side. She brushed against the car's fender and practically fell on it, but caught herself by putting her hand down on the hood.

"I can't even walk right," she said, laughing at herself. "Looks like your-a-drivin' us home."

I certainly was in no condition to be driving. And besides that, I didn't even have a driver's license.

My stomach sank as I sat down in the driver's seat. I put the keys in the ignition, but hesitated from turning them. Suddenly, my stomach felt as though it were in a knot and my heart raced, a surge of anxiety washing over me.

Driving was a very risky proposition for me on its own, seeing as how I didn't have a license. Drunk driving was absolutely, positively, downright stupid of me to even consider and I knew that, regardless of how drunk I'd gotten. I had so much more to lose than Bill and Doreen, more than they could've imagined.

Billboards all over the roads and commercials on television really drove the message home — drunk drivers go directly to jail. If I was pulled over, this meant I'd immediately be taken to the nearest jail, where they'd take my fingerprints and run them through the National Criminal Information System. In turn, they'd find out right then and there that I was a fugitive, a prison escapee. My vacation would be brought to an untimely, abrupt and definitive halt.

I thought about telling Doreen the truth. *Then she'd understand,* I thought.

But I just couldn't do that. It was too risky — for both me and them. Then I thought that maybe I'd just tell her I couldn't drive and we should sleep in the car, but that probably wasn't smart either. All it took was a cop cruising through the parking lot, looking for drunks, to get suspicious when our car was still there after everyone else had gone and then he'd be pointing his flashlight into the windows and rapping on them to wake us up. That, too, could end my vacation.

"What's the hold up?" Doreen asked me. "Let's get goin'. I wanna be asleep in my bed right now."

And so, I turned the keys in the ignition and started the car. Somehow I managed to drive us safely back to the apartment, but it was nearly as nerve-racking as hanging on to the train's handrail. I was acutely aware of my drunken state and thus very paranoid and anxious, and trying so hard to be as sober as possible and pay attention to the road.

The next day when I talked to Bill and Doreen, I shamefully admitted that I didn't have a valid driver's license. Surprisingly, they didn't seem all that concerned. In fact, Bill suggested that Doreen could drive me to the department of motor vehicles and I could use their Volkswagen to take the driver's test.

Naturally, I didn't hesitate to accept their offer. A couple of days later, Doreen drove me to the California Department of Motor Vehicles.

Driving a car is like riding a bicycle — you never totally forget how. Even though I'd only driven a car once in the past five years, I wasn't worried about taking the written test or the driving test. I was, however, feeling a little anxious about using my ex-brother-in-law's birth certificate.

I'd memorized all the information on the birth certificate — the birth date, hospital's name, parents' names and all that stuff — but I was still concerned that they might ask me a question I didn't have a good answer for. As it turned out, though, all my fears were for nothing.

The only thing the lady asked me was if I'd ever had a driver's license in the State of California.

"No," I said simply, and that was all.

I passed the written test and the driving test, they took my photo and issued me a temporary drivers' license.

Holding that piece of paper in my hand, I breathed a sigh of relief. I felt a lot less vulnerable knowing that I had a valid driver's license in another person's name.

I thought about buying a used car for transportation, but I didn't have enough money to purchase anything reliable. I had noticed a 1968 Triumph Bonneville motorcycle, a 650, at a motorcycle shop just down the street from my apartment complex. I thought it might be within my price range so I headed down there one day for a better look.

The bike appeared to be in excellent condition and when I took it for a test drive, it ran just as good as it looked. The price tag on it was five hundred bucks, but the guy at the store said he'd take four hundred in cash for it. Since I had the money, I bought the bike as a means of temporary transportation.

I rode around for about a half hour to get used to the bike before I went back to the apartment, where I wanted to let Bill and Doreen take it for a ride. Bill had owned a 250 Yamaha, but one night not too long ago someone had stolen it out of the parking lot at the apartments. Bill reported it stolen to the police, but so far, they hadn't recovered it. I thought he'd appreciate being back on a bike again and, without a doubt, I owed them a favor.

The weather in Southern California was, for the most part, decent for riding a motorcycle — all except for the smog. The smog was downright awful. If I rode from Santa Ana to Huntington Beach, by the time I reached my destination, my face would be covered in black soot from all the air pollution. Within a month's time, I was sick of riding a motorcycle everywhere I wanted to go. So, when one of the guys I worked with offered me $350 for the bike, I took it. What I really wanted was a good used car.

Finding one I could afford, however, was another matter. The only thing I could find for less than a thousand bucks wasn't worth buying.

When my boss heard that I was looking to purchase a used car, he offered to cosign on a car loan for me — telling me that I was one of the best workers they'd hired in a long time and that it'd be their way of showing appreciation for my work.

Normally, I'd have felt quite proud of myself. I wanted to feel proud. But I didn't. Instead, I felt terrible.

I felt especially bad because lately, I'd been thinking about leaving. The nagging worry that I'd already stayed far too long in one place was in the back of my mind and I knew that if I stayed, I could be making a huge mistake. But, I'd made a few friends and found a decent job — it was hard not to let my feelings about this new life cloud my better judgment. My attachment to these people was exposing me to a greater risk of getting caught and being sent back to prison. A person in my precarious situation should not become attached to anyone or anything that they're not willing to walk from without the slightest hesitation.

But the truth was that I really wanted to stay. So, I came up with excuses to satisfy that part of my mind that was in opposition.

I'll just stay long enough to pay for the loan on a used car, I told myself. And that would be smart because then, I'd have the means to move around as I needed to without worrying about buses and airports and, in general, traveling amongst others. I could travel frequently and instead of spending money on motel rooms, I could just sleep in the car.

With my decision made, I began shopping around for vehicles until I found a 1969 Chevelle for just a thousand dollars. My boss made good on his offer and cosigned a loan for half that amount. My plan was to keep working until I had the loan paid off, which would only take a couple of months.

Then, I'd simply drive away free and clear and find another temporary job somewhere else.

Doreen decided she wanted to find a job to make some extra money, but both she and Bill joked that she'd probably give up searching before she found one. Surprisingly, though, after just a couple days of looking she did find a job as a painter working on an all-female crew that painted the interiors of homes and office buildings.

There was only one problem — she had no way of getting to work because Bill had to drive their Volkswagen to the Marine Corps base each morning. The business that Doreen had to get to, though, wasn't far from the apartment and since I had to get up and go to work at about the same time, I offered to drive her to work. She checked with her new coworkers to see if one of them could drive her home and the answer was yes.

Early one morning, I was awakened by the sound of someone knocking on my apartment door. My heart leapt; it was too early for Doreen to be ready for work. I worried that it was the police coming for me and as I prepared to open the door, I took in a deep breath and readied myself to face the worst.

I pulled the door open and, instead of being confronted by officers, I saw Doreen standing there with a puffy, tear-streaked face.

"Are you okay?" I asked her, worried. "Come in, Doreen, tell me what's wrong."

Through her sniffles and tears, she told me that she and Bill had gotten into an argument last night and Bill stormed out of the apartment. She didn't tell me what they were arguing about, but I told her it probably wasn't all that big of a deal.

"I'm sure he just needs a little time to think things through," I reassured her. "By the time he comes home, I'm sure he'll have realized it was just a silly argument."

Doreen sat on the couch, sobbing and wiping the tears from her eyes.

At one point, she looked up at me and said softly, "It would be easy for you to take advantage of me right now."

I knew what she was trying to say. Perhaps under different circumstances, I might have accepted her proposal. But, Bill and Doreen were my friends.

"I understand that you're angry and you're feeling a lot of pain, Doreen, but you have to realize those feelings can affect your judgment," I told her. "I don't mean to reject you, because I wouldn't — you're a great girl. But you and Bill are my friends, and something like that would ruin our friendship and even worse, would ruin your marriage."

She nodded her head, sniffling.

"I don't want to do anything that could cause irreparable harm to your marriage, and I don't think you want to either," I added.

She didn't say anything for a couple minutes and I was a bit worried she might be angry with me. But, Doreen had better sense than that.

"Bill and I are lucky to have such a good friend," she told me.

"I'm lucky to have the both of you as friends too," I said back to her, and she cracked a small smile.

Shortly thereafter, Doreen left my apartment and sure enough, when Bill came home from the base that afternoon all was forgiven between the two of them. They apologized to each other and things went back to normal.

As for the conversation that Doreen and I had in my apartment that morning, nothing more was ever said of it.

About a week later, Bill and Doreen asked me if I'd like to move in with them.

"We know you're trying to pay off that car loan as quickly as possible," Bill said. "We just thought, if you were living with us, you could use the money you're paying in rent now to pay it off even sooner."

I felt bad, knowing I had an ulterior motive; a hidden agenda to pay off the car and get the heck out of dodge.

"You can sleep on the couch," Doreen piped in. "It's got a pull-out bed, so it'll be comfortable."

I was an escaped convict, supposedly a hardened criminal. I wasn't supposed to have a conscience, but I did and I vehemently disliked having to be deceitful and duplicitous to the two people who considered me their friend, and a good one, at that.

Nevertheless, I accepted their offer and at the end of the week, I moved in with them.

"But I want to give Doreen twenty dollars each week," I insisted. "There's no reason for you both to be paying for my food and other things. Let me at least help out by doing that."

Their apartment had a separate bedroom that they slept in, so it was a workable living situation. I slept on the couch, which folded out into a double bed, and tried to stay out of the way as best I could.

I soon discovered that Doreen was a meticulous housekeeper and a good cook as well. She cleaned the apartment every day and usually managed to have supper waiting for Bill when he came home. It was nice living with them. They treated me as if I was one of their own family members and I truly enjoyed their company. In the evenings, we played video games, watched television and occasionally, the three of us went out for pizza or a night out on the town.

Before I knew it, Christmas of 1977 arrived. It would be the first Christmas since 1971 that I was free to celebrate the holidays and with that in mind, it was particularly exciting.

When I was growing up, Christmas had always been the most wonderful time of the year for me. My fondest memories have always been of a house that was filled with large quantities of fruits, nuts, candy and lots of presents. I remember the joyous sound of innocent and enchanting laughter from four happy children — a house that was overflowing with an abundance of love from my parents and sisters. Of course, there were times when I didn't always get exactly what I asked for at Christmas, but the most important thing was that I felt loved by my parents and my sisters. I always felt safe and secure in the knowledge that mom and dad were always there to provide everything we needed, and to protect us from all harm, real or imagined.

I saved up money so I could give gifts to Bill and Doreen for Christmas. It felt good to give gifts at Christmas and I was excited

My Own Worst Enemy

to purchase and wrap items for them. I bought Bill a nice watch and for Doreen, a toaster, which is what she told me she really wanted and needed. And while I thought something a little more personal might've been more exciting for her, I wanted to give her what she asked for.

On Christmas day, Doreen spent hours preparing an excellent meal for the three of us. We feasted on turkey with all the trimmings and for dessert, Doreen served homemade pumpkin pie with ice cream. For a man who hadn't eaten a real holiday meal in years, it was incredible to taste the delicious meat of a home cooked turkey and all the traditional trimmings that went along with it.

With our bellies full of great food and our hearts full of cheer, we sat around after dinner sharing stories of our childhood experiences and memories of Christmases in the past. It was a great Christmas and I couldn't have asked for better friends to spend it with.

I was looking forward to celebrating the New Year with Bill and Doreen as well, but little did I know, my time had run out.

Two days after Christmas, I headed home from work looking forward to taking a shower and relaxing for the evening. When I arrived at the apartment, Bill and several of his buddies from the Marine Corps were sitting around the dining room table playing cards. Doreen was sitting on the couch, watching a show on television.

I said hello to Doreen and headed over to the table to say hi to the guys. After some brief chit-chat with Bill and his friends about the card game, I walked back toward Doreen and asked her if it would be all right for me to use their shower.

The only bathroom in the apartment was attached to their bedroom, and even though they said it wasn't necessary for me to ask to use it, I always felt I had to say something. After all, I had to go through their bedroom to get there and I felt it was important to respect their privacy.

I showered quickly and when I came out of the bathroom, the bedroom door was closed and the room was dark. Before rejoining the group of people outside the doors, I decided to lie down on the bed for a minute to grab a moment's relaxation. No sooner than I had laid down and closed my eyes, I heard what sounded like someone rapping on the front door. The sound was a bit muffled, but I thought I heard a female voice saying something along lines of there being an emergency phone call for Doreen at the front desk.

I heard the front door click behind Doreen as she walked out of the apartment and not long after, there was a bunch of scuffling noises in the living room immediately followed by a male voice yelling menacingly, "Get down on the floor! Get down, now!"

I knew immediately that it had to be the police and had no doubt they were looking for me. Suddenly, the bedroom door burst open and three men armed with shotguns rushed into the room, surrounding me on the bed and pointing their guns directly at me.

"FBI, don't move!" the men shouted repeatedly. I stayed just as I was, lying down on the bed.

One of the FBI agents grabbed my arm and leaned in to look at the tattoo on my right forearm. He asked me my name, but before I could answer, he gave me some choices.

"Is it Tom Crandel? How about Andrew Allen Lancaster? Or maybe it's James Anthony Goble?" he sneered.

I just looked up at them, not sure what to do. Clearly, they knew who I was. Another one of the agents stepped closer.

"James Anthony Goble, we have a fugitive warrant for your arrest," the agent said. "Roll over and put your hands behind your back."

After they placed me in handcuffs, one of the FBI agents went through my pockets, taking everything he found and tossing it on the bed for the other agent to examine. When the agent looked at my driver's license, he said something about charging me with a forgery case.

"I guess that won't matter much anyway, since you've already got a life sentence," the agent said.

I could hear the agents outside the bedroom questioning Bill and Doreen, trying to ascertain whether they'd had any prior knowledge about me being an escaped convict from Michigan. I felt good listening to their answers, knowing that because I'd never revealed my real identity or history to them, they could answer truthfully and not be in any trouble.

I'd known all along that in order to be a true friend to them, I had to protect them by not letting them know who I really was.

My arrest was inevitable, I suppose. I'd never had any delusions that I could remain free indefinitely, but I had held on to hope that it would be a very long time before I had to go back to prison. That proved to be nothing more than a pipe dream.

I reminded myself of the saying: "Hope is knowing that the outcome is possible and doing all you can to facilitate that end. Wishing is sitting on your ass and waiting for a miracle to happen."

Unfortunately, I'd given myself a false sense of hope by not doing all I could to facilitate my desired outcome — remaining free. I knew exactly what I should have done; remain detached from all people and everything, and all emotions, and never stay too long in one place or travel in a logical pattern. Despite that, I'd deliberately deceived myself by fabricating excuses and making compromises that, in the end, only hastened my return to prison.

As I was led out the front door of the apartment in handcuffs, I glanced back shamefully at Bill and Doreen.

"I'm sorry," I mouthed to them as I was pushed out the door. They watched me be led away with their jaws dropped in shock, no doubt confused at what was taking place in their living room.

A few days later, Bill and Doreen showed up at the Orange County Jail in Santa Ana to visit me. Needless to say, they were surprised beyond belief and hurt to find out the truth.

"This can't be right," Doreen said, sitting across the table from me. "Tell me that there's been a mistake."

I shook my head, casting my glance downward in shame.

"I am so sorry, guys. You both have been such great friends to me and I truly appreciate it, more than you can know," I told them, then looked both of them in the eyes. "But it's true."

Before anything else was said, I wanted to explain why I hadn't told them before.

"I'm sorry I never said anything to you; I felt horrible that I couldn't tell you who I really was, but I had no choice," I explained. "You were such good friends to me, and to be a good friend in return, I had to keep it secret from you. If you'd known anything about who I really was and you didn't notify the authorities about it immediately, you'd have been charged with harboring a fugitive. I just didn't want to cause you both any harm; I had to make sure you knew nothing to keep you safe."

"I know, buddy," Bill said. "We appreciate that you kept us in the dark. It'd have been hard to turn in a friend like you."

He asked if there was anything that they could do to help me, but I told him I was pretty much beyond helping.

"I don't think there's anything anyone can do for me now," I told them. "I was a fugitive and now it's time to face the music."

I appreciated their sincere desire to help and I thanked both of them for everything they'd already done for me.

"What do you want us to do with your clothes and personal things, and your car," Doreen asked.

I leaned back in my chair, I hadn't thought about that yet.

"Do whatever you want with my clothes and things — they're of no use to me anymore," I said. "As for my car, you both can keep it if you like."

I looked at Bill and continued talking. "It'd be a good car for Doreen to drive around, to get to and from work and grocery shopping and stuff. The only thing I'll ask is that you pay the remaining balance on the loan. It's just two hundred dollars and I'd hate for my boss to get stuck paying off the loan. Or, you could sell it and use the money from it to pay off the loan, if you don't mind."

They looked at each other while I talked and then Doreen said, "I think I'd like to keep the car. It'd be no problem to pay off the loan on it."

"Yeah, absolutely. And we thank you for it," Bill said.

When the visit was over, Bill said they'd come back to see me again.

"And just in case you need anything, we're going to leave some money for you at the front desk," Bill said.

"That's all right guys, it's really not necessary," I told them, but he insisted on doing it anyhow.

I knew that it was hopeless to try and fight my extradition back to Michigan, but I also wasn't in any hurry to return to prison. For that reason, when I went to court for my extradition hearing, I told the judge that I wanted to contest my extradition and requested to have a court appointed attorney represent me.

The judge had to grant my request, which he did and then set a date for an extradition hearing. He also set my bail at two hundred and fifty thousand dollars, which surprised me. It was a large amount but even so, at least it was an amount. The judge at my murder trial had refused to set bail before I was ever even convicted of a crime.

The Orange County Jail was about twelve stories tall and I was housed on the third floor. I was placed in a four-man cell with two other guys who were there for assorted lesser crimes.

The cell was divided down the middle by steel bars, but there was an opening at one end that allowed us to move freely from one side of the cell to the other. On one side of the cell there was nothing but two sets of steel bunk beds that were bolted to the wall. The toilet, sink, and shower were all situated on the other side along the back wall. There was also a stainless steel picnic table that was bolted to the floor and a color television mounted on the wall of one side.

The clothing that was issued to all prisoners consisted of a pair of blue jeans, a gray sweatshirt and a pair of tennis shoes, which was relatively comfortable for jail attire. The meals they served were edible, but the best thing about chow time was that we were allowed to come out of our cells and walk to the chow hall, which was located upstairs.

I'd been in the county jail for about two weeks when they placed a new guy in our cell. He introduced himself as Randy and as we were shaking hands, I couldn't help but notice that he had a perfectly round half-inch hole in his right forearm that looked an awful lot like a bullet hole.

When I asked him if that's what it was, he said yes and then twisted his arm around, pointing to another hole.

"And see there? That's where the bullet exited," he said.

It was none of my business to ask how he got shot and I fully expected him to tell me that. Even so, I asked the question and much to my surprise, he answered it.

"Me and a couple of my partners were robbing a jewelry store," he said. "During the robbery, one of the employees pulled out this handgun from under the counter and started shooting at us; that's when I got hit right here."

He continued, saying: "Well my partners were both carrying AK-47s, so when they saw I got shot they started shooting back. It was chaos; nothing but gunfire and by the time it was all quiet again, three people had been shot — including the schmuck with the handgun who shot me. They got him a bunch of times, fatally wounding him."

I asked him if either of his partners had been shot and he said they had not.

Randy had more than satisfied my curiosity about his gunshot wound and I wasn't about to press him with any more questions. Apparently, though, he wanted or maybe needed to tell his story to someone, so I just sat there listening as he continued to recount what happened.

"So right away, we all three turned around and ran like hell outta there. But the police had already showed up outside and they jumped out of their car, aiming their guns at us. Well, we were wearing bulletproof vests and using armor-piercing ammunition, so we just starting shootin' them up and we totally fucked up their cars, so then we ran over to ours and drove off."

It was one hell of a story and he shouldn't have been speaking a word of it to anyone, especially to another jail inmate who he hadn't known for longer than a minute. I told him that and, as an example, I gave him a brief version of what'd happened to me and how my so-called friends had betrayed me and testified against me.

"Be very careful about what you say and who you say it to," I advised him. "There's always someone listening and looking for information about other inmates that they could use to make a deal for themselves."

A few days later, one of the guys in our cell was released and later that afternoon, they filled his bunk with a Hispanic inmate. When I first saw the guy, he looked like he'd been beaten mercilessly — every inch of his body was covered in black and blue bruises.

"What the hell happened to you?" I asked him.

"I'm a heroin addict," he explained. "I've been cutting the heroin with some other chemicals; tryin' to make it last longer and, you know, maybe improve the high or something, but ever since I've been doin' it, my skin's gotten all discolored and shit. It ain't nothin' though."

It certainly didn't look like nothing. But whatever.

He told us that he'd been arrested on a misdemeanor charge several months ago and that he'd been out on bond until yesterday, when he went to court and was sentenced to five days in jail. He said he could have gotten more time, but he made a deal with the prosecution to plead guilty in exchange for a sentence of five days.

That evening, we were sitting at the picnic table watching television while the Hispanic guy was sitting on the toilet doing his business, or at least that's what it appeared he was doing. When he finished at the toilet, he went over to the sink and began washing his hands, but he was also washing off a package. When he came over to the table, he was holding a cylindrical shaped object about six inches long that looked like it was covered with a black condom.

Apparently, having been ready in advance to make the deal and go to jail for five days, the guy had prepared himself a little care package. He didn't want to go through withdrawals and so, he'd put a small syringe and several grams of heroin inside a plastic container that was wrapped in condoms, and inserted it in his rectum before going to court that day.

CHAPTER 9

BACK TO JACKSON PRISON

After being in the county jail for thirty days, the routine had become monotonous and I was ready to move on. I sent a letter to the Orange County Circuit Court stating that I no longer contested my extradition back to Michigan.

It took another three weeks before the department of corrections sent two prison guards to transport me back to Jackson Prison. The two guards had driven all the way to California in a station wagon and along the way, they'd picked up five parole violators who were also being returned to Michigan. The two guards had six prisoners to transport on an eleven day journey across the country, which meant they'd certainly have their hands full.

I was acutely aware that once I was back behind those prison walls, it would be almost impossible for me to escape again. But I had eleven days to come up with a viable plan. From the moment we left the Orange County Jail, the only thing I had on my mind was escaping. I was determined to take advantage of almost any opportunity that presented itself, as long as I didn't have to hurt anyone.

The six of us were bound in belly-chain handcuffs and leg shackles, which severely limited our movements and made it almost impossible to find a comfortable sitting position. With three prisoners to each seat plus the guards' suitcases, it was a very cramped and uncomfortable ride

The guards drove for eight hours every day, from eight o'clock in the morning until around four o'clock in the afternoon, with each guard driving for four hours at a time.

In the afternoons, they'd drop us off at the nearest county jail for the night while they checked into a motel. At around eight o'clock the next morning, they'd pick us up and drive until about noon, when they stopped at one of the ubiquitous fast food restaurants for lunch.

We were given takeout meals to eat in the vehicle. Surprisingly, the guards would always unlock one of our handcuffs, which made eating a lot easier. Even more surprising was that they often left our one hand free all afternoon, usually until we got close to the next county jail, and then they'd tell us to put the handcuff back on.

Both guards carried their handguns in shoulder holsters. I had observed that when they unlocked the handcuff and passed out our meals, they had to lean into the vehicle and over the person who was sitting next to the door. It would have been relatively easy for me to grab one of the guard's handguns. But I had to ask myself, *what would I actually do if I managed to get my hands on a gun?*

Even though I desperately wanted to escape, I wasn't willing to shoot anyone. For me to risk my own life was one thing, but I didn't have the right to place someone else's life in jeopardy and that was just how I felt. I talked to the other prisoners one at a time about trying to escape, but they weren't interested.

They were all parole violators and didn't have more than a few months to serve on their sentences. I decided that if I were going to attempt to escape, it would have to be on my own. I couldn't expect any assistance whatsoever from these guys.

During the time we were housed overnight in the county jails, I began looking for anything that I could possibly use to make a lock pick. A couple of days later, we stopped at an old, rundown county jail in Arizona and I was able to pry a small finishing nail out of a baseboard.

I bent the nail into the shape of a Z and I used the rough surface of the concrete floor in the jail cell to flatten and shape the nail into a crude handcuff key. The next morning when they loaded us in the

My Own Worst Enemy

vehicle, I made sure that I was sitting in the jump seat, the one that faced the rear of the vehicle, where the guards couldn't see what I was doing.

Just after finishing my lunch, I started working on unlocking the remaining handcuff that was still locked on my left wrist. There were two locks on each handcuff. The first one locked the handcuff in place and kept it from tightening around the wrist. That lock was easy to unlock. But the second lock, which unlocked the handcuff itself from around my wrist, proved to be more than a challenge. It wasn't working and so, as it neared four o'clock, I tucked the nail away and decided to give my design another look while at the next county jail.

The next day I tried to pick the lock again, but to my surprise, part of the lock pick broke off inside the handcuff. I didn't outwardly panic, but I truly thought I was going to have a heart attack right then and there. I knew that if I couldn't get that broken piece out of the handcuff, the guards would almost certainly know that I was trying to escape and I definitely wouldn't get another chance.

I frantically tried for hours to dig and shake the broken piece out, but it was hopeless. Finally, I resigned myself to the fact that it wasn't coming out.

When we arrived at the county jail, I held out my right hand and the guard unlocked the handcuff. When he tried to unlock the other handcuff, it wouldn't open. The key would go in the lock and turn, but it wouldn't unlock. Both guards tried their keys; they even tried a couple of the deputies' keys, but those wouldn't work either.

After about ten minutes, they finally gave up. One of the deputies said that the only way they were going to get the handcuff off was to either cut it off or try to force it open with a hammer and a pair of vise grips.

Finally, after another ten or fifteen minutes of persistent beating and prying, the handcuff suddenly popped open.

I was greatly relieved that I hadn't been discovered and that the guards weren't the least bit suspicious that I'd been tampering with the locking mechanism. In fact, the guards apologized to me for their defective handcuffs. They explained that it was rare for the handcuffs to malfunction, however, after prolonged periods of exposure to high humidity the internal locking mechanism would occasionally corrode and fail.

I considered the incident nothing more than a minor setback and I wasn't deterred from trying again. It took me a couple of days to make another lock pick that was similar in design and this time, I made a mental note to be gentle and refrain from trying to force the lock open.

The following day after lunch, I worked on the handcuff all through the afternoon but didn't make any progress whatsoever. That night in the county jail, I once again used the concrete floor to file and reshape the lock pick. I could only hope that I'd solved the problem.

The next day I was ready to try again and this time, I tried to be even more careful, but I'll be damned if I didn't break that lock pick as well! I stayed calm even though I knew that if my handcuff broke for a second time in a matter of days while all the other inmates had no problems, I'd definitely raise suspicions. The guards would know for sure that I was tampering with the lock and they would most likely double their security measures by placing me in two sets of belly-chains and leg shackles.

Incredibly, I got lucky. I shook my hand inside the cuff and amazingly, the broken piece of my lock pick just shook right out and fell on the seat before we stopped at the next county jail.

I began to realize that my plan wasn't going to work. I needed to come up with a different strategy.

I examined the handcuffs closely and decided that the weakest point was the swivel connector that connected the chain to the handcuff. I thought that if I could somehow bend this piece back and forth, it might just break. I began looking around inside the vehicle for something strong enough that I could use as a lever, but the only thing readily accessible was the seatbelt buckles.

Attached to the end of the seat belts was a piece of flat metal with a square hole in the center. I discovered that by placing the square hole over the swivel, I could use this like a bottle opener to bend the swivel connector back and forth until it broke loose.

If I succeeded in breaking the chain loose from the handcuff, I'd still have the handcuff around my wrist, but if I managed to escape, I could get that off later. The belly-chains were usually loose around my waist, and I knew that I could easily slide the chain down over my hips without any problem.

After the first week on the road, the guards decided that they didn't need to hobble us with the leg shackles, which I was thankful for. That was just one less obstacle I'd have to overcome. Nevertheless, we were still secured with the belly-chain handcuffs and once I managed to break the chain loose from the handcuff, I still had to find a way out of the vehicle.

During the day, if we had to use the bathroom, the guards would stop at a rest area along the expressway. One guard would stay with the prisoners in the vehicle while the other guard escorted us one at a time to the rest room.

I considered trying to make my move during one of these restroom stops but quickly discarded that idea because I'd have to overpower and incapacitate the guard. I didn't want to take the chance that the situation might get out of control. Someone could get seriously hurt or even shot in an altercation like that and I wasn't willing to go that far.

The inside door handle for the tailgate had been removed and could only be opened from the outside. The only way that I might possibly get out of the vehicle was through the tailgate window. The guards would always open the tailgate window whenever we asked them to, however, they were careful not to open the window more than a couple of inches — just enough to let some fresh air circulate. But with the window slightly opened, I'd be able to use my legs to push the window out instead of trying to kick it out, which would most certainly make too much noise and attract the guards' attention.

When we crossed the state line into Michigan, it was late in the afternoon and starting to get dark. We were only about three hours away from the prison though, so instead of stopping for the night, the guards decided to keep driving. I knew that if I was going to make one last attempt at escaping, it had to be now.

I took the metal piece from the seat belt, placed the square hole over the swivel connector on the handcuff and I pushed as hard as I could until I felt the connector slowly start to bend. The handcuff was cutting into my wrist though and I had to stop. I folded the material from my coat around my wrist several times in an attempt to protect my wrist and then placed the material between the wrist and my handcuff. With the padding tucked under the handcuff, I went back to work and couldn't feel any pain.

I was able to bend the swivel connector back and forth until it broke loose. With both hands now free, I slipped my coat on and sat there waiting for the right moment.

If at all possible, I wanted to wait for a semi truck to pass our vehicle in hopes that the noise from the truck would drown out the sound of breaking glass. I also had to make sure there wasn't any traffic directly behind our vehicle when I bailed out the window. After all, I had no desire to get run over by another vehicle at seventy miles per hour.

It wasn't long before the opportunity presented itself. A semi truck pulling an empty car-carrier trailer was coming up behind us in the passing lane and there wasn't any other traffic behind the semi or our vehicle. As the semi pulled up alongside our vehicle, I placed my feet against the top portion of the window and I pushed with my legs as hard as I could. When the window broke, it sounded like a gunshot blast and I heard one of the guards ask, "What was that?"

The entire back window was gone. It shattered into thousands of small pieces that fell to the pavement and bounced across both lanes of the expressway.

I was planning on climbing out the window, standing on the bumper and then jumping into the snow banks along the shoulder of the expressway. But at the last minute, I changed my mind because our vehicle was moving too fast and I wasn't sure if I could jump the distance necessary to reach the snow bank. If I fell short, it was definitely going to be a hard landing and I couldn't afford to sustain any broken bones, so instead I decided to improvise.

I straddled the tailgate door and climbed out to where I was precariously perched on the bumper. Then I reached down and I grabbed hold of the bumper with my right hand and I let my body fall to the pavement. At first, I was tossed around from side to side and I wasn't sure if I could hold on. Luckily, I was able to grab hold of the bumper with my other hand and pull my body up off the pavement to where only my shoes were dragging on the pavement. I held on until I saw the brake lights come on and when the vehicle slowed down, I finally let go. The vehicle was still doing about fifty miles per hour and as a result of the forward momentum; I was propelled down the expressway, rolling over and over again while I used my arms and hands attempting to stop myself.

Once I gained control of myself, I immediately leapt to my feet and looked to see where the vehicle was. I could see that it had pulled off the expressway and was still rolling forward, but it looked as though it was about to stop. I turned on my heels and ran for about a hundred yards in the opposite direction until there was a break in the traffic, then I attempted to cut across the expressway.

Just as I got to the median separating the north and southbound lanes, I heard one of the guards yell, "Stop or I'll shoot!"

At that point, I wasn't about to stop, especially since there was at least a hundred yards distance between the guard and myself. I was willing to take the chance that he wasn't that good of a shot, especially shooting a pistol over that distance. In fact, his warning to shoot may have only served as more incentive for me to pour on the coal and move my butt a little faster.

When I got to the other side of the expressway, there was heavy traffic in the southbound lanes and the vehicles were moving way too fast for me to safely traverse four lanes of oncoming vehicles. I stopped to wait for a break in the traffic and just then, I heard the sound of several gunshots. Since I didn't think the guard was shooting directly at me, I didn't panic. Besides that, there was too much traffic and I was pretty sure that the guards wouldn't take the chance of hitting one of the passing vehicles.

I looked back to see exactly where the guards were and caught sight of one of them running toward me while the other drove away in the vehicle. I presumed that the guard in the vehicle was going to try and cut me off on the other side, so I knew that I didn't have any time to waste.

At that point, I figured that I had three choices. First, I could stand there waiting for a break in the traffic, which would probably give the guard in the vehicle enough time to cut off my escape route. Second, I could keep running along the expressway with the guard taking potshots at me, or third, I could take my chances darting into traffic. I decided to take my chances with the traffic.

I started out slowly forcing my way into the oncoming traffic. I was hoping that the drivers would slow down just enough to where I could then duck and dodge my way through the steady stream of vehicles and to my surprise, it actually worked. When I got to the other side, I ran up an embankment. I was thinking that if I could make it into the woods, I could easily lose the guard, however, when I got to the top of the embankment there was a wooden-slat snow fence that was strung along the entire crest of the embankment. I didn't think that I had time to go around, and when I looked back to see if anyone was following me, I saw the silhouette of a man running across the expressway and coming in my direction. With no time to waste, I grabbed the top of the snow fence and I swung myself over.

I could see that the snow had drifted high on the backside of the fence and from past experience, I figured that it would be packed almost solid from the constant blowing of the wind. But when I jumped over the fence, I instantly sank up to my chest in deep snow and I couldn't move my legs at all. I frantically began pushing the snow away from my chest trying to dig myself out, but before I could make any progress, I heard a voice behind me telling me not to move or I'd be shot.

I turned my head to see who was behind me, even though I knew who I'd see. The guard was standing on the other side of the snow fence with his gun pointed directly at me.

I told the guard that I was stuck tight and couldn't move my legs.

In fact, I sarcastically quipped, "If I could move we definitely wouldn't be having this conversation."

It took me about fifteen minutes of digging with my hands before I finally managed to extricate myself from the snowdrift. By the time I climbed back over the snow fence, I was totally exhausted. The guard had me lay face down in the snow while he handcuffed my hands behind my back. Then, he helped me to my feet and walked me down the embankment where the other officer was waiting in the vehicle.

The guards immediately shackled me with two sets of belly-chain handcuffs and two sets of leg shackles just to make sure that I didn't try that again.

I was a little bruised and battered from my brief excursion. When I let go of the bumper I hit my head on the pavement, cutting a long gash in my forehead. And when I used my hands to stop rolling, the pavement scraped the skin off my fingers and the palms of my hands.

There was a lot of blood on my hands and face, but none of my injuries were life threatening. The guards still decided I ought to see a doctor so they took a detour to the nearest hospital.

The gash in my forehead looked a lot worse than it actually was, but when the doctor examined my head, he was concerned that I might have a slight concussion. After he put a few stitches in my forehead and the nurses bandaged the abrasions on my hands, they took several x-rays of my skull. When the doctor was satisfied that I didn't have a concussion or any other serious injuries, he told the guards that he was releasing me back into their custody.

Arriving back at the prison, I was taken directly to the infirmary and examined by one of the nurses. She too was concerned that I might have a slight concussion. As a precautionary measure, I was admitted to the infirmary for a twenty-four hour observation period. As soon as my twenty-four hours was up, I was released from the infirmary and taken straight to segregation — better known as the hole — which was what I'd expected but definitely not something that I was looking forward to.

I was placed in a cell on first galley, on the backside of the unit that faced the employee parking lot. The cell was bare except for a toilet, a sink, a bed and a disgustingly filthy mattress. At the bottom of the cell door there was a six-inch by eighteen-inch rectangular opening that had been cut from the steel bars, which was the food slot where they slid our trays into the cells. It reminded me of the food slots in the tiger cages at the Detroit Zoo, where I once saw the zookeepers feeding the tigers raw meat.

We were only allowed to come out of our cells once a week for a shower and to exchange our laundry. The only two privileges allowed in segregation were visits and the inmate store. We were still allowed to receive visits on a daily basis but the inmate store, which traveled to us, only came once every two weeks and the selection of items was limited to toiletries, tobacco, writing supplies, candy bars and cookies.

After two weeks in the hole, I went before the hearing officer for the escape ticket. The beginning of my punishment, he decided, would be thirty days detention in the hole.

A few days later, when I went to see the security classification committee, which was made up of a deputy warden, inspector and a counselor, my security level was raised to a six — maximum security. The committee told me that my security status would be reviewed again after my time in detention was served.

They also informed me that my escape had been referred to the Jackson County Prosecutor's Office for possible prosecution. When that was resolved, I'd be sent to the maximum security prison in Marquette, Michigan.

It took me a while to re-acclimate myself to the wretched environment of prison life. But, having been through this before, it wasn't totally unfamiliar.

I established a daily routine of exercising every morning for a couple of hours, doing sit-ups, push-ups, leg raises, standing on my head push-ups and I walked the walls. I progressed to a point where I could do thirty-five hundred sit-ups in one set, then one set of twenty-five hundred leg raises. I could do ten sets of push-ups with one hundred repetitions per set and eight sets of handstand push-ups at forty repetitions per set. Then, I'd simply walk the walls until my muscles were entirely exhausted.

Walking the cell walls was like doing an isometric exercise — you used a constant pushing tension. It was done by leaning forward and placing both palms flat against the wall, then placing one foot against the opposite wall — bare feet worked the best — and pushing against both walls until you were applying enough force to hold yourself suspended between the two walls. Then you placed the other foot on the wall and it was just a simple matter of moving one leg and the opposite hand at the same time.

Going up the walk felt like walking backwards and coming down it felt like walking forward. When I first started doing it, I had to overcome my fear of falling flat on my face. But just like with anything else, it took only a bit of practice to build my confidence.

I'd only been in the hole once before, when I first came to the prison back in 1973, but that was only for two days. Back then, it used to be so quiet in the hole that you could practically hear a pin drop. In the past few years, though, there had certainly been a big change.

There was a continuous babbling that droned on throughout the entire night, just like how I remembered it being in quarantine years ago. For some reason, most of the guys in the hole seemed to be on a reverse schedule — staying up all night and sleeping all day. I found this to be quite peculiar behavior and I never understood it. Perhaps it was nothing more than the way some of the guys liked to spend their time in the hole. On the other hand, maybe it was just easier for them to hide from themselves in the dark.

The cells on base were completely enclosed and had a solid, steel door. They were called quiet cells, which I found to be a complete misnomer based on the noise level. These cells were used to house the so-called management problem inmates.

One of the guys in a base cell had been in the hole for so long that he'd completely lost his grip on reality. Day and night, he'd constantly pound on his cell door for hours at a time without letting up. When the pounding finally did stop, I could only speculate that he must have exhausted himself and gone to sleep. The other inmates had given him the nickname of *Adam Twelve*, which was the name of an old television show about police officers. He was given that nickname because he was always making a loud whining noise that sounded a lot like the sirens on police cars.

After I served my thirty days of detention, I was given another security classification review. It was a waste of time. The committee reclassified me to administration segregation for another thirty days, which was no different from the detention I was already serving except for its designation on a sheet of paper.

Every thirty days for the next four months, they held their hearings and repeatedly reclassified me to administration segregation. I was beginning to understand how Adam Twelve turned so crazy.

After being in segregation for all those months, I began to experience periods of anxiety and depression from the incessant, monotonous boredom of isolation. Being locked in a six-foot by eight-foot cell for a prolonged and indefinite period of time is in no way conducive to a person's psychological well being. More often than not, the practice of sensory deprivation does not bring about positive changes in a person's behavior or personality. In fact, it tends to have the opposite effect.

The only thing I had to occupy my mind and my time was myself. For no other reason than to have something to do and to think about, I decided to go on a diet. It wasn't long before this diet of mine turned into something life threatening. In retrospect, I suppose that in more ways than one, it was more of an eating disorder than a diet.

I began starving myself for days at a time, consuming nothing more than water. When I did eat, I'd literally stuff myself with cookies and candy bars until my stomach hurt. Immediately after gorging myself, I'd force myself to vomit by placing my fingers down the back of my throat. It got to a point where I did this every time I ate anything for almost two months, until I realized that I'd become obsessed with binge eating and purging.

I'd heard about people who suffered from an uncontrolled binge eating disorder called bulimarexia, a type of disorder that shares characteristics of both bulimia and anorexia. I knew it could lead to a host of serious medical problems and even death. I began to think that I'd inadvertently incurred this same disorder and I knew that I had to make a conscious effort to stop the binge eating and purging before I did any serious damage to my health.

The first thing I did was to get rid of all the cookies and candy bars in my cell. I knew that my problem was psychological and that I had to change my idiosyncratic behavior by using my willpower. The one thing that really helped me to work through this problem was a book entitled Zen Buddhism.

My Own Worst Enemy

I never knew that Buddhism was a self-help religion, or that the name Buddha means the awakened one, or the enlightened one. I found it interesting that Buddha never claimed to be anything other than a man. He attributed all of his attainments and achievements to human endeavor and intelligence. I learned that Buddha taught and encouraged everyone to develop him or herself, as each person has the power to liberate themselves from all bondage through their own personal efforts and intelligence. Buddha also taught that our emancipation depends on one's own realization of the truth and not on the charitable mercy of a God or some other external power as a reward for their obedient good behavior. Buddhism teaches that the root of all evil is ignorance and false views.

Buddhists believe that everything is temporary, impermanent and subject to change. The Four Noble Truths of the Buddhist religion are: That life is suffering, and that suffering is caused by wanting. But there is the end of suffering, which is Nirvana. And The Eight Fold Noble Path is the way leading to the extinction of suffering.

I read this book over and over and I began to meditate every day, sometimes several times a day. I'd sit on the concrete floor with my legs folded and my back against the wall, concentrating on a single point of bright light. At first it was difficult for me to concentrate with all the ambient noise in the block. But the more I practiced emptying my mind and focusing my concentration on a single point the more I felt calm, tranquil and relaxed. I began to realize that I had the power within me to free myself from all past illusions and false beliefs.

Everything must first exist in the mind before it can become reality. I found that if I didn't give any energy to my perceived or imaginary problems, they simply didn't exist. I thought about what I'd read; that wanting is the cause of all suffering. From that point on, I made a conscious effort to end my suffering by not wanting.

During the next few months, I spent a lot of time contemplating some of my childhood experiences — the good right along with the bad. I wondered to what extent those experiences had contributed to the person I'd become. I was aware of my own insecurities and character flaws that I'd never taken the time to deal with or resolve. I grew up with the misconception that somehow these issues would eventually resolve themselves as I grew older. I was finally beginning to realize that over the years, I'd foolishly wasted a lot of time and energy attempting to hide my insecurities and faults from other people. Buddha is quoted as saying, "The only conquest that brings true peace and happiness is self conquest. One may conquer millions in battle, but he who conquers himself, only one, is the greatest of conquers."

Most people, including myself, don't generally live in the present moment. We live in the past, or in the future that is not yet born. We live somewhere else in our thoughts caught up in our imaginary problems and worries that are often memories of the past or desires of the future. As a result, we're frequently unhappy and dissatisfied with our present lives.

After six months in the hole, I was still on administration segregation status but was finally moved to the other side of segregation, which was somewhat better. I was allowed out of my cell for one hour a day, which felt really strange at first. Nevertheless, it was a welcome respite from what I'd endured over the past six months.

I was given my personal property, or at least what was left of it. My personal clothing, television and radio were all missing. The only items I got back after my vacation in California was my footlocker and a few toiletries. I wasn't angry about it; rather, I considered myself lucky to have gotten anything back at all. Normally, when an inmate escapes, his personal property is considered abandoned and the prison authorities may do what they please with the items.

I spent another five months in administration segregation before I was told that the county prosecutor had finally decided not to prosecute me for the escape. Apparently, he didn't want to waste the county's time and money since I already had a life sentence. About two weeks later, I was told to pack my property and get ready for my transfer to the Marquette Branch Prison in Michigan's Upper Peninsula.

CHAPTER 10

MICHIGAN INTENSIVE PROGRAMMING CENTER

At four-thirty a.m. the next morning, I was awakened by the sound of clanging chains and a guard telling me to get up and get dressed. I peered out the cell bars and saw four columns of inmates standing on the base at the far end of the cellblock. In between each of the two columns of the inmates laid a thick, heavy chain on the floor. The guards were securing each inmate in belly-chain handcuffs and leg shackles, then attaching each inmate to the heavy chain with a padlock.

By the time the guard finally came back for me, I was one of the last inmates in the group. As soon as they finished shackling the last of forty inmates, we were taken out through the front gate and seated on a bus that was aptly referred to as the Snowbird.

The ride to Marquette was an eleven-hour, arduous trek. If we had to relieve ourselves en route, we were given a stainless steel half-gallon pitcher and we took care of our business right there in our seat. Around lunchtime, we were given two bologna sandwiches, a small carton of milk and an apple. I didn't eat anything, hopeful that doing so would help me avoid having to use the steel pot.

Not long after we crossed over the Mackinaw Bridge, I began to notice that the snow was piled higher than the rooftops of some houses. I'd never been to the Upper Peninsula before and I was beginning to wonder just how far north we were going.

When we arrived at Marquette Branch Prison, I was taken across the street to a facility called Michigan Intensive Programming Center, commonly referred to as the MIPC. I was told that because of my escape and the assault on a prison guard, MIPC would be my new home for the next year.

The facility was mainly for those inmates who had a history of assaults and aggressive behavior. It housed only eighty-eight inmates and was divided into four color-coded wings, housing twenty-two inmates on each wing.

All inmates started the program in orange wing and were required to complete a specific criterion before they were allowed to advance to the next phase of the program. Blue wing was the second phase, but it wasn't really much different from the first phase. The third and final phase of the program was yellow wing. In that wing, inmates were given a few more privileges as a reward for their good behavior and as an incentive to apply themselves academically. They were even allowed to possess a few items of their personal property, such as their AM/FM radio.

The fourth wing was the green wing, which was the hole, or as the prison guards referred to it, segregation. There were no privileges in green wing and all the cells had an additional solid, steel sliding door to completely isolate each inmate.

MIPC was a behavior modification facility. They required all inmates to participate in their academic programs as well as psychological treatment, if needed. When I first arrived, one of the other inmates told me that I'd be given a written test to determine my academic level. He suggested that I refrain from doing my best on the test because at the end of the program, they'd give me the same test again and then compare the results to see if I made any noticeable progress. If I showed a marked improvement on the second test, they would think that their reprogramming had been successful.

It sounded like good advice, so I took it. I answered all the easy questions correctly but didn't give much thought to how I answered the difficult ones. I decided I'd wait until my second go at the test and then really apply myself.

During my first week at MIPC, I was interviewed by the psychologist. He gave me several questionnaires and asked me to answer each question as truthfully as possible. One of the questionnaires had more than a hundred questions and I actually found myself enjoying answering them. Some of the questions required that I explain how I felt about specific things while others required that I complete a sentence.

When the psychologist reviewed the results, I was surprised and impressed at how accurately he was able to describe some of my personality traits. He knew things about me that I wouldn't have openly revealed to him or anyone else. We discussed my so-called assault on staff and I explained the circumstances under which the assault occurred. I also brought up the fact that I hadn't injured the guard in any way, relaying to him that my sole intention was to escape. Based on the interviews and the questionnaires, the psychologist stated that he didn't find any abnormalities. In his opinion, there was no need for me to receive counseling or therapy. Even so, I'd still be required to participate in all the other phases of the MIPC's programming.

MIPC was a fairly new facility. The cells were clean and one of the first things I noticed was that the floors were made of tile rather than bare concrete. Everything in the cells — desks, beds, sinks and toilets — were all made of heavy steel and bolted securely to the walls. The complex had been specifically designed to restrict the inmates' movements and minimize direct physical contact between staff and inmates.

The cells were all concrete except for the cell door, which was made of steel bars with a six-inch by eighteen-inch food slot in the middle. In the back of each cell there was a small rectangular window that was mounted in the ceiling at a forty-five degree angle. The guards used these windows to observe each inmate and take count.

The control center was located in the middle of the complex and was sometimes called the bubble, a nickname it got because of its design. The bubble was circular and totally enclosed by shatterproof glass and steel bars, providing an almost unobstructed view of all four wings, which radiated outward from the center.

Everything was electrically operated from the control center, from the opening and closing of each and every door right down to the light switches in individual cells, giving guards in the control center total control over all inmate movement.

Attached to each cell door was a one-foot square card with the cell number printed on the front side. If we wanted to listen to one of the two radio stations that were available over the intercom, or if we wanted the light in our cell turned on or off, we had to swing the card outward to where it could be seen by the guards in the control center. The guard would then use the two-way intercom that was mounted in the ceiling to communicate with us.

Our meals were prepared by the inmate kitchen workers in trustee division at Marquette prison and then sent over to MIPC in hot carts. The guards brought the hot carts to each wing, where they served us in our cells. I was a bit surprised when a guard came to my cell and recited each item on the menu for that particular meal and then politely asked me what food items I'd like to have on my tray.

We were allowed one hour out of our cells each day, but only two inmates were allowed to be out at the same time. We were given a choice of being in the yard, activity room or gymnasium. The yard was actually nothing more than a twenty-foot by thirty-foot slab of concrete with a basketball hoop. It was surrounded by two chain-link fences with numerous coils of razor wire and an armed guard who observed our every move from a gun port overlooking the yard. The activity room was furnished with a table, two chairs and a color television set. The gymnasium was full size, but the only thing it had to offer was a full size basketball court.

When I was at Jackson, I'd completed my high school education and received my diploma. Even so, MIPC required me to participate in all phases of their academic program. An inmate could refuse to participate, but if he did, he was placed in segregation until he changed his mind or until the powers that be decided what they wanted to do with him. The quickest way to get a transfer out of MIPC was to complete their program.

MIPC was the same as being in the hole. We were locked in our cells twenty-three hours a day. If you wanted to maintain your sanity, you had to find a means of occupying your mind and your time. More importantly, you had to learn how to do your own time and in order to do that, you needed to look introspectively at your thoughts and feelings and ask yourself the really tough questions. Essentially, you had to become your own best friend. Part of this process is learning to discipline the mind to not give any energy to those random, negative and often self-defeating thoughts. In fact, you first must become conscious of what thoughts are best for yourself and your future and what thoughts are not. Then, as they say, it's all a matter of not putting any fuel on the fire. No fuel and the fire can't burn.

You had to adopt the philosophy that it doesn't mean anything and in fact, nothing means nothing. It was important to let it all go and move beyond the moment, detaching yourself from everyone and everything. Regardless of what happened, you had to believe that it couldn't touch you because it didn't mean shit.

To keep myself in shape, I got up around five-thirty every morning and would do calisthenics until breakfast, which was usually around eight o'clock. To exercise my mind and pass the long days, I worked crossword puzzles and spent a couple of hours every day going through the dictionary learning new words and their meanings. I tried to learn at least five new words a day. My method of putting new words to memory was to write them down on a piece of paper, along with their meaning, and test myself until I had the word, its spelling and its definition, memorized. It's kind of like those Word Power quizzes in the Readers' Digest magazines.

My stay at MIPC was, for the most part, uneventful. There were a few fights and two incidents where inmates were stabbed, but it was nothing serious like I'd seen at Jackson. One of my grossest experiences came after I'd finally made it to the yellow wing, the last phase of my program there, during my last three months. Several young kids would engage in shit-gun fights after lights out. It was very unpleasant to say the least.

They'd make their guns by mixing their feces and urine in an empty plastic shampoo bottle or hand lotion bottle. All they had to do was squeeze the bottle hard enough and a stream of feces would shoot across the hallway and into another inmate's cell. Out of necessity, I began hanging a blanket over the bars of my cell door at night to avoid waking up in the morning and finding feces in my cell.

There was also this one kid who liked to make explosive devices out of matches. He'd spend a whole day crushing match heads and packing the powder tightly into a small, empty deodorant bottle, which he then sealed with glue. To make a fuse, he rolled a thin line of the same powdered match heads in toilet paper and inserted this into a small hole in the top of the bottle.

Then, during the night when everyone was sleeping, he'd secure a lit cigarette to the device and slide it down the hallway away from his cell. When the lit cigarette burned down and ignited the fuse, it exploded into a fireball and sounded like a shotgun blast.

In October of 1978, after ten months at MIPC, I was transferred across the street to Marquette Branch Prison, where I stayed for the next four years.

CHAPTER 11

MARQUETTE BRANCH PRISON

Marquette Branch Prison was the oldest and the only maximum-security penitentiary in the state. It was supposedly where the most incorrigible, hard-core, worst-of-the-worst, die-hard inmates served their time.

I'd heard stories about how Marquette used to be, about how the inmate cells used to be called drums — a reference to being as tight as a drum. And in days gone by, if you went to the hole for a serious offense, they used to weld the cell doors closed for years at a time.

The first time I ever saw the outside of the prison, I thought it looked like an old stone block fortress or a medieval castle. It was an intimidating and depressing edifice; a sight that left me with an unsettling sense of foreboding. I almost expected to find a dungeon filled with prisoners living a wretched existence, huddled together in stinking, rat infested, dark, underground chambers. The uncertainty of not knowing what awaited me behind those walls allowed my mind to conjure up all sorts of unpleasant things.

My first few hours inside were spent in a holding cell waiting for a nurse to review my medical file, which was standard procedure at all prisons. All new arrivals were screened to determine if they needed treatment, medication or any sort of special accommodations detail before they were released into general population.

From the infirmary, I was sent to the control center, where I was assigned to a cell in G-block, the newest block on the compound. G-block was built exactly like the cellblocks at Jackson, but it did have one benefit over the rest of the cells at Marquette.

All the other cellblocks were built decades earlier and were designed totally different. The cells in the other blocks were a lot smaller, too. They were so small, in fact, that if you happened to roll out of your bed during the night you might wind up landing in the toilet — that's how close the toilet was to the bed. The other big difference was that the cell doors were mounted on hinges that swung outward, instead of sliding.

We were allowed to exercise in the common yard, which wasn't much bigger than the size of a football field. Even though everything was crowded together, there was still enough room for a softball diamond, a full-size basketball court, a small putt-putt golf course and four handball courts.

In the yard, there was also a paved area in front of the laundry that was about the size of a basketball court. Inmates were allowed to set up several rows of folding card tables during each yard period. Gambling wasn't allowed; however, it was usually overlooked, so long as it didn't cause any problems. It was just another means of passing the time, but it was probably the most popular way of passing time for the majority of inmates. Even in the dead of winter when the temperature was well below zero, there were always a few guys who were willing to brave the freezing cold just to play a few hands of blackjack or poker.

Tokens were the monetary exchange used by all inmates to purchase store items. They were also the accepted currency at the gambling tables. The tokens were made of aluminum and were approximately the same size and denominations as free world coins. The largest denomination was a five dollar token, which was about the same size as a silver dollar. Unlike the rest of the tokens, though, the five dollar ones were red in color for easy identification. All the other tokens were just a plain aluminum-silvery white.

Marquette was relatively easy time compared to what I'd endured over the past nineteen months. At least I wasn't still locked in a cell twenty-three hours a day with nothing to do. When I went to classification, I asked for a yard crew assignment because it was one of the easiest jobs to get and you didn't have to wait several months to start. Not many guys wanted to work on the yard crew because you had to shovel a lot of snow in the winter. That didn't bother me, though. From my perspective, it was just good exercise. I'd rather be outside where I could get plenty of fresh air, move around and hang out all day if I wanted to.

During the summer, the yard crew job was a breeze. The winter was pretty grueling though. When winter arrived, it snowed almost every day and we had to shovel every inch by hand.

The prison was located only a few hundred feet from Lake Superior and consequently, it usually received the brunt of the lake effect snow squalls and storms that regularly blew in off the lake. It wasn't unusual for us to get one- or two-feet of snow several times a week. Whenever it snowed during the night, the guards would wake the inmates on the yard crew at four-thirty in the morning to have them shovel all the sidewalks before they started running the chow lines for breakfast, which was usually around six a.m.

There wasn't much to do on the yard during the winter months. But when the temperatures dropped below freezing, the inmates who worked for the recreation department would set up a full size hockey rink in the middle of the yard. The enclosure for the ice rink was prefabricated out of fiberglass panels that easily bolted together, so it only took the inmates a couple of hours to assemble the entire enclosure.

Once all the panels were in place, they packed snow around the bottom edge of the panels to hold the water in and they used the fire hose to fill the rink with about an inch of water. When that had frozen solid, they repeated the process until the ice was several inches thick.

Each block selected players for league teams and games were played on the weekends. But whenever the league teams weren't practicing or a scrub game wasn't being played, anyone could check out a pair of ice skates and use the rink during yard time.

For the most part, all the inmates did their own time. Everyone had their own means of hustling a few extra dollars to support themselves. The hobby-craft program was one of the few legitimate and constructive ways for an inmate to earn extra money, learn a skill and pass the time. Inmates were allowed to send their finished products to the hobby-craft stand, where they were sold to the public. The hobby-craft stand was located outside the prison on the main highway and accessible to tourists and vacationers — some of whom would pay top dollar for quality, handmade items. Some of the guys who were skilled at making leather craft items were earning several thousand dollars a year from the sale of leather goods at the hobby-craft stand.

But apparently, some tourists didn't give a crap about quality or even common sense. They where literally buying anything as a souvenir that came from inside the prison walls. One inmate was even successfully selling small bags of rocks that he picked up off the yard.

Prison rules allowed us to make and sell three different hobby-craft items at one time. At Jackson, I had participated in the hobby-craft program making string art and doing woodworking. This time, I decided I wanted to try something different, like leather craft and jewelry.

Making earrings, necklaces and key chains was easy and the items always sold well on the hobby-craft stand, but I was more interested in learning how to tool leather. My first leather projects were key fobs and belts, which didn't require a lot of tooling and also helped me to learn from my mistakes and gain some experience. I soon discovered that if I was going to learn how to tool the intricate patterns on larger items like handbags, it was going to take a lot of practice and even more patience.

The hobby-craft program wasn't paid for with state funds. Instead, the funding came from charging every inmate a five-percent surcharge on all hobby-craft supplies ordered from vendors. In addition, we were charged another five percent on each item that was sold at the hobby-craft stand.

After my appeal was heard and then denied by Michigan's Supreme Court, I refused to pay my incompetent appellant attorney another cent. Instead, I worked on my own appeal for several months and then I filed a delayed motion for appeal in the Lapeer County Circuit Court. It didn't take long for the circuit court to deny my motion, which I'd expected. Appeals are rarely granted in the lower courts unless the prosecuting attorney has agreed to a deal.

A week later, I filed the same motion except this time, in the next court up — the Court of Appeals. I hoped for the best but I was also prepared for the worst.

My Own Worst Enemy

It took the court several months to rule on my issues. When I finally received their decision, the ruling was both good and bad. I was pleasantly surprised to learn the court chose to vacate my armed robbery conviction under the double jeopardy rule. They had not, however, overturned my first-degree murder conviction.

I felt somewhat ambivalent towards the court's decision. I was pleased with myself, in that I'd accomplished more than my so-called professional attorney. But on the other hand, having the armed robbery conviction vacated was irrelevant due to the fact that I still had the first-degree murder conviction with a life sentence. Nevertheless, I refused to give up all hope. I knew there was a case pending before the state's Supreme Court that could possibly affect all first-degree felony murder convictions.

Under Michigan's felony murder rule as it was, if a death occurs during the commission of, or in attempt to commit certain felonies, all participants can be held equally culpable, including those that did no harm, had no weapon and didn't intend to hurt anyone. Intent does not have to be proved for anything besides the underlying felony. If, during the commission of a felony, death occurs from heart attack, accident or fright, it's still automatically considered first-degree murder. If convicted, the mandatory sentence was life in prison without the possibility of parole.

The issue before the state's highest court was whether the jury should have been allowed to consider malice and intent as an essential element of the crime, which the jury was previously not allowed to consider. In my particular case, there was never any malice or intent to harm or kill anyone. Nevertheless, under the old felony murder rule, the jury wasn't allowed to consider that fact during their deliberations. In fact, all the evidence at my trail indicated that the shooting was accidental and yet I was still found guilty of first-degree murder.

Since Marquette was such a long way for my family to drive, I only received one visit a year during the summer months when my mother took her annual vacation from work. She and my three sisters would rent a motor home and plan their vacation around visiting me and sightseeing in the Upper Peninsula. Almost every day for a week, one or more or all of them would visit me for two hours in the morning and return in the afternoon for another two hour visit. I really enjoyed spending a few hours with my family. Every visit was memorable. The time I got to spend with my mother was special and I cherished every moment of it.

The worst thing about Marquette truly was its location. It was just too far for my mother and sisters to visit me on a regular basis.

When it was chilly outside in the morning, the yard crew workers would often stand in front of the laundry where there was a steel grate in the sidewalk that covered a hot air exhaust vent from the dryers. One morning when I was standing on the grate trying to keep warm, I heard what sounded like a pane of glass breaking over by the garment factory, which was located on the second floor above the institutional maintenance department.

At first, I didn't pay any attention to it, thinking that someone had accidentally broken a window. But when I heard another pane of glass breaking, I immediately looked up at the windows in the garment factory and I could see a hole in one of the windows right across from where I was standing.

There was no one else on the yard who could've broken the window. I didn't think that anyone could have been on the other side of the laundry building either, because that area was off limits. Just in case, I decided to check anyway.

When I looked around the corner, I didn't see anyone but I did noticed that one of the windows was wide open. It wasn't unusual; the windows were often kept open to vent the heat. Nothing more seemed to be happening and so, I figured I'd forget about it and maybe hear something later.

Just as I turned to go back to the grate and warm up, I saw what looked like a piece of copper tubing pointing out the window in the direction of the garment factory and I could make out a person inside the window, holding the tubing. Suddenly, I heard a forceful whooshing sound, like the sudden release of high air pressure, and immediately afterwards the sound of another window breaking.

I stood there for a minute, watching the window to see if the same thing would happen again. Instead, I saw one of the laundry workers, a guy named Sean, cautiously stick his head out the window and look around to see if anyone had noticed what he was up to. I decided to holler up to him.

"What are you doing?" I asked, puzzled.

He shrugged his shoulders in return. "Nothing," he said back.

"Nothing?" I said with a laugh. "I've been standing here watching you, man."

"Oh," he said, lifting the copper tube up to show me. "I was just trying to see if this air-gun I made had enough air pressure to shoot something that far."

I was curious about his air gun and I wanted to see how it was made, so I asked him to open the front door and let me in. As it turned out, Sean's so-called air gun was nothing more than a piece of copper tubing attached to the high-pressure airline. It functioned on the same principle as a pneumatic nail gun.

The projectiles he was using were like homemade darts. He'd made them from wire coat hangers cut into pieces about three inches long. One end of the wire was bent to form a small loop, through which he'd tied a strip of cloth to give the dart stability in flight. The other end, the tip, was blunt.

He demonstrated how it worked by placing one of the projectiles inside the copper tube and pointing it at the plywood cabinet door across the room from us. Sean pushed the lever that released the air pressure and with a whooshing sound, the projectile shot across the room, hitting the cabinet door with a loud thump. Sean opened up the cabinet door, grinning.

"Come here and check this out," he said to me.

More than an inch of the wire projectile had completely pierced and traveled through the half-inch thick plywood.

"Wow, that's a lot of force," I said.

"Hell yeah it is!" he said. "Imagine gettin' shot by one of these; it hurts like a bitch and I know that for a fact because one of the guys in here accidentally shot me in the leg with it."

As if he were a proud veteran showing off an old war wound, Sean dropped his pants and revealed the huge black and blue mark that practically covered his entire inner thigh.

"You guys are crazy," I told him. "You shouldn't be messin' around with something like that. At least be careful, dude — that thing could seriously hurt someone, probably even kill 'em."

All things considered, Marquette wasn't as bad as I'd first imagined. It was still a maximum-security prison, though, and bad things could happen to anyone at any time if they weren't careful. But typically, if an inmate just minded his own business and did his own time, he could usually stay out of serious trouble.

In some ways, Marquette was actually better than the other state prisons. We were allowed to order items like bed sheets, pillowcases, pillows and small area rugs, which the other prisons didn't allow. We also had cable television, which wasn't available at any of the other prisons. And for those who wanted a little extra back support while sleeping, they could even purchase a bed-board from the carpenter shop for three dollars.

The food was decent at Marquette, definitely much better than the food at Jackson. Not once did I find a cockroach in my food. The inmate store offered a wide variety of food items from canned goods to prepackaged cold cuts and occasionally fresh fruit like apples, bananas and grapes. If the store didn't stock a particular item that an inmate wanted to buy, whether it was a grocery item or a toiletry, as long as it wasn't a security threat the store manager would order it. The only stipulation was that you had to purchase the whole case.

In addition to the main store, there was also a small yard store that was operated by one of the inmate store workers. The yard store was open seven days a week whenever the yard was open. Everyone called it the pop-stand, but we could purchase a variety of items. Pints of ice cream, chips and candy bars, coffee and tobacco products were all sold at the pop-stand.

In 1980, some of Michigan's prisons experienced rioting and Marquette just happened to be one of them. About a week before the rioting occurred, almost the entire prison inmate population of Marquette united to make a statement of passive resistance by boycotting the chow hall for one day. The prison administration chose to ignore the incident, believing that the inmates could never put aside their petty bickering long enough to unite and become a serious threat to their omnipotent authority.

For the next week, there was a lot of talk amongst the inmates about a riot, but no one seemed to know exactly when it was supposed to take place. Then, one evening about a half-hour after they released the blocks for night yard, a fight broke out on the basketball court between two black inmates and that was the beginning of the riot.

Initially, the guards managed to separate the two inmates. Both men refused to let the guards handcuff them, though, until several more guards arrived and wrestled the inmates to the ground, forcing them to submit. In the process, one or two of the guards used excessive force, punching and kicking one of the inmates.

A crowd of about fifty inmates had been standing around watching a basketball game being played on the court when the fight broke out. They watched peacefully as the guards wrestled the inmates to the ground. But when the fifty or more men watched the guards blatantly abuse their fellow inmates, well, call it the *proverbial straw* that broke the camel's back.

"Hell no! It ain't goin' down like that!" yelled someone in the crowd, and just like a switch had been flipped on, all hell broke loose. Several inmates stepped out of the crowd and began punching and kicking the guards until they were lying on the ground. Within a matter of minutes, the guards were completely overwhelmed and powerless to defend themselves against the angry mob of maximum-security prisoners. The guards were entirely at the mercy of their assailants, and they were taking a thorough ass whipping.

As more guards responded, they soon realized that they were seriously outnumbered and that the situation had escalated beyond their control. The control center announced over the PA system that all employee personnel were ordered to clear the compound and report to the control center immediately. For those unfortunate guards who had to cross the yard in order to reach the control center, it was a bad day — they were forced to run the gauntlet of irate inmates and as parting gifts, the guards received a few extra licks for their trouble.

The emergency count siren was immediately activated, but it was totally ignored by all the inmates on the yard. No one on the yard had any intentions of locking up, at least not until they'd vented their pent-up frustrations. The guards in the gun towers began firing tear gas canisters into the compound, but it was no matter. The inmates simply moved to another part of the yard and began ransacking the other buildings, pillaging whatever they'd previously been denied.

When the guards realized that the tear gas wasn't having the desired effect, they began firing warning shots into the brick walls of the cellblocks and the other buildings on the compound. You could hear the distinct sound of bullets ricocheting off the brick and stone buildings and you could see where the bullets had gouged craters in the walls, sending fragments flying in every direction.

Still, the inmates weren't the least bit intimidated or dissuaded — everyone was caught up in the excitement of the moment. Surprisingly, only one inmate was superficially wounded in the leg by a ricocheting bullet, but even that didn't stop him. When asked about it later, he said he was having too much fun to let a little thing like a gunshot wound slow him down.

Once the guards had totally abandoned the inside of the prison compound, the inmates took complete control and began directing their anger and frustration at the prison itself, setting fires and destroying everything they could get their hands on. A group of inmates had broken down the door of the inmate yard store and men were carrying out cases of cigarettes, candy bars, Pepsi and whatever else they could get their hands on. Within a matter of minutes, there was store merchandise strewn all over the yard.

Someone started a fire in the institutional maintenance building and dense black smoke began pouring out through the windows. There was another fire burning in the lower level of the carpenter shop too, and that one was rapidly spreading to the upper floor — probably due to all the flammable materials like paints and solvents that were stored in there.

Several guys broke down the doors to the central store area in the basement, located underneath the laundry and the kitchen. The butcher shop, inmate store, quartermaster and hobby-craft were all located in this same area. The inmates were taking whatever they wanted and destroying everything else. Someone tried to start a fire, but the sprinkler system was activated and the fire was quickly suppressed. When it comes to wreaking havoc on a place, though, water damage from sprinklers is just as effective as any fire can be.

The water damaged all the food in the stores and other goods that were warehoused in the basement.

Many inmates began arming themselves too, grabbing pieces of pipe, steel bars, baseball bats and even large butcher knives from the butcher shop to wield.

Surprisingly, inmates didn't turn on each other like so often happens in riots. There were very few incidents of inmates assaulting other inmates, although one guy did claim he'd been assaulted and raped by several other inmates.

When the guards were ordered to report to the control center, they abandoned all the housing units without securing the block doors, allowing some of the inmates from the yard to re-enter the blocks. Several inmates were running up and down the galleries, passing out store goods to everyone. Another group of inmates were trying to open the cell doors of those who were still locked in their cells. But thanks to CNN News, which was broadcasting live pictures of the rioting while it was happening, even the guys locked in their cells had a front row seat to watch everything taking place. The news program was showing pictures of the burning buildings and they reported that the inmates at the North Side Complex in Jackson were rioting as well.

The counselor's office in G-block had been constructed out of two-by-fours and plasterboard, but that office had been completely destroyed. Pieces of plasterboard and two-by-fours were scattered everywhere on base and the inmate files that were kept in the counselor's office were strewn from one end of the block to the other — it looked as if a tornado had passed through the block.

The rioting went on unchecked for several hours, until the prison officials were finally able to muster enough prison guards and police to regain control of the prison. Dressed in full riot gear and armed with shotguns, they re-entered the prison through the control center and the sally port. Forming a line of skirmish, they began herding groups of inmates into the cellblocks and forcing as many inmates as possible into each cell, securing the cell doors behind them.

Once the yard was cleared and all the inmates were secured in cells, the prison officials allowed the fire department to enter the compound to extinguish the fires. But the building that housed the carpenter shop and the metal shop was a total loss. They managed to extinguish the fire in the maintenance building, but not before the fire had gutted the lower level. The upper level that housed the garment factory was untouched by the fire, but there was some damage from the rioting inmates.

It wasn't until later in the evening when things had calmed down, that several squads of guards still dressed in their riot gear began sorting out the inmates they'd earlier herded into cells. Inmates were removed from the cells one at a time, strip searched and then escorted back to their assigned cells.

There was still a great deal of unrest throughout the prison over the next few days following the riot. Inmates continued to start small fires by throwing burning rags and paper from their cells. They also continued to break as many windows as they could by throwing D-batteries and glass coffee jars from their cells. There was so much glass being thrown from the galleries that the guards didn't even bother to make their rounds for count.

For the next two weeks, we were given nothing but cold sandwiches to eat twice a day. No clean laundry, no showers, nothing — virtually everything was suspended. My substitute for a shower consisted of standing buck-naked over the toilet and pouring glasses of water over my head. I washed myself with a soapy washcloth, and I rinsed the soap off by pouring glasses of water over my head and body.

Three weeks passed before we were finally allowed to come out of our cells. We weren't allowed to come out of them, however, wearing or carrying anything except a bar of soap. Each one of us had to be completely naked for our brief trip to the shower.

Male and female guards were posted on the galleries and stairwells. For those unlucky guys who had cells on the front side of the block, it was a long walk to the showers in their birthday suits.

When we arrived at the showers, we were given a towel and a washcloth and told that we had five minutes to shower. When that five minutes was up, they turned off the water and it didn't matter if you were still soapy — you either came out or they came in after you.

When the kitchen was finally repaired, we were given one hot meal per day and several inmate workers were hired to run the kitchen. Not everyone was eligible for the assignment, though. The prison decided that only those inmates who weren't involved in the rioting could have the kitchen assignments.

The same week the kitchen reopened, the inmate store also went to each block selling a limited number of essential items. Soap, toothpaste, coffee and tobacco were on the cart.

After two more weeks, the administration finally decided to gradually reopen the prison and we were finally allowed to eat all three meals in the chow hall once again. A week later, we were given one hour of yard a day and the administration began reclassifying inmate workers to fill all the routine job assignments.

Instead of going back to work on the yard crew, I requested and received a job assignment working in the inmate store. The main store had gone through several changes because of the rioting, though. It was moved from its previous location in the basement to the same small building where the yard store was located. A wall separated the two stores but the building was so small that I had to restock the main store twice a day for each yard period. It was a real pain in the ass to say the least.

Moving the main store out of the basement was just one of several changes the administration made. Another change was that the inmate store would no longer sell any products which were packaged in glass containers, a decision that came from the fact that inmates used glass containers during the riot to break windows and assault guards.

The sale of Right Guard deodorant was also discontinued because of its alcohol content. Apparently, some of the guys had been purchasing the deodorant solely to extract the alcohol and become intoxicated. The extraction process was simple enough — several sticks of deodorant were placed in a sock, which acted as a filter, and then the alcohol was squeezed out. To lessen the terrible taste, the alcohol would then be mixed with Kool-Aid. Believe it or not, guys actually drank the foul tasting concoction just to get a buzz.

A new chain-link fence was also erected. It extended from the corner of the garment factory building all the way over to the chow hall. The new fence prevented inmates from having free access to other buildings on the compound. This also meant there was no more hockey rink or ice-skating and the putt-putt golf course was history as well. The area in front of the laundry that was previously used for the card tables was now on the other side of the fence, no longer a part of the main yard, so there were no more card tables or gambling either.

My detail as a store worker allowed me to be out of my cell from six in the morning until four o'clock in the afternoon, seven days a week. The main store, though, was only open for an hour during the morning yard period and another hour in the afternoon, leaving me with a lot of free time.

To pass the time, I'd help the central store supervisor fill the requisitions for the daily kitchen supplies first thing every morning. Once a week, we would also fill the requisitions for the block supplies.

In the afternoons, when I wasn't working in the store, I'd fill in as the central store's clerk, typing and filing the daily receiving reports. Occasionally, I'd also help unload the truck that delivered supplies.

There was one truck that no one ever looked forward to unloading — the meat truck. It was a backbreaking and dirty job.

Once a month, the butcher shop would receive a truckload of butchered beef and pork. The sides of meat weighed anywhere from one hundred and fifty to three hundred pounds. We had to carry each side slung over our shoulder and walk down a fifty-foot ramp to an overhead track, where the sides of meat were hung on meat hooks and then pushed inside the butcher shop. It was one of those jobs that made your muscles ache the next day. But the guys who did help unload the truck were always compensated for their hard work by the butcher shop supervisor, who would provide them with a special meal of steak and ribs.

Since the butcher shop was located downstairs next to the central store, I soon became good friends with the lead inmate butcher. Ironically, the guy's name just happened to be Butch. Every now and again when there was nothing to do at work, Butch and I would engage in long, drawn-out wrestling bouts, rolling around on the concrete floor for thirty minutes or more. The guards knew that we never lost our tempers, so they never tried to intervene. They just sat there, laughing at the punishment we inflicted upon each other.

Butch and I were pretty evenly matched in size, strength and endurance, but whenever Butch started to get the best of me, I'd unabashedly grab him by his testicles and squeeze just hard enough to force him into submission. At that point, he usually resorted to threatening me with all sorts of dire consequences if I didn't let go. But I knew he wasn't serious, and eventually he always gave up.

One afternoon, I was typing receiving reports when Butch came over to the guard's station and began talking to a guard. He was leaning on the desk with both arms stretched out and the palms of his hands placed flat on the desk.

A few minutes earlier, I'd grabbed the stapler sitting on the desk to staple a couple papers together, but it was empty. Knowing this and wanting to see what Butch's reaction would be, I walked over to the desk, picked up the stapler, placed it on the back of Butch's hand and without hesitation, I hit the stapler as if to drive a staple into the back of his hand.

And much to my surprise, it did.

Someone had refilled the stapler.

I could feel my face flush with heat and my stomach drop as I realized what I had done and wondered what would happen next. My eyes were glued to the staple, which was deeply embedded in the back of Butch's hand. In shock, I didn't say a word.

Butch looked down at the staple in his hand and then looked the guard in the eye.

"Did you see what he just did?" Butch said in a calm, nonchalant manner as he casually gripped the staple's edge with fingers from his other hand. He pulled the staple right out of his hand and kept on talking to the guard as if he didn't feel a thing.

Butch was one of those rare individuals who possessed a great deal of patience and tolerance. I don't recall ever seeing him lose control of his temper. He never seemed to get angry, he just did whatever he had to do without showing any emotion.

One of the guys who worked with Butch in the butcher shop was always trying to give him a hard time, usually in a taunting but playful way. Butch warned the guy several times to stop playing with him or there'd be consequences. The guy didn't heed Butch's warnings and day after day, they continued on in the same manner — the guy taunting Butch and Butch calmly warning the guy to stop.

Butch was working at boning a side of beef one day when this guy started running his mouth again. Without saying a word, Butch casually reached over with the boning knife and sliced the guy's finger almost completely off his hand.

Shocked at the sight of his finger dangling from his hand, the guy ran out of the butcher shop.

"I warned him," Butch said, shrugging his shoulders carelessly as he told me the story.

The incident could've gotten Butch in big trouble, but the guy was probably so terrified that he feared what would happen to him if he snitched. So, lucky for Butch, the guy told the guards he'd gotten careless and accidentally cut himself.

The two continued to work together in the butcher shop after that. The guy never taunted Butch again, though. He'd learned a valuable lesson about pushing people too far, and undoubtedly acquired a new respect for Butch too.

When the inmate who operated the yard store was transferred to a lower security level, I was asked if I wanted the position. I already knew everything about the job, since I'd been working with the yard store clerk on the weekends for the past several months. The position didn't pay any more than my current job and it was definitely a lot more work and responsibility, but I took the job for the extra benefits.

My new detail allowed me to be out of my cell from six in the morning until nine o'clock at night, seven days a week. I was usually one of the first inmates out of the block every morning and often the last inmate to return in the evening.

Besides running the store, I was responsible for picking up the Sunday newspapers from the front gate and delivering them to those inmates who had paid in advance.

The store clerk assignment was one of the best jobs to have. Not only was I able to come and go as I pleased, but I was practically my own boss. As long as I did my job, no one ever bothered me. One of the perks of the job was that whenever there was any outdated, damaged or discontinued merchandise, my supervisor would tell me to sell the items for half price and keep the money.

Just after I arrived at work early one morning, the guard working the central store told me I needed to report back to my block. When I got to the control center, the guard there said I had received a telephone call from my sister regarding a family emergency and that I needed to call home immediately. Naturally, I automatically assumed the worst. I knew that it had to be something serious or my sister wouldn't have called the prison. I went straight to the telephone and dialed my sister's number.

"Mom's okay, but she had an accident at work," my sister said as soon as she picked up the phone.

"What happened?" I asked.

"She was working on a stamping press when the machine malfunctioned. It caught her arm inside the press," she said. "They rushed her to the hospital, but her arm just couldn't be saved. It was mangled too badly and the doctors had no choice but to amputate her arm just below the elbow."

"Jesus," I said in disbelief. "Which arm?"

"Her right one," my sister said. "It gets worse; her heart stopped on the operating table. She'd just lost too much blood, the doctors said, but they were able to bring her back to life."

"What?" I said. "But you said she's okay?"

"Yeah, I mean, she's supposed to be," she told me. "She's still in serious condition, but she's stable now."

I was totally devastated by what my sister had just told me. I was trying to hide the fact that I was crying. Mom meant more to me than anything — she was my lifeline. Without her love, moral support and guidance, I sincerely believed I wouldn't be strong enough to survive in prison. My sister assured me that mom was going to be okay, though, and that I shouldn't worry.

"I've just been home for a little while to change my clothes and wash up. I'm headed back there in a bit, you know, to make sure Mom's got everything she needs," she said. "I just wanted to call you right away and let you know."

I called my sister again later that evening and she told me that Mom was doing a lot better.

"When I got there, she was sitting up in bed, waiting for someone to help her apply her make-up and fix her hair," my sister said.

I laughed a little — that sounded exactly like the mom I knew. My mother had always been very meticulous and fastidious about her appearance.

When my sister talked to the doctor who performed the surgery, he told her that mom was out of danger and the prognosis for her recovery was excellent. I asked my sister for the telephone number of the hospital and I asked her to tell mom that I'd try to call her the following day.

Inmates weren't allowed to make direct telephone calls and the hospital wouldn't accept a collect call. Since it was a family emergency, though, my counselor called the hospital from his office and allowed me to speak with my mother.

When I heard my mother's voice, I felt a surge of emotions and my eyes welled up with tears. I felt profoundly sorry for my mother and at that moment, I'd have given anything to have held her in my arms and comforted her. But the only thing that I could do was to tell her how very much I loved and needed her, so I did. If it would've been possible, I'd have gladly given both my arms to have spared my mother from the pain and suffering she was going through.

"How'd it happen, Mom?" I asked her. "Do you remember?"

"The foreman assigned me to operate this press that everyone knew wasn't working right," she said. "I even told him about it, said I didn't want to work on that machine because of it, but he said, 'The job still needs to be done' and walked away."

My Mom said that when she turned the machine on and placed a part inside, the press suddenly activated by itself, before she pushed the start button and before she could even pull her arm out of the press. The machine came down on her arm twice, crushing it, before she even realized what happened.

"One of the guys nearby saw what happened and ran over to help me," she said. "He pushed the emergency stop button and helped me get my arm out."

Clearly, the foreman had been negligent. He'd acted in an inappropriate and irresponsible manner when he insisted that an employee operate a machine that was known to be defective.

The company had also been negligent by not installing the proper safety devices that would have prevented an accident like this from ever happening in the first place. It was later discovered that the electrical switch on the press was defective and that was what caused the press to malfunction.

My sister retained a personal injury attorney to represent my mother in a lawsuit against the company she worked for, as well as against the company that manufactured the defective electrical switch. There was no doubt that my mother would win the lawsuit.

The attorney assured my mother that she'd receive a large enough settlement to ensure that she'd never need to work again. It took more than a year of negotiating with both companies before they finally decided that it was in their own best interest to settle with my mother out of court. She eventually received a monetary settlement that allowed her to retire comfortably, but no amount of money can truly compensate my mother for the loss of her arm or the pain and suffering she was forced to endure because of it.

She underwent physical therapy and psychological counseling for more than a year, which helped to a certain degree. But she still experienced phantom pain in her right arm and was haunted by vivid, horrible nightmares of her accident for many years.

A few months after my mother's accident, The Michigan Supreme Court finally handed down the ruling that I'd long been anticipating. The constitutionality of the old felony murder law was being reviewed and the state's high court ruled that the law was indeed unconstitutional. The new ruling was dubbed the "Aaron Ruling."

The court changed the interpretation of the law and also ruled that in all future felony murder trials, the jury must be instructed as to malice and intent. First-degree murder could no longer be imputed from the underlying felony. It must be proven that a person committed the crime with malice, intent to kill, or to do great bodily harm.

This was good; however, the court chose not to resolve any erroneous felony murder convictions that happened prior to November 25, 1980. By the provisions of the Aaron Ruling, the authority to resolve erroneous felony murder convictions was given to the state's governor, who could execute commutations, or to the legislative branch of the state's government, which could pass a house bill to overturn the erroneous convictions.

I couldn't understand how the court could rule that a law was unconstitutional but then stipulate that their ruling wasn't retroactive — it didn't make any sense to me. If the law was found to be unconstitutional, how could it have been constitutional two years earlier, or for that matter, ten years earlier?

The mere fact that no one had challenged the constitutionality of the felony murder law before this time didn't make it constitutional. As far as I knew, the constitution had not been changed. What about fair and equitable justice? If I were to be tried today for this very same crime I couldn't be convicted of first-degree murder due to the fact that all the evidence at my trial indicated that the shooting of the victim was accidental.

It was quite evident to many people that the court was more concerned with the politics of their ruling rather than the concept of fair and equal justice. To apply their ruling retroactively would have meant that a number of highly publicized convictions might have been overturned. Their judicial ruling was nothing more than a matter of self-serving politics.

The history of the felony murder doctrine dates back to England in the 1630s. Pennsylvania adopted England's felony doctrine in the eighteenth century and the State of Michigan adopted Pennsylvania's felony doctrine word-for-word in 1937. Michigan, however, doesn't have a legal statute for felony murder. In 1957, England abolished its felony murder doctrine, which many have called barbaric.

The felony murder rule states that any death that occurs during the commission or attempt to commit certain felonies, including arson, burglary, kidnapping and others, is first-degree murder and all participants in the felony can be held equally culpable, including those that did no harm, had no weapon and didn't intend to hurt anyone. Intent doesn't have to be proved for anything besides the underlying felony. Even if the death occurs from fright or a heart attack, it's still first-degree murder so long as the person keels over dead during the commission of a felony. In reality, felony murder is merely used to enhance punishment as well as raise second-degree murder charges to first-degree murder.

The problem with the felony murder rule is that it operates as a matter of law once the intent to commit a felony, such as burglary, has been established. The prosecution is then relieved of its burden to prove intent to kill, which is otherwise and should always be a necessary element to prosecuting murder. The intention to burglarize someone's home does not prove there was intention to kill, nor does intention to commit armed robbery equal intention to kill. The bottom line is, the intention to commit a felony just doesn't equal intention to kill. Additionally, the intention to commit a felony, like burglary or robbery, by itself is not sufficient to establish a charge of murder.

Aside from just being plain wrong, the felony murder rule is unconstitutional because in some cases, it violates the Eighth Amendment regarding cruel and unusual punishment. The punishment — a mandatory life sentence — is grossly disproportionate to the crimes actually committed, considering the death occurred as an accident or other anomaly.

The law also violates the Fourteenth Amendment, which guarantees a right to due process, because no defense is allowed on the charge of first-degree murder. The person is only allowed to defend him or herself against the underlying felony.

The rule of felony murder can be and is currently being used by prosecutors to greatly influence disproportionate sentencing. The purpose of creating varying degrees of murder charges is to punish intentional killing more severely than accidental killing. Is it right that an unplanned, unintentional or accidental death be treated the same as a premeditated, cold-blooded murder?

A few years after the Michigan Supreme Court's ruling, a number of state representatives introduced legislation that was aptly called the Felony Murder Bill. The proposed house bill would have allowed for those individuals who were convicted of felony murder before November 25, 1980, to file a right of appeal in The Michigan Court of Appeals. The following is the actual bill as it was proposed:

A bill to amend 1927 PA 175, entitled "The code of criminal procedure" (MCL 760.1 to 777,69) By adding section 13 to chapter X.
THE PEOPLE OF THE STATE ENACT: CHAPTER X
Sec. 13.

(1) An individual convicted of first-degree murder in violation of Section 316 of the Michigan penal code, 1931 PA 328, MCL 750.316, has a right to appeal that conviction to the court of appeals, regardless of any appeal taken or not taken, if the individual meets all the following conditions, as applicable.

>(a) The individual was convicted before November 25, 1980 of murder committed in the perpetration of, or attempt to perpetrate, arson, rape, criminal sexual conduct in the first-degree, robbery, burglary, breaking and entering of a dwelling, larceny of any kind, extortion or kidnapping.

>(b) The individual's intent to kill, intention to do great bodily harm, or wanton and willful disregard of the likelihood that the natural tendency of the individual's behavior was to cause death or great bodily harm wasn't submitted to the jury or considered by the judge sitting as trier of fact.

>(c) If the individual was convicted of murder as described in subdivision (a) by aiding and abetting, the individual's knowledge of the principle's intention to kill, intention to do great bodily harm, or wanton and willful disregard of the likelihood that the natural tendency of the principle's behavior was to cause death or great bodily harm wasn't submitted to the jury or considered by the judge sitting as trier of fact.

(2) If the court of appeals determines that the individual meets all applicable conditions described in subsection (1), the court shall vacate the individual's first-degree murder conviction and remand the case to the trial court. The trial court shall enter a conviction of second degree murder or a lesser included offense based on the transcript and other evidence in the record, conduct a sentencing hearing, and sentence the individual on the conviction. The sentencing hearing shall comply with all current sentencing statutes, court rules, and case law.

(3) An individual sentenced under subsection (2) shall receive credit for time served on the vacated first-degree murder conviction.

(4) The Court of Appeals shall determine an appeal under this section within 270 days after the appeal is filed.

Enacting section 1. The section added by this amendatory act applies only to those persons convicted of first-degree murder before the Michigan Supreme Court's decision in people v Aaron. 409 Mich 672; 299 NW2d 304 (1980).

In the past, adjectives like fair and equitable haven't been a priority of the politicians in Michigan, especially when it comes to criminal justice. Understandably, in today's political climate, no politician wants to be perceived as being soft on crime. And certainly the news media doesn't help matters by endlessly nurturing the public's fears.

Without a doubt, people who commit despicable acts against others deserve to be dealt with severely. However, that severity should always be balanced by a sense of fairness, for there can be no justice when laws are absolute.

Consequently, men and women who were erroneously convicted under a law that was ruled unconstitutional by the Michigan Supreme Court in 1980 are still sitting in Michigan's prisons waiting for fair and equitable justice. We're waiting for the politicians to do the right thing and hoping they'll do it before we all die of old age.

A year after the riots, no positive changes had been initiated to improve prison living conditions inside Marquette. In fact, we'd lost a number of privileges. But in prison, you survive by learning to adapt to the same old monotonous routine day after day.

Time seems to pass ever so slowly — the days seem like weeks and weeks seem like months. The only noticeable change, other than the weather outside, is the face that stares back at you from the mirror, now with a tinge of gray and those little, indelible lines etched into aging skin.

Whenever an inmate threatened a guard or got out of hand, the guards usually called the goon squad — a group of the prison's three or four biggest guards — to deal with the inmate. If the goon squad visited the block, everyone knew that someone would be going to the hole. The squad never left empty-handed.

If a guy tried to resist, they'd simply wrestle him to the floor, place him in handcuffs, throw his butt in a laundry cart which we all jokingly called the Cadillac, and push him over to segregation.

If you were unfortunate enough to lock on first or second gallery and they had to come and get you, there was always a chance that you might be taking the express elevator directly into the Cadillac waiting on base. The express elevator being, of course, a free fall courtesy of the guards. If that sounds bad, the alternative wasn't much better, especially if you'd managed to really piss off the guards. They'd handcuff your hands behind your back, grab your feet and drag you down the steel stairs, bouncing your head off every step.

Another method they used to transport unruly inmates was a two-wheel pushcart with leather restraining straps attached to both sides. The straps were used to immobilize the inmate's hands and legs and once he was securely strapped to the pushcart, the guards would wheel him to segregation or to the infirmary just as if they were moving a piece of furniture around.

In October of 1982, the counselor called me to his office to inform me that my father had passed away and that I needed to call home as soon as possible. The counselor always behaved genuinely sympathetic, which I found surprising because most people working in the prison system are not.

"You can attend your father's funeral," he told me, followed by a heavy sigh. "But it'll cost thirteen hundred dollars. That's what they charge for having two guards escort you and for the transportation cost."

At that time, I didn't have that much money in my inmate account. When I left his office, I went directly to the telephone and called home.

When my mother answered the telephone, I could tell from the sound of her voice that she'd been crying, which in turn made me start crying.

"Don't cry Jim, please," she said. "If you cry, I'll start crying again and then I won't be able to say a word."

She told me that my eldest sister, Jenna, had found my father lying on the bathroom floor early that morning. Jenna immediately called for an ambulance but it was too late; my father had died sometime earlier in the morning. When the paramedics arrived, there was nothing they could do for him. They told my sister that my father had most likely suffered a massive heart attack and died instantly.

I told my mother what the counselor said about me attending the funeral and I asked her to send one thousand three hundred dollars by Western Union as soon as possible. Both of us were grief stricken and having a hard time holding back the tears. I knew there wasn't much that I could say to lessen the profound psychological pain and sorrow that we were feeling, so I told her that I'd call her back later on.

I went back to work thinking that if I kept busy, I'd be able to suppress my grief. But all that day I felt like there was a ponderous, invisible weight pressing down on me. Later that evening, when I was alone in my cell, I was overwhelmed by the insuperable psychological pain and I finally broke down and cried like a baby. As I laid there on my bunk absorbed in my grief, I suddenly realized what the family of Alex Blake must've gone through after losing their son.

Before my father died, I'd really had no firsthand experience at losing a loved one. I had no idea, no way to truly understand how the death of a loved one could be so excruciatingly painful. I realized this, as I laid there crying, and became overwhelmed with guilt and sadness on top of the other emotions I was feeling. I was so profoundly ashamed of myself for being responsible for other people having to feel the way I felt about my Dad. I felt so wretched that all I wanted to do was curl up on the floor in the corner of my cell and die.

I began to think about the relationship that I had with my father when I was growing up. My father was a strict Southern Baptist who believed in preaching fire-and-brimstone sermons. He fervidly believed in the proverb, "spare the rod and spoil the child."

I loved my father dearly, but I could never understand his inexplicable inclination to discipline me by inflicting physical pain upon my person. Whenever I did something wrong, I usually received a spanking, which was a lot more like a beating. I was punished often, even for the most trivial offenses such as leaving the yard without his permission.

My father never hit me with his hand. Whenever he gave me a spanking, he always used his thick, leather belt or a freshly cut hickory switch — both were extremely painful. During the spanking, my father would grasp me tightly by my wrist to prevent me from sitting down or running away.

With each painful lash, he'd ask me angrily, "Are you going to do that again?"

I found it extremely difficult to answer him, my mind so focused on the intense pain of the stinging lashes. I'd be crying and screaming at the top of my lungs, but I had to force myself to answer him. If I didn't answer, he'd continue beating me until I could barely move.

"No Daddy," I'd cry out through my screams and sobs. "I won't do it again, I promise!"

I remember begging him to stop, telling him it hurt and promising I'd never commit whatever offense it was that landed me in that terrible position again.

"Please stop, Daddy!" I remember crying out. But my pleas always fell on deaf ears. Only when he'd satisfied his anger and fully spent his wrath would he finally stop beating me.

There were times when I'd look him directly in the eye and tell him that I hated him. I wanted to hurt him like he hurt me. The truth, though, was that I didn't hate him at all. He was my father and one of the most important people in my small world. I suppose that by telling him I hated him, I was really hoping he'd realize how much he was hurting me, not just physically but psychologically as well.

After each whipping I'd have numerous painful welts on my legs and buttocks for several days. Occasionally, the whippings were so severe that the welts would actually bleed. There were also a number of times when I cried so hard that I lost my breath, almost passing out from oxygen deprivation. I'd be gasping for air, but it was like my lungs had collapsed. The pain in my chest was even worse than the spanking itself. It felt like there was a knife in my chest and in those moments, I seriously believed I was going to die from suffocation.

My father often told me that he loved me and I had no doubt that he truly did. In my mind, though, if you love someone you do not intentionally inflict pain upon that person. As a child, I could never understand this paradox. No doubt all those spankings left a few scares on my psyche and probably contributed to my inappropriate, irrational and irresponsible behavior as a young adult.

One time, after my father had given me a spanking, I was reading aloud to myself and he, apparently still angry with me, accused me of talking back to him.

"No sir, I was just reading out loud to myself. I was trying to be quiet," I said softly.

"You're too stupid to read," he told me scornfully. "And if you don't stop mumbling, I'll give you another spanking."

I closed the book. I didn't know what else to do.

There were many times like that. In retrospect, I can see my father was being insensitive and even acting irresponsibly.

I remember breaking something one time, though I can't remember what it was that I broke, but it belonged to my father.

He got very upset about it and angrily said, "I can't have anything because of you damn kids."

I've never forgotten those words and I've always wondered exactly what he meant. I've drawn a variety of conclusions, of course, but none of which make me feel good.

I wouldn't necessarily say he was a bad parent. In fact, I believe his goal was to be a good parent. He just had a tendency to speak his mind without giving careful consideration to what he was actually saying and how it might affect his children.

At that time, I had no way of knowing the significance or the impact that his callous statements would have on my life. I was raised to think of my parents as if they were Gods, all-knowing and all-powerful. And as a child raised in such a manner, I wanted nothing more than to please my parents and accepted everything they said to me. When my father told me I was stupid, then, I accepted his statement as the gospel truth. From that point on in my life, I felt there was no need for me to apply myself in school or put forth an effort to succeed at anything academic or otherwise.

I know that my father often felt frustrated, stuck in a dead-end job that he never really cared for and working paycheck to paycheck. He was a blue-collar worker at a nearby automobile factory, trying to support his wife and children on the meager paycheck. It was a lot of responsibility and I imagine that it weighed heavily on his mind. In fact, I imagine it had a lot to do with how much anger and frustration got vented on us kids — especially me, being the only boy.

My father never talked much about his childhood, but I know that he was raised by his stepmother. From what little my mother told my sisters and I, his childhood wasn't a very happy or carefree experience.

When I was a child, I was never allowed to play with any of the neighborhood kids or visit their house unless their parents attended church and practiced the same Christian dogma as my father. Consequently, my social skills didn't develop as well as a normal kid's. When I finally was old enough to choose my own friends, I made poor choices and really didn't know any better. I just wanted to be accepted as one of the guys and have friends. My mistake was, I was not very selective.

Without a doubt, the character of some of the individuals I chose to hang around with should have raised flags. Very few of the so-called friends I selected possessed any esteemed attributes like morals, scruples or integrity.

I hold no malice in my heart or my mind toward my father. In fact, I still love him dearly to this very day and I always will. I often think of him and I miss him.

It took me many years to realize that my father did the best he could with what he had. I've learned to move beyond the moment. I no longer live in the past, which is dead and gone and cannot be changed. Nor do I live in the dreams of the future, which is not yet born. Each day I make a conscious effort to live in the present moment, my real life, instead of imaginary problems and worries.

The day after I spoke with my mother, I was notified that thirteen hundred dollars had been deposited into my account. I went to see the counselor about arranging for a trip to my father's funeral, but the news wasn't good. The warden wouldn't allow me to attend my father's funeral after all.

I was never given an explanation, but I suspect it had a lot to do with my past history of escape. I was probably considered too high of a security risk for such a trip.

Later that day, I spoke with my mother on the telephone and explained to her that my request to attend the funeral had been denied by the warden. Since I wouldn't be there for the funeral, I asked her to have one of my sister's take a few pictures and to keep them for me just in case I ever got out of prison and wanted to see them.

"We can send them to you, Jim," she offered.

"No, I don't want to see them while I'm in here," I told her. "I just don't think it would be good."

What I didn't tell her was that I didn't want to see the pictures in prison because I already had too many painful memories in my mind. I had no desire to be haunted by the image of my father lying in a casket on top of it all.

My mother told me that my father didn't have any life insurance, savings or any other assets that would help cover the cost of his funeral and burial.

"I am not about to let your father be cremated or buried in a pauper's grave," she said staunchly. "He was a good Christian man and he'll have a decent and proper Christian burial."

I knew my mother didn't have much to pay for his funeral. I'd managed to save a little more than two thousand dollars for an attorney and offered to put it toward his funeral expenses.

"You really don't have to do that, Jim," she assured me. "I'll figure it out somehow."

I really wanted to, though. Sitting behind prison walls doesn't allow for many opportunities to help the people you love. After I explained to her why I felt it was my obligation to do what I could, she graciously accepted my offer.

My father had worked for General Motors for thirty years. In all that time, he had very little to show for his lifelong effort. All his life, he built new cars for other people and yet could never afford to buy one for himself. When he finally retired, the only thing he received was a cheap, stupid wristwatch. You give a company a lifetime of blood, sweat and tears and when it's all over, what do they give you in return? A watch, perhaps to remind you of the all miserable time you wasted working for them.

When he died, he was living in an apartment with my eldest sister and her daughter. During the last few years of his life, he lived off his pension and monthly checks from social security. He left nothing behind except a few personal items that my sisters kept as mementos.

In May of 1982, the state had just finished building another maximum-security facility in Ypsilanti, Michigan. The new facility was named Huron Valley Men's Facility and it was scheduled to open the following month. There was a rumor going around the prison that the counselors were accepting transfer requests and reviewing inmate files for possible transfer.

I desperately wanted to get closer to home and Ypsilanti was even closer to where my mother lived than Jackson was. The day after I heard the rumor, I went straight to the counselor's office.

"I've heard you guys are reviewing files for possible transfers to the new facility in Ypsilanti," I said.

"Yes, we are," he said.

"I'd really like to put in a request for transfer," I told him. "I'd be a lot closer to my mother. It'd be really nice to be able to see her more often."

After he looked through my file, he told me that he'd submit my name to the transfer coordinator.

"There's no guarantee that a transfer will be approved, though. You understand that?" he asked.

"Yes sir," I said. "But I'll hope for the best."

I thought that my chances of being transferred to another maximum-security facility were pretty good. I hadn't had any major disciplinary tickets in the last four years and I'd always kept a work assignment.

About three weeks later, I was working in the yard store when a guard told me that I had to report back to the block. I immediately began to wonder what was happening now. I certainly didn't need any more bad news. But when I got to the block, the guard told me that I needed to pack my property and bring it to the desk as soon as possible.

"You're being transferred tomorrow morning to the Huron Valley Men's Facility," he said.

Finally, some good news. It was exactly what I wanted to hear.

I was so excited about the transfer that I didn't sleep much that night. It was doubly exciting because not only would I be much closer to home, but I'd also be in a new, clean facility.

I'd gotten up early — wide awake with excitement and not at all feeling the effects of a mostly sleepless night. When my supervisor from the prison store came to my cell, I thought he'd just come to say goodbye.

"I've asked the deputy warden to postpone your transfer for thirty days," he said to me. "I need you to stay on a little longer here so you can train another inmate to take your place at the yard store."

He apologized for the inconvenience and assured me that I would definitely be on the next transfer to Huron Valley. My supervisor had always treated me with respect and kindness and so, I reluctantly agreed. After all, I knew it was certain that I'd be on the next bus out of there.

My supervisor interviewed several guys before he hired one that had some previous experience in the free world as a store clerk, which made the task of training him a lot easier for me. There wasn't all that much to running the yard store in the first place. As long as the inventory and the money balanced out at the end of the day, that was usually all it took to satisfy my boss and the business office.

The month went by rather quickly and the week before I was supposed to leave, I spent some time saying goodbye to the guys. I knew that I'd be seeing most of these guys again, since most of the guys at Marquette were serving a long, indeterminate or life sentence.

A long, indeterminate sentence was usually considered to be twenty years or more. Some of the guys had been sentenced to a number of years that resembled basketball scores. There was one guy who had been given the nickname ninety-nine, because that was the number of years that the judge had sentenced him to.

I was thrilled with the prospect of leaving Marquette behind. I could only hope that once I got on that bus, I'd never see Marquette prison again. With all things considered, though, Marquette actually hadn't been that bad of a place to do time, especially before the riots. A lot had changed since then, though, and I'd spent almost five years behind the walls at Marquette. I was more than ready for a change of scenery.

My time at Marquette had definitely been a learning experience and I'd made a few friends. The most important thing, though, was getting closer to my family. Being able to receive regular visits from my loved ones trumped all else.

I'd called my mother as soon as I could after I found out about my transfer to share the good news. She too was excited and relieved that I was being transferred to a place where she'd be able to visit me at least once a month instead of once a year.

When I was told to pack my property for the second time, I didn't have much to pack. I knew that I'd be leaving at the end of the month so I didn't bother to completely unpack from the first time.

The next morning, forty inmates were secured in belly-chains and leg shackles and we were placed on the bus for the long ride back to the Lower Peninsula. The worst part of the whole ordeal was having to wear the black box that they always placed over the handcuffs on every high-security prisoner.

The black box was made of dense, hard, black plastic. It was designed to deter and prevent prisoners from tampering with the handcuff locking mechanism. However, it was also painfully restrictive, especially after having to wear the device for an eleven-hour bus ride.

If a prisoner didn't keep his arms pulled in close to his body at just the right angle, the handcuffs would literally cut into the flesh of the wrist. Besides the black box, I really didn't care much for having to use a stainless steel pot to piss in either.

But whatever it took to get closer to home, I was willing to endure.

CHAPTER 12

Huron Valley Men's Facility

When we arrived at Huron Valley Men's Facility, it was late in the afternoon and the prison was lit up with more halogen and sodium vapor lamps than I'd ever seen before.

We were taken directly into the control center where the guards removed our shackles and told us to have a seat in the visiting room while they processed the paper work.

When that was done, we were given bedrolls, assigned to housing units and given directions as to where the housing units were located on the compound.

When I stepped out of the control center, it was almost like walking onto a college campus. The compound was huge. It must have been at least eight times the size of Marquette.

The landscaping was all hills and valleys with numerous trees and shrubs, which was totally unexpected. The most noticeable aspect was that there were no concrete walls, which made the prison seem even larger. The open expanse of the grounds gave me the distinct feeling of being less confined.

The complex was enclosed with two chain-link fences, motion sensors, and five guard towers along the perimeter of the fences. The inside fence had three coils of razor wire strung along the top. And the outside fence was completely covered with multiple coils of razor wire.

There were five housing units on the compound and I was assigned to housing unit two. Segregation was designated as housing unit one and housing units three, four, and five were general population. The units were two tiered — a base and first gallery — with the cells facing inward. There were two wings of cells, designated A-wing and B-wing, with twenty-two cells upstairs and another twenty-two downstairs on each wing.

Some of the first things I noticed when I walked into the unit were the colorful murals painted on the base area walls. I was surprised to see how bright and colorful the housing unit was painted. It definitely wasn't the usual drab prison atmosphere that I'd become accustomed to over the years. I could hardly believe that I was in a maximum-security prison.

Each unit had two day rooms, one on each side of the base area. The activity room was furnished with a regulation size pool table, Ping-Pong table and several card tables. The other day room had a color television set, several rows of soft padded chairs and several sofas that were upholstered in different colors of vinyl. I'd never seen anything like this in a prison before.

In 1982, Michigan prison guards suddenly changed their designation and insisted on being called corrections officers. I'm not really sure why, possibly to boost their morale or maybe it made them feel more professional. At any rate, the inmates had no choice but to comply or suffer the consequences of their wrath, which was usually in the form of misconduct tickets or unwarranted shakedowns.

The officer's station was a cubicle situated in the middle of the base area, giving the officers a complete and unobstructed view of the entire unit. The bottom segment was enclosed with cinder block walls while the top section was constructed with tall panes of shatterproof glass.

Three officers were assigned to each housing unit. And except for making an occasional round through the housing unit, they usually stayed inside the cubicle. From there, they'd take turns at operating the computer that controlled the locking mechanisms on every cell door in the unit. On the inside of each cell door was a small black button. When an inmate wanted to come out of his cell, he simply pushed the button and his cell number would appear on the computer screen at the officer's station. The officer would then type a command into the computer and the lock on that particular door would open.

I was assigned to a cell on first gallery where I could look out the window and see the traffic on the I-94 expressway about a half-mile away. Each cell had a window that was approximately thirty-six inches by sixty inches and surprisingly, the bottom section of the window actually opened for fresh air circulation. There were no bars on the windows but on the portion of it that opened, there was a security screen on the other side.

The room itself was a little bigger than any other cell I had previously occupied. The rooms were furnished with a steel bed, a small desk with four shelves and a doublewide wall locker. One side of the locker had several shelves while the other side had a rack for hanging clothes.

The toilet didn't have a seat or a lid, but the standard size bathroom sink did have turn on faucets — a welcome change from the push button type. There was also a twenty-four by thirty-six inch real glass mirror mounted above the sink, which was totally unexpected. Mirrors were usually an eight-inch by twelve-inch piece of polished stainless steel that was bolted to the wall.

Each housing unit had it's own laundry facilities where our clothes were washed in individual nylon-mesh laundry bags. If a guy was willing to pay the inmate laundry man two dollars a month, he could get his clothes washed, folded and delivered to his cell twice a week.

On my first morning there, I was surprised to see the modern architectural design of the chow hall when it was time for breakfast. The entire front of the building was covered with large panes of dark, smoked glass — it looked more like a restaurant in the free world than a prison chow hall. The double door entrance led into a small vestibule, where two serving lines divided the chow hall into two separate dining areas.

Most of the black inmates were seated on one side and most of the white inmates ate on the other side. There was no forced segregation or integration — it was simply a matter of choice. The meals were served on blue polystyrene plates and trays instead of the old style stainless steel trays that were used at Marquette. At the end of the serving line, we were allowed to select one eight-ounce beverage of coffee, milk, or a soft drink.

I was told that during the first week that the facility was open, the inmates in segregation were allowed to come out of their cells and eat in the chow hall. But that soon came to an abrupt halt when an officer found an inmate stabbed to death in his bed. Evidently, whoever stabbed the inmate had taken the time to lay him on the bed and cover his body with a blanket. Supposedly, the person who killed the inmate had also placed a hand written note in the window of his cell door that said, "Do not wake for chow." After that incident, segregation was permanently locked down and its inmates were fed in their cells.

When they opened the yard after breakfast, I decided to go for a walk on the yard and have a look around at my new surroundings. The main yard was located behind housing units three, four and five and extended from one end of the compound to the other. The yard was huge compared to Marquette's small yard and there was even a half-mile long oval asphalt track that the inmates used for walking and jogging.

Behind housing units three and four, there was a football field and two tennis courts. At the other end of the compound, by the gymnasium, there was a softball diamond. But when I looked over toward the kitchen, I saw the most amazing sight of all — someone had excavated an area directly behind the kitchen and created a manmade pond.

Naturally, the area was posted as off-limits to all inmates, but it was a welcome sight just to be able to look at something different. I especially enjoyed watching the ducks and geese as they swam around the pond.

From the softball diamond, it was easy to see the women's facility just across the fence. Every day, rain or snow, male and female inmates would stand as close to the fence as they were allowed and try to have a long distance conversation by yelling back and forth or by using hand signals to spell their words.

Occasionally, the female inmates would pull their tops up to expose their breasts, but they were too far away for us to really see anything. One of the inmates who was transferred on the first bus from Marquette told me that when they first arrived at Huron Valley, the female inmates were working in the kitchen. That only lasted about a week, he said, because the male and female inmates couldn't keep their hands off each other or their pants up.

Special activities like hobby-craft, music and the library were located in the school building, along with the quartermaster and auditorium. The carpenter shop and the mattress factory were situated in the back part of the school building. The inmate store and barbershop were located in the front area of the gymnasium.

It had been over a year since my last visit with my mother, but in my first week at Huron Valley, she came to visit. As a prerequisite to all visits, the visitors were subject to a search for contraband before entering the visiting room. I knew that my mother was self-conscious and easily embarrassed when anyone happened to notice that she had a prosthetic arm so I was thankful that the officers didn't make her remove her prosthesis during the search.

When my mother first lost her arm, the only type of prosthesis available was the one with steel hooks. It mortified her. Within a few short years, though, there had been a great deal of progress in the field of bionics. She'd been able to get a new bionic prosthesis that looked almost exactly like a real arm and functioned much more like one as well.

The old prosthesis was strapped on to her shoulder while the new one fit snugly over her forearm and was held in place by suction. The old one was operated manually by a cable; the new one was battery powered and equipped with sensors that reacted to the muscle contraction in her forearm. When she contracted or relaxed the muscles in her forearm, the prosthesis made the same movements a hand would, either opening or closing. If a person wasn't aware that she had an artificial arm, it was hard to even notice the difference.

The new technology, materials and specialized techniques used to individually produce each prosthesis made it expensive to get one, costing around ten thousand dollars. Fortunately, my mother's insurance covered most of the cost.

"Oh Jim, I have the funniest story to tell you about when I first got this thing," she told me during our visit.

She said that when she first brought it home and began wearing it, it often became uncomfortable until she really got used to it. So in the beginning, she'd take it off frequently around the house.

"One afternoon, I was watching some television and had taken it off and put it on the couch beside me. During a commercial break, I decided to get up and make myself something to eat, so I went into the kitchen," she said. "Well, when I came back, I sat down on the couch right where I'd been sitting before, right next to the prosthesis, and all of a sudden I felt something pinch my leg."

She continued, "I looked down and saw the hand of the prosthesis was squeezing my thigh and I was so scared, I didn't know what to think! I just jumped straight out of that chair, thinking that arm had grown a life of its own!"

Evidently, when my mother sat down, she must've brushed up against the prosthesis and inadvertently activated the sensors, causing the hand to close.

We both laughed heartily at the story. As funny as the story was, I enjoyed just watching my mother laugh even more.

It was always extremely difficult for me having to say goodbye at the end of each visit, especially to my mother. The psychological anguish of having to watch my loved ones leave after our visits often left me heartbroken and feeling empty inside.

Regrettably, for many years I failed to realize that my loved ones shared these same feelings. They too had always felt my pain and suffered my misery. They were painfully aware of all those silent, unshared birthdays and those many lonely nights — nights that were filled with heartache, desolation and the never-ending isolation of a lonely prison cell. They too had experienced the profound pain of finding themselves separated from a loved one by mere inches, yet years and worlds apart.

I often think back to when I first came to prison and my mother would drive all the way to Jackson just to visit me. I'd intentionally manipulate her emotions and make her cry, but my intentions were never to hurt her. I was hurting inside and I didn't know how to deal with the pain and misery I was experiencing. I desperately wanted and needed someone to understand what I was going through, but I was unable to articulate the psychological pain I was feeling. Unfortunately, I took my frustration out on the one person who loved me the most, probably because I knew that she'd forgive me.

It took me years to realize that she, more than anyone else, had always understood and shared my pain. To this very day, I'm ashamed of my atrocious behavior in the past. I profoundly regret the way that I treated my mother. She gave everything of herself and asked for nothing in return. I was simply too absorbed in my own self-pity to see the truth. Throughout the years, I've apologized to her many times, seeking her forgiveness, and each time she has responded with the unconditional love and forgiveness of a mother.

"There's nothing for you to apologize for," she'd tell me time and time again. "I've always felt your pain and suffering."

I went to classification for a job assignment a few days after my arrival. I requested an assignment for either the inmate store or the yard crew. But because there were no job openings in the inmate store, I was assigned to the yard crew. However, with my previous experience working in the store at Marquette, my name was placed at the top of the waiting list for the inmate store.

There wasn't much to the yard crew job. We mowed the grass almost every day but we used power mowers, which made the job a lot easier. The hard part was pushing the mowers up the hills in front of the school area. The facility had a full-size Ford tractor with a rotary mower attached to the rear and occasionally, I was allowed to drive the tractor to mow the larger areas along the perimeter fence and the big yard.

On the days when I got to drive the tractor, I didn't consider it work. To me, that was more like fun.

When Huron Valley Men's Facility was built, it wasn't designed to be a maximum-security prison. All of the facility's existing gun towers were positioned along the outer perimeter of the fences, providing no protection for the officers and staff who worked inside the housing units or any of the other buildings inside the compound. The inmates realized this and as a result, very little deterred or prevented them from assaulting the staff and one another.

From the very first day Huron Valley was opened, the facility was out of control. Within a few months, drugs were plentiful throughout the facility. Just about anything an inmate wanted was available if you had the money — cocaine, heroin, marijuana, hash, and all kinds of pharmaceutical drugs as well. If it wasn't coming in through the visiting room, then the inmates were paying the officers cash to smuggle it in.

But drugs weren't the only contraband being smuggled in. Street knives like slim jims started showing up inside the facility. For a twenty dollar bill, you could buy a street knife — the knives were definitely not coming in through the visiting room. One day, when the maintenance man was working on the dryer in housing unit two, he discovered a dozen knives wrapped in plastic that someone had stashed in the duct pipe for the hot air exhaust.

After a while, things started to really get crazy. On three separate occasions and in different housing units, several individuals went on rampages using the pool balls to break out the windows in the day rooms, and it was never just one or two windows. The guys would throw pool balls until there were no more left to throw, breaking as many windows as they possibly could. At around that same time, all the nice soft chairs and sofas began to mysteriously fall apart. A few inmates were indiscriminately destroying everything they could get their hands on.

It wasn't long before one of the inmates in housing unit four decided that he wanted to take a female officer as a hostage. The officer was making her rounds on first gallery when the inmate grabbed her and forced her into his cell. He barricaded his cell door by using the wall locker and the desk. The facility immediately went into lock-down and the Michigan State Police S.W.A.T. team was called in to handle the situation.

The S.W.A.T. team arrived by helicopter and landed inside the facility on the softball diamond behind the gymnasium. At first, they tried to talk the inmate into letting his hostage go and surrendering, but the inmate refused to negotiate.

They couldn't gain access to the inmate's cell through the solid steel door and the only other possible means of gaining entry was through the cell window. While they considered using the window as a possible means of entry, they first wanted to make sure they could enter the cell quickly and rescue the officer before the inmate had a chance to harm her. To make sure it would go smoothly, the S.W.A.T. team used an empty cell to simulate the plan.

The empty cell was on the other side of the housing unit, far away from the inmate with the hostage so he couldn't see what they were doing. I had a clear view from my cell window, though, and watched the simulation. One of the state troopers came around the housing unit carrying a ladder. He placed it against the building, next to one of the windows, and climbed up to where he was standing next to the window. He then grabbed a sledgehammer from his utility belt and took a good swing at the window. Surprisingly, the sledgehammer bounced off the shatterproof glass without even cracking the window.

The trooper gave the window a second good whack with the sledge hammer and this time, it finally cracked. I suppose they figured that it would take too long to get into the cell that way for the plan to work because the trooper didn't take a third swing. He climbed back down the ladder, grabbed it and left.

The state police continued to negotiate with the inmate all that day for the release of his hostage but they didn't make any progress until early the next day, when they tricked the inmate into opening his cell door to get some Kool-Aid and cigarettes. As soon as he cracked the door, the troopers rushed in and wrestled his dumb ass to the floor. The female officer was rescued unharmed and the inmate was taken to segregation.

Not long after that incident, two health care porters — custodians who were assigned to clean the health care building — planned and executed an escape by breaking out the window in the dental clinic. Evidently, the porters had managed to talk their supervisor into letting them clean the carpet in the dental clinic on a Saturday, when it was closed for the weekend.

Health care and the dental clinic were both located in the same building as the control center, which was the only building on the compound that wasn't completely enclosed by the perimeter fences. The fences merely abutted each side of the building and being as such, only a small portion of the health care building was actually inside the perimeter fences. The dental clinic was situated on the other side of health care, toward the front of the building, and was completely outside the perimeter fences.

The window in the dental clinic was covered with a heavy, mesh security screen that could only be opened with a special security key. However, the key was kept in a desk drawer in the dental clinic and the porters knew exactly where it was.

After the officer unlocked the dental clinic door, he left the two porters unsupervised and went back to the control center. While one porter was cleaning the carpet, he was also acting as a lookout for the other porter, who was busy getting the key out of the desk drawer.

Once they had the key, they unlocked the security screen and used a mop wringer to break through the shatterproof glass. The loud whining noise of the carpet cleaning machine prevented anyone from hearing the pounding required to break through the shatterproof glass, which doesn't break like normal glass. With shatterproof glass, the glass merely shatters into small fragments but the hard part is getting through the plastic laminate stuck between the panes of glass.

When the hole was big enough to squeeze through, they crawled out the window and dropped about two feet to the ground. Then, they walked around the building to the parking lot, where they had someone waiting for them and they simply drove away. They weren't gone for very long, though. Two months later, both men were arrested in Las Vegas.

About three weeks after that escape, another inmate managed to escape by climbing up and over the control center building. Supposedly, he'd somehow managed to remove the security screen from the inside of his cell window. Somewhere around three o'clock in the morning, he crawled out his window in housing unit two and made his way across the yard to the control center.

The control center building was only about twenty feet high, but all along the top edge of the building there were several coils of razor wire and electronic sensors that were designed to detect the slightest movement. In addition, several more coils of razor wire were stacked on top of the building in an effort to deter inmates from attempting to escape.

The clever inmate, though, was able to use the razor wire to his advantage. He tossed one of his blankets towards the roof until it snagged the razor wire and then used the blanket to pull himself on top of it. But at the same time, he inadvertently set off an alarm inside the control center.

When the control center radioed to all units that there was an alert in that particular zone, the officer in the sally port gun tower saw the inmate on top of the building. The officer fired a warning shot, but this particular inmate was determined to escape. He ignored the warning shot and continued to work his way through the multiple coils of razor wire.

The officer in the gun tower fired several more shots directly at the inmate, but the bullets missed their target. Once the inmate got through all the razor wire, he ran to the front of the building, lowered himself over the edge and dropped to the ground. He then ran across the parking lot and into a nearby wheat field.

Once the facility notified the state police and the local authorities that they had an escaped convict on the loose, the police immediately cordoned off the surrounding neighborhood and initiated a thorough foot search of the adjacent area. After searching for about an hour, one of the police officers came across the inmate lying in the wheat field where he was trying to hide. Supposedly, the officer ordered the escaped inmate not to move, but the inmate jumped up and lunged at the police officer. In self-defense, the officer fired one shot from his revolver, hitting the inmate in the face and killing him instantly.

It seemed like every couple of days, an assault between inmates or inmates and officers would take place. Whenever there was trouble, the officers would call a code blue over their radio and give the location of the incident.

One afternoon, a fight broke out between several inmates in housing unit four. The officer called a code blue and every available officer immediately responded to the call.

Three officers ran across the yard and entered housing unit four, but as soon as they were inside, they were overpowered and assaulted by an unknown number of inmates. One of the officers was stabbed in the upper chest and his life was saved thanks to a training manual that he happened to be carrying around in his shirt pocket.

A female officer stepped through the door and was blindsided with a punch to the jaw, falling to the floor unconscious. The other officer had also been punched and kicked numerous times and was lying on the floor by the officers' cubicle groaning in pain.

It was several minutes before the unit officer finally managed to contact the control center and inform shift command of the situation. The control center immediately sounded the emergency count siren and tried to initiate an emergency lock down of the facility, but by then, there was mass confusion on the yard and the inmates weren't paying any attention to the siren.

The officer manning the gun tower in the far corner of the compound, behind housing unit three, apparently thought he could intimidate the inmates with the sound of gun fire. He began firing shots indiscriminately and luckily, no one was shot. One of the bullets did, however, go through a window in the school building and barely missed some of the inmates attending class.

After about forty-five minutes, the inmates slowly began returning to their housing units on their own. Once the officers finally managed to get everyone back in their cells, the prison was locked down. We were expecting to be locked down for at least a couple of days, but much to all of our surprise, everything was back to normal by the next morning.

When Huron Valley first opened, it was indeed the best thing that Michigan prisoners had going for them. A number of the inmates housed there had already served too many years in the filthy, dilapidated and hostile environments of Jackson, Ionia, and Marquette to really care or appreciate what they'd been given. They'd become victims of the wretched, artificial environments they'd been forced to live in. Many of the guys had forgotten what it was like to be treated as a human being.

Eventually, my request for an assignment at the inmate store came through. By the time it did, the store was experiencing a number of problems. Ever since the store first opened, it had made very little in profits — partially due to a lack of supervision, I'm sure.

While inmates had been allowed to operate the store, the only supervision they received was from the yard officers, who merely locked and unlocked the doors. Making matters worse, some of the yard officers had also taken to using the inmate store as their own personal party store, helping themselves to whatever they wanted.

The business manager of the facility finally took charge of the situation and began implementing a number of changes and procedures. One of the prison's warehouse staff members was placed in charge of the store to supervise its daily operations, making one person accountable for the store's profits or losses. All of the inmate store workers were fired and all of the locks were changed to prevent any unauthorized entry. I was hired as the store clerk and one other inmate was hired as the store worker. Within three months after the new procedures had been implemented, the store was finally showing a profit, and most of the previous problems had been resolved.

The staff supervisor operated the cash register and the inmate store worker filled the store orders. As the clerk, I took care of all the miscellaneous paper work. It was my responsibility to fill out procurement requests for merchandise and to keep the store stocked with enough inventory to last a two-week period. I also typed the daily receiving reports and calculated the retail cost extensions for every item sold. The store was easy work, but it was also monotonous. After a few months as the store clerk, I decided to go back to the yard crew for the summer.

During my time at Huron Valley, I met an inmate by the name of Paul. Paul was one guy that you definitely didn't want as your enemy. Physically, he wasn't a big guy, but he had a lot of heart and was considered one of the most dangerous inmates at Huron Valley.

Paul told me that when he first came to prison he was serving a two-year sentence for auto theft. He'd tried to avoid all the bullshit, but he was young and a few of the other inmates were always trying to take advantage of him. Not long after Paul came to prison, he got into a fight with another inmate and they both went to the hole for thirty days. When he got out of the hole, the same inmate kept trying to intimidate him and he had another run-in with the guy.

With few viable options, Paul felt that he had no other choice but to settle the matter once and for all. He made himself a shank, which is basically a crudely fashioned knife made by inmates out of whatever materials they can find. Paul used a piece of metal that he removed from a desk drawer.

He waited and watched the guy for two days until Paul caught him alone in the shower. When the guy was washing his hair and couldn't see what was going on, Paul ran in and stabbed him twice in the stomach.

Paul told me that he wasn't trying to kill the guy, he just wanted to make a point so the inmate would stop trying to intimidate him. The guy didn't die either, but Paul was prosecuted for assault with intent to do great bodily harm over the incident. He was sentenced to an additional ten years in prison but what really angered Paul was that the inmate testified against him during the trial.

"After that shit, I really just didn't care anymore," Paul told me. "About that time, I decided I'd try to make my way through the alphabet."

In prison, when a person is convicted of a crime and enters the system, he or she is given an alphabetical pre-fix, A, B, C, etc., followed by a six-digit prison identification number. The alphabetical pre-fix corresponds to the number of times that person has been sentenced to prison. For instance, one conviction gets you an A pre-fix before the number, two convictions gets you a B, three convictions gets you a C and so on. When I met Paul his pre-fix, was K, meaning he'd already been convicted and sentenced eleven times. He had the highest pre-fix of anyone I'd ever met. And it's quite possible that Paul still holds that infamous distinction today.

Every one of his convictions was for stabbing other inmates. He'd been convicted of everything from the lesser crime of assault to first-degree murder.

Paul had an infinite dislike for inmates who had testified against other people or who were in the process of testifying against someone. His personal agenda was to eliminate these individuals as he found them. During the short period of time that I knew Paul, he stabbed two of these individuals in the gymnasium's weight room.

The first inmate Paul stabbed had supposedly testified against his codefendant in a drug case as part of a plea bargain agreement. Apparently, someone told Paul about this guy's case and that was all it took to set him in motion.

Paul stalked the guy for several weeks, watching every movement he made, before he decided the weight room would be where he'd stab the guy. A few days later, when Paul saw the inmate head for the gymnasium, he got his shank and went after him.

"I walked into the weight room and the guy was doing bench presses," Paul told me. "So I, all polite and stuff, asked if I could do a couple sets with him. He said, 'sure, go ahead.'"

They did a couple sets, Paul said, before the guy built up to lifting so much weight he couldn't really move. It was then that Paul stabbed the guy several times in the chest and abdomen.

His injuries were serious but he didn't die, at least not right away. The inmate was taken to an outside hospital and spent a couple weeks there before he had healed up enough to come back. When he came back, he was placed in segregation on protective custody status.

Seven months later, while he was exercising in his cell doing push-ups, he suffered a heart attack and died. The authorities believed that the heart attack was directly related to the injuries he received when Paul stabbed him, but for whatever reason, they were unable to charge Paul for the inmate's untimely death. Instead, he was convicted of assault with the intent to do great bodily harm and served six months in the hole.

The other inmate Paul stabbed was self-nicknamed Dangerous. This wannabe rapper made the mistake of telling some so-called prison buddies that he'd made a deal with the prosecutor to testify against his rap partner in exchange for a time cut. Unfortunately for him, someone passed that information on to Paul and once again, Paul was on a mission.

A few days before Paul stabbed Dangerous, he and I were walking the yard when he pointed to another inmate and said, "That guy's a snitch!"

Evidently, Paul had been stalking this guy for some time because he said that he was just waiting to catch him in the right place at the right time.

Several days later, it was about three o'clock in the afternoon and I'd just gotten off work. I was on my way out the gymnasium door when I noticed Paul and Dangerous inside the weight room.

Not even thinking about what Paul had told me a few days earlier, I went in to say hello. No sooner than I had stepped one foot into the room Paul was walking toward me, gesturing with his head and eyes for me to leave. I knew right away what was about to happen.

"I gotta go," I said to Paul. "But I'll catch ya later on the yard."

I left the gymnasium and walked around the building to the big yard, but before I even got to the track, I heard the call come over an officer's radio.

"Code blue in the gymnasium," I heard on the radio and suddenly, several officers from every direction took off running toward it. There was no doubt in my mind what had happened.

Two officers brought Paul out of the gym in handcuffs and walked him over to segregation. It took a while for the nurses to finally arrive and when they got there, they didn't seem to be in much of a hurry. One of them was casually pushing a wheelchair and the other nurse had a satchel slung over her shoulder that was filled with medical supplies.

They were only in the gymnasium for a few minutes before they came back out with Dangerous sitting in the wheelchair. He had an oxygen mask over his nose and mouth and the whole front of his shirt was soaked with blood. Evidently, Paul had punctured one of the guy's lungs when he stabbed him because there was blood coming out of his mouth and he appeared to be gasping for air, breathing as if he'd just finished running a marathon.

Nevertheless, it must have been the guy's lucky day because there just happened to be an ambulance in the parking lot of the facility. Dangerous was immediately transported to an outside hospital and when he came back a couple of weeks later, he was placed in administrative segregation on protective custody status. A few weeks later, he was transferred to another prison.

Paul was convicted of another assault with intent to do great bodily harm and he spent the next seven months in segregation. But this time, when he got out of the hole, he told me that he'd decided to stay out of trouble and keep a low profile. He said that he was getting tired of doing hard time.

There used to be a time when most inmates settled their disputes by fist fighting. Those days seemed long gone. During the five years I spent at Huron Valley, more inmates and staff were stabbed than at any other prison in the state.

Whenever a good meal was served in the chow hall — hamburgers, pizza or steak — there was always a problem with inmates being disrespectful toward their fellow inmates by cutting the line in front of them. If an inmate allowed other inmates to disrespect him in that manner without voicing his disapproval, then that inmate was usually perceived as being a weak individual and easy prey.

One afternoon, I was standing in the chow line talking with Josh, who I knew from Marquette, when a young white kid walked right past the two of us and cut in front of Josh.

"Hey kid, I don't mind giving cuts so long as you ask, but I don't appreciate the disrespect," Josh said. "Why don't ya go find someone else to cut in front of."

Apparently, the kid had only been in prison a short time and didn't think that he'd done anything wrong. Instead of just walking away, he raised his voice and tried to start an argument. Josh didn't feed the argument, though.

"If you got a problem, kid, we can settle it on the yard after chow," Josh retorted.

By the time we got through the serving line and sat down at a table, we didn't think anything more about the incident with the kid. But just as we started eating, the kid suddenly walked up behind Josh, pulled a shank out of his pocket and stabbed Josh in the side of the neck before anyone could warn him that the kid was behind him.

Watching the incident so close made it seem like slow motion. As the kid pulled the shank out of Josh's neck, a stream of blood gushed from the wound and shot across the table. Josh grabbed his neck with the palm of his hand, trying to stop the bleeding, but the blood was pumping through his fingers at an alarming rate.

A nearby officer had seen the kid stab Josh and almost immediately, several officers had the guy surrounded, ordering him to drop the shank. As soon as he did, officers rushed in to handcuff him and whisked him away to segregation.

Josh looked like he was in pretty bad shape. The officers had him lay on the floor while one of them placed a hand towel over his wound. I heard one of them tell Josh they needed to keep pressure on the wound to slow the blood loss. Fortunately, the nurses arrived quickly and they managed to get Josh to an outside hospital before he bled to death.

Josh lost a lot of blood but recovered quickly. Within a few days, he was back on the yard talking about how lucky he was to be alive. As for the kid, about a month later he was transferred to maximum-security in Marquette. About three months later, we heard that another inmate had stabbed the kid, only the kid's luck wasn't as good as Josh's was — he died on the way to the hospital.

There was one time when an inmate was stabbed so many times that I honestly don't know how he managed to survive. Everyone knew that this particular inmate was dealing drugs and it just so happened that the two inmates who stabbed him were also drug dealers. It was rumored that they were having some sort of dispute over drug turf inside the facility.

One Saturday morning, my neighbor and I were out walking the yard over by the gymnasium. We'd just turned the corner by the front door when we noticed two inmates who had another inmate pinned in the corner of the building. At first glance, it looked like they were punching the other inmate with their fists, but as we got closer, we could see that they were actually stabbing the inmate. Whatever was happening was none of our business, so we made a quick detour and took a lap around the track. When we came back about ten minutes later, there was so much blood on the ground and the sidewalk that it looked like someone had butchered an animal.

Incredibly, the inmate survived the assault. He was never the same again, though. One of his kidneys had to be removed and he walked with a pronounced limp from nerve damage.

During my time at Huron Valley, I became interested in ultra-light aircraft. I'd always had an interest in flying but I never took the time to actually learn about aviation. Now that I had nothing but time on my hands, I decided to learn all that I possibly could about flying fixed and rotary wing aircraft.

I was still holding on to the hope that one day I'd be released from prison and I thought it was best not to completely waste all this time I had. The more knowledge I could acquire in prison, I believed, the better off I'd be if I were ever released.

Actual flight lessons were out of the question, of course, but I could study and learn just about everything else from aviation books. If I memorized the books, I could effortlessly breeze through a ground school course in the free world.

I ordered several training courses on how to fly fixed-wing aircraft and helicopters and I was rather surprised when the facility approved the order. But, all the books were considered educational material. Therefore, they were allowed by department policy.

Nevertheless, once I actually received the books, several of the officers believed that the material posed a security threat to the facility. They surreptitiously conspired with one of the housing unit officers to perform a so-called routine shakedown of my cell and confiscate the training courses under the pretense that they were contraband.

My only recourse was to file a grievance citing department policy on educational material and requesting that the material be returned. My grievance was denied at its first two steps, which didn't surprise me. Step three of a grievance is when the matter goes before the director of corrections. At that level, the director determined the material was indeed educational and ordered the facility to return my property at once. From that point on, I never had a problem ordering and keeping aviation related materials.

I studied all the Federal Aviation Administration's rules and regulations and I even wrote to the Government Printing Office to request my name be placed on their mailing list to receive free circular advisories that were routinely issued by the FAA. I acquired all the textbooks necessary to complete a ground school course, reading books on aeronautical knowledge, weather and anything else that I could get my hands on that pertained to aviation.

I even purchased subscriptions for Private Pilot and Flying magazines, ordered several sectional aeronautical charts, a navigational plotter and a small hand held flight computer that was essential in learning how to navigate. I continued to study aviation for the next few years, hoping that perhaps one day I'd be able to use that knowledge to become an Emergency Medical Service helicopter pilot.

Years later, I eventually came to the realization that my dream was nothing more than wishful thinking. Nevertheless, I don't consider all that time I spent studying to be wasted time — I learned a lot about aviation, navigation and weather. Learning is never a waste and besides, maybe the knowledge will prove to be useful at some point in the future. Even today, when I look up at the sky, I can still identify all the different types of clouds, what they're composed of and their altitudes.

Some inmates studied or focused on hobbies, like myself. Other inmates just seemed to get in a lot of trouble. One thing that has always puzzled me were the inmates who took hostages. The end result was always the same and it was always a no-win situation for the inmate. Nevertheless, it happened two more times while I was at Huron Valley.

During one incidence, two inmate kitchen workers decided to take two of the food service staff workers as hostages. Both inmates were armed with crudely fashioned knives when they forced their hostages into one of the small rooms located in the rear of the kitchen. After the inmates barricaded the doors, they just stayed there like the idiots they were until finally realizing their situation was hopeless.

Once again, the state police S.W.A.T. team was called to handle the hostage situation. The whole facility was locked down for two days while the state police negotiators talked with the inmates about their demands.

From what I was told, the inmates wanted to be transferred to a federal prison instead of serving their time in the state prison system. By the time two days had passed, though, the inmates gave up and released their hostages unharmed.

They were prosecuted and given an additional number of years, which they'd have to serve in the same state prison system.

The third hostage situation happened almost exactly like the first. The inmate grabbed a female officer while she was making her rounds in housing unit two and he used the desk and wall locker to barricade his cell door. Different from the first guy, though, this inmate was apparently infatuated with the female officer that he took hostage.

He wanted to spend some quality time alone with the woman to express his romantic feelings, but the inmate's burning passion was quickly extinguished when the officer abruptly informed him that she didn't have any romantic feelings for him. Although he probably felt pretty stupid, he wisely decided to release the officer unharmed.

During the summer of 1985, I was working on the yard crew again when two inmates attempted to escape by driving a semi tractor-trailer through the perimeter security fences. Several times a week, semi tractor-trailers were allowed to enter the facility and deliver food provisions to the kitchen. The trucks would enter through the sally port and drive the short distance to the kitchen's back loading dock, where inmate kitchen workers would then unload the supplies.

Once the drivers had parked their vehicles at the back dock, they'd turn off the ignition and usually go inside the kitchen to obtain a signature from one of the staff food stewards for the merchandise. Every now and again, though, one of the drivers would inadvertently leave the keys in the ignition of the vehicle and their oversight never went unnoticed by the kitchen workers.

On this particular day in 1985, two of the inmate workers who had been conspiring to steal one of the semi trucks got their lucky break. The two men intended to ram through the sally port gates with the giant truck and once they were far enough away from the facility, they were going to ditch the semi and steal another, less obvious vehicle.

Like most prison escapees, though, they never considered that something might go wrong and played it by ear, counting on a lot of luck. They simply got their idea together and waited for the opportunity to present itself.

Early one morning when they were unloading an eighteen-wheeler, they noticed that the driver had gone inside the kitchen and left the keys in the ignition. When they finished unloading the trailer and the other two inmate workers went back inside the kitchen, they made their move. They climbed into the cab of the semi and started the engine but just as they were pulling away from the back dock, they noticed that another truck was sitting in the sally port waiting to enter the facility.

They'd already committed themselves to their ill-conceived plan and at that point, their only other option was to try driving the semi through the double set of chain-link perimeter fences adjacent to the sally port. They attempted to gain as much speed as possible in the short distance from the kitchen to the fences but it was quite apparent that these two morons didn't have the slightest idea as to what they were doing — the sally port gun tower was no more than two hundred feet away from where they attempted to crash through the fence. And to make things even more difficult, the slope of the terrain was all up hill.

When the kitchen officer saw the truck veer from the driveway and head off across the yard, he knew immediately something was very wrong. He radioed the officer in the sally port gun tower and that officer fired a warning shot. However, the inmate who was driving the semi kept the pedal to the metal and continued driving toward the fence.

The officer in the gun tower fired several more shots that were meant to take the driver out, but the bullets merely struck the vehicle, shattering both the windshield and the driver's side window. When the semi hit the chain-link fence, there was a distinct sound made by all the wire fasteners suddenly being torn away from the steel posts of the support structure. But the semi didn't have enough speed or momentum to push completely through the first fence, causing the fence not to collapse, but rather engulf the front of the semi truck and act like a crash barrier net.

It slowed the truck down so much that when they hit the second security fence, the engine stalled and the semi stopped dead in its tracks.

The facility had what was called an ERV, an emergency response vehicle. One officer armed with a pistol and shotgun patrolled the outside perimeter fence twenty-four hours a day in the vehicle. The ERV responded quickly to the botched attempt at escape and the officer stood on the other side of the fence, ready to shoot if the inmates made any further attempt to escape.

When the officers approached the semi-truck, they ordered the inmates to exit the truck and had them lay face down on the ground with their hands behind their backs. Once both men were handcuffed, they were taken straight to the hole and never seen on the yard again. The facility was locked down for the next three days and we were given bag meals until they replaced the section of fence that had been damaged.

In 1986, the store supervisor requested that I come back and work there again, so I did. One of the clerks had been transferred and the store supervisor needed someone with experience until he could hire and train another inmate.

For the next couple of months, it was business as usual. The busiest days were always right after they passed out tokens. The line would stretch around the building and the inmates had no choice but to stand outside for hours at a time with no protection from the rain or cold weather. No one liked the hassle of having to stand in a long store line. To avoid this problem, some of the guys would offer to pay me and the other store clerk to fill their store orders.

When the store closed at three o'clock in the afternoon, our supervisor would always allow us to fill a few extra orders. He told us that he didn't mind as long as it didn't interfere with the normal store operations. We only charged the guys a dollar for each store order we filled and the few extra dollars we made every month helped to supplement our slave wages of twenty-three dollars a month.

Tokens were passed out every two weeks and what they called pay script was the monthly wage that inmates earned from their institutional job assignments. At the end of the month, that money was credited to the inmate's personal account and was available for inmates to spend during the first week of every month.

But for some unknown reason, the business office decided to change the week that pay script tokens were passed out to the inmate population. The problem was that they decided to implement the change during the same week that pay script was supposed to be available. And to make matters even worse, they never even bothered to give anyone prior notice.

Because of this, most inmates had to wait an extra week to receive their pay script and that put a lot of inmates in an awkward position. Many were unable to pay their debts to other inmates, causing considerable anxiety and a number of unnecessary problems throughout the facility.

During the next couple of days that followed, the business office received numerous complaints and even a few anonymous threats from irate inmates about the impending change. That, of course, only made things worse for the inmates. In response to the complaints and threats and supposedly to avoid any further problems, the business manager ordered the store closed for the remainder of the week. That, in turn, created a big problem for me.

Several inmates had paid me in advance to fill their store orders, which, with the store closed, I couldn't do. There wasn't anything I could do about the situation except return their money to them. Most of the guys were understanding of the situation and accepted my apologies — all except for this one guy. No matter how many times I tried to explain to him that the store was completely shut down, he didn't seem to comprehend one word of what I was saying. My apologies, too, fell on deaf ears. Finally, I came to the conclusion that I was wasting my time by trying to reason with this asshole.

Besides being an idiot to begin with, I could also tell that the guy was either drunk or high on drugs because his speech was slurred and his eyelids were half closed. From my own past experience, I knew that there was usually no reasoning with a drunk, so I decided to just walk away. But when I went to walk around him, he stuck his arm out to the side to block me.

"Either you get my shit or you get stuck!" he yelled.

I didn't think much of his threat, since he was high, but when I tried to step around him he reached inside his front pants pocket, pulled out a street knife and flicked the blade open.

The knife had a thin blade about six inches long and the handle was shiny black. He was clutching the knife in his right hand and weaving from side-to-side, trying to keep me from getting around him. I kept my eye on the knife and tried to anticipate his next move.

When he lunged at me, I immediately stepped to the side — unfortunately, I didn't move fast enough. I felt a burning sensation when the blade pierced my left forearm and for a moment, I thought about trying to take the knife away from him. His reactions were slow, after all, and he seemed a little unsteady on his feet. Things have a way of getting out of control, though, and I didn't want to exacerbate an already bad situation, so I decided against it.

We were standing in the bathroom area of the gymnasium. It was just down the hall from the inmate store and partially enclosed by a four-foot-high concrete block wall. I decided the easiest way out of this dilemma was flight rather than fight.

I placed both my hands on top of the concrete partition and swung my legs and body up and over the wall. At the same time as I was going over the wall, the guy once again lunged at me with the knife. Just as my feet hit the floor on the other side of the wall, I felt the blade penetrate my left forearm again.

As I ran down the hallway toward the front exit of the gymnasium, I could feel the warm blood running down my arm and dripping from my fingertips. I knew there would be an officer sitting at the desk by the front door, so just before I turned the corner where the front door exit was located, I slowed my walk to a casual pace and folded my arms to hide the blood on my shirt.

When I rounded the corner, I tried to act as nonchalant as possible. I cordially addressed the officer.

"Afternoon sir. How are you?" I said as politely as could be.

The officer was writing something and didn't pay me any mind, looking up only to give me a quick glance and then going right back to what he was doing.

The officers who sat at the desk in the entrance to the housing unit also didn't notice my wounds. In fact, they didn't even so much as look in my direction.

When I got to my cell, I called out to the officer sitting at the computer to open number twenty-six and a few seconds later, the door popped open. I pulled open my shirt sleeve to inspect the damage as soon as I got behind the closed door.

Thankfully, the bleeding had stopped. There was a lot of dried blood on my forearm and because of it, I couldn't really see how large or deep the cuts were. I carefully washed some of the blood off and afterward, saw there were only two small puncture wounds in my forearm that looked strangely like button holes. I figured they weren't big enough to even require stitches.

I'd just finished drying off my arm when I heard the sound of an officer's keys jingling outside my cell and suddenly, the cell door opened. I thought I'd made it past all the officers, but apparently, someone knew what happened.

I looked up at the housing unit officer, trying to act natural and hope for the best. "Orders from the control center are to strip search you," the officer said. Definitely, they knew.

I removed my clothes and then he told me to raise my arms above my head and turn around in a circle. As I was getting dressed, he questioned me about the blood on my shirt and the cuts on my forearm. I refused to tell him anything because I knew that whatever I said, it wasn't going to matter one way or another. I was going to the hole and that's just how things worked.

When the unit officer left, he top-locked my door, which meant that I wasn't coming out of that cell until they wanted me to. About ten minutes later, two officers unlocked my cell door, placed me in handcuffs and escorted me to the infirmary.

I was taken into one of the examining rooms where they removed the handcuffs and put me through the same routine again — strip down and turn around in a circle. They were looking to see if I had any other marks or cuts on my body.

After I got dressed, the officers took several photographs of my forearm and allowed the nurse to treat my wounds. Once she finished bandaging my arm, she gave me a tetanus shot and told me that someone would check on me tomorrow.

The officers handcuffed me again and I was taken to housing unit two pending a notice of intent hearing.

When the facility first opened, only housing unit one was designated as segregation. However, due to the inordinate number of inmates going to the hole, the administration decided to use housing unit two as an administrative segregation housing unit. As a result, more than one-third of the prison's population was in segregation.

The next day, my arm was sore and badly bruised. Practically my whole arm was black-and-blue, along with shades of nearly every other color in the rainbow. There wasn't anything I could do about the dilemma I was now faced with.

At my hearing, I was told that I had two choices — I could either identify the inmate who assaulted me and I'd be released back to general population or, I could stay in segregation until they decided to transfer me to another prison. Needless to say, I chose the lesser of the two evils, which was to remain in segregation.

It was about a week later when I found out from one of the officers how they knew so quickly that someone had been injured in the gymnasium. The gym officer had noticed drops of blood on the floor in the hallway and since only one other inmate and myself had left the gymnasium, they knew it had to be one of us.

Fortunately for me, the counselor in segregation used to be my supervisor when I worked on the yard crew. I was almost certain that if I sent him an intramural correspondence explaining my current situation that he'd hire me as a porter in segregation. When I worked for him on the yard crew, he once told me that he could make a million dollars off me if I worked for him in the free world, a compliment in regard to my work ethic. I wrote him and before the end of the week, I was moved to housing unit one to work as a porter, which basically means custodian.

There were three porters in housing unit one. Our job was to clean the unit and prepare the food trays for the eighty-eight inmates housed in segregation. I was assigned to the detention side of the unit where they kept the inmates who were considered to be incorrigible and dangerous. Whenever one of these individuals was brought out of his cell, for any reason whatsoever, he'd be placed in belly-chain handcuffs, leg shackles and accompanied by two officers. Two of the inmates were considered so dangerous that they required an escort of four officers whenever they were brought out of their cells.

There really wasn't much to being a segregation porter because all the inmates were kept locked up in the cells. The worst was when one of the inmates would flood the base area by flushing sheets and blankets down the toilet. It'd happen every now and again and meant I'd have to spend several hours mopping up the water.

The job I disliked the most was cleaning out the cells. On my side of the housing unit, there were two guys who literally lived like pigs. They never came out of their cells for showers unless they were forced to, and once a month, the housing unit officers would do just that. The officers would lock the guys in the shower until I completed the unpleasant task of cleaning their pigpens.

Even though most of the garbage was paper cups and Styrofoam food containers, the cleaning job was overwhelming. I always had to use a shovel to work my way into their cells and the amount of garbage I'd remove was unbelievable. The worst part of the job, though, wasn't the garbage but the putrid, rotting smell that went along with it. Both cells reeked of a stench so foul and disgusting that I had to wrap a towel around my face to breathe and keep from gagging. I never understood how anyone could live like they did.

The segregation officers didn't appreciate any disruptions of their normal routine. Whenever an inmate created the slightest disturbance, the officers didn't hesitate to retaliate. They'd take him out of his cell, lock him in the shower, order him to strip down and leave him standing there buck-naked for hours at a time. That was one of the officers' favorite ways of dispensing summary punishment.

Every prison always has a few unethical officers, those who don't have any compunction about lying and setting inmates up for major misconduct tickets. Apparently, these officers believed all inmates are sent to prison to be punished and forget that being sent to prison alone is the punishment.

On several different occasions, I observed officers removing pieces of metal from the inmate's bed springs, sharpening it to a point and then writing a major misconduct ticket alleging that they'd found a shank in the inmate's cell during a routine shakedown.

One particular inmate had assaulted an officer at Huron Valley and had been in segregation ever since — for about eight months. Two of the regular segregation officers despised this inmate and they'd frequently harass him with their petty and vindictive acts of retaliation. Often, they'd put disgusting things in his food, ranging from flies to spiders to spit. On two separate occasions when this individual was sleeping, I watched these officers quietly open his food slot and throw cold water on him, or at least that's what I thought it was. It very well could have been urine.

One evening, they took this individual out of his cell and locked him in the shower for more than two hours, naked as can be. At around eight-thirty, one of the officers told all the porters that we had to lock up early.

"We've got some unfinished business to take care of," the officer told us.

We knew what was about to happen. They were planning to physically abuse the inmate and they didn't want any witnesses. We'd seen it happen before. To cover their own asses, they'd just claim that the inmate had initiated the confrontation by assaulting one of them.

There was another inmate in segregation who had been there since the facility first opened in 1982. In the mid-1970s, this individual was doing time at Marquette Branch Prison. Supposedly, he and another inmate were in the auditorium when a guard unexpectedly walked up on them and caught them in a homosexual act. For whatever reason, the inmate reacted by stabbing the guard and unfortunately, the guard died.

The inmate was kept in a special cell on base located at the far end of the unit and his door was secured with several extra locks. Whenever the officers brought him out of his cell, they first had to secure him in two sets of belly-chains and two sets of leg shackles. The guy never went anywhere without a mandatory four-officer escort, not even to the shower.

Every now and again when I was sweeping or mopping in front of his cell, I'd hear him talking to himself as if there was actually another person in the cell with him. He'd already spent about ten years in the hole and had lost all touch with reality.

His whole world existed only within that tiny concrete prison cell. And as far as anyone knew, he'd most likely spend the rest of his natural life in the hole.

At that point in time, it wasn't unusual for an inmate to spend years in the hole. Just being in the hole was a very unpleasant experience in itself. But as bad as it was, things could always get worse. If an inmate was caught throwing food or plastic eating utensils on the floor outside of his cell, he was placed on food loaf for thirty days.

Food loaf was the name given to a gross concoction made at the prison. All the food items listed on the menu for that day's particular meal would be mixed together, placed into a small square pan about the size of a pound of butter and baked into a loaf. It looked and tasted terrible. Sometimes, it was the only thing an inmate would be fed — three times a day for weeks and even months at a time.

If an inmate said or did something really stupid to provoke the segregation officers, he usually didn't have to wait long for their response. Several officers would suit up in riot gear, spray a little gas in the guy's cell and rush in with a riot shield, pinning him to the wall or the floor. Once he was handcuffed, they'd drag him out of the cell and lock him in the shower, leaving him there for several hours.

When the officers finally decided to return the inmate to his cell, all of his bedding would be gone — no mattress, no pillow, no blankets and no sheets. He'd be made to sleep on a cold and hard concrete slab. To make things even more miserable, the officers would shut off the water to his cell so the inmate couldn't flush the toilet, wash his face or even get a drink of water.

Even more cruel than that was the practice of shackling inmates with belly-chain handcuffs and leaving them in their cells until the next day. I always empathized with those poor, wretched guys because I knew it could of just as easily have been me. Nevertheless, there wasn't much I could do for the guys other than to slip them the occasional cigarette or something to read.

When the inmates in segregation wanted to get the officers attention, they usually kicked on their cell door until the officer came to see what they wanted. I generally didn't pay much attention to the guys kicking on the doors, but one afternoon when I was mopping the galley, there was one individual that had been kicking and beating on his cell door for more than an hour and the officers were just ignoring him.

My Own Worst Enemy

I knew from firsthand experience that being in those cells twenty-four hours a day, seven days a week with nothing to occupy a person's time or mind could sometimes push a guy over the edge. Not surprisingly then, when I got close enough to the guy's cell door where he could see me, he began screaming obscenities at me and kicking the door even harder. I tried to ignore the guy because I didn't think that he was directing his anger at me, it was just that I happened to be there. But suddenly, the cell door burst open, almost knocking me over the railing.

I was more than a little surprised when that door flew open and slammed into my shoulder. In fact, I instantly got angry, throwing the mop on the floor and grabbing hold of the door with both of my hands before shoving it as hard as I could. In the process, the door hit the inmate in the face and knocked him backward.

My main concern was to keep this raving lunatic off of me and the best way to do that was to keep him in that cell. I pushed on the door as hard as I could, trying to get it shut, but somehow, his leg had gotten caught in the door. He began screaming that I'd broken his leg. At about that same time, I heard an officer call over the radio that there was an unsecured door in segregation.

As soon as I saw the guards running up the stairs, I let go of the door, picked up my mop and I walked away. The most incredible and amusing part of this whole incident was overhearing this guy telling the officers that I had broken his leg and assaulted him.

In an effort to prevent anyone else from kicking their cell door open, the warden ordered the maintenance department to weld an extra deadbolt lock to every cell in segregation.

Four years after it first opened, the prison's administration finally accepted the fact that Huron Valley Men's Facility was simply not manageable as a maximum-security prison. Around that time, they began instituting a number of changes to tighten security.

One of the first changes made was the removal of all the wall lockers and beds with springs from every cell. The maintenance department removed and replaced them with steel footlockers and solid steel beds that were bolted to the floor. By removing all the wall lockers and bolting everything to the floor, the inmates wouldn't be able to use the cell furnishings to barricade themselves in their cells.

Several chain-link fences were also erected on the main yard to better restrict and control the movement of all inmates.

In 1986, construction was completed on a new, multi-level regional facility in Lapeer County. It was the first of many new regional facilities that the state would build during the next few years.

At the time, I was only a few months away from having served ten years in maximum-security for my escape. Due to the fact that I hadn't had a major misconduct ticket in all that time, my security level had already been reduced from a level six to a level two.

The next best thing to actually going home would be a transfer to the new facility in Lapeer, which was only about a mile from where my mother lived. I considered myself fortunate that my counselor was a decent and fair person. I knew if there were any chance of me getting a transfer to Lapeer, he'd be the person to make it happen. When I talked to him, though, he told me that he didn't have the authority to transfer anyone from a level six facility directly to a level two facility.

"Only the regional transfer coordinator can approve that," he said. "But I'll tell ya what, I'll submit your name and write a favorable recommendation for you too."

Most of the officers who were hired to staff the new facility in Lapeer had been training at Huron Valley for about the past eight months. During that time, I'd gotten to know most of them when they worked in segregation and I'd mentioned to several of them that I'd already requested a transfer to Lapeer because it was the region where my family lived.

One of the officers who was hired to work at Lapeer told me that the facility was scheduled to open at the end of the month.

"I'll be transferring there at the end of this week to make final preparations," the officer told me. "The facility is supposed to open in July."

By the time the month of August had come and gone, I began thinking my transfer request had been denied. After all, the new facility had been open for almost two months and I hadn't heard a word about my request.

One afternoon, though, my counselor finally called me to his office and told me my transfer had been approved. I was ecstatic — now I'd be able to get a visit every week from my mother and sisters. Plus, after spending the past ten years in maximum-security, I considered myself lucky just to be leaving Huron Valley alive.

The day before I was scheduled to transfer, I heard that one of the inmates I'd known ever since I first came to prison had been stabbed to death at Jackson. His real name was Dennis but everyone called him Lucky — a nickname he earned for serving two tours of duty in Vietnam yet making it back home each time.

During his time in Vietnam, Lucky had acquired an impressive war record. He was a trained sniper who was an expert in field craft and survival. Lucky was one of those individuals who possessed certain qualities and talents that allowed him to deal with being inserted deep into enemy territory for long, disquieting periods of time.

Lucky was credited with one hundred and eight confirmed kills. His commendations included eight Purple Hearts for wounds received in action, two Bronze Stars for meritorious achievement and bravery as well as two Silver Stars for gallantry in action. Lucky was undeniably a real, live war hero.

Like so many other soldiers who served in Vietnam, though, Lucky began using heroin. He soon found himself addicted to the almost pure dope that was readily available practically everywhere in Vietnam, where it cost only about two dollars for a vial.

When Lucky was discharged from the Army, he returned home and brought his habit with him, quickly spending everything in his bank account just trying to get high. Without money or a job, it wasn't long before Lucky began to pull armed robberies to support his habit. His life of crime was short lived, though, and he soon found himself behind bars. A jury of his so-called peers found him guilty of armed robbery and the judge sentenced him to life in prison.

Once Lucky came to prison, he found that heroin was just about as easy to get as it was on the streets. The only difference is, in prison, heroin costs about four times as much and was usually cut to hell with quinine and mannitol, which meant you had to shoot a lot more of the stuff to get high. Nevertheless, like so many other lost souls that come to prison, Lucky felt that he had nothing else to lose and so, he started using again.

Lucky paid for some of his heroin with the money he made from selling other peoples' drugs. Mostly, though, he relied on the monthly disability checks that he received from the Veterans' Administration to pay for his habit. Eventually, Lucky got in over his head with an inmate drug dealer and he wasn't able to pay the money that he owed for drugs. The drug dealer retaliated by stabbing Lucky in the neck. An artery in Lucky's neck was punctured and before the prison staff could get him to a hospital, he bled to death.

Personally, I always felt more sorry for Lucky than I did for myself. He was actually one hell of a nice guy. Lucky was a whiz at electronics and he was always willing to help a guy out. But moreover, he deserved much more than he ever received or asked for. He was a true war hero in every sense of the word. In my opinion, this country owed Lucky a great debt of gratitude for his selfless service in Vietnam. I found it rather ironic that no one ever bothered to offer him a helping hand to fight the addiction that he had picked up while serving his country so valiantly.

At the very least, the courts should have considered his outstanding war record and given him a break. The fact that Lucky was killed by a low-life drug dealer in prison has always deeply troubled me. He deserved better. I, for one, will always remember him as the true war hero that he was.

CHAPTER 13

THUMB CORRECTIONAL FACILITY

It used to be that once a lifer served ten years of his sentence with a good record, he was eligible for level one status and he was usually sent to the trustee division, a camp or one of the farms.

That practice came to an abrupt halt after a couple of inmates walked away from the trustee division at Jackson and committed a murder. Neither of the inmates was serving a life sentence, but that fact seemed to be lost on the politicians and corrections officials in Lansing.

As a direct result of the incident, the department of corrections would no longer allow lifers to be placed in a level one facility. As for those inmates who were serving a life sentence and who were already in a level one facility, their security level was raised and they were transferred back to a level two facility.

Thankfully, the incident didn't affect my transfer to Lapeer, which accepted multiple levels of prisoners. The prison was called the Thumb Correctional Facility and commonly referred to as TCF.

The first thing the officers did when I arrived at TCF was to go through my property and confiscate several items that weren't allowed at their facility. After they finished nitpicking through my property, I was assigned to housing unit Durant-A and given directions on how to get there. I didn't really know what to expect but when I walked out of the control center, I immediately knew that I was in a much better facility than the one I'd left behind.

The first thing that I noticed was a large concrete amphitheater that had been constructed in a half-circle configuration. It had five tiers of elongated, concrete steps that I assumed were for seating and the backside had been landscaped with yew shrubs and honey locust trees. Ornamental crab apple trees adorned the front of every building and the yard had been covered with sod that looked like a deep green carpet. The setting looked more like the grounds of a college campus rather than what one would normally expect to find inside a prison.

The housing units were designated by name — Auburn, Burns, Cord, Durant, and the level four housing unit was called Essex. Each housing unit was divided into two separate wings — A and B. Durant-A and Durant-B were connected by a corridor they called the bow-tie area, which was kept off limits to prisoners unless we received special authorization to enter it. Situated in the bow-tie area was the laundry room, two small storage rooms, two counselors' offices, a staff bathroom and a small multipurpose room for the officers.

The wings housed forty-eight inmates with twenty-four upstairs and another twenty-four downstairs. There were two triangle shaped day rooms on each level that were enclosed on three sides with large panes of shatterproof glass and the floors were covered with squares of deep blue indoor-outdoor carpet, which was totally unexpected and actually quite nice.

Each day room was furnished with a color television set and a dozen chairs made of molded plastic that were colored blue to match the carpeting. In addition to the day room, there was also an activity area on base with about a dozen tables, where we were allowed to play cards, chess, dominoes and other board games.

There were no sinks or toilets in any of the level two cells. Each level had two communal bathrooms with two single showers that were located on opposite sides of the unit. The cells were furnished with a doublewide wall locker, a small desk with four shelves, a solid steel bunk and a bulletin board to post personal photos. There was also a window with a small section that opened, allowing fresh air circulation from the outside. Lighting in the cell was provided by two fluorescent light fixtures above the bulletin board and lights were covered with a valance that was painted deep blue to match the color scheme of the unit.

I was surprised by a number of things when I first arrived at TCF but the thing I found most astonishing was when an officer issued me a key to my cell door. Up until that point in time, inmates weren't allowed to possess any key other than a footlocker key. If an inmate was caught with a key, they were promptly escorted to the hole for possession of escape paraphernalia with no questions asked.

The yard area was about the same size as Huron Valley's yard and included a half-mile asphalt track. Two softball diamonds were located on opposite sides of the compound and there was also a football field, two tennis courts, four handball courts and a full size basketball court. A couple months after the facility opened, prisoners enrolled in the vocational building trades class built an outside weight pit, two shuffleboard courts, and four horseshoe pits.

The opposite side of the compound, which was separated by the school and the gymnasium, was where the level four inmates where housed in Essex unit. The level two and level four inmates were not allowed to interact with each other. Because of this, level four had it's own separate yard with a small asphalt track and weight-pit that was enclosed with a chain-link fence. All of their movements and activities, for things like access to the gymnasium, library, store, school and chow hall, were scheduled at different times to ensure minimal contact with the level two inmates.

In the far corner of the compound, over by the sally port, was the Michigan State Industries Laundry, which was also called MSI. The MSI laundry was actually one of the many MSI laundries within the prison system throughout the state that contracted with numerous outside hospitals and other institutions for their services.

There was never a shortage of customers since MSI was able to secure contracts by underbidding their free world competitors. This, of course, was due in part to the substantially lower labor costs at MSI, which paid inmate workers just twenty cents an hour.

The building, machinery and utilities were all paid for with taxpayer dollars. Therefore, there were very little, if any, overhead operating expenses. The MSI supervisors, right along with the truck drivers who picked up and delivered the laundry, were all employees of the department of corrections.

The MSI laundry employed mostly level two inmates. They paid the highest wages of all the institutional job assignments, but even that was still slave wages. MSI was also the most difficult job assignment to obtain because of all the prerequisites that were imposed upon the inmates. Nevertheless, there were always plenty of guys who were willing to wait a year or more to procure an MSI job assignment.

The housing unit officer who worked the first shift was Ms. Maxfeld, one of the female officers who had trained at Huron Valley. At Huron Valley, I'd spoken to her on several different occasions and she seemed to be a reasonable and fair-minded person. Even though the officers weren't supposed to discuss their personal lives with the inmates, Ms. Maxfeld often talked freely about her two children and other personal matters. She told me that before becoming a corrections officer, she'd been a registered nurse. I found that rather interesting and personally, I couldn't understand why anyone would want to give up a perfectly good career as a registered nurse to become a corrections officer.

"It's a matter of economics," she told me once. "The only reason I applied for this job is because the state pays much higher wages."

Unlike Huron Valley, there was much less tension amongst the staff and inmates at TCF. It was a totally different atmosphere from what I'd become accustomed to over the past fifteen years.

Most of the inmates in level two were serving a relatively short sentence, which gave them something to look forward to and focus on. Having an out date was a big incentive for those guys to avoid all the bullshit and stay out of trouble. On the other hand, the lifers or guys with long, indeterminate sentences who were at TCF had already served a number of years before they got there. The majority of these guys had already learned from past experience how to do their own time and avoid the many pitfalls of prison life. In fact, some of those individuals were considered stabilizing factors with the prison population and in some instances, even looked at as role models for the younger inmates.

When I went to classification, I requested a job assignment in the inmate store or the yard crew.

"Well, you might just be in luck," said the friendly classification director, a female. "We're looking for an inmate with experience as a store clerk. I see on here that you have a lot of experience."

"Yes, I do," I told her. "I've worked the stores at Marquette and Huron Valley."

"If you're interested, I should have a detail available for you within the next couple of days," she said.

"I am," I said. "Thank you."

The pay was only ninety-eight cents a day, but more important than the money was getting something to occupy my time. When I mentioned to my neighbor that I'd been assigned to the inmate store, he told me the store's supervisor was a civilian who'd never worked in a prison before.

"I heard he's really screwin' things up," my neighbor said. "He don't know what the hell he's doin' so there's stuff all over the place and they're always running out of everything."

Apparently, the two inmates who worked in the store had been taking advantage of their supervisor's kindness and inexperience, stealing the inventory as fast as the supervisor could order it.

A few days after I went to classification, the inmates who were working the store were told their details had been canceled and I was sent to work in their place as the new store clerk.

With my past experience as a store clerk at Marquette and Huron Valley, I was confident that I'd be able to help the store supervisor organize and rectify the problems he was having. When I met the store supervisor, I immediately understood why the inmate store had been having so many problems. Kindness is often taken for weakness in prison and the store supervisor was not only an all-around nice guy, he was also naïve and trusting to a fault. The previous inmate store workers had been shamelessly abusing his kindness.

He asked me to call him by his first name, Frank. But that was actually against prison rules — staff and inmates weren't supposed to address one another on a first name basis because of a belief that the use of first names promotes familiarity. The thought is that it erodes the authority figure's ability to direct and maintain control over the inmate and his behavior.

Frank had originally been hired as a worker in the prison warehouse. It wasn't long after the facility opened that he was placed in charge of the inmate store, he told me. No one had bothered instructing him on how he was supposed to operate and maintain the store, though, and so he'd been learning through trial and error.

All prison employees are trained to never believe anything that an inmate tells them, no matter what the circumstances are. Because of this, many employees have a tendency to construe an inmate giving advice to them as a personal affront. They seem to resent that an inmate would have the audacity to question their competence and ability to perform their job in a professional manner.

Frank wasn't like that, though. He knew he needed assistance so he wasn't about to indulge in a frivolous insecurity. He was willing to listen and learn from the past experience of an inmate.

To alleviate the problem of long lines at the inmate store on script days, the business manager contracted with one of the local vending machine companies to install a candy and soft drink vending machine in every housing unit. And to eliminate the need for coins, which inmates weren't allowed to possess anyhow, the vending machines were converted to accept debit cards.

Each inmate was issued two debit cards and whenever we went to the store, so long as we had money in our inmate accounts, we could charge up to thirty-five dollars worth of items on the card. And each time a card was placed in the vending machine, it would automatically display the amount available to spend and the remaining balance after each purchase.

Whenever Frank took a day off from work, Ms. Baldwin, who was one of the other warehouse workers, usually filled in for him. Part of Ms. Baldwin's warehouse job was delivering supplies inside the facility. One week, she'd deliver supplies to the housing units and the following week, she'd deliver supplies to the school, health care, MSI laundry and other departments.

When she was filling in for Frank one day, she told me that she'd asked the classification director for two inmate workers to assist her with the deliveries she made inside the facility. The problem was, no one wanted the assignment. It was only for one day per week and the pay was just seventy-five cents a day.

"If you can get Frank to agree to it, I wouldn't mind helping you out," I told her. "I can probably find someone else who would volunteer to help out too, just for something to do."

"Really, you wouldn't mind?" she asked me.

"Not at all, so long as Frank doesn't mind," I said.

"All right, well, I'll talk to him the next time he's working," Ms. Baldwin said.

"In the meantime, I'll ask around and see what I can do about finding a volunteer to help us out," I offered, and she thanked me.

Ever since I first arrived at TCF, I'd hung around with a guy named Don. He was serving a life sentence for possession of cocaine and not for a sex crime, which was important to know when looking for someone to work with a female employee. Don also didn't have a job assignment, so when I asked him if he was interested in taking the part-time job delivering supplies once a week, he agreed without much coaxing on my behalf.

At eight o'clock every Thursday morning, Don and I would wait at the back door of the school building for Ms. Baldwin to clear the sally port. If there were no unexpected delays, we were usually finished delivering all the supplies in about forty-five minutes.

One morning, Don and I were inside the back of the truck loading supplies on the pushcart that was destined for the MSI laundry and Ms. Baldwin — who we called Cathy when no one was around — was delivering a package to the school building. When we finished delivering the supplies to MSI, we went back to the truck and began loading the supplies for health care. Before we could finish, though, Ms. Baldwin came running back to the truck, excitedly waving her hand in a "come here" type of fashion.

"Come here guys! Come here!" she hollered at us. "You guys have got to see this!"

"See what?" I asked.

"A guy over at the school has his pants down and he's flashing me!" she said.

Don and I laughed. "Quit bullshitting, we don't have the time for this," I told her lightly.

"No, I swear," she said firmly. "Come here and look for yourself."

From the look of disbelief and astonishment on Ms. Baldwin's face, we finally realized that she had probably seen the TCF Flasher. Don and I climbed down off the truck and we followed Ms. Baldwin back to where she'd seen the Flasher, but of course, he was already gone.

Nevertheless, Don and I knew exactly who the inmate was. His name was Ferrick, but everyone called him by his nickname, Flash. The guy was notorious for flashing everyone. It didn't matter, male or female, he just liked to flash people. He'd been busted numerous times for flashing staff and received several sexual misconduct tickets, but he wasn't about to let a few major misconduct tickets slow him down because that was how he got off. He was a genuine pervert, and he didn't care who knew it.

Flash locked on B-wing in the Durant unit, on the side that faced the employee parking lot. One afternoon at four o'clock when the administration and business office personnel were leaving for the day, Flash stripped down buck-naked and stood in his cell window flashing anyone who dared to look in his direction until one of the employees notified the control center. The control center contacted the housing unit officer and when the officer went to Ferrick's cell, he found him standing there naked in the window and stroking himself as if there were no tomorrow.

The offense wasn't considered serious enough to put Flash in the hole, so the officer told Flash to put some clothes on and he wrote him another sexual misconduct ticket.

Not long after that incident, Flash decided to make a surprise appearance when the warden was giving a tour of the facility to a group of Christian men and women from the local community. The kitchen was one of the last stops on the warden's tour; however, it was also where Flash worked washing pots and pans in the dish tank area.

When the group entered the food service building, they proceeded through the dining room area to the main kitchen where the meals were prepared. Just as the warden began to explain the operation of preparing meals, lo and behold, out stepped Flash. He was buck-naked except for a pair of bright yellow rubber boots and a big smile on his face. He didn't say anything, he just stood there with his penis in his hand as if he was caught up in the rapture of the moment — the look on his face was one of sheer ecstasy.

But his moment of pleasure was short lived. The officer who was with the tour group immediately grabbed Flash and hustled him out of the kitchen. I can only imagine what must have been going through those good Christian folks' minds when they saw Flash. The warden apologized to the abashed and bewildered tour group and he assured the good Christian citizens of the community that Flash wasn't a scheduled attraction on their tour. As for Flash, after that escapade, no one at TCF ever saw hide nor hair of him again.

The hobby-craft department was supervised by Mrs. Bishop, who was hired as an officer but promoted to the position of hobby-craft director. Before Mrs. Bishop became a corrections officer at TCF, she was employed as a schoolteacher. She was one of the few staff who made a sincere effort to help the inmates make positive changes in their lives.

Mrs. Bishop often went out of her way to encourage inmates with her positive and reassuring comments. Unlike others, she seemed to actually like her job and it was readily apparent from the outstanding manner in which she organized and supervised the hobby-craft department.

When I first got into hobby-craft at TCF, I had no intention of getting seriously involved. I merely wanted to make a few macramé plant hangers for my mother and sisters. Once I learned how to tie all the different kinds of knots, though, I actually began to enjoy what I was doing. Not only did I find each macramé project to be an excellent way of relieving stress but upon completing the projects, I also felt a sense of accomplishment and pride — emotions that were hard to come by in prison. Moreover, I discovered that there was money to be made in macramé, which was a big incentive.

After a few months of practice, I was making everything from dream catchers to Santa Clauses. I was amazed at the endless variety of things that could be created with just a few simple knots. I could usually make a four-foot plant hanger in one day. Larger plant hangers that were more than seven-feet in length would take me about a week to finish. Each of the seven-foot hangers required more than three hundred yards of six-millimeter braided macramé cord.

I designed each hanger to hold a piece of circular cut glass, twelve- to eighteen-inches in diameter. Hardly a day went by that I didn't make something and most of the items I made were unique and of my own design. After a while, I had so many items on the hobby-craft stand that it began to look more like a macramé stand than anything else.

In order to promote and foster good public relations with the local community, Mrs. Bishop would often purchase hobby-craft supplies from some of the local vendors in downtown Lapeer. One of the vendors, Meesha's Knit and Stitch, was where I purchased most of my macramé supplies.

Meesha, the lady who owned and operated the store, not only sold a variety of craft supplies but she also sold a number of finished items, such as custom designed aluminum lawn chairs woven with macramé cord. Customers were able to order a chair with practically any design they desired. The most requested designs were the ones with the letter 'M' to represent the University of Michigan or the letter 'S' to represent Michigan State University. Using the colors of each university, the design was woven into the back of the chair and the seats were usually done in a herringbone or a checkerboard pattern.

I never got much into making chairs because the cost of materials was rather high and made for a negligible profit margin. When Meesha lost one of her workers and couldn't keep up with the orders, though, she asked Mrs. Bishop if I'd consider helping her out and I readily agreed.

Whenever Meesha needed me to do a chair, she'd bring the material to the facility and drop it off at the hobby-craft stand, which was located in the lobby of the administration building. Usually on the same day, Mrs. Bishop would walk up front and bring the materials back to me. I could typically finish most chairs in a couple of hours and have them ready for Meesha to pick-up the next day.

There was nothing complicated about weaving the designs into the chairs. Each chair came with a numbered pattern. After securing one end of the cord to the frame of the chair, it was a simple matter of counting the number of over and under cords, and securing the other side with a looping stitch with a crochet hook. I usually received ten dollars for each chair I completed and so long as the chairs didn't require an intricate pattern, I could usually finish two chairs in a day.

Another of the most requested patterns was the logo of the Detroit Red Wings. That particular pattern was especially intricate and woven with three-millimeter cord, requiring twice as much work and time to complete. Still, I only charged an additional five dollars because I knew Meesha wasn't making a lot of money from the items she sold.

During the holiday season, I usually made around three hundred dollars just from the chairs, and another three hundred bucks from the hobby-craft stand for plant hangers and other macramé items.

Not long after TCF opened, the inmates were allowed to start an organization called the "Child of the Month Club". The objective of the organization was to provide a number of under privileged children in the local community with a Christmas party and several gifts for as many children as possible. We specifically wanted to help the children who would otherwise have very little to celebrate during the Christmas holiday.

Most of the inmates who were involved in the organization were also involved in hobby-craft. In order to raise the necessary funds needed to purchase gifts, food and other items, everyone got involved in making hobby-craft items. The money generated from the sale of these items was placed in a special account and by the end of the year, the inmates had managed to raise over two thousand dollars.

The liaison and coordinator for the Child of the Month Club was Mrs. Bishop, the hobby-craft director. Without her tireless efforts and selfless dedication, the club probably would have never existed. She spent countless hours of her own time coordinating every detail and was instrumental in obtaining the warden's permission to hold the Christmas party in the facility's kitchen dining room. She also arranged for the county's social services department to select and invite more than twenty families to attend the Christmas party that year.

The party was supervised by members of the administration staff and several officers. They not only volunteered their time but also contributed food items and many gifts, making the event an overwhelming success.

At the end of the evening, many parents expressed their profound appreciation to all the staff and inmates. One mother was so overcome with emotion that she cried tears of joy at the sight of her child having his Christmas wish come true. I remember her saying that there was no way she could ever have afforded to give her child all the wonderful Christmas presents that he'd received. Many of the children had been given remote control cars and trucks as gifts and almost everywhere you looked, there was a remote controlled toy speeding around the dining room floor or running the obstacle course through the legs of the dining room tables and chairs. It was a sight that I never could have imagined seeing inside a prison.

TCF was full of such surprises. During the month of December, the base area of each housing unit was decorated with a seven-foot-tall artificial Christmas tree and the inmates were allowed, even encouraged, to help make additional decorations for the tree and housing units as well.

A couple of days before Christmas, every inmate received a free Christmas gift bag that was filled with a variety of food and snack items like meat sticks, cheese and candy. In all my years in prison, TCF was the only facility I ever saw that actually allowed the inmates to celebrate Christmas. Of course, all the Christmas decorations, including the gift bags, were paid for by the inmate benefit fund and not the state or facility.

The inmate benefit fund was a special account that received funding directly and entirely from the profits generated by the inmate store. Other sources of inmate revenue, such as photo tickets, vending machines and hobby-craft sales, also benefited the fund. All special activities were paid for by the fund, including things like cable television, the library and hobby-craft and any other special activity. The department of corrections didn't pay for anything other than the required basic necessities — food, clothing, housing and medical care.

It wasn't long after TCF opened that an inmate managed to escape by climbing up and over the wall in the level four visiting yard. The outside visiting yard used by the level four inmates was enclosed by a brick wall and monitored by electronic sensors. And surprisingly, only a single coil of razor wire was strung along the top of the wall, which really wasn't much of a deterrent.

A major design flaw with the wall was that only the section facing the employee parking lot was thirty feet high. The other section, the one situated inside the facility's perimeter fence, was only about twelve-feet high and there were no electronic sensors or razor wire on that wall.

The inmate had no problem climbing on top of the twelve-foot wall. By using the steel mounting brackets for the electronic sensors as a step, he was able to reach the top of the thirty-foot wall and pull himself up. Once on top of the wall, he carefully stepped over the razor wire until he reached a point beyond the perimeter fence, where he then lowered himself over the edge of the wall and dropped to the ground.

He walked right by the window of the warden's office and passed the front entrance of the lobby without anyone ever noticing him. He walked through the parking lot, across the street and into a field that was adjacent to the prison grounds. But for all his efforts, he didn't get very far.

About thirty minutes later, he was taken into custody by a Department of Natural Resources officer who spotted him walking in a nearby wooded area. He was the only inmate to ever successfully escape from TCF.

In an attempt to deter anyone else from trying the same thing, the maintenance department installed numerous coils of additional razor wire along the top and sides of both walls. Nevertheless, about a year later, another inmate tried to escape by using the same route. He managed to get to the top of the thirty-foot wall, but he couldn't avoid becoming entangled in the multiple coils of razor wire. He was soon spotted by an employee in the parking lot, who notified the control center of the inmate's precarious situation. The guy became so entangled in the razor wire that before they could bring him down off the wall, they had to cut sections of his clothing off.

The second year after TCF opened, Warden Roberts began what became known as the warden's annual picnic. Every year, the picnic was scheduled during the month of August and held in the amphitheater, which had plenty of room for everyone to sit, eat their meal and listen to the live entertainment that was provided by several of the inmate musical groups.

The maintenance department had constructed two large grills by cutting an old, two-hundred and fifty gallon oil tank in half. Legs were welded to each half and for the gridirons, sections of diamond shaped security screen were laid over the top.

The main entree consisted of barbecued chicken and hot dogs, which were grilled by the warden and his deputy wardens. The potato salad, baked beans, and corn on the cob were prepared in the kitchen and then delivered to the serving lines in hot carts.

Tables from the school classrooms were used as serving tables and arranged in two rows along the sidewalk between the school building and health care. Administration and business office employees volunteered to participate and they served the food. The picnics were always a big success and sincerely appreciated by all the inmates. By far, the best thing about the picnics was the real banana splits served for dessert. Administration secretaries and several other female employees from the business office were responsible for whipping up these delicious desserts.

Since my escape in 1977, I'd managed to avoid receiving any major misconduct tickets. I'd spent almost ten years in two different maximum-security prisons. In all that time, I'd never received a single ticket, which wasn't an easy thing to do. In every prison, there, are always at least one or two corrections officers who possess a malicious nature and TCF was no exception. These officers appeared to suffer from more psychological problems then the inmates themselves — they were often petty and vindictive, frequently abusing their authority and tended to treat all inmates as if we were pieces of shit. They seemed to think that we were somehow directly responsible for everything that was wrong with the world and their personal lives.

One such person was a female officer by the name of Leggett. She was a heavy-set older woman with scraggly gray hair who was spiteful and exhibited a wretched disposition that she didn't mind sharing with anyone and everyone who happened to cross her path.

Ms. Leggett was a hateful, despicable old bitch. I can only speculate that at some point in her miserable life, she must have been victimized — beaten, battered, abused and perhaps even molested. Something terrible must've happened to cause her to become the sorry excuse for a human she turned out to be. Ms. Leggett seemed to hate everyone, especially inmates, and she never missed an opportunity to punish us.

She wasn't much liked by her coworkers either. Whenever she worked the housing units, she disrupted the normal routine and created a hostile environment for the inmates and staff alike. The guys in the housing units would often antagonize her by placing feces on the telephone and hoping that when she answered the telephone, she'd get a mouth full of shit. They often set fires in the trash cans, placed voodoo dolls on the officer's podium and sometimes, the guys would even steal the officer's podium from the base area and place it in the shower with the water running. The podium itself was insignificant, but inside the podium was a locked drawer where the officers kept the housing unit security log book. If an officer was to lose the log book, they could also potentially lose their job.

Officer Leggett had received several disciplinary write-ups from her supervisors for miscounting the number of inmates during formal counts. As a result, she'd received a progressive number of days off work without pay for each offense. If she made one more mistake during a formal count, she would have been fired.

Not surprisingly, it was rumored that she did make another mistake during count one afternoon when she was working overtime on second shift. But supposedly, the second shift lieutenant and the old bitch worked out an amicable arrangement that was to their mutual satisfaction. She got to keep her job and the lieutenant got what he wanted, when he wanted it.

One morning, Don and I were working for Ms. Baldwin delivering supplies to the housing units when Leggett tried to give Don a hard time. We were stacking the supplies against the wall in the hallway as we always did when Leggett decided that she wanted the supplies placed in the office.

"You aren't going to put those boxes there," she scoffed in her usual, scornful voice. "Bring it over here and put it on the desk."

But Don refused.

"The housing unit porter's job is to put the supplies away," he said, avoiding eye contact with the old hag. "It ain't my job. My job is to deliver them."

Naturally, she took this as a direct challenge to her omnipotent authority.

"I am giving you a direct order to take the supplies into the office and put them on the desk," she said coldly. "If you don't comply, I'll have your butt in big trouble. How about a major misconduct ticket for disobeying a direct order?"

Don wasn't so easily intimidated.

"I don't care," he told her nonchalantly. "You go right ahead."

But just in case Leggett decided to write that ticket, Don told Ms. Baldwin about the incident so he'd have a witness to help him set the record straight.

"Don't worry about her, Don," Ms. Baldwin reassured him. "She's just mean. I don't think she'd actually write a ticket for something so silly."

But sure enough, Leggett did write the ticket. And when she took it up to the control center for her supervisor to review, the sergeant threw the ticket out. I'm sure that irritated the old bitch to no end.

Little did we know, that while we finished delivering the supplies, Ms. Baldwin had it in her mind to also pay the control center a visit. She complained to the shift commander about how Officer Leggett had harassed her inmate workers.

"You know, it's their job to deliver the supplies to the back door of the housing unit. That's what I hired them for," Ms. Baldwin said. "Now, I don't need some mean old woman ordering them around like they work for her. She tried telling them they had to bring the supplies in and put them away — that's not their job and if it was, we'd never have enough time in the day to get everything delivered."

Ms. Baldwin was clearly upset.

"Now listen, these are two good guys, hardworking guys, that I've got working with me," Ms. Baldwin continued on. "If any of them gets pulled away from their job because of some silly ticket written without any basis by that woman, well, you won't hear the end of it from me."

Don and I knew well enough that Leggett was a petty and vindictive old hag. Having her misconduct ticket torn up was a blow to her over-inflated ego that wouldn't be easily forgotten. We knew she would seek revenge on us, biding her time until she could set up a trap to get us. And we were right too — the old bitch never did get over that incident.

It was a few weeks later when Leggett came to my cell and said she wanted to do a routine shakedown. She thoroughly trashed what had been my tidy little living area and after it all, didn't find any contraband or rule violations. But, the bitch was determined to have my ass for something. She narrowed in on two safety pins that were attached to my sheet and mattress. I'd been using them to secure my bottom sheet to the mattress, keeping the sheet from sliding off the plastic covered mattress while I was sleeping.

When she finished her shakedown, she didn't say anything to me but unclipped the safety pins and took them back to the bow tie area. About an hour later, she came back by my cell, put her hands on her hips and stared coldly at me until I returned her gaze.

"Technically, I could write you a ticket for destruction of state property," she told me with her nose turned up like the snobby, petty bitch she was.

"For what?" I asked, flabbergasted.

"For those holes in your mattress," she chastised.

I didn't say anything. It took me a second to realize she was talking about the safety pins. There was nothing to say back to that; I just thought to myself about what a petty bitch she was and knew there was nothing I could say to appease her.

After realizing I wasn't going to give her any fodder by replying, she moved on to barking orders at me.

"You need to bring your mattress to the bow-tie area and exchange it with the mattress lying by the back door," she said.

"No thanks," I tried to say as nicely as possible. "I've already got a used mattress."

"This is a direct order, mister," she barked at me. "You will get up right now and do as I say."

"Not in this life time," I mumbled under my breath.

"You've got until eleven o'clock to exchange your mattress," she declared.

"I don't care if you give me eleven days, I'm not doing it," I told her, now looking her directly in the eyes.

If she had wanted me to exchange my mattress for a new one, I would've had no problem doing it. But I knew of the mattress she was talking about; I'd seen it lying there. It was being thrown out as garbage.

In fact, I was responsible for delivering the new mattress to the housing unit that morning. It went to an inmate who was exchanging his old mattress for a new one, and the old one was supposed to be headed for the dumpster. I was not about to exchange my mattress for what I knew to be someone else's garbage.

"You'll do as I say and you'll do it by eleven o'clock or else I'll write you a major misconduct ticket for disobeying a direct order," she said to me before turning on her heels and walking away, no doubt feeling quite good about her high-and-mighty self.

Just as she promised, the old bitch wrote me that ticket.

A few days later, Ms. Maxfeld told me that Leggett had told her in confidence that the only reason she wrote that ticket was because I hadn't had a ticket in years. The mattress was just the perfect excuse; Leggett knew I wasn't going to exchange a perfectly good mattress for one that was literally headed for the trash.

Disobeying a direct order is an all-inclusive ticket and as such, it is regularly abused by officers seeking retaliation against an inmate. There are only two extenuating circumstances in which a

DDO, which stands for disobeying a director order, can be considered invalid.

If the direct order places the inmate's safety in jeopardy, the ticket can be invalidated. The other circumstance that can invalidate a DDO is if an inmate is given conflicting orders by two different officers. Neither of those circumstances applied to my mattress situation.

I went to court for my DDO ticket the following week. When the hearing officer asked why I refused to follow Leggett's order, I informed the officer that it was because the mattress in question was old and being thrown out because it was soaked with urine.

The hearing officer phoned Ms. Maxfeld and asked her if she could verify my statement.

"I didn't personally examine the mattress," Ms. Maxfeld said. "However, I know the mattress was being thrown out because it was non-serviceable."

It was all for moot. Regardless of the facts, the hearing officer found me guilty and he gave me two days top-lock in my cell, which meant that I wasn't allowed to come out of my cell for anything except for meals and to use the bathroom.

When I got back to the housing unit, Ms. Maxfeld came by to visit me.

"I know I could've gotten you out of that ticket, but I would've had to lie about the mattress being soaked with urine and I know you wouldn't have wanted me to lie for you," she said to me.

"I understand, but truly, you wouldn't have been lying to assume the mattress was soaked with urine," I told her.

The following week, when we delivered supplies to the housing unit where Officer Leggett was working, she stood in the hallway and gave us the evil eye as we unloaded the supplies. Just to aggravate her, I told Don that it smelled like a pig farm in this unit and made sure I said it loud enough for her to hear me.

There was another inmate standing in the hallway and I took the opportunity to drive my point home.

"What stinks in this unit?" I asked him loudly. "Are you guys raising pigs in here or what, because it sure smells like pig shit in here to me."

Leggett didn't say anything, just shot me a dirty look with those cold, heartless old eyes of hers. She knew my derogatory comments were directed at her but she couldn't write me an insolence ticket for something that I said to another inmate.

Two weeks later, though, I was told to pack my property because I was being transferred elsewhere. I didn't find out until almost two years later that the old bitch Leggett had written a statement to the deputy warden saying she felt threatened by me. As a direct result of her vengeful actions, I was transferred.

Once again, I'd find myself far, far away from home and my family. If Leggett's goal was to make my life as miserable as hers, I suppose she'd succeeded.

As the old saying goes, "misery loves company." And that old bitch spent her life trying to make sure each and every inmate was as miserable as she was.

CHAPTER 14

Hiawatha and Kinross Temporary Facilities

The next morning, I was placed in belly-chains and two officers transported me to the Riverside Correctional Facility. From there, I was placed on a transfer bus headed to the Upper Peninsula.

On the bright side, my second trip to the U.P. wasn't nearly as bad as the first time, when I was sent to Marquette. The bus they had us on looked like a regular school bus, except it was painted white and all the windows were covered with security screens.

The bus was only half-full, which was a pleasant surprise that worked out to my advantage. I had two seats across from each other all to myself, allowing me to stretch out and be relatively comfortable on the long ride. I also was not placed in leg shackles or the dreaded black-box and I thanked my lucky stars for that.

I was sent to Hiawatha Temporary Facility near Sault Saint Marie, Michigan. As the name implies, it was supposed to be a level two temporary facility built to house the influx of new inmates and temporarily ease overcrowding.

However, the state had built several of these so-called temporary facilities with another objective in mind — to offset the loss of manufacturing jobs in the automobile industry by keeping a steady flow of construction work available. Using the word temporary in the names of these facilities was a joke. There was no doubt, at least in my mind, that the department of corrections would most likely still be using these "temporary" facilities for conceivably the next fifty years, or at least until they run out of funding.

The housing units were nothing more than pole barns with a plasterboard partition running down the middle of the unit. Each side was divided into ten, six-man cubicles and one hundred and twenty inmates were housed in each unit. There were a total of eight housing units on the compound.

The front section of each cubicle was enclosed with a four-foot-high partition and had a four-foot-wide doorway in the middle. And even though the sidewalls between the cubicles were eight-feet-high, they were still about four-feet-short of touching the ceiling, allowing all the noise to pass freely between cubicles.

Situated on each side of the doorway was a single-man bunk, a small metal desk and a wall locker for each inmate. Along the back wall, there were two sets of bunk beds, four desks and four wall lockers. From the moment I walked in the housing unit and saw those six-man cubicles, I knew this was definitely not a place that I wanted to be. There was absolutely no privacy whatsoever and from the constant clamor of voices, televisions and radios, it was quite apparent that there would be no peace and quiet in the days to come.

The yard was a lot smaller than TCF's yard, but there were individual common yards in front of each housing unit and every common yard had a few picnic tables and a basketball court.

The weight-pit, a small dirt track and a pole barn they called the gymnasium — which was rarely open to the inmates — were all located on the back yard.

Reluctantly, I resigned myself to the fact that I was going to be in the Upper Peninsula for at least the next few months. I'd just have to make the best of a bad situation.

To pass the time, I requested a job assignment on the yard and a week later, I was given a yard crew detail. Fortunately, it was early spring, which meant I wouldn't be spending my time shoveling snow. I didn't really have any interest in cutting grass or picking up cigarette butts either. But at least I'd be outside all day long, where I was allowed to pretty much come and go as I pleased. Quite unexpectedly, I received a Notice of Action from the parole board that was dated May 15, 1992.

"The parole board will begin actively processing your case in the near future. However, the parole board will not be requesting placement in level one security for any prisoner serving a life sentence who is not already in level one."

My Own Worst Enemy

I could hardly believe what I'd just read. The parole board had held an executive session and voted by a majority to begin actively processing my case for a commutation — that meant I stood a good chance of being released!

First, though, I'd have to go through the process of a public hearing. The hearings are typically scheduled within ninety days from the time the parole board decides to process an individual's case.

The purpose of having a public hearing is to protect the public from the release of an inmate who might pose a risk to society. It also provides the public the opportunity to voice their concerns for or against the inmate's release. And while the parole board must determine the inmate's state of mind; the inmate must accept responsibility and express remorse for his crime.

After the public hearing, the parole board would then review the transcripts from the hearing and consider all relevant comments. If there were no strong opposition, the board would then submit their recommendation to the governor requesting that my sentence be commuted to second-degree murder. If the governor grants the commutation, the parole board then has the authority to grant a parole.

I was ecstatic. It'd been a long twenty years in prison and finally, after all that time, there was a little ray of light at the end of the tunnel I called my life. I could actually be home within the next couple of years.

For about two months after receiving the letter, it was as if a great weight had been lifted off my shoulders. Forget that I was in such an unpleasant, "temporary" living environment. Forget that I was in the Upper Peninsula again, hundreds of miles and hours from my mother and family.

Suddenly, for the first time in many years, all the little trivial annoyances of prison didn't bother me. I walked around as though I didn't have a care in the world. The noisy housing unit seemed to fall mute on my ears. The cramped cubicles, lack of privacy — none of it mattered. I had my sights set on being home again.

My carefree attitude was short-lived, however.

A convicted sex offender by the name of Leslie Williams, who was on parole, kidnapped, raped and murdered four young women in the tiny town of Fenton, Michigan. The public was understandably outraged and demanded action.

The media had a field day with the murders. Pressure was put on the governor's office, the department of corrections and the parole board. Everyone wanted an answer to one question — why was this person paroled in the first place?

The heinous crimes were relentlessly sensationalized by media outlets throughout the state. Everyone seemed to arrive at the conclusion that only a broken system would allow such a travesty.

Making matters even worse, it was an election year. Every politician wanted to look as though he or she had no hand in creating the problem but had just the solution to fix it. Consequently, the politicians' reaction was swift and every inmate in the State of Michigan would suffer the consequences for the horrible crime committed by one individual parolee.

Michigan's legislature hastily passed a number of new laws and within a matter of months, a new, ten-member parole board was appointed to replace the seven members who had previously served.

Unlike their predecessors, the new members were appointed to serve a specific term and now, they could be held accountable if they paroled an inmate who then went on to commit another crime. If that happened, the board members would lose their job. As a result, the number of inmates who did get paroled was significantly reduced.

The new parole board adopted the philosophy that a life sentence meant exactly that — life in prison. A life sentence essentially became a death sentence.

Furthermore, the new parole board refused to honor the previous parole board's decisions and recommendations. Most of the pending paroles and commutations that had not yet been finalized were rescinded with no explanation, including mine. Shortly thereafter, I received a notice from the parole board stating that they had no interest in taking any action in my case at that time and that my case would be reviewed in five years.

For the life of me, I couldn't understand how the parole board could justify holding all inmates in the State of Michigan accountable for the heinous crime that was committed by one individual.

I personally believe that anyone who commits a crime against women, children or the elderly should be punished severely. But why does every person who ever committed a crime, no matter how long ago it was, have to be punished as the result of one person's heinous crime? Why are we all punished as if we're all somehow responsible for that one person's actions?

Apply the same logic to doctors and see how fair it sounds then. If one doctor harms a patient, irrespective of his intent, and that patient is seriously injured or even dies, should all doctors be judged and punished based on that one doctor's actions?

We all make mistakes and errors in judgment and some people will never learn from their mistakes. There are also some truly evil people in this world who unquestionably need to be locked up to protect the public. However, it's not only morally and ethically wrong to hold one individual liable for the unforeseen acts and/or consequences of another individual's actions, it's a violation of the fundamental principles of individual criminal culpability, and therefore, unjust.

In today's society, it's unacceptable and politically incorrect to discriminate against people simply because of their race, religious beliefs, ethnic affiliations and even their sexual preferences. Yet, people who are convicted of a crime are often stereotyped, treated like pariahs and routinely discriminated against as if they're somehow directly responsible for all that is wrong with the world.

Society needs to remember that people in prison are still human beings and that we have the capability to change. The belief that all people in prison are bad and all free-world people are good is a misconception. We are not simply bad people who committed bad crimes against good people. This stereotypical mindset only further ostracizes people who have found themselves on the outskirts of society.

I'd only been at Hiawatha for about six months when I received a ticket for fighting. My state of mind, by then, had gone from happy and hopeful to the point that nothing could bother me to very irritable, unhappy and annoyed. It was the first ticket I'd received for fighting in twenty years.

The guy who bunked right across from me was one of those individuals we called a bible thumper. His name was John and he pretty much spent his entire day reading the bible and trying to talk about the bible or recite verses from it to anyone who would listen.

Lenny, one of the other guys in the cubicle with us, was for some unknown reason, constantly trying to pick a fight with John. I think it had something to do with John's religion, I'm not sure if his constant bible thumping irritated Lenny or if he actually had different beliefs. But the bible thumper wouldn't allow himself to be goaded into a fight, even when Lenny would shove the wannabe preacher against the wall or wrestle him to the floor.

One afternoon, John and Lenny were embroiled in another of their petty altercations when, against my better judgment, I decided to say something to Lenny. I knew I should've kept my mouth shut but I was so sick and tired of listening to their constant bickering, hour after hour, day after day, week after week. Lenny was always the aggressor, so I turned my remarks to him.

"Why don't you just give the guy a break?" I asked Lenny. "He's not bothering anyone. Just leave 'em alone for once."

Lenny looked over at me, one hand still pinning John to the ground.

"This got nothin' to do with you," he sneered, delivering a few other choice words that I decided to ignore.

I knew he was right. I had no business opening my mouth in the first place, so I returned to trying to ignore their incessant fighting and focused my attention on the television. The next day while I was on the yard, John came up to me with his head down.

"There is something important I must tell you," he said in a hushed voice.

I worried that he was going to start one of his religious lectures and just stood there, waiting for him to get started.

"Lenny told me that I ought to be careful or he'll do to me what he plans to do to you," John said, leaning in close and speaking as softly as possible. "He said he was going to stab you in the neck while you're sleeping."

He stepped back from me.

"I just wanted you to know," he said, then turned his gaze toward the ground and walked away.

I didn't know whether to believe the guy or not. The thought certainly crossed my mind that John could be trying to manipulate me, trying to turn me against Lenny as a means to solve his own problem with the guy. Perhaps he was hoping that by telling me such a thing, I'd take the initiative to stab Lenny in the neck first.

Living in an open dorm setting, though, I didn't want to take any chances. As much as I hated life in prison, I didn't have a death wish. I figured the best thing to do was to confront Lenny and hear what he had to say about it.

Later in the afternoon that same day, everyone was out on the yard and I was enjoying some quiet time alone in the cubicle. Lenny came in and went over to his wall locker. I watched him carefully and when he finished what he was doing and turned around to go back outside, I called out his name.

"Hey Lenny," I said calmly but with a very direct tone. "Did you tell someone you were going to stab me in the neck while I'm sleeping?"

"Who told you that?" he shot back at me, turning around in a flash.

"That doesn't matter," I said. "Just answer my question. Did you tell someone you were going to stab me, or not?"

He avoided my question by asking another question and then, without giving me a chance to answer, began ranting and raving, his voice growing louder with each word. The guy was definitely off-kilter.

"Whatever," I said, turning around to walk away.

I had taken two steps before I felt something hit me in the side of my head. When I turned around, Lenny was standing there with his fists clenched, wearing an angry, menacing scowl on his face.

At that point, I had no choice but to defend myself. I threw a hard right punch and landed it directly on his left eye, causing him to immediately drop to his knees. He was only stunned momentarily, though, and then he grabbed me around the waist with both his arms and began ferociously biting into my stomach like a mad man.

To fight back, I began wailing on the top of his head with my fists, but it didn't do any good. My third strike finally knocked him back to the floor, where he laid for a minute. Since he didn't get right back up, I assumed the fight was over. As he finally began pulling himself off the floor, I let him get up. That was a big mistake.

When he got off the floor, he charged me like a bull with his head down — grabbing me around the waist again and knocking me backwards until we landed on one of the other guy's bunks. Lenny was on top of me now and I tried to push him off with one hand while I blocked his punches with the other. I laid my right hand flat against his face and pushed as hard as I could, trying to push his neck sideways to convince him that he had to get off me. Suddenly, I felt him bite down on my thumb and lock his teeth into my flesh like a snapping turtle that refuses to let go.

There was a desk right next to the bunk and when I saw Lenny reach over and grab a large afro-pick, I immediately sensed that he intended to use it as a weapon. There wasn't much I could do when he began stabbing at my face except move my head from side-to-side, and that didn't work for long. I felt the afro-pick's individual teeth tear into the flesh of my cheek and became acutely aware of the precarious situation I was in.

Lenny was a much bigger guy than I was, outweighing me by probably eighty pounds or more, and here I was pinned underneath him. With him still biting down on my thumb, I had only my left arm to use against him while he was wielding a weapon — aimed at my face, of all places. One good stab with that comb and I could be blind for the rest of my life. I was in deep shit.

Adrenaline surged through my body and I struck him three more times, solid hits with my left arm in quick succession, and landed all three of the punches on the right side of his head. He stabbed me again, this time in the forehead, and that's when I suddenly heard the housing unit officer.

"Break it up!" boomed the officer's voice and within a matter of seconds, several officers were pulling us apart. They handcuffed both of us and told me to sit on the bunk while they transported Lenny to health care, where the individual holding cells were located.

There was blood running down my face from my stab wounds and my thumb was also pumping out blood from where Lenny had bitten me. Through the blood, I could just barely see the wound on my thumb, and it looked like a rat or some other type of dirty vermin had been gnawing on me.

When I got to health care, they put seventeen stitches in my cheek plus another eight in my forehead. They bandaged my wounds and I was placed in one of the temporary segregation holding cells.

Later that afternoon, I was given a major misconduct ticket for fighting and told that when I was released from temporary segregation, I'd be on top-lock status until I went to court. That meant I wasn't supposed to leave my cubicle without permission, not even for the bathroom. It didn't matter that I didn't throw the first punch; in prison, it rarely does. If an officer doesn't clearly see who starts the fight, then a ticket is typically given to everyone involved in the fight.

When they released me from temporary segregation, I was assigned to a different housing unit where I spent the next two days on top-lock. After that, I was transferred across the street to the Kinross Temporary Facility, or KTF.

KTF was another temporary level two facility. The housing units were all pole barns, exactly the same as Hiawatha. The only noticeable differences between the facilities were the layout of the buildings and the size of the yards. KTF had two weight-pits, one on the front yard and another on the back yard, which was unusual.

Surprisingly, KTF also had a hockey rink that looked vaguely familiar to the one we had at Marquette before the riots. After asking around, I finally found out from one of the guys who had been at KTF for years that it was indeed the same hockey rink. All of the guys at Marquette, myself included, had thought the administration had thrown the rink away along with all the rest of the recreation equipment after the riot. Come to find out, it was just shipped somewhere else.

I went to court in an attempt to fight the ticket I'd received for fighting at Hiawatha, but it was of no use. I was found guilty and sentenced to thirty days loss of privileges. I could've gotten thirty days in the hole, but luckily, none of the temporary level two facilities had a segregation unit. I also could've been sent to a level four facility for punishment, but a fighting ticket wasn't considered a serious enough infraction of the rules to raise my security level.

From day one, I didn't care for KTF any more than for Hiawatha. I was tired of living in a dormitory setting where there was absolutely no privacy and you had to practically sleep with one eye open. Besides that, I was fed up with having to worry about someone stealing my property every time I left the cubicle. It was a pain in the ass having to lock up all my property, even when I went to the bathroom.

I knew that most administrations would eventually transfer an inmate who created a lot of unnecessary paperwork for them and so, I decided to go on a grievance writing campaign.

I wrote as many grievances as I possibly could. I wrote grievances for just about anything and everything, even for the most minor policy violations. I even filed a request for a legal name change just to create more paperwork and I kept at it until I finally became enough of a nuisance to warrant a transfer back to TCF.

It was early morning when we were loaded on the bus for the trip back down to the Lower Peninsula. Once again, I counted my blessings that we weren't required to wear leg shackles or the odious black-box.

Since I knew exactly where I was going and what to expect when I got there, the long ride back to the Lower Peninsula was a lot less stressful and I was able to sit back and enjoy some of the scenery. It was late in the afternoon when we finally arrived at Riverside Correctional Facility in Ionia, Michigan. It was also a Friday and none of the facilities transferred inmates on the weekends unless it was an emergency. So, we had to spend the weekend at Riverside until the transportation officers came from TCF to pick us up on Monday.

Riverside was a multilevel facility that housed both level two and level four inmates. It was one of the oldest prisons in Michigan and at one time, it was used to house the criminally insane. Over the years, though, it had been converted into a resident treatment program for inmates who received psychotherapy and counseling. Because of its central location in the state, it was also being used as a transfer point for inmates coming and going from prisons in the Upper Peninsula.

I was assigned to housing unit seven-one-east and placed in a cell that was freezing cold. For some reason, there weren't any heat registers in the cells. All the steam heat registers were in the hallway and this provided very little heat to the cells. The main reason it was cold in my cell, though, was because someone had broken out several panes of glass in the window. Every so often, a gust of wind would blow snow right through the broken panes and into my cell. For what it was worth, I politely complained to the officer, but it didn't do much good.

After a few minutes, the asshole came back to my cell with a plastic garbage bag.

"Why don't you try rigging this up to cover those holes," he said, holding the garbage bag out to me.

Then, to add insult to injury, he also handed me a half-gallon plastic jug.

"If you need to relieve yourself during the night, you can go ahead and use this," he said.

It turned out to be a very long, cold and sleepless night. At around six o'clock the next morning, an officer unlocked my cell door and told me that I could use the bathroom and take a shower before breakfast.

It definitely would have been nice to take a long, hot shower. I was chilled to the bone and the idea of hot water and steam sounded like a slice of heaven after the cold night I'd endured. But, I didn't have any shower shoes and in prison, you just don't take a shower without shower shoes. All sorts of fungi and unpleasant pathogens live on the shower floor and I just wasn't about to expose my bare feet to all that lurks there.

I skipped the shower but was glad for the opportunity to use a toilet. When I went to the bathroom, I was disgusted by the rundown conditions. Standing water was all over the floor from the leaky toilets, paint was peeling off the walls and the plaster was falling by the chunks from the ceiling — everything was literally falling apart. I'd never seen a prison in such a state of disrepair.

I was just glad that I was only passing through this little piece of heaven. When I finished in the bathroom, the officer told me that I could use the day room and the outside airing room. The airing room was where the inmates were allowed to smoke, since smoking was prohibited inside any of the buildings. It was similar to a porch except it was totally enclosed with steel bars, kind of like a big cage.

Half of the day room was being used as a dormitory for inmates in transit, so it was almost impossible to watch or hear the television. Fortunately, I was able to borrow a couple of books and I sat in the corner of the day room, reading. It was a little noisy, but at least it was better than sitting in a freezing cold cell, staring at the decrepit walls.

After a long and miserable weekend in Ionia, I was ready to go first thing Monday morning when the transportation officers arrived from TCF. I knew both of the officers and was almost glad to see their familiar faces. I was even looking forward to the ride back to TCF.

Most of all, I was just glad to be leaving Riverside. It was a real shit-hole if there ever was one. Sure, there's no such thing as a good prison, but I can say from experience that there are some that are worse than others. If I had to be locked up, I'd prefer to do my time at TCF.

The most important thing to me was being close to my family, where I could get weekly visits. In the past ten months, I'd only received one visit from my mother. The trip to the Upper Peninsula was just too far for her to drive. However, now that I was back close to home, I was looking forward to our weekly visits once again.

CHAPTER 15

BACK TO THUMB CORRECTIONAL FACILITY

When I arrived back at TCF, I discovered there had been a big change in the cell accommodations. Due to the overcrowding in the state prison system, the governor had ordered all level two and level four facilities to begin double bunking. The state had built more than thirty new prisons and yet they still didn't have enough beds to accommodate the steady influx of new prisoners.

At the same time as the automobile industry began downsizing its workforce, business was booming for the department of corrections — it was expanding by leaps and bounds. The state was diversifying its economy by creating and providing new jobs in the department of corrections. Hundreds of new prison guards were being hired and trained to staff all the new facilities. There was even a plan to take people off welfare and hire them as corrections officers. Prison guards were being paid higher wages and receiving more comprehensive fringe benefits than what was provided to schoolteachers, nurses and many other professionals.

It's a sad commentary on the State of Michigan and its citizens when the politicians continue to appropriate an annual budget in excess of almost two billion dollars to the department of corrections. At the same time they're sending all this money toward the prison system, the quality and quantity of education and healthcare for regular citizens continues to decline. In my mind, the education and good health of all the state's residents ought to be far more important than warehousing prisoners. I wonder if politicians have ever heard the old proverb, "An ounce of prevention is worth a pound of cure."

The politicians have become fixated on the concepts of revenge, retribution and retaliation. Today, we live in a throw-away society with the misguided mentality of, "lock 'em up and throw away the key". Building more prisons and keeping people in prison longer will never decrease the crime rate. In time, it will merely bleed the state coffers dry. And even though prisons provide jobs, the taxpayers must pay their salaries. Currently, that cost is around four million dollars a day for the nearly eighteen hundred prison employees.

Prisons are not like a conventional business — there's no profit. It's like flushing your money down the toilet. You get nothing back on your investment.

No one ever grew up wanting to become a criminal and spend their life in prison. There are a myriad of reasons for criminal, deviant and antisocial behavior. But, merely treating the symptoms and choosing to ignore the root cause simply because it's too time consuming and too costly will never solve the problem of crime.

The current system is broken but society has become too cynical and indifferent to care. Politicians are allowed to waste billions of dollars to punish those who have gone wrong rather than invest an equal amount of funding in education and intervention programs that could prevent, deter and change inappropriate behavior. I believe the problem of crime will remain a fact of life in our society until people change their misguided, hardheaded and hardhearted philosophy.

Prison, in my mind, should be a last resort — a place for only those who commit the most vile and heinous crimes and serve no other useful purpose on the planet. Alternative forms of punishment that are less costly to the public and perhaps even serve a benefit to the public and the offender should be found. The majority of people, however, never realize the truth about their judicial system or prison system until it directly affects them or a loved one. Then, suddenly, they become acutely aware of the cannibalistic monster they helped to create.

TCF was the first facility to implement double bunking. If the inmates had stood up then and voiced their disapproval, in all likelihood, double bunking probably would have been stopped or had never taken place at all. Instead, though, the inmates went right along with the program like passive sheep being herded into a pen.

Inasmuch as I'd just spent the past ten months living in a cubicle with five other inmates, I could deal with the current situation. I wasn't about to become a martyr — I'd already been there and done that.

My bunkie turned out to be a sixteen-year-old kid. He tried not to show it, but he was scared to death of everyone. It didn't take long for me to figure out that he lived in a fantasy world all his own. Some of the guys had warned me about the kid. They said he'd been moved around from one cell to another because he couldn't get along with anyone, and that he had a bad habit of snitching on people.

Nevertheless, I thought that if I tried to be nice to the kid, if I treated him with respect and consideration, he'd reciprocate in kind. But then again, that philosophy doesn't always work. Some people take kindness for weakness and they never seem to appreciate anything.

For the first few days, we got along okay. It became obvious right off the bat, though, that he had a big problem with always running his mouth. The little shit was constantly making up stories about the things he'd done and the places he'd been. After several days of listening to his bullshit, I tried to tell him in a helpful manner that there was absolutely nothing he could possibly say that would impress me. I offered him a bit of advice, too — good advice.

"I've been in here for nearly half my life, kid," I told him. "In prison, it's often best that you keep your mouth shut and your eyes and ears open. The less anyone knows about you, the less they can use against you."

The kid had been convicted of arson. He told me that he'd broken into a school, ransacked the classrooms and stolen several items. In an attempt to cover up the break-in, he started a fire that happened to spread quickly and caused extensive damage to the school.

The kid was as hardheaded as they came. In his arrogance of youth, he thought that he knew everything and no one could tell him anything. Watching and listening to the kid, I couldn't help but wonder if I was that bad when I was a teenager. Regrettably, I have to admit that in some ways, I was. I was also incredibly hardheaded. I refused to listen to those with more life experience and wisdom who knew better than I did. Like the Nietzsche saying, "Ignorance is bliss where knowledge is folly."

At KTF in the Upper Peninsula, the inmate store sold chewing gum. I'd brought several packs in my property down to TCF with me. However, when the property officer began sorting through my stuff and came across the gum, she pointed at it and told me it wasn't allowed.

"I'll let you keep what you have, but don't say anything about it," she said.

Since gum wasn't allowed at TCF, I thought that maybe the kid would appreciate the gesture of having something that he couldn't normally get. One day, when I was feeling particularly nice, I gave the kid a pack of gum.

"Don't tell anyone where you got it," I told him.

Evidently, the little shit didn't appreciate anything. The next day, one of the yard officers came to our cell and directed his gaze at me.

"I've got orders from the control center to shakedown your property, specifically to confiscate chewing gum," he said.

It wasn't something I was going to fight about or make difficult for this guy. It was just gum.

"It's in the top of my locker, on the right," I told the officer. "There's about eight packs. I ain't got any stashed anywhere else, but you're welcome to check."

This wasn't one of those gung-ho officers, so even though he walked over to my locker and looked right at it, he turned around, said he didn't see any chewing gum and walked back out of the cell.

I don't know if the kid was hoping I'd get in trouble or what, but I enjoyed the outcome of that. Afterwards, though, I wasn't about to keep the gum in my cell just in case the control center sent another officer to shake me down again. I decided to get rid of it and distributed the gum amongst some of the older, wiser guys in the housing unit. They actually appreciated having it and had enough sense to keep their mouth shut.

I also kept my mouth shut about what I did with the gum. I didn't want the little snitch kid to hear a word about where it was.

A few days later, Officer Maxfeld called me off to the side to speak with her privately.

"That kid cellmate of yours has complained to one of the other housing unit officers that you've been smoking marijuana in the cell," she whispered.

Most of the officers there had known me for years and knew me well enough to know I gave up using drugs years ago. The kid's complaint was so off base it was almost comical, even to the officers.

In a hushed voice, I told Ms. Maxfeld all about the chewing gum incident.

"One of us has got to go," I told her, finishing my story. "Either the kid needs to be moved or they need to move me."

"I understand," she said. "I'll talk with the counselor and try to arrange a move as soon as possible. You just hang in there and be as patient as you can, okay? He isn't worth getting into any trouble for."

I nodded my head, "Absolutely, and thank you very much."

She told me later that other people in the housing unit were also tired of listening to the kid's bullshit and that there'd been a lot of complaints about him. That same afternoon, they moved the kid to another unit. The whole incident reminded me of how glad I was to be back among officers like Ms. Maxfeld.

Before I left TCF, Don had been complaining about not feeling well. He wasn't sure exactly what was wrong but shared with me that he was concerned he'd somehow developed a serious medical problem.

"My stomach is all screwed up, and I'm in a lot of pain." He told me once. "Almost every time I take a crap there's blood in my shit — it's really nerve-wracking, man. It's just one of those things, where you just know something ain't right."

He'd seen the facility's doctor several times, but as usual, prison health care merely treated the symptoms and not the cause. After complaining to health care for several months, the doctor at TCF finally decided to send Don for additional testing.

Unfortunately, when the test results came back, they showed that Don had colon cancer. About a week later, he was transferred to the prison hospital in Jackson and began receiving radiation treatments. By the time they finally discovered what was wrong with Don, though, the cancer had already progressed to an advanced stage. He died just a few weeks after being diagnosed.

Throughout the years, I've watched while many of my fellow inmates have died unnecessarily from a variety of diseases that the prison health care system simply refused to treat until it was too late. It's sad. For far too many years, the health care providers for the department of corrections have been much more concerned about their bottom line than providing adequate health care services to inmates.

Inmates are routinely patronized and treated with deliberate indifference. Medical procedures are routinely deferred, which I believe is a denial of inmates' right to proper medical care. Medical personnel also frequently and deliberately disregard inmate complaints, even when they're well aware that there is an excessive risk to the inmate's health and safety. Put simply, nobody believes our lives are worth proper medical care. What is probably an emergency for a regular person is nothing to see a doctor about in prison. We're provided with inadequate and inconsistent health care that is so deficient that it amounts to cruel and unusual punishment.

The issue of health care is an issue of fairness and humane treatment. When it comes to America's incarcerated populace, however, the issue of health care is yet another wrinkle in the American fabric. Here in Michigan, as elsewhere around the country, there is a large prison population — more than fifty-one thousand inmates, in fact.

A growing segment of that population is older inmates who have special needs. The cost of maintaining the health of these older inmates, like myself, has become astronomical. In addition to the older inmates, there is also a large population of HIV infected people and those who have AIDs. Add to that the number of disabled inmates or those suffering from mental illnesses and it's clear why the cost is so great.

In order to rein in the high cost of health care associated with prisoners, in 1999, former Governor John Engler appointed a private corporation known as Corrections Medical Service, or CMS, to address all medical concerns with the department of corrections. The very same company had been fired and ran out of eleven other states prior to being invited to Michigan in 1999. The reason given by the other states: killing through negligence. Basically, inmates and jail detainees would receive such woefully inadequate and incompetent medical care and practices that it could be directly attributed to their death.

In Michigan, there have been hundreds of lawsuits filed against CMS since December of 1999. The company has a meat ax approach when it comes to cutting health care. Cuts made at the expense of inmates' pain, suffering and death can be directly related to the dramatic decrease in the department of correction's health care costs in Michigan. The state doesn't have a death penalty, but merely getting sick while serving time in a Michigan prison can very well turn into one.

Since CMS took over, Michigan inmates have felt the squeeze. Some have died or been seriously injured due to inadequate treatment. For instance, medications needed by some inmates have been discontinued or substituted for cheaper and weaker generic brands that yield too little to no results. Necessary surgeries are arbitrarily denied. Patients are misdiagnosed. Broken bones and torn tendons are ignored for weeks at a time. Medical treatment is denied solely on cost considerations and not an inmate's medical needs.

The standard policy of CMS is to deny inmates' proper health care. Their goal is to frustrate the inmates because they know that an inmate will often give up trying to battle bureaucracy. This tactic is generally employed and its purpose is to prevent inmates from properly filing complaints, grievances or lawsuits. So long as an inmate doesn't formally complain, CMS and the regional health administrator can simply say, "We're sorry, we didn't know he was sick." Consequently, they can avoid any sort of responsibility or liability and at that point, the silence conspiracy has succeeded.

The person at CMS who writes inmate treatment and care guidelines doesn't have any medical training. This person goes by a book to create guidelines and that is the book of treatment and cost. The unwritten policy, of course, is money first, care second.

If an inmate requires surgery or the cost of the treatment is expensive, it is a tactic of CMS to ignore the inmate's request for an entire year. The contract provision between CMS and department of corrections, under section 11(3) (c), reveals the details and ominous ploy being played out by the CMS and the department. This contract, believe it or not, is available to the public via a simple Freedom of Information Act request.

The United Nations Commissioner for Human Rights has adopted a Body of Principles that states, "medical care and treatment shall be provided free of charge to prisoners."

However, every inmate who initiates a health care request is charged a five dollar co-payment for every health care visit unless it's prompted by a medical emergency, work related injury or for chronic care. Although a five dollar co-payment doesn't sound like much, when you consider the fact that an inmate's average monthly income is only around fifteen dollars, a five dollar co-payment is totally absurd.

As a direct result, some inmates avoid requesting medical assistance even when they know they need treatment. This sometimes results in a routine medical problem eventually becoming a serious medical problem that, in turn, costs even more money to treat. Unfortunately, it also sometimes costs the inmate his life. In addition, it's still uncertain and unknown where the money from this charge has gone.

My mother had been telling me for a couple of months that she hadn't been feeling well. During one of our weekly visits, she told me that she felt tired and listless most of the time and that she was having trouble keeping food in her stomach.

"Everything I eat just comes right back up," she said, sighing. I could hear the tiredness in her voice.

She finally went to see the doctor for a routine check-up and the doctor found several unusual lumps. Some were under her right arm and more were found behind her left ear. The doctor took tissue samples and sent them to the lab for a biopsy. The results weren't good.

The biopsy showed that the lumps were indeed malignant, or cancerous. At that point, the only thing her regular doctor could do was give her a referral to a specialist. He referred her to one of the best cancer doctors in the state, she told me.

Once she'd seen the cancer specialist, he scheduled her for a more comprehensive series of tests. My mom went through CAT scans, an MRI and a number of other tests she'd never heard of. After all the results came back, the doctor finally had a diagnosis for her — lymphoma.

"He told me I've got to have the lumps removed as soon as possible," my mother told me during one of our visits. "That means surgery but, he said it will help prevent the cancer cells from spreading further throughout my body."

Surgery was scheduled quickly. Thankfully, there were no surprises or complications on the operating table. The doctor told my mother he'd successfully removed all the cancerous growths, but it wasn't the end of the road just yet. She still needed several months of chemotherapy treatments to rid her body completely of the cancer.

My mother's cancer was in the second stage and the doctor said that made it easier to treat than if it were in the first stage.

"He said he's very confident I'll make a full recovery," she told me by phone after the surgery. "Of course, there's no guarantees, but that's just the nature of this thing."

The chemotherapy treatments were scheduled every two weeks. For six days each month, Mom would check into the hospital and undergo daily treatments of chemotherapy.

A couple of weeks later, she'd receive another treatment at the doctor's office where the chemotherapy was given to her intravenously through a port that had been surgically implanted under her skin, just above her right breast.

The whole ordeal made me think of all that my Mom had already been through in her life and now, she's got to go through this too. She was a lady with tremendous inner strength and courage but nevertheless, when she came to see me, I could see the fear in her eyes and hear the uncertainty in her voice. She was waging the biggest and most frightening battle of her entire life.

Knowing my mother, though, it didn't surprise me that her number one concern was losing her hair from the chemotherapy. Personally, I was scared to death at the very thought that my mother might not survive the ordeal of cancer. I'd heard the treatments were sometimes worse than the cancer itself. I'd read about people who had refused to undergo the treatments, braving the cancer rather than submitting themselves to the radiation and chemotherapy.

I'd also heard many terrible stories about cancer, about how it could ravage a person's body and cause intense pain and great suffering. I wouldn't have wished cancer on my worst enemy, though I would've gladly suffered through my mother's cancer for her if it meant she'd be spared from all the pain and misery of it.

My mother had always been there for me. She never abandoned or disowned me, not even when she learned that I was responsible for the death of another human being or when I was sent to prison for life. All those years when everyone else forgot about me, when no one else bothered to write a letter or visit me, my mother had always been there when I needed her. But when my mother needed me the most, I was unable to be there for her — stuck behind bars.

I felt profoundly ashamed of myself. If it were possible, I'd have moved heaven and earth to be there at her side. I'd have given anything just to have held her in my arms and comforted her.

Whenever my mother was in the hospital receiving chemotherapy, I was unable to call her from the prison telephones that were designated for inmate use. Inmates were only allowed to make collect calls and the hospital wouldn't accept a collect call.

Thankfully, my unit counselor Ms. Chaplan, was a very understanding person, who empathized with my mother's illness and the situation I was in. She'd call the hospital from her office, allowing me to speak with my mother each time she was in the hospital.

It was from those phone calls that I was able to get a feel for just how much the chemotherapy affected my mother. The treatments always sapped a great deal of mother's strength from her. There were times when she was so weak she couldn't even talk. Even then, as long as I knew that she could hear my voice, I was more than happy to do all the talking. I just wanted her to know how much I loved and needed her.

When my mother started to lose her hair from the chemotherapy, she broke down and cried. Her hair was always so important to her. I remember how she would spend the good part of an hour sitting in front of a mirror, brushing her long black hair until she was satisfied that every little hair was in just the right place. She was always very meticulous when it came to her appearance and her hair was a big part of that.

Rather than toss her beloved hair in the garbage, she would place each handful of hair that fell out in a brown paper bag to save it. Each time she put more of her hair in the bag, she'd also shed a few tears.

"I just don't ever want to forget," she told me once. "Who knows what will happen. Maybe it won't grow back in the same or maybe, maybe someone can make a wig out of it. I don't know, Jim. I just can't part with it."

One time when my mother was in the hospital, she became terribly sick from the chemotherapy and didn't think she was going to live through it. She told me that as she was lying there in the hospital bed, she suddenly got the distinct feeling that she was dying.

"I could feel myself slipping away," she told me later. "It was the strangest sensation, almost as if I were floating upwards and there was some invisible force pulling me toward a very bright light."

"Then what?" I asked her.

"Just before I got to the light, this figure of a person — not a distinct person but almost like a shadow or something — appeared and told me it wasn't my time, that I needed to go back," she said.

Her words sent chills up and down my spine, not just thinking about how close I'd come to losing my mother but also knowing that she'd had such an otherworldly experience.

"After that person appeared and told me that, I began feeling like I was being pulled in the opposite direction, away from the bright light," she told me. "And then suddenly, I knew I was back in my body. It was the strangest thing, Jim."

Oddly enough, as my mother awoke and regained her bearings, the first thing she noticed was that the chair was missing from her hospital room.

"My blood just boiled as soon as I realized it was gone," she said. "And I know, it's a weird thing to get upset about just after having almost died, but still, I was just so angry."

She told me that earlier in the evening, one of the nurses had come in and asked to borrow the chair. My mother asked the nurse politely not to take it because she didn't have any other place to sit.

"When I get up the strength, I like to go and sit in it," my mother said. "It's a nice change, you know, especially when you spend the entire rest of the day in a hospital bed."

Evidently, the nurse waited until my mother fell asleep and then took the chair anyhow. The fact that the nurse had surreptitiously taken the chair is what really made my mother angry, and anger is a rare emotion for my mom. In fact, it's totally out of character for her. In my whole life, I've only seen my mother get angry one time and I knew she was truly angry because she said "damn." That's also the only time in my life I heard her curse.

"Jim, you wouldn't believe this, but after all I'd been through, feeling so weak and nearly dying and all, I actually got up out of the bed and went walking around, looking for my chair," she said. "I finally came across that nurse and I was so angry, I told her 'I want my chair now!' "

The nurse apologized, explaining that she'd borrowed the chair during the night to use for a visitor in another patient's room and that she'd had every intention of bringing it back before my mother woke up, but simply forgot.

"I don't know why I got so angry about that chair," my mother told me. "But it felt good; it made me feel strong."

The really strange thing wasn't just her emotional reaction to a missing hospital chair, but the fact that right after her perceived encounter with the afterlife, she began to get better. Her will to survive grew stronger and she began to regain her strength.

The chemotherapy had destroyed most of my mother's T-cells, which are the cells that defend the body against pathogens. This left her immune system seriously weakened and she was highly susceptible to infections of all types. Because of that, she was instructed to avoid crowds and anyone who had the slightest hint of a cold.

It didn't stop her from visiting me, but as a precautionary measure, whenever she did come to the prison we were allowed to sit in the far corner of the visiting room, away from all the other visitors. Occasionally, when the visiting room was crowded, the deputy warden would allow my mother and I to visit privately in the deputy's conference rooms. Even the deputy warden's secretary, a very gracious lady named Ms. Tanner, was exceptionally kind to my mother. Ms. Tanner would go out of her way to make sure that my mother had everything she needed. She'd even offer to bring us items from the vending machines in the visiting room, which we greatly appreciated.

Warden Roberts was also sympathetic to my mother's medical condition. When he received a letter from my mother's cancer specialist regarding her weakened immune system, he allowed my mother to visit me every Wednesday morning prior to the regularly scheduled visiting hours. This way, her chances of coming into contact with other people, especially those who might be carrying viral infections, would be greatly reduced.

My mother and I both greatly appreciated the staffs' empathy and compassion. I must admit that I was humbled by the staffs' display of kindness and respect for my mother. As a small token of her appreciation, every year at Christmas she would send a large Poinsettia plant to the facility with a Christmas card expressing her profound gratitude. Over the years, she also donated numerous plants and supplies to the facility's horticulture program. Staff and inmates alike enjoyed and appreciated her donations.

After a year of intensive chemotherapy, my mother was finally in remission. Even so, she still felt tired and weak most of the time. Her doctor said that was partly due to her low white blood cell count. In an effort to increase her white blood cells, she began receiving blood platelet injections. The cost was steep at twelve hundred dollars per injection, but the most important thing was that Mom had survived her battle with cancer. And hopefully, it was a battle she'd never have to fight again.

During my brief stay in the Upper Peninsula, I didn't bother to get involved in their hobby-craft program since I didn't plan on being there that long. Upon returning to TCF, though, one of the first things I did was rejoin the hobby-craft program. Unfortunately, I learned that Mrs. Bishop, the hobby-craft director, was leaving to become a parole officer.

It was rumored that the athletic director, Bessie Casper, would most likely be replacing Mrs. Bishop. Most of the inmates, myself included, were desperately hoping the job would be given to someone else. Ms. Casper had been the athletic director for the past several years and it was well-known, and often the source of many jokes, that Ms. Casper did nothing all day long except sit on her fat ass, drink coffee and shovel food into her bloated face.

Frankly, I could never understand why or how Ms. Casper became an athletic director in the first place. The only way that I could ever imagine her participating in any athletic activity would be as a sumo wrestler or a linebacker. Weighing in at around three hundred pounds, she was definitely in dire need of a little vigorous athletic directing herself.

Perhaps the administration was beginning to see the irony in it all because unfortunately, Ms. Casper was appointed as the new hobby-craft director, and she didn't waste any time making changes.

First to go was macramé. Suddenly, the macramé cord became a security risk and inmates were no longer allowed to order or have the cord in their possession. That was that and we were never given a reason for the decision.

A couple of months later, though, Ms. Casper called me over to hobby-craft and had the audacity to ask me if I'd make a macramé chair for her.

"One of the female officers here is retiring and I'd really like to give her a personalized lawn chair as a retirement gift," she told me. "Now, I understand you're quite good at macramé. I'll purchase all the necessary materials for you and I'll pay you for your time."

That really angered me. So, macramé was a security risk when it became something the inmates had success with, but when she decided she wanted something made for a personal reason, it was no longer a security risk?

"No thank you," I said politely, but sternly.

From that moment on, Ms. Casper behaved like a real bitch towards me.

Suddenly, whenever I tried to place an order for supplies for a hobby-craft project, my paperwork would somehow manage to get lost. Pretty soon, my monthly sales receipts from the hobby-craft stand also began mysteriously disappearing.

It became quite apparent to me that Ms. Casper was just another one of those sorry-ass, petty and vindictive state employees. She even went so far as to try to set me up for a major misconduct ticket that would have placed me in the hole. As the saying goes, though, "the best laid plans of mice and men often go astray."

Her plan was in writing, literally. She wrote a memo to the day shift commander alleging that I was in possession of dangerous contraband — a pair of scissors.

I did have a pair of scissors. However, the scissors had been legitimately purchased from a local vendor in Lapeer and they were listed on my hobby-craft card that I kept in my cell.

Hobby-craft cards were provided to every inmate who participated in hobby-craft and it was required that we have a valid hobby-craft card in our cells at all times. The card listed each hobby-craft item in the inmate's possession and had to have the signature of the hobby-craft director.

The nasty old bitch wanted me punished so badly that she took the time to go through my hobby-craft file and remove the purchase order forms and receipts from when I ordered the scissors. Throughout the years, I'd purchased two other pairs of scissors. She actually went far enough back through my files to have those receipts taken out as well. The only thing she didn't count on was that my last property pack-up receipt listed all three pairs of scissors and the receipt was signed and dated by the prison's property officer.

When the officers came to shakedown my cell, the scissors were hanging in plain sight on the inside of my locker door. One of the officers took the scissors and the other officer placed me in handcuffs. When we got to the control center, they placed me in the level four visiting room and told me to have a seat. I waited for a few minutes and then the lieutenant came in.

"Do you know why you are here?" he asked me.

I shook my head, "I don't, sir. I have no idea."

He told me about the memo that Ms. Casper had written and immediately, I knew what was going on.

I explained to him how Ms. Casper had previously asked me to make a personalized macramé lawn chair for her to give to a retiring officer, but I'd refused.

"I wasn't mean about it or anything, I just said no thank you," I told him. "I just thought, it was deemed a security risk for us to have the macramé cord and just figured what's fair is fair. If we can't have the cord on a regular basis like we used to, why should there be a special exception?"

I continued on: "After that, she got pretty angry with me. Ever since that day, I've had the feeling she's been on a mission to get back at me. It's strange that all my hobby-craft orders and sales receipts began mysteriously disappearing right after that."

"Is there any way to prove you got these scissors legitimately?" he asked me.

"Yeah, there should be several purchase orders and receipts on file for all of them," I said.

"We've checked already, Jim," he told me. "There aren't any."

I sat back in my chair, trying to digest it all. I couldn't believe this was happening to me again — a vengeful prison employee trying to make life even more miserable for me.

"She must've gone through my file and threw them all away," I said. "Is there any chance you could contact Mrs. Bishop and ask her about it? I'm sure she'd remember when I purchased a couple pairs from Meesha's Knit & Stitch."

"Something doesn't seem right about what's being alleged in this memo," he said. "Hang on a minute. I'll see if I can make sense of this."

He left the room and he went back inside the control center, where I could see him talking to the other female lieutenant. When he came back, he told the officer to remove the handcuffs.

"I'm going to personally investigate this matter further," he told me. "I have a feeling Ms. Casper is being a bit duplicitous and I don't want to punish you without reason."

About two weeks later, the lieutenant called me back to the control center to tell me that he'd completed his investigation.

"Listen, Mr. Goble, I'm going to be honest and level with you here." he said. "I do believe Ms. Casper acted improperly, but I can't prove it. I've tried, but there's just no way I can prove that she's actually violated any administrative rules, policy, or procedures."

I nodded my head.

"With regard to your scissors, we aren't going to write a major misconduct ticket," he said. "However, since there's no record in your hobby-craft file to verify that you legitimately purchased them, we can't let you keep them."

I nodded my head again. All in all, it wasn't such a bad outcome. At least I wasn't getting the ticket.

"I'm sorry," he said. "You can go now."

When TCF first opened, they offered vocational training in building trades, food tech and custodial maintenance, but they didn't have the funding to hire a teacher for the horticulture program.

However, when they hired a new custodial maintenance teacher, he was also hired to teach a horticulture class. I'd always wanted to learn more about flowers, shrubs and trees, so I decided to enroll in the horticulture class.

The custodial maintenance class was scheduled during the morning period and the horticulture class was held in the afternoon for three hours Monday through Friday.

At that particular time, TCF didn't have a greenhouse. The facility's business manager was trying to purchase a greenhouse that was within their budget constraints. There also wasn't much for supplies, leaving the new teacher, Mr. Sosnick, with practically nothing to work with.

The business office finally approved a small budget of eleven hundred dollars, allowing him to purchase two dozen new horticulture text books, a few tools for working in the garden and two grow-light carts that students could use to germinate the seeds of annual flowers and vegetables. We also began propagating several different genus of tropical houseplants from cuttings, which were placed in other classrooms and staff offices throughout the facility.

I was given the job of watering and caring for all indoor plants on a weekly basis. Because of that, I made sure that the inmate store, quartermaster and kitchen had several plants, giving me a reason to go there once a week. That way, whenever I needed clothing, store items or food, I never had to stand in line.

Whenever I went to the kitchen to water the plants, Ms. Archer, one of the food service supervisors, would always ask me to make sure I remembered to water the banana tree in the back room. There was no banana tree in the back room — it was just her way of telling me that I could help myself to the bananas that were kept back there. Ms. Archer knew that I liked bananas and she always looked out for me whenever I came to the kitchen.

Once I had completed the required bookwork for the horticulture class, Mr. Sosnick hired me to be a tutor for other inmate students. I'd always been fascinated with cacti and succulents and after reading several books on the subject, I asked Mr. Sosnick if he'd allow the class to grow a few cacti and succulents from seed.

As I became more interested in cacti and succulents, I purchased magazine subscriptions to *The Cactus and Succulent Society of America* and *The Amateurs' Digest*.

The society had established their own seed bank called the Seed Depot, where seeds could be purchased by members at a marginal cost. However, the number of seeds sold to each person was limited. Every other month the magazine published a newsletter with a list of all the new seeds that they'd recently acquired from members all over the world, including seeds from rare and endangered species that were extremely hard to find.

I'd mentioned to my mother that I worked as a tutor in the horticulture class and that I was thinking about trying to grow a few cacti and succulents. She didn't say anything to me, but about a month later the horticulture class received several boxes in the mail that contained dozens of different species of cacti and succulents. My mother had purchased the plants from a mail order business in California and donated them to the horticulture class.

After about a year, Mr. Sosnick left TCF to teach custodial maintenance at Huron Valley. He was replaced by Mr. Dontell, who was a counselor in Durant unit. Mr. Dontell didn't have much experience in horticulture, but he enrolled in the Master Gardener Program that was offered by the Michigan State University County Cooperative Extension Program to become knowledgeable.

Not long after Mr. Dontell became the horticulture teacher, the facility finally purchased a greenhouse. Instead of contracting with an outside company to erect the greenhouse, it was decided that the horticulture and building trades classes would do the construction work. This way, the students would get some hands-on experiences, especially for those in the building trades courses. Additionally, installation of the electrical wiring, plumbing and the mechanical equipment was done by the institutional maintenance department.

The horticulture class only taught the basics. For those students who were interested in learning more and willing to pay a fifty dollar licensing fee, Mr. Dontell would contact the Michigan Department of Agriculture and arrange for one of their representatives to visit the facility. The representative would administer certification tests to students who were interested in becoming Certified Pesticide Applicators. He also arranged for one of the other tutors and myself to take the Michigan State University Master Gardener course, which we were required to pay for out of our inmate accounts in advance.

Before Mr. Dontell came to work for the department of corrections, he was employed as a teacher at a junior high school in a neighboring county. From what we heard, he was forced to resign from that position after one of his female students accused him of inappropriately touching her.

He'd worked at TCF for several years as a corrections officer until he was promoted to the rank of sergeant. Two years later, he became an assistant resident unit supervisor in the Durant unit. He retained that position until he was finally given the job as the horticulture teacher.

For the most part, Mr. Dontell seemed to be a nice person. Although at times, he did behave a little strangely. He'd often talk to one of the other inmate tutors about explicit sex acts and we were aware of the magazine pictures of naked women that he kept in his desk. Beyond that, though, he was always decent with the inmates. He treated everyone with respect and consideration and overall, he contributed a great deal to the horticulture program.

We were all aware that, as state employees, the prison's staff had great benefits that allowed them a lot of vacation time and sick days. Being as such, it wasn't uncommon for TCF's schoolteachers to take several days off from work every month. So, when Mr. Dontell didn't show up for a couple days, we didn't concern ourselves with it.

After a whole week passed without Mr. Dontell, though, everyone began wondering what happened to him. We asked other staff members but no one seemed to know anything about him, or at least they weren't telling us.

A few days later, another inmate passed me a local newspaper and pointed to an article on the front page.

"Check this out, Jim," he said, holding the newspaper out for me to see. "Isn't that the horticulture guy?"

I took the newspaper from him and began reading the article. Apparently, Mr. Dontell had been arrested for molesting a three-year-old girl. He was being charged with first-degree criminal sexual conduct and the article also said that he'd been suspended from his job with the department of corrections pending the outcome of his trial.

This was a very serious crime that Mr. Dontell had been charged with. If convicted, he faced a possible life sentence in prison. A couple of months later, though, the newspaper printed that Mr. Dontell had plead guilty to the lesser charge of second-degree criminal sexual conduct and was sentenced to five years in prison.

It seemed like a light sentence for such a heinous crime. After all, it's a three-year-old toddler who was hurt by this man. The court had to have taken his years of service with the department of corrections into consideration and given him a break because of it. Naturally, his employment with the department of corrections was terminated. I did, however, hear a rumor that he was allowed to keep his pension.

Early one morning, around seven o'clock, I was outside in the weight-pit doing a few bench presses, when I saw several officers running toward the chow hall. Rarely do officers run if there isn't some sort of trouble brewing. Sure enough, the emergency count siren went off a few minutes later and all the inmates were ordered to return to their housing units.

We'd only been locked down for a couple of hours when they announced over the PA system that the facility was back to normal operations. When I came out of my cell, I overheard some of the guys saying that one of the female food service employees had been killed by an inmate kitchen worker.

"Which one?" I heard one guy ask another.

"I don't know," I heard the other guy reply.

Two guys who locked just down the gallery from me were morning shift kitchen workers. I figured if anyone knew what happened, they would. When I spotted one of them standing on the gallery talking to a couple of the other guys, I went over to ask if the rumor about an employee getting killed was true.

As I walked up to the group, it was obvious that's what they were talking about. Just as I entered the conversation, I heard the kitchen worker tell the guys it was Ms. Archer who'd been killed.

I was shocked. I couldn't believe anyone would intentionally hurt Ms. Archer. She'd always been so nice to me, making sure I got a couple of bananas whenever I stopped by to water the kitchen's plants, but it wasn't just a special thing for me. Ms. Archer was a super nice lady who was always so considerate of everyone.

I edged my way into the circle of guys that had made a small crowd around the kitchen worker to hear what had taken place. The guy hadn't actually seen what happened, he said, but added that everyone had known the offending inmate was upset.

"Apparently, he was infatuated with Ms. Archer," the kitchen worker said. "When Ms. Archer told all of us that she was planning on retiring at the end of the month, the inmate just became more and more upset. Every day, he seemed to get more agitated in the kitchen."

The guy had become so infatuated with her that he didn't want her to retire because he wouldn't be able to see her anymore.

"He was working as a prep cook this morning, cutting up the vegetables," the kitchen worker told us.

That meant he was allowed to check out a knife by turning in his inmate ID card, which ensured he had to give the knife back before he'd be permitted to leave the kitchen.

"Maybe an hour or so went by and he was sitting back in the supervisor's office — you know, that's located all the way in the back of the kitchen," said the guy. "He was back there talking to Ms. Archer, which wasn't unusual or anything, so nobody thought anything of it."

He continued: "We think he was back there trying to talk her out of retiring and when he finally realized he couldn't change her mind, I think he just snapped."

When he first hit Ms. Archer, she managed to activate her personal protection device, which set off an alarm in the control center. Before help could arrive, though, the inmate barricaded the office door with a desk and filing cabinets.

The officers in the hallway could hear Ms. Archer screaming for help, but since there was no other way of getting inside the room, they were powerless to do anything. They could only stand by, listening as Ms. Archer's agonizing screams faded away.

After several minutes of eerie silence, the inmate finally began removing the barricades and surrendered to the officers. When they entered the room, they found Ms. Archer's lifeless body lying on the floor in a pool of blood. The medical staff immediately began trying to revive her, but it was too late. She'd been stabbed several times and was so severely beaten; that there was nothing anyone could do to save her.

The inmate had tried to cut his own throat before he opened the door, but he botched the attempt and his wound was only superficial. He was taken to health care, where the nurses treated his wound, and then he was placed in segregation. The inmate was on suicide watch throughout the night and transferred to a maximum-security facility the following day.

The inmate who killed Ms. Archer was a convicted rapist. He was known as the pancake rapist — an infamous nickname given to him by the newspapers that reported on his crime. The story was that he'd broken into a woman's home, raped her repeatedly throughout the night and then, the next morning, demanded that she make him pancakes for breakfast before he'd leave. According to his victim, even after she told the man that she didn't have any pancake mix in the house, he still insisted on pancakes and wouldn't accept anything else.

Apparently, he wanted pancakes so badly that he sent her to the grocery store to buy pancake mix, foolishly believing that she'd actually come back. Once out of his sight, the woman went straight to the telephone and called the police, telling them everything that'd happened and that her assailant was still at her house, waiting for her to return.

After Ms. Archer was murdered, the pancake rapist was charged with first-degree murder. The prosecuting attorney, however, allowed him to plead guilty to second-degree murder and he was sentenced to life in prison. He and several other inmates who had also killed corrections employees would almost certainly spend the rest of their natural lives in a maximum-security prison. They'd never again be allowed to come out of their cells without first being secured in belly-chain handcuffs, leg shackles and accompanied by a four-officer escort. Without a doubt, inmates who kill corrections employees will eventually die a lonely death in their eight-by-ten prison cell.

My younger sister Louise was working for the county government when she decided to take the civil service test. Anyone who wanted to become a state employee with the department of corrections had to pass the test, and Louise did.

She'd previously worked for an alarm system company where her job had been to program and maintain the company's computers. Soon after she got word that she'd passed the test, a job opened at TCF for a data processing coordinator. Louise had plenty of experience to qualify her for the job and she was on the list of applicants to be interviewed by the warden for the position.

Since I was an inmate at the facility, I really didn't think she had a very good chance of getting the job. However, from what she told me, her interview went quite well. Louise told the warden that I was her brother and instead of responding negatively, he simply told her that he also knew our mother.

"Very nice lady, she's made many donations to our horticulture program here," the warden told Louise.

Once the warden had interviewed all the applicants and reviewed their resumes, he decided that Louise was the most qualified applicant for the position. She was notified that she'd been "tentatively selected for the job."

"The warden would like to meet with both you and your mother before making his final decision," said the secretary who called my sister about the job.

The warden had some concern regarding me being an inmate at the same facility where my sister would be working. As the data processing coordinator, she'd have the security codes to control all of the security systems at the facility. Naturally, this created a lot of cause for concern.

Louise and my mother met with the warden soon after and the warden decided that the situation was workable. He did, however, suggest it would be in everyone's best interest if only a minimum number of people knew that we were related.

My sister, needless to say, was thrilled that she'd gotten the job. My mother, on the other hand, was worried that my sister's employment at the prison could eventually lead to me being transferred elsewhere.

My mother told me that during their meeting, she told the warden that if hiring Louise was going to create any sort of problem for me, then my sister wouldn't be taking the job. The warden assured my mother that as long as he was warden, I wouldn't be transferred because of my sister's employment there, not unless there was a major problem.

My mother and sister had their own private talks and agreements about the situation too. To reassure my mother that I wouldn't be transferred because of her job, Louise promised my mother that she'd transfer to another facility or quit before she'd let that happen.

After the meeting between the three of them, Louise was officially hired and the warden called me down to the control center later that same day.

"Well, I wanted to talk to you about Louise. I've decided to hire her as our data processing coordinator," said Warden Roberts. "Do you anticipate this causing any problems, with yourself or with other inmates?"

"Not at all," I told him. "I love my sister and respect her very much. I would never, ever consider placing her in a compromising position that could endanger her safety or her job here."

I added, "I'd give my own life before I'd let something bad happen to one of my sisters."

"It should never come to that," the warden said. "If there is any sort of problem that comes up, I want you to come to me directly and immediately. We'll work it out."

"Absolutely, and thank you," I said. "I know my sister looks forward to working here and there won't be any problems from me."

"I've never considered an arrangement like this before," he said, leaning back in his chair. "But your family seems very nice. I'm willing to give it a try."

When my sister started working at the facility, I didn't see her very often. Whenever we did happen to cross paths, I'd address her as if she was just another state employee. We were polite, respectful, and impersonal.

Eventually, some of the staff found out that the computer lady was my sister. Personally, I saw nothing wrong with the staff knowing. If an employee who I'd known for years asked me about it, I'd usually nod my head and ask them not to say anything. If an inmate asked me if my sister worked at the facility, though, I'd usually just play dumb and ask them where they heard that rumor. I was pretty good at avoiding their questions.

My sister had been working at TCF for about three years when another inmate told me he'd seen my sister in the control center.

"When I first saw her, I wasn't sure if it was really your sister or not," he told me. "But then I saw her name tag and I knew it had to be her."

I kept quiet, just looking at him as he continued to talk.

"Oh yeah, I remember the good 'ol days, hangin' with your sister in Lake Orion," he told me. "I used to go over to her place all the time when her and her husband were living there. Me and her husband were good friends, hung around a lot, played pool together and stuff. Ain't that where you guys were all raised?"

I kept my face expressionless as I looked him directly in the eyes and said, "Listen, pal, I don't know what you're talking about and I think it'd be in your own best interest if you just forgot about the whole thing."

I called my mother the next day to tell her about the inmate.

"Can you tell Louise that there's another inmate here who claims he knew her and her husband when they lived in Lake Orion," I told my mother.

I gave her the guy's name and asked her to let me know what my sister had to say. When I called home again a few days later, my mother said that my sister acknowledged that she knew who the guy was, but that my sister hadn't seen him in years. Supposedly, that was all that was said, or at least that's all my mother told me but my gut told me there was more to the story. Nevertheless, I trusted my mother and decided to forget all about it. Then a few weeks later, the guy was suddenly transferred to another facility.

When Warden Roberts eventually retired he was replaced by Warden Anderson. A short while after taking over the job, Warden Anderson was informed that his data processing coordinator had a brother who was an inmate at the facility.

Warden Anderson turned to Deputy Warden Pembroke to discuss the Matter. Deputy Warden Pembroke had been at the prison for a long, long time and knew my family and I about as well as Warden Roberts had. After their discussion, the new warden agreed that there were no problems with the current arrangement.

A year later, Deputy Warden Pembroke was promoted to become the warden at another facility in the Upper Peninsula. After he left TCF, everything changed. The new deputy warden who came to TCF had been reassigned from the Macomb Correctional Facility, where she'd held the same position. The rumor was that she'd placed herself in quite the compromising situation with one of her male officers and to avoid any hint of impropriety, she was reassigned to work at TCF.

This new deputy warden had her own way of doing things and that much quickly became clear. For some reason unbeknownst to me, she suddenly decided that I wouldn't be allowed to stay there so long as my sister was an employee at the prison.

I was working in the greenhouse when I found out. One of the yard officers approached me and told me I needed to report back to my housing unit. As soon as I got there, the officer on duty informed me that I was being transferred.

"I've got orders from the control center to lock you in your cell until your property is packed and ready to go," she said.

It took me about forty-five minutes to pack all that I owned. I then sat there on my mattress, staring at the wall while I wondered why I was being transferred and dreading where I might be going. My thoughts kept going back to my sister. It was the only thing I could think of.

When the officer finally came back, she told me to load my property in the laundry cart and to report directly to the property room. Everyone was asking me what was going on, but the only thing I could say with certainty was that I was being transferred. When I passed by my horticulture classroom, my boss came out to ask me the same thing. Apparently, no one had told her that I was leaving because she seemed just as surprised as I was.

When I finally got to the property room, the property officer told me that the inspector had called her and said I wasn't allowed to leave the property room until the transportation officers arrived to pick me up. No one seemed to know why I was being transferred, not even the officers. In fact, most of the officers seemed just as surprised as I was.

I waited in the property room for more than two hours before the transportation officers finally arrived. I wasn't told where I was headed until we were actually on the road, though.

"Saginaw Correctional Facility," said one of the officers when I asked if I could find out where I was going. "It's in Freeland, north of here. It'll take us about an hour and fifteen minutes to get there. Not too bad of a drive."

I was not a happy camper. I searched my mind over and over again, trying to think of any and all possible reasons as to why I was being transferred. Even though I didn't want to accept the fact that it was because of my sister's employment, it was the only plausible explanation.

I never had any expectations that my sister would somehow use her position to try to help me in any way, shape or form. In return, I never expected or thought she'd do anything to make my life more miserable either and being transferred was about the worst thing that could happen to me. I'd spent almost thirteen years of my life at TCF and during that time, I'd developed a rapport with the staff. It was enough time to prove myself to the staff as being about as trustworthy as an inmate can be. But the most important thing was my weekly visits with my mother. Now suddenly, all those things were gone. I felt uprooted, sad, nervous and betrayed.

My mother was only getting older and I knew she'd be unable to drive the distance to Saginaw by herself. She'd have to rely on someone else to bring her, meaning our visits would be few and far in between.

I called home as soon as I could and found out that my mother already knew I'd been transferred.

"Louise told me that an inmate at another facility had written a letter to the inspector at TCF," my mother told me. "Apparently, the inmate alleged that your sister was smuggling drugs into the facility for you."

It was the same inmate who had approached me at TCF saying he knew my sister and her husband from when they lived in Lake Orion — the same guy who had been quickly transferred after my sister found out about him. I wanted to believe what my mother said, but something just didn't sit right with me about it.

My Own Worst Enemy

Throughout my years in prison, I'd known a lot of inmates who were suspected of smuggling and dealing drugs. If an inmate is suspected of such a thing, he was usually subjected to almost daily shakedowns of both his person and his cell. Oddly enough, I had not been subjected to any of that.

The story that my sister told our mother just didn't make any sense. No inmate would send a snitch letter to the facility and use his real name. He wouldn't take the chance that other inmates might discover his identity. He'd be branded as a snitch for life and nothing has quite the adverse affect on an inmate's prison social life than being labeled as a snitch. Snitches were known to be highly susceptible to serious accidents, often of the fatal kind.

In order to find out exactly why I was transferred, I went to the counselor and I asked him if he'd look at the transfer order in my file. I wanted to know the specific reason given for my untimely departure and the name of the person who signed the transfer.

The counselor pulled my file from the cabinet, thumbed through the pages and when he found what he was looking for, he spun the file around on his desk. The document had a red striped border inscribed with the letters SPON, which stood for Special Offender Notification. It was signed by Assistant Deputy Warden Eiser and the reason given for my transfer was, "Inmate has a relative employed at TCF and will not be allowed back at the facility while that relative is employed at TCF."

I believed then, and I still believe today, that my sister knew all along that I was going to be transferred. Apparently, her job at TCF was more important to her than the promise she'd made to our mother. I found it to be incredibly selfish.

She'd decided her job was more important than my mother being able to see me regularly, and vice versa. There was nothing in my life more important than that. Simply because she liked working where she was and didn't want to transfer elsewhere, she took away the last vestiges of everything and the only thing I'd spent the last thirteen years caring about. Louise took more from me than she could ever possibly imagine.

With a new warden and deputy warden at the facility, I realized that my sister had very little input and no control whatsoever over the decisions that were made by the administration. However, my sister had been duplicitous when she intentionally deceived our mother by fabricating the drug smuggling story. Our mother might've believed the story, but it was far too convenient. Besides that, the transfer order in my file disputed Louise's version of the facts.

Ultimately, it didn't matter what excuse my sister tried to use as justification for my transfer. She'd broken her promise. There were no other options open to me, but my sister could've easily pleaded my case to her bosses and requested a transfer to one of the other facilities located in the surrounding area. In addition to that, her son worked at a computer company that had already offered her a better paying position than what she had at TCF.

It was evident that my sister didn't really care about what she took from me and I seriously doubt that she ever gave it a passing thought. About a year later, she told our mother that the department of corrections had trained her to be a bitch. Be that as it may, I'd argue that no one can make you into anything that you are not willing to become.

I suppose they also trained her to be an insensitive liar. It was readily apparent that something had changed my sister during the past few years. She'd become a cynical and vain person, filled with her own self-importance to the point of being an arrogant bitch.

My mother wasn't one to take sides and she never did say who she believed, my sister or I, regarding the reason for my transfer. A year later, though, I wrote Louise a scathing letter telling her exactly how I felt about her broken promise and acts of duplicity. She and I have not spoken in the past seven years.

I know the saying is that time heals all wounds. So long as Louise continues to conceal the truth, though, the deep wound she inflicted upon me will most likely never heal.

CHAPTER 16

SAGINAW CORRECTIONAL FACILITY

Like TCF, the Saginaw Correctional Facility was a multi-level facility. Despite that one similarity, Saginaw had been designed and built completely different from TCF.

There were six housing units with two hundred and forty inmates per unit. Three of the housing units were designated as level two and the other three units were level four.

The main yard was located at the south end of the complex and was only about half the size of TCF's yard. But there was still a quarter mile asphalt track for jogging, a softball diamond, two basketball courts, a weight-pit and two handball courts. Both level two and level four inmates used the main yard. The level four inmates, however, were only allowed one hour in the main yard per day in the afternoon.

In addition to the main yard, the level two inmates were also allowed to use the smaller common yard that was located in front of the level two housing units. With the exception of count times and when the chow lines were running, the common yard was usually open from seven-thirty every morning until a quarter to nine at night.

I knew several of the officers at Saginaw because many of them had previously worked at TCF. Fortunately for me, one of them just happened to be the inspector. The inspector used to be a sergeant at TCF and knew my mother wore a prosthetic arm. At TCF, she wasn't required to remove the prosthetic arm when she came to visit, and I knew that meant a lot to her.

To make the process of her visiting me a little easier, I wrote a letter to the inspector asking if he'd please consider granting my mother an exemption from having to remove the prosthesis during the shakedown process. Thankfully, he granted my request and an exemption was logged in the facility's visitor tracking computer system at the information desk.

None of my sisters ever made themselves available to bring my mother to Saginaw to visit me. By the grace of God, though, my niece Sandy volunteered to bring her at least once a month.

Sandy was my eldest sister's daughter and throughout the years, she'd come to visit me more often than any of my three sisters. She never forgot about me and I couldn't be more grateful for it. During one of our visits, Sandy told me that when she was a little girl, she thought I was a God — that really made me smile. She probably thought that simply because I used to go to my sister's house on a regular basis and whenever I was there, I always paid attention to Sandy.

I remember walking in the door to my sister's house and Sandy, as a little girl, would come running up to me saying, "Uncle Jim, Uncle Jim, pick me up and spin me around!"

She was always so excited to see me that she'd stand there twisting her little body from side-to-side as fast as she could. She reminded me of an excited little puppy dog. One Christmas when Sandy was about three years old, I gave her a doll that was bigger than she was. To this very day, she still talks about that doll.

When I thought about my situation at Saginaw, I knew that things could have been worse. I could have been sent to the Upper Peninsula again or even to the west side of the state, which also would've been a horrendously long drive for my relatives.

Therefore, I decided that it was probably in my own best interest to accept what I couldn't change and count my blessings. For the time being, I'd just have to bite the bullet and try to settle in.

Saginaw had two greenhouses and since I already had several certificates in horticulture, I thought that maybe I could get a job assignment as a greenhouse worker. I sent a letter to Mr. Wagner, the horticulture teacher, detailing my experience and requesting a job assignment there. The response, though, was that there were no openings at that time.

I needed something to occupy my time and since all inmates were required to have a job, I decided to accept a yard crew assignment until something else was available. I really wasn't interested in spending hours cutting grass with a push mower, but I tried to look at it from the perspective that it was good exercise. At one time, the inmates were allowed to use power mowers, but that was a thing of the past.

Rather than continue to purchase expensive power mowers that required fuel and regular maintenance, the state began purchasing inexpensive push mowers and relied on the blood, sweat and muscle power of the inmates to get the job done. On the days when we weren't cutting grass, we walked around the yard picking up trash and cigarette butts for about fifteen minutes and that was the extent of our workday. The starting pay on the yard crew was ninety-six cents a day. After sixty days on the job, my pay would be increased to a dollar and fourteen cents a day.

On Monday, Wednesday and Friday mornings, I went to the weight-pit for an hour. After that, I usually walked around the common yard until it was time for the eleven o'clock morning count. After lunch, I played dominoes on the yard with a few of the guys until the clock struck two, which was when I had to report for work. It was pretty much the same old routine day after day. I found Saginaw to be a pretty laid back facility with only the occasional fight or stabbing.

Just after I arrived at Saginaw, the lifers received permission from the warden to start a lifers' club. A guy I'd known for years asked me if I was interested in becoming a member and I decided to check it out and see what the club was all about. The only requirements to be a member was to pay a five-dollar membership fee and have the willingness to do a little manual labor.

Despite the club's name, not all of the members were serving life sentences. The main purpose of the club was to gather and disseminate judicial and legislative information pertaining to those inmates who were serving a life sentence. However, the lifers' club was also active in many other things.

We organized fundraising events for projects that were not only beneficial to the inmate population, but also helped the less fortunate residents of local communities.

The facility participated in the Prison Built Project, which was analogous to that of Habitat for Humanity. As part of this project, the level one inmates housed outside of the facility's perimeter security fences actually built houses from the ground up.

The lifers' club was responsible for growing all the trees, shrubs and perennial flowers that were used to landscape the yards of the new homes once they were moved to their permanent locations. In addition, the lifers' club cultivated several gardens of vegetables and donated the produce to local soup kitchens and food banks.

After a couple of months on the yard crew, I received notice that there was a job opening at the greenhouses. I eagerly accepted the assignment and it worked out very well for my role with the lifers' club and the Prison Built projects we were working on.

My daily routine changed so that after exercising for an hour each morning in the yard, I then worked in the greenhouse until the eleven o'clock count. Once count cleared, I went to lunch and then directly back to the greenhouse until four o'clock in the afternoon.

There was another count at four-thirty and then dinner was served at about five-thirty. Evening yard was from seven o'clock until quarter to nine, but instead of hanging out on the yard, some of us — myself included — chose to spend our time working in the flowerbeds. It was something to do and personally, I enjoyed working with the flowers. I always seemed to get more out of the experience than what I put in to it.

I'd been locking in housing unit nine for about three months when I decided that I wanted to move to housing unit seven, where I knew more people. When I asked the counselor if he'd consider moving me, I was surprised when he didn't give me the usual run around.

"I'll approve the move so long as there's an open bed," he told me.

About a week later, my move was finalized, but when I arrived at seven unit, I was led to a cell where I'd be bunking with a cigarette smoker. I refused to lock with the guy, trying to explain to the officer that I had COPD, or Chronic Obstructive Pulmonary Disease. Even though it didn't bother me much to be around cigarette smoke while outside, being in a confined space with cigarette smoke was entirely different.

In a small space like a cell, cigarette smoke exacerbated my condition and caused me to experience spasmodic episodes of coughing, to the point where I couldn't breathe.

"I understand," the officer told me. "But there's just nothing I can do. The move has already been finalized on the count sheet. You have to stay here until Monday, at least, when the counselor's back at work and then we can ask for another move to a nonsmoking cell."

I thought about the situation for a minute and decided I could probably put up with the smoke for a few days. When I opened the cell door, though, I knew instantly I couldn't live in that room for even one day. It reeked like an overflowing ashtray. The white walls were covered with so much nicotine that they were instead a dingy brown color and everything in the cell was covered with a thick layer of sticky, stinking nicotine.

Frustrated, I went back to the desk and I told the officer that I had no choice but to refuse the room.

"You're aware of the repercussions of refusing to lock in your assigned cell?" he asked me.

I nodded my head, but he continued to inform me of the punishment.

"If you refuse to lock in your cell I will be forced to write you a major misconduct ticket for disobeying a direct order," he told me. "This means you will be taken to the hole and will have to stay there at least until you go to court for the ticket. Do you still wish to refuse the cell?"

Before deciding, I took a second to think about it. Seeing as how my property was already packed and I'd at least be able to breathe normally in the hole, I decided to suffer the consequences.

"Yes, sir. I understand. Go ahead and write the ticket," I told him.

He called the control center to tell the captain that I was refusing to lock in my assigned cell and was being issued a major misconduct ticket. In a matter of minutes, two yard officers showed up to escort me to the hole.

I spent the next six days in a quiet, single-man cell with room service. I passed the time by reading, exercising and practicing my juggling skills. Though I didn't have anything to juggle with, I'd learned from my past experiences in the hole how to make a variety of things out of wet toilet paper. I made several balls by wetting wads of toilet paper in the sink and then, as I squeezed out the excess water, I shaped the toilet paper into balls that were approximately the same size as tennis balls. After drying overnight, they were almost as hard as baseballs, albeit much lighter.

When I went to court, the hearing officer gave me seven days top-lock with credit for the six days I'd already served in the hole. I was released from the hole and sent back to housing unit seven. When I got to the housing unit, the officer gave me a door key and he told me what number cell I was assigned to. Before I even bothered to carry my property up the stairs, I wanted to make sure my new bunkie didn't smoke. I walked up the stairs and was thankful that when I opened the door, the cell didn't reek like a dirty ashtray.

I introduced myself and told the guy I'd been assigned to bunk with him.

"I've got some medical conditions, though, and I can't be in a cell where someone's smoking," I said. "Are you a smoker?"

"I am, but you ain't got nothing to worry about here," he said. "I never smoke in the cell."

For the time being, I was good. I walked back downstairs, picked up my property and set about moving in.

Whenever an inmate at Saginaw was found guilty of a major misconduct ticket, it was practically automatic that he lost his access to the weight-pit for six months as part of the punishment. This applied to me as well, but since I'd never been one of those guys who sits around on their butt day after day, I started doing other things to keep myself in shape.

In the beginning, I did calisthenics — push-ups, pull-ups and other exercises. After a couple weeks, I still felt that I wasn't doing enough. I wasn't into playing basketball, so that was out of the question. I also didn't care much for the idea of jogging, but my options were rather limited.

When I was in the army, I vehemently disliked running. The last time I had tried jogging was twenty years earlier at Jackson and I didn't like it then either. Nevertheless, I made up my mind to give it another try.

I knew that jogging wasn't going to be any easier for me than it was before, especially now that I had chronic obstructive pulmonary disease. On the other hand, I was no longer a smoker and that had to work in my favor. During my first attempt at jogging, I couldn't even complete four laps around the track, which would've equaled a mile. I had to quit early and when I stopped jogging, I was gasping for air and coughing my guts out.

Despite my miserable first try, I kept at it and was surprised and pleased at the quick progress I was able to make. By the end of the fourth week, I was running twenty laps on the quarter mile track, putting me up to five miles. After two months, I was able to jog throughout the entire morning yard period of an hour and fifteen minutes. The longest sustained period of time that I ever jogged was two hours straight.

I found irony in the fact that, as a robust, young, eighteen-year-old man, I hated jogging and yet, thirty plus years later, I looked forward to jogging six miles a day, four days a week.

I was only at Saginaw for about eighteen months. I'm not exactly sure why I was transferred, though I have my suspicions.

One afternoon, I was sitting out on the yard playing dominoes with three other guys when someone said something about a new hobby-craft director. The inmate pointed to a person who had just walked out of the control center and though I couldn't see her face, the silhouette of her sumo wrestler's body coupled with that waddling duck walk was unmistakable. It was none other than that old bitch Bessie Casper, the incredibly fat and lazy athletic director turned hobby-craft director from TCF — the same old hag who'd practically ruined the hobby-craft program at TCF and then tried to get me in trouble for not doing her a personal favor.

Apparently, TCF had finally managed to get rid of her.

There was no doubt in my mind that she hadn't forgotten about me. Likewise, I hadn't forgotten about her. During the next two months, I didn't say a thing to her. In fact, I went out of my way to avoid her completely. If I caught her waddling down the sidewalk, I'd turn and walk in the opposite direction. I even made sure to not make eye contact from the furthest distances away.

Despite my best intentions to make sure we didn't cross paths, it was two months after she arrived that I was transferred to the Riverside Correctional Facility in Ionia, Michigan.

CHAPTER 17

Riverside Correctional Facility

Riverside Correctional Facility was one place I definitely didn't want to be. Not only was it still the same old filthy place that I remembered from my previous weekend visit eight years ago, but also, it put me even farther away from my family than when I was at Saginaw.

When I arrived at the facility, the department of corrections was in the process of changing it over to a level two, general population prison. About half of the facility was still classified as RTP, which stood for Resident Treatment Program. Inmates in the RTP were being treated for psychological problems. The remaining inmates in the RTP were slowly being transferred to Huron Valley Men's Facility, which had been converted from the maximum-security facility it was when I was there to a psychiatric facility.

I was placed in housing unit seven-one-west. It was one of two buildings at the prison that were each four-stories tall. Housing unit eight, the so-called honor unit, was a pole barn that had been erected to be an open dorm-style unit with six-man cubicles. Though it was called the honor unit and was supposedly for the well-behaved prisoners, most of the guys wanted nothing to do with the noisy, open dorm-style living environment.

The other housing units — nine, ten and eleven — were all two-story buildings.

The facility didn't have a main dining area where all the inmates were fed, but it did have a kitchen where all the meals were prepared. The food was placed in hot carts and then delivered to housing units seven and eleven, where the prison used a couple of the old treatment rooms as dining areas.

The yard was run on a rotating schedule, which was unlike any other level two facility I'd ever seen. Every other day from seven-thirty to ten o'clock in the morning, housing units seven, eight and nine had morning yard time. On those days, housing units ten and eleven had yard time from twelve-thirty to three-thirty in the afternoon.

In the summer months, when it was lighter out for much longer into the evening, we were given evening yard time too. Whichever units had morning yard also received the evening yard time from six o'clock to eight-thirty. To me, it seemed like the whole facility was ass-backwards.

The entire recreation yard was encircled by an oval, quarter-mile asphalt track. The track was plagued with numerous large potholes and cracks, making it especially difficult and dangerous for jogging. A softball diamond covered most of the area inside the track, but there were also four horseshoe pits, a handball court, and a small weight-pit, with a few weight lifting machines. Thankfully, the prison was in the process of building a larger weight-pit by the gymnasium.

The so-called gymnasium looked like a big greenhouse. The entire structure was covered with the same type of plastic used to cover greenhouses. It had originally been constructed to temporarily house inmates, but was now being used as the gym.

The cells were furnished with a small wall locker, a metal desk and a steel bunk bed for each inmate. There was also a small window that could be partially opened if you spent some time scraping away the many layers of old paint that had sealed it shut. Throughout the years, the cells had been painted so many times that in the summer when the temperature and humidity was high, the layers of old paint would expand and cause the cell doors to occasionally stick.

As a result, the doors occasionally had to be forcibly opened and closed. The floors in the cells also had a similar problem with layers of old wax — there must have been at least ten or fifteen years of old wax build up. The cell floors were actually an off-white marble color with flecks of brown, but they didn't look that way anymore. All the buildup of old wax gave them a brownish-yellow color, almost like an amber color. It took me two days of scraping the floor with a putty knife just to remove all the old wax from my small cell.

The facility offered a horticulture class and maintained a greenhouse. When I asked the instructor for a job as a greenhouse worker, though, he told me he wanted me to attend his class as a student instead. I explained to him that I'd already completed the horticulture program while at TCF, including the Master Gardener Program offered by Michigan State University and was also a licensed and certified pesticide applicator in six different categories. My experience and credentials seemed to fall on deaf ears, though.

"If you want to work in the greenhouse, I'm still going to need you to enroll in my class first," he insisted.

What he really wanted was the funding that the school received for each student enrolled in a class. It was quite obvious to me that I wouldn't be working in the greenhouse, and I really wasn't interested in working on the yard crew. I was tired of cutting grass, shoveling snow and picking up someone else's trash and cigarette butts. I decided that for the time being, I didn't need a job.

When the facility transferred the last of the Resident Treatment Program inmates, everyone locking in housing unit seven-west was moved to housing unit eleven. And they moved all the kitchen workers into seven-west after we moved out.

Eleven-unit wasn't much better than seven-west, but there was less noise and each wing had its own day room. The unit was divided into four wings; two upper and two lower. Each wing housed forty-eight inmates and more inmates were also housed in one or two of the old treatment rooms on each floor. The rooms were converted to a dorm-like setting for their new purpose.

The day room was furnished with a color television set, four rows of chairs and a Ping-Pong table. There were also two smaller day rooms, one of which was furnished with a pool table and several card tables. The other day room only had a few tables and chairs and was designated as a quiet room, meant specifically for inmates who wanted to read or play board games.

The so-called airing room located on the backside of the housing unit was where the inmates were allowed to smoke whenever the yard was closed. It was used by everyone who wanted to get some fresh air, though, and not just the smokers.

The airing room was kind of like a front porch, except it was totally enclosed with steel bars like a big, human-sized bird cage. The bars stopped us from going out, but they didn't stop the prison's resident raccoons from coming inside to look for something to eat. In fact, the airing room was one of the raccoons' favorite hangouts because the inmates were constantly feeding them.

It always amazed me how agile and adept the raccoons were at climbing up and down the perimeter security fences without ever setting off the alarms. Equally amazing was their ability to navigate through multiple strands of coiled razor wire without ever getting snagged.

The only thing I really liked about Riverside was all the different wildlife that lived in and around the facility. Almost every day, I saw at least one or two deer. Occasionally, small herds of about ten or fifteen deer would walk right up next to the perimeter fence. They were seemingly oblivious to all the people and movement around them.

Not long after I moved to housing unit eleven, the unit's inmate painter was transferred to another prison. I was getting bored with sitting on my butt all the time and I decided to apply for the job. When I told the housing unit officer that I was interested in it, he said that painters are hired by the institutional maintenance staff and I'd have to send a written request to classification and institutional maintenance.

Usually, there was a long waiting list for all institutional maintenance jobs. I sent written requests to both departments as I was instructed to, but I didn't expect to hear back from classification for at least a month. Much to my surprise, the following week I was called to the officer's desk and given a detail as the unit painter. The pay was a dollar and thirty-four cents a day, but the money wasn't important to me. I just wanted something to do.

My new job detail opened my eyes to just how filthy and dilapidated housing unit eleven really was. The whole facility needed a lot more than just another coat of paint — it was literally falling apart.

The bathrooms in every housing unit were atrocious. The plumbing was so old that the drains barely functioned and the toilets were either constantly overflowing or wouldn't flush at all. Everything in the bathrooms that was made of metal, such as the privacy partitions between the toilets and the light fixtures that hung from the ceiling, were all covered with rust and corrosion from excessive moisture, lack of proper ventilation and years of neglect.

These same factors were also responsible for the large cracks and craters in the plaster walls and ceilings. In addition to the squalid living conditions that we were forced to endure, we were also compelled to drink — out of necessity only — the extremely unpalatable drinking water. The water came out of the faucet a deep brown color and tasted as bad as it looked.

The officers and staff didn't really care. They had no reason to — they didn't have to drink the water. Instead, they brought their own bottled water to work with them every day.

The entire facility looked like it should have been condemned years ago.

When I first got the job as the unit painter, the counselor told me that he wanted his office painted. Since I badly wanted a transfer to another facility, I saw the paint job as a great opportunity. I didn't come right out and blab to him about how desperately I wanted out of that prison. I knew I had to be patient and bide my time, and meanwhile, I decided to go along with whatever he wanted and to do my very best to be kind, personable and downright friendly.

I probably could have painted his office in one day, but instead, I took my time and tried to make it look like I was just being a perfectionist because I wanted it painted just right for him. I thought that if I could talk to him and perhaps engender a little sympathy, then maybe, just maybe, he'd be more inclined to transfer me closer to home.

When the opportunity presented itself, I told him about my mother's battle with cancer and how it was almost impossible for her to visit me at Riverside. I told him about the traumatic loss of her arm years ago and how the physical disability made it even more of a challenge for her to drive long distances.

"Maybe — I mean, not until I finish painting the entire housing unit, of course — but maybe then, you might consider transferring me somewhere closer to her?" I asked as innocently as possible. "It sure would mean a lot to me."

No doubt, the counselor had heard his share of hard luck stories before.

"I'll think about it," was the only thing he said, hardly looking up from the stack of papers he was going through.

I painted for six hours a day, five days a week for the whole month until the entire north wing of the housing unit had been completely painted, from top to bottom. The maintenance supervisor praised my work ethic and he said that he was more than happy with the quality of my work. The unit officers and the counselor were also pleased with the job I'd done, but the only thing that I was interested in was getting out of that stinking place as soon as possible — which I soon found out was only a grievance and a telephone call away.

One afternoon when I went to the quartermaster to exchange several items of my state issued clothing, they refused to exchange my prison issued thermal underwear, claiming that they were seasonal only. I was told they wouldn't be issuing any winter clothing again until October. However, I was somewhat familiar with the state-issued property policy.

I told the supervisor that the property policy specifically states that, "All state issued items shall be replaced at all facilities as needed due to normal wear and tear or loss, regardless of season or the length of time in the prisoner's possession."

The guy copped an attitude with me and told me to write a grievance. He obviously wasn't impressed with my knowledge of policy since he also told me to leave or he'd write me a major misconduct ticket for disobeying a direct order.

For the past few years, there had been an ongoing lawsuit over prisoners personal and state issued clothing. Previously, inmates had been allowed to purchase and wear their own personal clothing whenever they wanted. The department of corrections put a stop to that, though, when they implemented a new policy that effectively took away almost all personal clothing and required all inmates to wear state-issued prison uniforms.

Consequently, this provoked a group of inmates to file a class action lawsuit against the corrections department. The court ruled that the department did have the authority to limit inmates' personal property and require all inmates to wear a uniform. The court also stipulated, though, that each inmate must be provided with a specific minimum number of each state issued clothing items and allow these items to be exchanged as needed. To ensure that the court's orders were being followed, the court also appointed a monitor to address all complaints of noncompliance from inmates.

I took the officer's directions and filed a grievance. Of course, it was rejected by the grievance coordinator as a nongrievable issue. When that happened, I immediately called the court appointed monitor and explained my problem to her.

She agreed that the facility was violating a court order by refusing to issue the state clothing that I'd requested and she instructed me to file another grievance. In the interim, she promised to personally telephone the facility and read them the riot act regarding the court order and policy concerning state issued clothing.

Within a couple days, the business office manager of the facility called me to the control center for an interview regarding my grievance.

"Have you been given the thermal underwear you requested?" he asked me, to which I plainly stated I had not.

"Well then, you'll have them by the end of the day," he said. "Can you sign off on the grievance as being resolved?"

I refused to sign off on it. After all, I hadn't received the thermal underwear yet. Telling me I was going to get it did not satisfy my grievance.

About an hour later, I was called to health care to review another grievance that I'd filed against the nurse for inappropriately charging me a five dollar co-payment. The nursing supervisor told me that due to the fact that I'd never signed the health care request authorizing the co-payment to be deducted from my account, and because a Notice of Intent Hearing was never held to remove the co-payment, the five dollars would be returned to my prisoner account.

"Thank you," I said. "But I want a copy of the signed document stating that the money will be returned to my account."

"OK, I'll have it mailed to you at the facility," he told me.

"What do you mean, mailed?" I asked.

"Oh, you're being transferred this afternoon," he said. "You didn't know that?"

Evidently, when I filed a grievance against the quartermaster and notified the court monitor that the facility was violating the court order, the court had ordered the facility to immediately purchase and issue all state clothing to inmates whenever it was requested, regardless of the season. This was a big expense for the prison and it was a common practice at most facilities to transfer any inmate who filed a grievance that resulted in the facility having to spend money. This too was a violation of department policy — inmates were not supposed to be transferred solely because they filed a grievance. Even so, it's a well-known fact that most facilities routinely violate department policies.

The people who make up prison administrations know that most inmates will become frustrated with a worthless grievance procedure, which is why grievances are routinely denied. They know inmates are more likely to give up their battle against the bureaucracy rather than go through the hassle of taking the issue to court.

On the other hand, the intent of many inmates who do file grievances is often just to obtain a transfer in the first place. All things considered, I guess you could say that sometimes, the end justifies the means.

At around one o'clock that afternoon, I was told to pack my property and be ready to leave in an hour. I was so glad to be leaving that it only took me twenty minutes before I was packed and ready to go.

When I got to the control center, there was one other inmate who was also waiting to be transferred. The both of us were strip searched, secured in belly-chain handcuffs and escorted out the main gate to the transportation van. Shortly after we got on the road, one of the officers told us we were being transferred to the Carson City Correctional Facility. It was only about a twenty-minute drive north from Riverside.

It wasn't any closer to home, but all the same, I considered myself lucky. I'd only had to spend eight months living in the squalid slums of Riverside.

CHAPTER 18

CARSON CITY CORRECTIONAL FACILITY

Carson City was another multilevel facility that housed a little more than twelve hundred level two and level four inmates. It was built almost exactly the same as Saginaw, which was probably due to the fact that both facilities were built at around the same time in the early 1990s.

The only noticeable difference between the two facilities was the positioning of the buildings and the layout of the yard. The main yard had the usual oval, quarter-mile asphalt track, weight-pit, softball diamond and about a dozen picnic tables. Both levels used the main yard, but at different times. The level four inmates were only allowed to use the main yard for one hour in the afternoons.

In addition to the main yard, the level two inmates had a smaller common yard with two tennis courts, four handball courts, four horseshoe pits, two shuffleboard courts and four basketball courts.

All new arrivals at Carson City were placed in housing unit eight for approximately two weeks until they completed the orientation process. Most inmates were assigned to either housing unit seven or nine. Nonsmoking inmates, however, were allowed to request placement in the nonsmoking wing of housing unit eight.

When I first arrived at Carson City, I was surprised to see so many guys that I hadn't seen since my time at Jackson prison almost thirty years ago. Most of them had aged so much, though, that I didn't even recognize them when I first saw them.

There was no greenhouse or horticulture program, but the yard crew did have a small area where they started their seedlings for the flower beds and the vegetable garden. The inmates were allowed to grow their own vegetables, but space was limited so there was a long waiting list.

Only sixty guys were given a garden plot and in order to be eligible for one, an inmate had to be free of any major misconduct tickets within the past six months. Additionally, inmates who did receive plots were required to sign a disbursement of funds for ten dollars, which covered the cost of seeds, seedlings, onion sets and fertilizer.

The plots were only about twelve feet by twenty feet, but we could grow just about whatever vegetables we wanted with the exception of corn, which was too tall. It was something to do to pass the time. Besides that, the reward of fresh produce was well worth all the time and effort it took to grow it.

When I went to classification, I was told that all inmates were required to have a job assignment. I was allowed to choose two job assignments, however, I was also told that one of my choices had to be a housing unit porter or a yard crew worker.

Essentially, I was being forced to choose between cutting grass and shoveling snow or cleaning toilets. I'd have to do one of the two jobs while I waited for the job assignment I really wanted to open up.

Seeing as how I had no desire to get stuck cleaning toilets, I reluctantly chose the yard crew. As for the job assignment that I actually wanted, I requested housing unit recreation because it was one of those assignments that required no effort whatsoever. It consisted of passing out board games and officiating during the pool tournaments that were held on the holidays.

When I received my detail for the yard crew, I had no intention of busting my butt. Five days a week I reported to the yard shack, where I checked in to get paid for the day. While the other guys were checking out tools and lawn mowers, I'd grab a plastic trash bag and act as if I was going to pick up trash. Instead of working though, I headed straight for the back yard where the track was located.

On my way there, I might stop to pick one or two pieces of paper here and there. As soon as I got to the back yard, though, I'd throw the plastic trash bag in the garbage can and run laps on the track.

After a couple of weeks in housing unit eight, I was moved to housing unit nine and placed in a cell with an older guy. The guy smoked in the cell and at first, I thought it was going to create a problem for me.

Before I even started to unpack my property, the other inmate and I had a conversation about smoking in the cell. I explained to him about my Chronic Obstructive Pulmonary Disease and how it made breathing difficult for me, especially when I was around cigarette smoke. Fortunately, he offered not to smoke in the cell.

The cell had actually been painted white, but you couldn't tell. The walls and ceiling were a dingy brownish color from all the nicotine and similarly, everything in the cell was covered with a thick layer of nicotine. It smelled like a dirty ashtray.

The first thing on my to do list was to give the cell and everything in it a thorough cleaning. The other inmate didn't offer his help, but I didn't care. He probably would've just gotten in my way anyhow. Besides, if I cleaned the cell myself, I could be sure it was done properly.

My new bunkie's name was Edgar and he was an older guy, probably in his late fifties. He didn't strike me as a bad guy; he was quiet, polite and he kept to himself. He often spouted off bible verses as if he were a devout Christian.

It wasn't long, though, before I found out from one of the other guys in the unit that he was a child molester. The guy had molested his own five-year-old granddaughter. I immediately lost all respect for the guy and I couldn't help but feel dirty and disgusted whenever I was in his presence. I wanted nothing more to do with him and from that point on, my attitude changed dramatically.

I began trying to find another bunkie right away. I couldn't knowingly live in the same cell with a despicable, lowlife child molester. I was sure Edgar noticed the sudden change in my attitude toward him and I'm sure he'd figured out that someone had told me about him being a child molester. He was probably worried I might try to hurt him, as inmates often do attack child molesters, and before I could even arrange a move, Edgar went to the housing unit officers and told them I'd stolen his bathrobe.

At nine o'clock one night, when I was already in bed, one of the housing unit officers came to our cell.

"Inmate Goble, you need to pack your property," he told me. "You're moving to another cell prior to the nine-thirty count, so move fast."

I asked him why I was being moved, especially so late in the evening, but he wouldn't answer my question.

"There's no way I can get everything packed up and moved in less than a half hour," I told him.

"It's outta my hands," the officer said. "I've got strict orders from the lieutenant to make the cell move."

"That's fine, but I just can't do it in less than a half hour. It's impossible," I said.

He told me to come to the counselor's office with him and when we got there, he explained what happened. Edgar had accused me of stealing his bathrobe and the lieutenant had decided it'd be best to just move me to another cell until they could find out exactly what was going on. I was dumbfounded.

"You've got to be kidding me," I told the officer. "That old, senile child molester uses his bathrobe as a blanket. If he'd taken the time to actually look for it, he'd have found it laying right there behind the bunk on the floor where it fell off his fat ass while he was sleeping last night."

Evidently, the pervert never considered that his bathrobe might have fallen behind his bunk. I knew it was there, lying on the floor. Earlier in the day, when I pulled my footlocker out from under his bunk, I noticed it lying there next to the heat register.

Ironically, my first thought was to pick it up and put it on his bed, but then I decided that I wasn't going to get in the habit of picking up after him.

When I finished telling the officer my side of the story, he went straight to our cell and found the bathrobe exactly where I said it was. However, since the child molester had inadvertently but all the same falsely accused me of stealing, which was tantamount to snitching, the officer was concerned that I might do something to him and so, I still had to move.

I knew that whatever I said wasn't going to do me any good, but I told the officer that it didn't make any sense to punish me for Edgar's senility. The right thing to do was move the person who had started all the bullshit in the first place. I was actually nothing more than an innocent bystander who had been falsely accused.

I'd already made up my mind what I was going to do, so when the officer gave me a direct order to pack my property and move, I told him that I wasn't packing shit.

"As far as I'm concerned, you can take me to the hole," I told him.

The officer didn't say anything else, but instead just turned around and got on the phone to call the control center. I didn't hear the conversation, but evidently when he informed the shift commander that I was refusing to lock in my assigned cell, the captain must have told him to write me a major misconduct since he sent two officers to take me to the hole.

The next day when the sergeant reviewed the ticket, I waived my right to a hearing investigator. There was no sense in trying to fight the ticket. Without a doubt, I'd been railroaded, but that didn't matter. In their minds, I'd disobeyed a direct order and they weren't about to recognize or care about any extenuating or mitigating circumstances.

Corrections employees simply did not make mistakes; at least none that they'd admit to. Right or wrong, it was all about giving the impression of being in complete and total control and nothing beyond that mattered.

I went to the hole Sunday evening and the first thing Tuesday morning, I was brought to court for my ticket. As I expected, the hearing officer found me guilty.

She also gave me thirty days loss of privileges, which I found to be utterly absurd for something that was not at all my fault.

"Whatever happened to progressive discipline?" I asked her before leaving the office.

When she didn't answer, I couldn't help but add, with a bit of sarcasm in my voice, "Thirty days loss of privileges is a rather inordinate amount of time for a DDO ticket, isn't it?"

Apparently, she didn't like my tone of voice because when she looked up from her desk, she gave me a contemptuous leer as if I'd just called her a bitch or something worse.

"Disobeying a direct order is a serious offense," she sneered coldly.

I thought that was just more bullshit and laughed as I walked out of her office.

That afternoon, I was released from segregation. I was given my property and told that I'd been assigned to housing unit seven. I could only hope that my new bunkie wouldn't be another child molester or rapist.

Loss of privileges meant that I was confined to my cell. There was no time on the yard, no phone calls allowed, nothing. I even had to ask permission to use the bathroom and take a shower.

The only time I was allowed to leave the housing unit was for chow. For the next thirty days, I occupied my time by running in place every other day for an hour and on the opposite days, I did calisthenics for an hour. I also did a lot of reading, writing and watching television to alleviate the ever-present boredom.

When my thirty days was completed, the yard sergeant asked me if I wanted my job back on the yard crew, but I declined. About a week later, I was assigned to housing unit recreation, which was the job I had wanted all along. If I had to have a job, I wanted something that didn't mean anything to me. That way, the next time they decided to take it away from me, I wouldn't care. The less I cared about, the less I had to lose.

When I first came to prison back in the early 1970s, any inmate who committed a sex crime was treated like a pariah — hated and shunned by all the other inmates. Child molesters and rapists were particularly despised. They were considered to be the lowest forms of life in prison and were ostracized by all inmates.

Out of fear for their own safety, they served their entire sentence in protective custody. They didn't dare show their faces on the yard at Jackson or Marquette.

However, prison has drastically changed during the past thirty years and nowadays, sex offenders are prevalent throughout the prison system. Through the years, I've noticed that most child molesters or rapists will suddenly find religion when they come to prison. But even so, I've never seen one sex offender who had a sincere desire to change his perverted behavior.

They fervently proclaim to be devout Christians attending church services every week and spouting bible verses word for word, but it's nothing more than a ruse, a superficial attempt to pass themselves off as God fearing Christians. They are, in fact, actually trying to hide behind the Christian faith because they're afraid and hoping that no one will do to them what they did to an innocent woman or child. Their only concern is their own self-preservation.

Invariably, as soon as most sex offenders are paroled and walk out the front gates to the free world, their mindset suddenly becomes "Thank you Lord, I'll take it from here." Religion is put behind them and they revert back to the same illicit and perverted sexual behavior that brought them to prison in the first place.

In their minds, they see nothing wrong with their perverted sexual desires. Most of them feel no remorse or shame whatsoever for their despicable acts. There are also those who claim that they were molested as a child, but I've never believed that. If that truly were the case, then they'd know firsthand what a horrible experience it is to be molested and would never inflict the same upon another innocent and helpless child.

While I was at Carson City, my eldest sister Jenna, who was only four years older than me, passed away. During the last few years of her life, she'd suffered from a number of health related problems. She was diabetic, which most likely contributed a great deal to her failing health.

Jenna had also spent a lot of time in the hospital, undergoing a number of surgical procedures for a variety of stomach ailments. There were times when she seemed to be getting better, but then she'd relapse suddenly and her illness would get worse. The last time Jenna came to visit me at TCF, she weighed only about ninety pounds. She was only fifty-seven years old, but she looked so much older.

Her health deteriorated to the point that she was physically unable to take care of herself. Eventually, she even had to be fed through a feeding tube. Her daughter, my niece Sandy, took on the responsibility of caring for her, but even Sandy was limited in what she could do. There came a point when Jenna's condition was so severe that she required professional medical care around the clock. Reluctantly, Sandy decided to move her to a hospice.

It wasn't a decision Sandy wanted to make, I know. But it was the only thing to do to ensure Jenna was as comfortable as possible and had twenty-four hour professional care and medication to alleviate her pain and discomfort.

The last time I spoke with Jenna on the telephone, I told her that I loved her very much. I expressed my regret for not being the brother that I should have been and I apologized to her for not being there when she needed me. I also told her that if we didn't see each other in this life again, I'd see her on the other side.

Sandy and I had previously talked about her mother's deteriorating health and the inevitable fact that it was only a matter of time before Jenna lost her battle. She told me that when her mother passed away, she wanted to tell me in person and not over the telephone.

When the day came that an officer approached me and said I had a visit that I wasn't expecting, I immediately suspected that I was about to have a very unpleasant experience. I walked into the visiting room and took a seat against the wall by the officers' station, where all the inmates wait for their visits. As I sat there waiting, I was hoping that everything was okay, but my gut told me otherwise and it was right.

Sandy and one of my other nieces, Candice, came through the visiting room door and I could see at once that Sandy had been crying. I gave Candice a quick hug and hello and then turned to Sandy, who embraced me emotionally.

"My mom's gone," she whispered in my ear, her voice trembling and tears beginning to fall again down her reddened cheeks.

Though I'd pretty much known this was coming, I couldn't help but feel an overwhelming wave of grief and sympathy surge through my entire body. I wanted to cry, but I fought back the tears. I knew that if I were to break down, it would only make Sandy and Candice feel even worse.

I didn't know what to say. I'd lost my big sister, whom I'd always loved and looked up to. I felt terrible and I was profoundly hurt. I tried to console Sandy as best as I could, but I knew there was nothing that I could say that would lessen her heartache and grief.

Sandy had lost her mother and her best friend and nothing could fill that void. I knew something about the insuperable mental anguish that Sandy must have been going through. I'd never forget the excruciating psychological pain and the profound grief that I felt when my father passed away.

I didn't care much for Carson City. It was just too far away for my family to visit on a regular basis. I asked the counselor if he'd consider transferring me to the Macomb Correctional Facility, which was less than an hour's drive from where my family lived, but he told me that I had to do a year at Carson City before he'd consider transferring me.

Nevertheless, I wasn't discouraged. There were always other ways of getting a transfer, the problem was the gamble you took doing it. You never knew where you might be transferred to and mostly, it depended on who you pissed off.

I was willing to take that chance, though. I decided to write a few grievances and see what happened.

As it turned out, I didn't have to wait long for a response from the administration. Within a matter of weeks I got what I wanted, however, it wasn't exactly what I asked for. I was being transferred to the E.C. Brooks Correctional Facility in Muskegon, Michigan, which was located on the other side of the state about five miles from Lake Michigan.

I definitely wasn't happy about how things had turned out, but that was the gamble I took when I wrote the grievances. There wasn't anything I could do except deal with the situation for the next few months.

CHAPTER 19

E.C. Brooks Correctional Facility

When I arrived at Brooks, the female property officer spent more than an hour going through my property with a fine-toothed comb. She confiscated several items of my personal property that I'd legally purchased and owned for years. I tried my best to stand up for myself without pissing her off.

"I've had that for more than a decade — it's been okayed by property officers at least two prisons, if not more," I said at one point.

"This is considered contraband here at Brooks," she said coldly. "You can request a hearing to have your stuff returned, but I can't let you have them now."

I did request a hearing, which was held by the resident unit manager. He determined that not all of the items were contraband and ordered them returned to me.

The trouble was, somewhere between the property room and the housing unit, all those items mysteriously vanished. That was when I first began to realize that they had their own way of doing things at Brooks. It was apparent they didn't care about department policy.

I was assigned to housing unit-B and from the very first day I set foot in that unit, I had nothing but problems. To start, the mattress in my cell had several long rips in it, one which ran across the entire width of the mattress. The cotton batting was falling out and the mattress looked completely totaled. Before unpacking my stuff, I found the assistant resident unit manager and requested a new mattress.

"We can't do that," she said matter-of-factly. "There's a budget crunch right now and we won't be replacing any of the mattresses until the next fiscal year."

I politely reminded her of department policy.

"I believe the policy is that all cell furnishings must be clean and in good repair. This just doesn't meet that standard," I said kindly. "There's another policy too that specifically addresses mattresses. If I'm not wrong, I think the policy states that if the covering on a mattress or pillow has been compromised, those items have to be replaced."

"I hate to be a bother, but clearly, this mattress covering is compromised," I added.

She really wasn't interested in hearing about policy from an inmate.

"I'm going to need you to return to your cell now," she said. "You'll have to make do with the mattress that's in there."

And so, I had to go through all the hassle of filing a grievance. She received it the following week and suddenly, she decided to just order me a new mattress and resolve the issue rather than letting the grievance go to the warden at step two.

It never ceased to amaze me how the inmates were always expected to adhere to all department policies, procedures and rules, and yet, the officers and support staff did not. In fact, they often had the tendency to totally disregard those very same policies and procedures as if those rules pertained only to the inmates.

My bunkie acted as if he wasn't playing with a full deck. He appeared to have some sort of mild learning disability or something, which was no problem for me. What I did have a hard time dealing with, though, was his incessant snoring. The guy snored all night long and sounded like a freight train.

At first, I tried using earplugs to block the snoring. It didn't work. With the extreme snoring coming from a matter of mere feet above me, the earplugs only slightly muffled the noise.

After that, I tried talking to the guy to work out an amicable solution.

"I know it's bad," he said. "But it's a medical condition. There ain't nothing I can do about it."

In my opinion, that was bullshit. He only snored when he was lying on his back.

"Well, it seems like you only snore when you're lying on your back," I said. "What if I just hit the bottom of the bunk whenever you're snoring really bad, and then you can try just rolling over to your side and see if that works."

"Yeah, we can give it a try," he said.

We tried that for about a week, but he quickly got tired of me waking him up. He actually expected me to let him sleep while I had to lie there all night long staring at the bottom of his bunk, listening to him snore. Apparently, he didn't care if I slept or not. He wasn't willing to make any other compromises.

A couple days later, when I couldn't get to sleep because of his snoring, I hit the bottom of his bunk trying to get him to rollover.

He jumped down off the top bunk like a wild animal and began ranting and raving about how he couldn't live like this. I was at first shocked that he woke up so quickly, but then grew angry as I listened to him complain. After all, he wasn't the only one putting up with a less than ideal sleeping situation. The more he ranted and raved, the madder I got.

"You know what, pal? Why don't you take your sorry ass down to the officers' desk and tell it to them because I am sick and tired of hearing about your bitch ass medical condition," I finally yelled.

It was about two o'clock in the morning when he stomped out of the cell and he didn't come back for the rest of the night. Evidently, the third shift officer let him spend the night in the day room. I was glad for a decent block of uninterrupted sleep.

Early the next morning, one of the day shift officers came to our cell and it was clear there was a problem.

"We have a complaint that you've been hitting your cellmate's bunk and harassing him during the night," the officer said. "What's been going on in here?"

I tried to explain the problem to him, how my bunkie's incredibly loud snoring was keeping me up and we had agreed to work the problem out by me knocking on the bottom of the bunk whenever it got too bad.

The officer dropped his tone of professionalism.

"Listen, man, your cellmate has got some mental problems," he whispered. "You gotta cut him a break."

The officer pointed to his head and said, "He's working with less up there than the rest of us, you know."

So apparently, it didn't matter that I wasn't getting sleep.

The issue was resolved, though, because the officers decided to move my bunkie to another cell. Unfortunately, my new bunkie turned out to be an even bigger idiot.

His name was Greg and he had some real psychological issues. Greg was one of those individuals who wanted to regulate everything in the cell, including me. He was a total and complete control freak.

The guy was forty-three years old, which came as a huge surprise to me. After living in the same cell with Greg for only a few days, I was simply amazed that he'd managed to stay alive for forty-three years. Greg wasn't only controlling and obnoxious, he was also as ignorant as a box of rocks. It was clear to me that Greg would never die of old age. He was living on borrowed time and sooner or later, especially here in prison, someone was going to put him out of his misery.

Greg was full of epic tales of how he'd severely beaten people within an inch of their lives. He was constantly trying to find listeners for his stories, trying to impress and intimidate anyone who'd stop for even a second to listen to his bullshit. It was the biggest ego I'd seen on a prisoner since I'd had to bunk with that punk teenager at TCF.

Greg was also a very insecure and defensive person, often taking offense at the most trivial things and always trying to bully just about everyone. I think it was all nothing more than a distraction, an attempt to hide his many character flaws. He was definitely a deeply emotionally troubled person and clearly carried around a number of unresolved issues.

He spent most of his time and energy belittling and maligning other people. I wrote it off as something he did simply so he could feel better about himself. No matter what issues were creating his behaviors, though, I thought poorly of him for not taking advantage of his time in prison to work things out with himself and work on being a better person. In my opinion, he was simply evil.

I soon discovered that Greg was also a cell thief, when an item of my personal property mysteriously vanished into thin air one day. At first, I was hesitant to complain. My neighbor kindly informed me, though, that while I was out running the track every morning, Greg kept himself busy by going through all my personal belongings.

"I saw him going through everything in your footlocker," my neighbor said. "I even saw him pull out a bunch of papers from under your mattress."

I kept all my personal papers neatly organized in file folders under my mattress. While it certainly disturbed me that he was going through my stuff, it wasn't at all a surprise. After all, Greg had never shown any respect or consideration for anyone or anything, not even himself.

One morning after I'd finished my daily run on the track, I returned to the housing unit to take a shower and was going to stop by the cell to pick up some fresh clothes and toiletries. When I opened the cell door, though, I was surprised to find my bunkie and some young kid sitting next to each other on Greg's bunk.

They were sitting close enough to one another to give the appearance of intimacy, which made me hugely uncomfortable. I said nothing, turned around and closed the door behind me, deciding I'd skip the shower and just hang out in the day room. Later that day, Greg tried to cover up what had happened with that kid.

"You ever met him before?" he asked me.

I shook my head. "Nope, can't say I have."

"Cool kid, he brought over some dope to smoke," Greg said. "Yeah, we were just sitting around, getting high and talking 'bout shit.'"

He wasn't hiding anything from me. I'd heard stories from a bunch of the other inmates that Greg was a notorious homosexual predator who especially liked the young boys. I didn't want any problems, so I just kept my mouth shut and acted like I bought his cover-up.

A few days later, Greg was taking a nap and I was lying in my bunk, the top bunk, watching television when I had to use the bathroom. I always tried to be as quiet and careful as possible when I climbed down off the top bunk, but I inadvertently hit my knee against the side of the bed. The noise woke up Greg and because he was such a defensive jackass, he naturally assumed that I had deliberately kicked the bunk. Greg rolled over and made some sarcastic, pugnacious remark about me intentionally waking him up.

"Yeah, well, you don't hear me complaining about all the times you've woken me up, so why don't you just go back to sleep and forget about it," I said.

In keeping with his nature, Greg couldn't let my comments pass without taking them as fighting words. He jumped up from the bed and a heated altercation between us began. By the time we finished arguing, we both knew there was no way we could spend one more night in a cell together without some serious bloodshed.

I skipped the bathroom trip that started the whole argument and marched myself right down to the assistant resident unit supervisor's office and told her, in no uncertain terms, that she was going to move me to another cell today. I didn't ask her, I told her. I didn't want there to be any misunderstanding or doubt in her mind about what needed to happen. One way or another, I was moving to another cell today.

"Calm down, okay?" she said. "Why don't you just tell me what's going on."

"Don't bother," I said, my fists still trembling with anger. "Just arrange the move."

Evidently, it was clear to her that I was in a highly agitated state and beyond the point of talking. She immediately called C-unit to arrange a move. It took me about twenty minutes to get my property packed and I was out of there.

During all my years in prison, there had only been two times when my back was up against the wall — just two times where I thought I'd have to make the choice between stabbing someone or getting stabbed. Luckily, it never came to that. This was the third time and once again, I was lucky to have avoided that scenario.

My new bunkie in the C-unit was a young guy who seemed to be a reasonable person. At the very least, he was clean, quiet and considerate. Thankfully, he was nothing at all like my last two bunkies.

At least for the time being, I figured I had straightened out my living situation and resigned myself to being at Brooks for a while.

My Own Worst Enemy

And actually, Brooks wasn't as bad as some of the other facilities I'd been to in the last five years.

Each housing unit had an ice machine, two microwave ovens and vending machines where we could purchase soft drinks, candy, chips and pastry items. We were also allowed to order from the inmate store on a weekly basis, where most of the other facilities only allowed orders to be placed on a biweekly schedule. The facility was designed almost exactly the same as Saginaw and Carson City, but the level two and level four inmates had their own separate yards. That was a big plus because it meant the level two inmates, like myself, were afforded more yard time.

The weight-pit was located on the back yard right across from the softball diamond. All of the weight lifting equipment was old and worn out; the weight bars were all bent, the padding on all the benches was in tatters and the cables on the two weight machines were always broken. The worst thing about the weight-pit, though, was that it had a dirt floor. The dirt was constantly being blown around and by the time you finished working out, you looked like you had been digging ditches all day. The only good thing about the weight-pit was that during the winter months, they enclosed three sides with clear plastic to keep the wind and the snow out.

I was surprised when one of the guys told me that they had bicycles at Brooks that we were allowed to ride during the summer months. I knew that Huron Valley Women's Facility used to have bicycles for the female inmates, but I'd never heard of a mens' facility that allowed bicycles.

During the evening yard period, we could check out one of the six bicycles and ride around the quarter-mile asphalt track in the level four yard for twenty minutes at a time. The track in the level-four yard was used because the level four inmates weren't allowed to use the yard in the evenings.

One of the few things I liked about Brooks was the big oak trees around the housing units. The trees must have been close to a hundred feet tall and were beautiful to look at. In the summer, the trees provided welcome shade and were the playground and home of some very large, fat and friendly gray squirrels.

The squirrels became so tame that they'd eat right out of our hands. Some of the guys purchased bags of mixed nuts or trail mix from the candy machine every day just so they could feed the squirrels. The squirrels seemed to especially like chocolate chip cookies, which was what I usually fed them. Without a doubt, these were the best fed squirrels in the entire state. I always thought the squirrels looked especially cute when they stood on their hind legs and begged for food.

When I went to classification for a job assignment, I was pleasantly surprised to learn that because I had a certificate from the Michigan State University Master Gardener Program, the prison would pay me three dollars and four cents a day to work on the yard crew. That was far more money than I'd made before. However, there was still snow on the ground and I really didn't want to shovel snow.

For three dollars and four cents a day, though, I decided I could handle a few weeks of snow shoveling. When my detail came through, I learned that I had been assigned to the second shift yard crew. I got to work quickly and just as quickly learned that a couple of the officers who supervised the yard crew were real assholes.

Before I got to work, I was issued a pair of thermal coveralls that were a size XXL, which was way too big for me. I usually wore a size large, not an extra, extra large.

"Can I get a size large?" I asked the yard officer who'd handed me the coveralls.

The officer snapped at me like a drill sergeant, saying "This is prison! You take what you can get. I don't have time to look for your size. What are you, anyhow, some type of girly girl? Gotta have just the right fit?"

I thought to myself, who does this idiot think he's talking to? I could tell just by looking at the kid that I'd been in prison for more years than he'd been alive. I'd probably spent more time sitting on a prison shit-bowl than he had as a corrections officer. Before I opened my mouth, though, I reminded myself to speak calmly.

"Listen, I'm not your kid, and I'm not your dog. You must have me confused with someone else," I told him, keeping my voice low and calm.

Some of the officers have a tendency to stereotype and treat inmates as if we were born in the penitentiary, like we're some sort of retards who are completely oblivious to the world around us. They seem to think that just because we've been given the discriminative label of inmate, convict and prisoner that we're somehow lesser human beings than themselves. We're considered to be irrational, irresponsible and ignorant — totally incapable of making a logical or intelligent decision on our own behalf. Incredibly, these very same people attempt to make all of our decisions for us when they can't even manage their own lives.

I tried to resolve the clothing issue with a different officer the next day, but I got the run around once again, so I filed a grievance. A few days later, the sergeant called me down to his office and took care of my problem, issuing me a large pair of coveralls.

After that, though, the yard officers made it known they weren't happy about the fact that I had filed a grievance. They gave me all the shitty jobs. Looking out for my own best interests, I wrote to the classification director and requested placement on the first shift yard crew. My request was granted and I was quite happy about it.

The officers who were in charge of the day shift yard crew were more laid-back and had a totally different attitude. They were less concerned about projecting an image of authority and omnipotence, probably due to the fact that they were all older than the officers on second shift and had likely spent many years working as corrections officers. Like many officers, the guys who spend a lot of time working in the prisons gain a lot of insight and wisdom about dealing with inmates — attributes that their second shift counterparts had not yet acquired.

During the summer months, each yard crew worker on the day shift was assigned to maintain a specific area on the yard. It was his responsibility to keep the grass cut and the trash picked up within that specified area. I was assigned to a small area in front of A-unit that didn't require a lot of maintenance. I cut the grass twice a week and it only took me about twenty minutes each time.

My detail was Monday through Friday from six a.m. to two o'clock in the afternoon, but every day before I went to work, I spent at least an hour running the track or working out in the weight-pit. As long as the grass was cut and the trash was picked up, the officers didn't care what we did with the extra time.

Brooks was one of several facilities that provided a strict vegetarian diet to inmates of the Buddhist faith. Since I was interested in learning more about Buddhism, I sent a letter to the chaplain requesting that I be allowed to participate. Before the chaplain would approve me for the diet, though, I had to undergo a question and answer screening process to see if I actually knew anything about Buddhism.

During the interview, the chaplain asked me numerous questions about the faith — none of which were any problem for me to answer. I'd been actively reading books to learn about the Buddhist faith and had acquired a wealth of knowledge over the past few months. When she was satisfied that I knew enough about the Buddhist faith to qualify for the strict vegetarian diet, she approved me and said she'd send her recommendation to the special activities director for his approval as well.

I'd only been on the strict vegetarian diet for about a week when I discovered that the kitchen workers didn't follow certain guidelines in the preparation of the meals. They often served Jell-O, cottage cheese and bread that were made with animal byproducts. They also used the same plastic serving trays to feed the strict vegetarians as they used to feed the medical diet lines, which they weren't supposed to do because the medical diets included meat and animal byproducts.

I began writing grievances regarding these issues and shortly afterwards, I found out just how duplicitous and vindictive some of the staff could be. The food service director seemed to be a nice person when I first met her, however, once I began filing grievances against the kitchen, she turned out to be a real petty bitch.

She started checking my store order receipts to see if I'd purchased any items that contained animal byproducts. When she found one of my old store receipts showing that I'd purchased a Honey Bun, she automatically assumed that it contained an animal byproduct. She was so determined to get back at me that without even reading the ingredients listed on the package label, she wrote a notice of intent to remove me from the diet for a period of sixty days.

A notice of intent, or NOI, is a formal written notice to inform the inmate that a hearing will be held to establish the basis of the alleged policy violation and to determine what course of action should be taken by policy.

It was about a week later when the assistant resident unit supervisor called me to his office for the notice of intent hearing. To prove there were no animal byproducts in the Honey Bun, I took one with me to show the assistant resident unit supervisor the ingredients listed on the package. I'd even gone through the dictionary and written down the definition of every ingredient listed.

But before I could even present my evidence the assistant resident unit supervisor said he was dismissing the NOI. Apparently, the food service director had neglected to list exactly what animal byproduct was allegedly in the Honey Bun. Meanwhile, the food service director was so confident that I'd be found guilty that she didn't bother to wait for the hearing officer's disposition on the hearing.

That afternoon, she instructed her staff to remove me from the strict vegetarian diet line. When I went to the chow hall that evening, the stewards refused to serve me a strict vegetarian tray. I didn't bother to argue with them but instead went straight back to the housing unit and informed the assistant resident unit supervisor of the issue. He claimed there was nothing he could do and suggested that I write another grievance.

I'd already made up my mind to do that, but this grievance would be different. This grievance was filed specifically against the food service director and was for violating my religious and due process rights, a very serious charge.

The next morning when I went to breakfast, I took a copy of the hearing officer's disposition with me just in case they refused to give me a strict vegetarian diet tray.

Sure enough, when I got to the chow hall, one of the day shift supervisors told me I'd been taken off the diet line. I showed her the copy of the disposition from my hearing and pointed directly to a specific sentence that read, "The inmate is not to be removed from the strict vegetarian diet."

She suddenly changed her tune and instructed one of the inmate kitchen workers to prepare a diet tray for me. When the food service director was told that I'd been found not guilty and that I hadn't been removed from the strict vegetarian diet line, I'm pretty sure she was more than just a little pissed off because she then doubled her efforts to remove me from the diet line.

A few days later, she had an officer shakedown my cell to see if I had any food items in my possession that contained animal byproducts. Of course, the officer didn't find any. We received our store orders from the housing unit the day after the first shakedown. And so, the housing unit supervisor himself — who never does shakedowns — came to my cell again looking for items that had animal byproducts in them.

He was in the cell for about fifteen minutes before he came back out with a bag of nacho chips and a box of snack cakes that were under the bed in a plastic bag. I tried to explain to him that the items belonged to my bunkie and I attempted to show him my store receipts, but he said the items were found in my area of control and as far as he was concerned, the items belonged to me. He refused to listen to anything that I had to say.

With two inmates sharing the same cell, the cell was divided into two supposedly separate areas of control. Each inmate was responsible for whatever was found in his area of control regardless of whether it actually belonged to him. Half of the space under the bottom bunk was my area of control, which is where I stored my footlocker. The other half was where my bunkie stored his footlocker, dirty laundry and his store items.

Instead of simply asking what property was mine and what belonged to my bunkie, the supervisor was using an invisible line to determine ownership. Obviously, his supervisors weren't pleased that he'd found me not guilty on the first notice of intent.

In order for him to redeem himself, his supervisors had probably suggested that he find a way to remove me from the strict vegetarian diet by whatever means necessary and that was exactly what he was trying to do.

Throughout the years, I've seen many corrections employees who were unethical and had no scruples whatsoever. But Brooks was one facility that seemed to have more than its fair share of these individuals. When the powers that be decide to abuse their authority, to disregard their own policies, procedures and rules, then the inmates will undoubtedly always pay the price.

During the past three decades, I've seen very few fair and impartial men and women working for the department of corrections. Altruism is just not their forte. They could care less about us as human beings. To them, we're nothing more than job security.

With the assistant resident unit supervisor alleging that he personally found items containing animal byproducts in my area of control, there was no doubt what the outcome of my hearing would be. My guilt was virtually assured.

Not surprisingly then, the resident unit manager who held the NOI hearing refused to even consider any of my evidence. The evidence I brought, my store receipts and the receipts from my bunkie, would, after all, prove my innocence and the prison's staff had already decided they couldn't let that happen again. I was found summarily guilty and removed from the diet.

Many years ago, I adopted the philosophy of keeping everyone at a distance. Seldom did I ever let anyone get close enough to me where I'd consider him or her a true friend. There was one individual at Brooks, though, who I became close friends with. His name was Dave and I first met him a couple of years earlier when we were at Riverside together.

Dave and I both started working on the yard crew at about the same time. Without a doubt, Dave was the funniest guy I'd ever met. He had a natural talent for making people laugh. The guy really should have been a professional comedian. He could keep me laughing all day long at the crazy and silly things he said and did.

Dave stood six-feet and four-inches tall, weighing in at more than three hundred pounds. Not only was he big in stature, he was also a big-hearted person and one of the friendliest people I'd ever met.

The one thing about Dave, though, was to never mistake his kindness for weakness. The last thing you wanted was to end up on Dave's bad side. If his physical size wasn't intimidating enough on its own, Dave also wouldn't hesitate to use a shank if he thought he was in a position where it was necessary.

He was serving forty to sixty years in prison for robbing a bank. Dave had been fighting his conviction in the court system for years but so far, all of his appeals had been denied. The last time I heard from him, he was once again in the process of filing a motion in the courts to have his sentence reduced.

Dave was full of stories about the adventures he'd had before coming to prison, including some of the robberies that he and his partners had pulled off in the past. One time, he told me about how he and his partners had robbed this place in Las Vegas and gotten away with enough money to fill several grocery bags. He said that after the robbery, he and one of his partners were parked in the parking lot of a strip mall waiting for their other partner to arrive when they noticed a young couple walk by their vehicle and go to their van.

Unfortunately, when the couple got to their van, they discovered that someone had broken into their vehicle and stolen practically everything they owned. They noticed Dave and his partner sitting in their car and approached them, asking if they'd seen anyone around their van. Dave told them they hadn't been sitting there long and no, they hadn't seen anyone.

The couple told Dave they were newlyweds from Ohio and were on their way to San Jose, California, where they planned to live. But now, since they'd lost almost everything they owned, they didn't know what they were going to do.

Dave said that he and his partner felt so sorry for the young couple that they decided to give these total strangers one of the grocery bags full of money, which he said was at least twenty thousand dollars. Dave told the couple that he and his partner had just hit the jackpot at one of the casinos and that they were more than happy to share their good fortune with them to help cover their unexpected loss.

I believed the story, since that's just the way Dave was. Whenever he had more than he needed — whether it was food,

My Own Worst Enemy

money or anything else — he was always willing to share with others, no strings attached, and he never expected anything in return.

In all the years that Dave had been in prison, he'd never gotten into lifting weights until I talked him into giving it a try. Surprisingly, for as big as he was, he wasn't very strong. When we first started lifting weights together, Dave had a hard time bench-pressing one hundred and thirty-five pounds for just eight repetitions.

I didn't push him hard because I knew from experience that he'd be sore for the first few days and I didn't want him to get frustrated or discouraged and quit on me. We started a regular routine of working out three times a week for an hour at a time and rotating our workouts. One day we did a chest workout and the next day we worked our arms.

For the first couple of weeks, Dave worked out with whatever weights he felt comfortable with. But as soon as he began to notice that he was getting stronger, he started pushing himself harder. Within two months time, Dave was bench-pressing two hundred and twenty-five pounds for six repetitions. It was a huge improvement.

When I found out that Dave's birthday was coming up, I decided to surprise him with a bag of goodies as a birthday present. I also made him a special birthday card. To be funny, I wrote, "Happy Birthday Dick-Head!" in large letters on the front of the card and drew a picture of a large penis with an equally sizable pair of testicles underneath it. On the inside of the card, it said, "Who's your Daddy? Who's your Man?" and I signed the card Uncle Jim, an inside joke we had.

The joke came from our weight-lifting sessions. Whenever we were doing bench-presses and Dave couldn't push the weight off his chest himself, I'd insist that he call me Uncle Jim before I'd lend him a hand.

I knew that Dave liked junk food, so as a birthday present I put together a big bag of goodies with several different kinds of candy bars, bags of candy, boxes of snack cakes and a few other food items as well. Then, on the morning of his birthday, I waited until he left for work and I asked his bunkie to lay the birthday card on his pillow where he could easily find it when he came back.

Later that morning, I was sitting in the day room when Dave came in with a big smile on his face and said, "You're a dickhead!" Immediately, I knew he'd gotten the card. We laughed about it and I told him to wait there until I came back because I had something else for him.

When I walked in the day room with the bag of goodies I said, "Happy Birthday!" and held out the bag of goodies to him. From the expression on his face, I could tell he was totally surprised. For a brief moment, I thought the big guy was going to get emotional.

Dave said he couldn't believe that someone had actually thought of him on his birthday. In all the years he'd been in prison, no one had ever bothered to give him so much as a birthday card, let alone a gift. He thanked me several times, telling me how much he appreciated the kind thought. But when he tried to give me a hug, I told him that the party was over and I wanted my shit back — making the both of us laugh.

It was a rewarding feeling to know I'd helped make Dave's special day just a little more special.

A couple weeks later, the warden was making her rounds in the housing units when Dave and a couple other guys complained to her about the lack of tissue paper and hand soap. They reminded her that the items were supposed to be issued to each inmate on a weekly basis. Apparently, whatever they said to her must've really pissed her off because the following week, two of the inmates were transferred to Carson City.

A few days after that, Dave was also transferred, except he was sent all the way up to the Kinross Correctional Facility in the Upper Peninsula. That was the last time I saw Dave. He spent the next eight months at Kinross before he was transferred back to Brooks. By the time he returned to the corrupt Brooks prison, I'd already been transferred elsewhere.

We still correspond on a regular basis, though, and I'm sure that sooner or later, we'll both wind up at the same facility again.

My Own Worst Enemy

For the next few months, it was the same old boring routine every day. I was still working on the yard crew, but shoveling snow and cutting grass was no longer a part of my job description. Instead, I was assigned to pick up trash on the yard at six o'clock every morning and again at eleven o'clock after the count cleared. Surprisingly, I was still getting paid three dollars and four cents a day for what amounted to no more than twenty minutes of work.

I'd tried just about everything I could think of to get a transfer, but nothing seemed to work. I knew there was one sure way of getting a transfer, but it was one of those desperate, last resort options and definitely a hard way to go.

If an inmate received a major misconduct ticket for displaying threatening and intimidating behavior toward an employee, he wasn't allowed to remain at the same facility with that employee. I'd already decided that I wasn't ready to seriously consider that as a practical solution to my problem.

I was lying on my bunk watching television one evening when, quite unexpectedly, my efforts finally paid off. I wouldn't have to take any extreme measures and I was glad about that.

The housing unit officer simply walked up to my cell and told me I was scheduled to be transferred the next day. I had no idea where I was going, but I spent the night hoping it was somewhere closer to home.

Early the next morning, myself and four other inmates were secured in belly-chain handcuffs and loaded into a transportation van. The first thing we wanted to know was where we were going, but we didn't ask because we knew the transportation officers weren't allowed to tell us until after they'd left the facility. That way, if an inmate didn't like where he was going, it was too late for him to do much about it.

When we turned onto the interstate highway and headed east, one of the guys asked where we were going. The officer looked at his paperwork and announced that three of the guys were headed to the Mound Correctional Facility near Detroit. Then, he said that me and the other guy were going to the Macomb Correctional Facility in Macomb County.

I breathed a sigh of relief. I would finally be at Macomb.

CHAPTER 20

MACOMB CORRECTIONAL FACILITY

In December of 1999, I was transferred from Lapeer to Saginaw. From there, I went to Riverside in 2001. A year later, in 2002, I arrived at Carson City. In 2003, I moved to Brooks. Finally, in 2005, I got to Macomb.

That means it had taken me six miserable, long years of writing grievances and in general, being a pain in the ass at every facility I'd been to, just to get back to where I was relatively close to my family.

My mother and my niece Sandy were practically the only relatives I had left who still cared about me. I couldn't have been happier to just be closer to them, at a prison where I could get visits on a regular basis again.

Therefore, I told myself that I was going to put all the bullshit that had happened over the past six years behind me. I was going to make every effort to keep a low profile and try not to file a grievance unless it was absolutely necessary. The only important thing was seeing my family again.

Macomb was almost exactly like Saginaw, Carson City and Brooks. In the early 1990s, the state had built eight of these multilevel facilities. Originally they'd been designed to house six hundred inmates. But since they implemented double bunking and built an additional housing unit at each facility, there were more than fourteen hundred inmates being housed at each facility.

All the buildings were designed exactly alike. The only noticeable difference at each facility was the slight variations in the way they'd positioned the buildings, which changed the layout of each facility's yard.

Even though the yards might have been laid out differently, they all pretty much had the same recreation activities and equipment — a paved quarter-mile track, softball diamond, handball court, basketball courts, horseshoe pits and a weight-pit.

The first thing that I noticed about Macomb was how clean the housing units were. I was told that two years earlier, the institutional maintenance department had repaired and repainted everything in each of the housing units, and from the way it all looked, they did a fine job.

The units looked as if they'd just been built. The most noticeable improvement was the off-white linoleum floor tiles, which made the housing units look cleaner and brighter. At Saginaw, Brooks and Carson City, the housing unit floors were bare concrete — drab and dreary looking.

When I went to classification, I requested a job assignment as a greenhouse worker but was told I'd have to write to the horticulture teacher.

"He usually hires his own workers for the greenhouse," I was told.

Before I wrote the teacher, I talked with one of the inmates who worked in the greenhouse. He told me the teacher wouldn't hire anyone who wasn't enrolled in his class and I really had no interest in sitting in a classroom for the next several months.

I decided to forget about working in the greenhouse and instead wrote a letter to the classification director inquiring about a yard crew assignment. Specifically, I asked her what my rate of pay would be if I were to accept a yard crew assignment. I explained to her that I had several certificates in horticulture and landscaping, including one from the Michigan State University Master Gardener Program. I also wrote that I'd worked on the yard crew at Brooks Correctional Facility, where I was paid three dollars and four cents a day.

No one ever responded to my query and I presumed it was because they didn't want to pay me more than ninety-four cents a day — that's what all the other yard crew workers were paid at Macomb.

I decided it didn't make much of a difference to me whether I worked or not. Most of the time, the meager salary wasn't worth the hassle of the job assignment anyhow. I could always find other ways to occupy my time.

My Own Worst Enemy

During my years in prison, I had always tried to spend at least an hour every morning doing some type of physical activity. I found it helped to maintain both my physical and psychological well being.

At Macomb, I ran four days a week for an hour in the morning and on the other three days, I worked out in the weight-pit for forty-five minutes. In the afternoons, I did a few sets of pull-ups and walked the track for about an hour. In the evenings, I didn't do much of anything. I'd usually just stay in my cell, watch television or occasionally read, which was pretty much the extent of my day.

When I first arrived at Macomb, my niece Sandy came to see me and brought my mother with her so they could both visit me. I hadn't seen Sandy or my mother in about a year and when they walked into the visiting room, I almost didn't recognize Sandy. She'd lost seventy pounds since I last saw her at Carson City and she looked like a totally different person — even better than she had looked as a teenager.

My dear mother had just turned eighty-two years old, but she'd always looked much younger than her actual age. In fact, she looked as if she were only in her sixties, which was generally the age that everyone guessed her to be. My grandmother had lived to be ninety-six years old and I was hoping that mom had inherited her mother's longevity.

It was nice to see my mother and niece again. They were my lifeline and honestly, I don't know what I'd do without their love and support.

Whenever they came to visit me and whenever I talked to them on the phone, I'd always be sure to tell them that I loved them and how profoundly I appreciated all that they did for me. I've tried to be ever mindful of the fact that even though I'm serving a life sentence in prison, I still have many things to be thankful for. I've always felt blessed to still have family members who care about me. In my opinion, there is nothing more important than family.

During my first six months at Macomb, I tried to ignore all the minor inconsistencies and policy violations that were perpetrated against the inmates. I adopted the mindset that as long as it didn't directly affect me, I wouldn't give it any energy.

But eventually the inmate store pushed me past my abilities to not complain. Repeatedly, my store orders were filled with granola bars and other items that were four months or more past their freshness date. I felt forced to start writing grievances.

A few weeks later, when I requested several state issued clothing items from the quartermaster, they either didn't have my size or refused to issue the items on the grounds that they were seasonal. Once again, this was in direct violation of department policy and I knew it. After all, it was a fight I had won before. I felt I was left with no other recourse but to write a grievance.

Supposedly, the problem with the quartermaster had something to do with budget cuts. We were being told that due to a state budget deficit of four billion dollars, the facility's funding had been cut. However, while the state legislature was cutting funding for education, social service, Medicaid and most other state agencies, the department of corrections had their budget increased to nearly two billion dollars.

Regardless of this fact, the department of corrections decided to use the budget deficit as a pretext to make cutbacks in areas that only affected the inmates — food service, quartermaster and cleaning supplies.

The food service departments at all correctional facilities were ordered to discontinue the purchase of coffee for inmate consumption. Since there was no more coffee, they also felt it was appropriate to decrease the amount of sugar apportioned to each inmate by half.

The department also discontinued purchasing whole milk and replaced it with two percent milk, which was processed and sold by Michigan State Industries. And even though policy was never changed in regard to the minimum size of food portions allotted to each inmate, the food service supervisors routinely issued smaller size serving ladles to the inmates working on the serving lines in an attempt to cut costs.

Despite this subterfuge, the majority of inmates never complained or filed grievances regarding this practice because they were afraid that they'd be transferred. The inmate kitchen workers, of course, were well aware of this deceptive practice but they too refused to say anything about it, more concerned that they might lose their monthly bonus of forty dollars or even their jobs.

Before the department of corrections got into the business of Michigan State Industries, all cleaning supplies were purchased from outside vendors. Laundry soap, bleach, disinfectants, bathroom cleansers, hand soap and other cleaning supplies were readily available to the inmates.

In an attempt to save a few dollars, some facilities discontinued the use of bleach to wash inmate clothing. In addition, the disinfectant that was used to clean the inmates' bathrooms and their cells was routinely diluted to the point of being ninety-eight percent water. The staff, however, insisted that their bathrooms and work areas be cleaned with entirely undiluted disinfectant.

Every two weeks, we were issued two small bars of state-made soap and two rolls of toilet paper. Some facilities, we heard, stopped issuing hand soap to inmates.

Inmates were also issued five envelopes and ten pieces of writing paper for the entire month.

While these were the types of things the department cut back on to save money, if they were really serious about saving a few bucks, they could've just as easily paroled some of the fourteen thousand inmates who are currently still imprisoned past their minimum release dates. The average savings for each inmate paroled would be around thirty-two thousand dollars a year. Even if only half those inmates were paroled, it would still add up to two hundred and twenty-four million dollars a year, reducing their overall budget by about half.

Every month, Macomb had an emergency count, fire drill or mobilization for training purposes. It was during these training exercises that we were frequently ordered to evacuate the housing unit and report to the gymnasium, where two hundred and forty inmates were packed like sardines into an area that was half the size of a basketball court.

The training exercises sometimes lasted for more than two hours at a time. Usually, a state police K-9 unit officer was brought in to search the housing unit for drugs.

Meanwhile, every inmate was subjected to a strip search before we were allowed to return to our cells. But for all the administration's efforts, they usually didn't find anything. Nevertheless, that didn't stop the officers from trashing the inmates' cells.

Sometimes, the administration would even lock down the whole facility just to do a cell-by-cell search for extra toilet paper. I could never understand how the department of corrections — which inmates so often referred to as the department of corruption — could justify paying corrections officers twenty-five dollars an hour to search inmates' cells for extra rolls of toilet paper that cost about thirty-five cents a roll.

There just wasn't a whole lot of savings there.

These are some of my thoughts and experiences from the past thirty-five years of my life. The true reality of prison itself cannot be expressed or understood by mere words alone. I can only say that it's an experience best left undiscovered and unknown — an experience to be avoided at all costs.

Over the years, I've come to realize that there is no amount of money in the world worth coming to prison for. If I had fifty million dollars, I'd gladly give it all to get out of prison today. For what good is all the money in world if you can't spend it? Without your freedom, you have nothing.

After all these years in prison, I no longer remember what it feels like to be a free man. Whenever I look back on my life, it seems as empty and meaningless as watching an old television movie.

For many years, I've felt disconnected from the real world. I used to miss all the small, common and often unnoticed everyday things in life, most of which I often took for granted before I came to prison.

I never realized just how much those little things meant to me until they were gone; simple things that are too numerous to begin to mention. But that was so many years ago that today, I don't even remember what most of those things were.

Occasionally, something vaguely familiar will trigger an old memory and my mind will flashback to a long forgotten experience. But the moment is fleeting, and invariably the memory is quickly lost and forgotten once again.

I often wonder what the point is in keeping a man locked up for thirty-five years for a crime the judge deemed an accidental shooting. Surely, after all these years, I'm not a threat to society — at least not in my mind. To me, it appears that I've become nothing more than job security for state employees.

Change is inevitable in everyone and everything. I personally believe that I've changed a great deal in the past thirty-five years. I'm somewhat wiser now than I was as the twenty-two-year-old young man who came to prison more than three decades ago.

My priorities and perspective have changed immensely over the years. I have finally become my own best friend instead of my own worst enemy.

I've made a conscious effort to change my inappropriate behavior and become a better person. I'm no longer willing to compromise my morals, scruples and integrity just to be accepted by others. I've learned to be self-reliant, self-sufficient and to avoid conflict situations. I know that I'm capable of fitting back into society without ever having to resort to criminal behavior or drugs. I've learned that we change our circumstances by changing our attitudes. And despite living in these warehouses we call prisons, I've become a decent and caring human being who is no longer a threat to society. I'm acutely aware that I have responsibilities in this life, and that every decision I make has consequences affecting the lives of my family and many others as well.

Death is another inevitability of life — a fact that I've come to accept without any fear of dying. I guess it's a lot easier to accept when you have nothing to look forward to, and nothing to live for.

To say that, through all these difficult years, the thought of suicide and ending this madness hadn't crossed my mind would be simply untrue. Frankly, though, I have never possessed the courage to end my own life.

Nonetheless, I'd gladly welcome death this very day, rather than continue to exist in this wretched, artificially created environment for another twenty or thirty years. When my mother was seriously ill with cancer and suffering terribly from the adverse effects of the chemotherapy, there was a time when she wanted to give up. She thought the alternative — death — might be the lesser of the two evils.

She once told me that, "Life is more about the quality, and not necessarily the quantity."

After thinking about what she said, it made perfect sense to me. I understood and I totally agree with her sentiment.

There is an old Chinese proverb that says, "The only difference between a long life and short life is but a moment in time."

At this point in my life, I want nothing more than to go home and assume the responsibility of caring for my elderly mother. To fulfill my obligation as a grateful son and to try and repay a portion of the great debt of gratitude that I owe her for never giving up on me.

I continue to hope that one day in the not so distant future, the governor will take a long, hard look at the facts in my particular case and accept the recommendation of my sentencing judge to commute my life sentence.

Until then, I'll be here. But regardless of what happens, I'll no longer be my own worst enemy.

ACKNOWLEDGMENTS

During the course of writing this book, I have included information and quotes from the book *What the Buddha Taught*, by Walpola Rahula. The Rev. Dr. W. Rahula's book is one of the most enlightening and readable books on the fundamental principles of the Buddhist doctrine that I've ever read.

Citizens Alliance on Prisons & Public Spending, a nonprofit public policy organization that is concerned about the social and economic costs of prison expansion. Because policy choices, not crime rates, have caused our prison population to explode, CAPPS advocates re-examining those policies and shifting resources to public services that prevent crime, rehabilitate offenders and address the needs of all our citizens in a cost-effective manner.

Selected commentary and research on the Felony Murder Rule was prepared by students from the Inside-Out Prison Exchange Program, Ryan Correctional Facility, 2007.

The experience of writing this book has been both rewarding and extremely frustrating at times. I wish to thank my sisters Nancy and Janet, along with my nieces Sandy and Crystal, who have been unwaveringly supportive and immensely helpful. I'd also like to thank my niece Lisa Klepoch, who did an excellent job designing the book cover.

ABOUT THE AUTHOR

James A. Goble was twenty-two years old in 1973, when he was convicted and sentenced to twenty to thirty years for armed robbery, and life for first-degree felony murder. He is now sixty years old, and has spent the past thirty- eight years in Michigan's prison system. Over the years James has earned sixteen educational and vocational certificates. He has worked for over twenty years in horticulture, and has written a number of articles on the propagation and cultivation of Cacti and Succulents that have been published in international magazines. James is an honorably discharged veteran, A Member of the Vietnam Veterans of America and Veterans of the Vietnam War Inc. He is divorced, and has two sisters.

James is hopeful that his book will have a positive influence on others and help readers gain insight by reading of his mistakes and experiences. James offers no excuses and freely admits he was once a very cynical, irresponsible and ignorant young man. He believes that when he started using drugs, he destroyed any chance he might have had for a decent life. It took James many years to realize he was his own worst enemy, but since that time, he has made a sincere and conscious effort to become his own best friend. James concedes that he did many irresponsible and harmful things to himself that he would have never allowed anyone to do to him. But change is inevitable and today, James is a totally different person from that young man who entered the prison system thirty-eight years ago. He's learned that he has many responsibilities in this life and that every decision has consequences. James expresses many regrets in life, but none more insuperable than being responsible for the death of another human being.

James still remains hopeful that one day he will be released. To read more about James, please visit his website at www.freejamesgoble.com.

Made in the USA
Monee, IL
13 October 2022